RED SUMMER

RACHEL GREEN

BY RACHEL GREEN

Madame Renard Investigates:

Body on the Rocks
Five Dead Men
No Tears for Sandrine
Red Summer

Red Summer

Copyright © Rachel Green 2025

Get the free short story, *Christmas Past*, when you sign up at: https://www.rachel-greenauthor.com/freeshortstory

PROLOGUE

She got off the bus in Rue Grimaldi. Her first time in Monaco, but Esmée knew exactly where to go. She'd spent so long studying the street plan that she knew the route by heart, although nothing could have prepared her for the thrill of actually being there: the fancy hotels, the swanky apartment blocks, the glitz, the glamour... you could almost taste the money in the air.

She stepped out from behind the bus, right into the path of a yellow Lamborghini. Too eager to get by, its throaty engine on a leash, tamed to a paltry ten kilometres per hour in the cramped and congested streets. Everyone wanted to be there, to see and be seen. After letting the Lamborghini go by, Esmée crossed the street, then she went down some steps to a subterranean passage, following the signs to the casino. Only in Monaco would the subways be lined with mirrors, polished to immaculate perfection – one wouldn't want to miss an opportunity to admire how good one looked. Esmée was briefly caught out when she caught sight of her own reflection; she so easily fit in. Dressed up for the day, her torn jeans (€20 from the market in Arras) looked no different from the designer ones worn by the other women waltzing by. Even cheap concealer, if you put enough on, covered the worst of her acne. To the casual observer, she was a cosmopolitan bright-young-thing, out for an afternoon of shopping, all her anxiety hidden behind dark sunglasses. Ever conscious of the scar on her neck, Esmée pulled up the collar of her shirt.

She emerged on the edge of Port Hercule, back into strong sunshine. Out in the marina, the sight of the sleek white mega-yachts caused Esmée to pause. A millionaire's playground, enough money floating on that water to feed an impoverished nation. Maybe one day, you too could afford a boat like this. Then again, most probably not. It was hard not to be intimidated by the wealth, but Esmée gave herself a nudge of encouragement. It was imperative she stayed focussed. Keep her mind on the job. She quickly got back into her stride.

She peeled off onto Avenue de Monte Carlo, the whiff of money growing stronger by the second. Esmée unfastened the buckles on her messenger bag. Not long to go now. Just a few more turns and she would be there. Nearing the Place du Casino, she eyed up the shops: Gucci, Valentino, Hermès. She was spoilt for choice.

A dozen Ferraris were lined up outside the Hotel du Paris. Red, yellow, and blue ones, no sign of their owners, posing elsewhere. What was the collective noun for a group of supercars? A vulgarity of Bugattis? A ludicrousness of Lamborghinis? Esmée's pace slowed again as she passed within inches of the expensive hot metal, doubts creeping in. She'd always been a rebel, but this was new territory. Her sister should have been with her, if only for moral support, but had dropped out at the last moment. Esmée took a deep breath. *This is every bit our world as theirs*, someone had once said to her. Her confidence came back and she quickly refocussed. There was no reason to feel intimidated.

One more turn and she was there. Fred. Louis Vuitton.

Chanel... Esmée had already chosen Dior. A voice in her head wished her *bon chance* as she went inside.

The guard on the door was as big as a sofa; any more doughnuts and he would probably burst. He flicked Esmée an inquisitive look, but didn't seem troubled. As long as you were attractive or looked well-heeled, you could have been walking in here with a bomb. It was that easy.

Inside the hallowed premises, Esmée took off her sunglasses, eager to take it all in. Even the air seemed finer in here; it was a wonder they didn't charge you to breathe it. A fake plastic lady behind the counter was the next to latch onto her. Suspicion oozed from every filled crack on her face as she checked out the new arrival, concerned they might have been invaded by a member of the great unwashed. Apparently reassured, the phoney went back to counting her money.

Free to move on, Esmée moved casually around the store, casting her eyes over the finery. Handbags in glass cases, too pristine to touch. Watches on pedestals, glistening under spotlights. Nothing came with a price tag, of course (if you had to ask, you couldn't afford it), but Esmée knew the score. Some of these handbags sold for more than her father had paid for his first house; the dresses cost more than a nurse earned in a year. Esmée felt her cheeks start to burn. It may have been everyone's world, but look what some people had done to it.

Esmée slipped a hand into her messenger bag. What would people think when they heard? Would her parents disown her? Would she get kicked out of college? All the questions that had been worrying her on the bus started to bounce around in her head once more. But Esmée pushed them aside. None of that mattered anymore. She felt it in her heart: her cause was just, right was on her side.

Giddy with excitement, Esmée took out one of her packets of powder paint. Something close to euphoria flooded her system as she tore open the packet and began dousing the finery with bright orange dust. "Attack the rich!" she cried out, meekly at first, but then, as the air around her began to turn orange, her inhibitions melted away. "*Liberté, égalité, fraternité!*" she shouted. "An end to capitalism! Now!"

The overstuffed sofa looked like an elephant had just sat on him. As many as five seconds went by before he sprang into action, moving with a speed that belied his bulk. The delay was long enough for Esmée to empty two of her pouches and cover half the finery with orange dust. She had plenty more in her bag, but the phoney came out from behind the counter and started attacking her with an umbrella. A pampered customer looked on in disgust before fleeing out the door and calling for the police. *How dare you despoil our finery? Arrest her, at once!*

It didn't take long for them to tackle her to the ground, but then Esmée didn't put up a fight. The guard pinned her to the floor with a knee to the chest; the phoney grabbed hold of her foot and attempted to drag her back into the street. Esmée reeled from a heel in the face, got winded when the fat guy toppled over and crushed her stomach, but she felt no pain. Close to ecstasy, all she wanted to do was laugh. Her cause was just, her heart pure. And none of the jostling clowns could take that away from her.

1

Madame Janvier had an unusual method of cataloguing her books. Instead of organising them by genre or alphabetically by author, she arranged them by the year of publication, the earliest going all the way back to the eighteenth century. Margot had been visiting her bookshop, tucked away in the maze of lanes down by the harbour, most Saturday mornings for the past few months, and had often been pleasantly surprised by the discoveries she made. No hierarchy – first edition gems stacked next to mass-market paperbacks; classics rubbing shoulders with pulp. Here, for example, was 1965: *Catch-22; Do Androids Dream of Electric Sheep? A Clockwork Orange; The Man with the Golden Gun.* Then came *Charlie and the Chocolate Factory, The Electric Kool-Aid Acid Test, The Autobiography of Malcolm X* – an eclectic mix, crammed onto shelves fixed to every available upright surface. Often the smallest of shops had the biggest of hearts.

Margot ascended two steps, rounded a corner, and arrived in 1942. Her eyes lit up when she spotted *West with the Night* – one of her favourites. When she took it down from the shelf and looked at the title page, she was delighted to see that it was a first edition. As a teenager, Margot had been captivated by Beryl Markham's tales of adventure in 1930s East Africa. The story of how she'd spent her childhood hunting barefoot with the local tribes, and later, night-flying over the bush, had been remarkable by anyone's standards. At the tender age of seventeen, when her father left her to embark on a journey to Peru, Beryl had determined to begin a new life of her own and had set off on her horse, carrying only a toothbrush and a spare pair of slacks in her saddlebags. Later, aged thirty-four, she'd flown solo across the Atlantic, the first person ever to have done so from East to West, against the prevailing wind. Margot flipped the book over, wincing when she saw the price tag. €400. Could she afford it? It was tempting. She hadn't yet replaced all the books she'd lost in the fire, but then her finances were already a little stretched this month.

The sound of soft crying brought Margot out of her thoughts. She looked around curiously, but there didn't appear to be anyone else there. The crying continued, so she put the book back on the shelf and followed the source of the sound to the back of the shop where she found Madame Janvier, hidden away in the small room behind the counter, sobbing quietly into a handkerchief.

"Madame Janvier!" Margot said, unable to keep the surprise out of her voice. "Whatever's the matter?"

Madame Janvier gave a small gasp of surprise. She turned her head just far enough for their eyes to meet through the curtain of pearls and beads. She bravely tried to gather herself. "I'm sorry, Margot. I don't know what came over me. Do you need some help?"

"No. I couldn't help overhearing..."

Margot waited, hoping for an explanation, but despite Madame Janvier's best efforts, another wave of emotion washed over her. She retreated behind the curtain and promptly broke down into tears.

Margot's heart went out to her. Despite being well into her eighties, Madame Janvier was a robust woman who wouldn't normally let anything get the better of her.

"I don't wish to intrude," Margot said, delicately parting the curtain, "but if there's anything I can do..."

Madame Janvier bravely got a grip on herself and reappeared, her nose covered with the handkerchief. She gave Margot a sad, dejected look. "I've done something incredibly foolish."

"Haven't we all?"

"I've lost it."

"How do you mean?"

"I can't believe I was so gullible. I usually see right through them."

Margot began to catch on. "Are you saying someone's conned you?"

Madame Janvier's state of bewilderment showed no signs of abating, so Margot decided to take charge. "Why don't I make us some coffee?" she smiled reassuringly. "Then you can tell me all about it."

The shopkeeper relented. She told Margot to turn out the *FERMÉ* sign and then welcomed her into the back room. It was a cosy little hideaway: one small window, a simple kitchenette, two comfortable armchairs flanking a table full of books. Margot put the kettle on while Madame Janvier made space on the table.

"You hear about people falling for these scams, but you never think it will happen to you. You think you'll be smarter."

"Don't blame yourself. They're usually very convincing."

"Oh, they were."

"When did it happen?"

"These past few weeks. But I don't think it really sank in until this morning."

The kettle came to the boil. Madame Janvier spooned some coffee into the cafetière, and then Margot added the water. They took it to the table along with two cups and then settled into the armchairs. "It's no use bottling these things up," Margot said, pushing the plunger on the cafetière. "You'll feel better once you've got it off your chest."

"I know. I just feel so ashamed."

"Don't," Margot poured the coffee and handed her a cup. "People like that are parasites."

"Yet they both seemed so nice."

"What exactly happened?"

Madame Janvier put down her cup after taking just one sip. "Well, it started with a telephone call from my insurance company. They said my policy was due for renewal and they were sending someone out to do a review. It was just to make sure that everything was in order and that the policy was suitable for my needs. I already knew the renewal was coming up so I wasn't suspicious.

"A few days later, a young woman called round. She seemed to know all about the history of the building, and she had a good look around. But then, after she'd been outside, she said she thought there might be a problem with the roof. She asked to see the attic, so I took her upstairs. She stood at the top of the ladder and told me the roof was in a very bad state. She said they wouldn't be able to renew the policy until it had been repaired."

"Have you been up there yourself?"

"No, but it did ring true. There's been a damp patch on the bedroom ceiling for years. I think she was worried a tile might fall off and injure someone in the street – everything she said made sense. She told me not to worry, that it could certainly be fixed. She gave me a list of their approved contractors, so as soon as she left, I started phoning around. Everyone I spoke to was busy apart from one man who said he could come the next day. True to his word, he arrived the following morning. I showed him the attic and told him what the insurance lady had said. He took a good look and said that many of the timbers were rotten. If I didn't get it treated soon, he said the rot would spread and it would end up being a much bigger job. I was so worried."

"I can imagine."

"He assured me he could fix it. He gave me an estimate of three thousand, which seemed quite reasonable. I offered to give him some money up front to pay for the materials, but he wouldn't accept it. He worked on it for three days, all on his own. And when he'd finished, the insurance agent came back and said she was happy with what he'd done. I thought I'd had a great deal, especially when he gave me his bill and said he was charging me less than the estimate since he'd managed to re-use more of the old tiles than he'd expected."

"Hmm," Margot said dubiously, suspecting what was coming next.

"Anyway, I wrote him a cheque, and we got chatting over coffee. He'd been telling me about a piece of land he'd acquired on the edge of town. He'd wanted to build a house on it, but couldn't get planning permission, so he'd come up with the idea of turning it into a residents' car park instead. Apparently, it's a very sound investment."

Margot nodded knowingly. When she'd lived in Paris, she'd heard of people paying over twenty-five grand a year for a single parking space.

"The plot was big enough for forty spaces, and I soon did the maths. The problem was that one of his investors had dropped out at the last minute, and it had left him in quite a pickle.

Unless he found another investor, he was going to have to call the whole thing off. I asked him how much he needed."

"How much?"

"Forty thousand."

Margot winced. "Please tell me you didn't."

"It seemed too good an opportunity to miss. He assured me I would double my money in less than a year. He'd got all the permissions. Everything looked official."

Margot's heart sank. "So you gave him the money?"

Madame Janvier nodded. "The whole forty thousand. In cash."

Margot reached over and squeezed her hand. "It's shocking what these people will do."

"The thing is, I had some cash put aside and had been looking for a way to invest it. When my aunt died last year, my sister and I found a horde of notes hidden in her wardrobe, which, I'm rather ashamed to say, we never declared." She tutted, annoyed with herself. "I knew it would come back to bite me."

"What happened then?"

Madame Janvier had another sip of her coffee. "I signed the agreement, and he wrote me out a receipt. He was going to take me to see the piece of land, but then something cropped up and he had to leave. A few days went by, and then a week. When I still hadn't heard from him, I called the number on the card he'd given me. Lo and behold, the line was dead. So then I went to try and find this plot of land myself, only to discover that the address he'd given me didn't exist. Then it dawned on me – I'd been conned."

"The insurance agent was in on it, I suppose?"

"Oh yes. When I phoned them, they knew nothing about her. They said they hadn't sent anyone round and had never heard of this builder. As far as they were concerned, there was nothing wrong with the building and the policy would have renewed without a problem."

Margot tutted in sympathy. "It's easy to get drawn in."

"I felt such a fool."

"You say the builder gave you a business card."

"Yes. I've still got it." Madame Janvier stood and went to her bureau. She opened a drawer and immediately found what she was looking for. She handed the card to Margot: *Rémy Demis. General Builder,* followed by an address in Narbonne.

"In case you're wondering, that address is false, too. I went there on Monday, but it was just an empty office."

"And the woman who posed as the insurance agent... did she give a name?"

"Probably, but I can't remember it now."

Margot glanced around. "Any CCTV in the shop?"

Madame Janvier shook her head. "My granddaughter, Natalie, keeps telling me I should get a camera, but I'm not very good with technology. Besides, who steals books?"

Somewhat ironically, Margot had just seen a copy of Abbie Hoffman's notorious *Steal This Book* on one of the shelves.

"When the insurance lady called you, was it on the phone here at the shop?"

"Erm... yes, it must have been."

"If you can remember the exact time and date, we might be able to trace her number from your phone records."

"Of course." While she was still standing, Madame Janvier took a calendar down from the wall. She leafed back. "It was the week after Whitsun, I remember that. Either the Tuesday or the Wednesday. That would make it the 11th or the 12th of June."

Margot made a note on her phone. "I'll see what I can find out."

"Would you? That's most kind."

"Not at all. Have you told the police?"

Madame Janvier shook her head. "I was worried about the undeclared cash. I didn't want *Impôts* getting onto me."

"You should at least report it, if only to stop other people falling into the same trap."

Madame Janvier nodded. "All right. I'll do that."

Margot picked up her cup and finished her coffee in one mouthful. Like a hound sensing blood, she was keen to get on the trail. She rose to her feet. "I'll hold onto this card, if I may."

"Of course. What are you planning on doing?"

"Not sure yet. But people rarely disappear completely. He may have left a trace."

Margot turned to leave, but then paused at the curtain. "One last thing: if you saw them again, would you recognise them?"

"Oh, yes," Madame Janvier said without hesitation. "I might not be good with technology but I never forget a face. The builder was quite a big man, solidly built. I'd say he was in his early forties. He had quite a sympathetic face, and I did rather like him. The insurance lady was much younger. No older than early twenties. Quite serious-looking. She had black hair down to her shoulders, and a fringe that covered her eyebrows. Oh, and she had a scar. Right here, on the side of her neck. A nasty-looking thing. She kept lifting her collar to try and hide it."

2

Disturbed by a rattle of the front door, Margot and Madame Janvier peeked out through the bead curtain. A customer was waiting outside.

"Sorry, Margot," Madame Janvier said, easing by. "I'll have to open up. She's one of my regulars."

"Of course."

They said their goodbyes on the doorstep.

It was a hot July morning and the tourists had already descended. The tiny cobbled streets were choked with pedestrians as Margot walked to the end of the lane and back again, searching the shopfronts for cameras. The only one she found was above the door of the atelier on the corner, but when she went inside and asked, the assistant told her the camera hadn't worked in years.

Back on the sunlit street, Margot took out her phone, unsure what to do. Opening Maps, she zoomed in on Narbonne and found the address on the builder's card to be close to the centre of town. She wasn't familiar with the location. It was ten o'clock. Narbonne was a hundred kilometres away, which would mean a pretty expensive taxi ride. At times like this, Margot wished she owned a car (or maybe a motorbike – wouldn't that be fun?), even though there was nowhere to park at her cottage. She looked up the train times and found a service ran every hour from Argents to Narbonne, with the next train departing in twenty minutes. Margot's heart began to beat a little more quickly. If she hurried, she was certain she would catch it.

———

Margot smiled contentedly as the train pulled out of Argents station. There was something special about travelling by rail, looking out the window and watching the scenery roll by – the villages, the farmland, people's back gardens. One day, she would have to undertake one of those epic train rides, coast-to-coast, or a transcontinental trek.

An hour and ten minutes later, they arrived at the *Gare de Narbonne*. Margot walked out through the bustling ticket hall and found a quiet spot outside to light a cigarette. She used her phone to calculate a route to the builder's address and, as soon as she had her bearings, set off down a tree-lined avenue.

A ten-minute walk took her to a row of single-storey office units. Number 5 was the one she sought; the only one not to have a sign on its floor-to-ceiling windows. The smoked-glass door was locked. Margot moved her face closer to the glass and, with her palm blocking out the glare of the sun, looked inside. The room was bare, with four plain walls and a simple wooden desk. A pile of unopened mail sat on the doormat.

She took a step back. Her attention switched to the *Immobilier* next door, its window lit up like a sweetshop for property hunters. It took her a few moments to realise that a man inside was looking at her, smiling in a way that suggested she go in. Margot took him up on his offer.

"Bonjour, Madame. Seen something you liked?"

There must have been a school somewhere that turned out men who thought they were God's gift. If there was, this one was certainly a graduate. Flattering though it was, Margot wasn't in the mood to play along.

"Any idea who rents the unit next door?"

Crestfallen, he replied, "What's your connection?"

"A friend of mine used a builder who gave her that address."

"Ah."

"That sounds ominous."

He gave her a nod of affirmation. "You're not the first who's come looking for him. There was a woman in here last week, a couple the week before, maybe two more last month... all telling a similar story."

"Which was?"

"He'd got them to put some money into an investment scheme that turned out to be fake. Something to do with a car park. Is that what happened to your friend?"

Margot nodded. "Pretty much."

"If it's any consolation, he had us fooled, too." It turned out the *Immobilier* was the letting agent and hadn't faired well. "He paid a month's rent in advance, but we've received nothing since. His references all checked out, as did his ID. But with all these people turning up, we've been beginning to wonder."

"I presume he gave a name on the tenancy agreement."

The man took her to his desk, where he consulted a computer. After a few moments, he said, "Rémy Demis. He gave us some contact details, but we've had no response." He straightened. "Look. I'm sorry this has happened to your friend, but we let it out in good faith. There's nothing we can do."

"I understand. Can you remember the last time you saw him?"

"It must have been a few weeks ago."

"Did you ever see him with anyone else? A young woman, perhaps."

The man thought about it, then shook his head. "Don't think so. Someone must still be around, though. They get mail delivered every day, but by next morning it's gone."

"You mean someone's being going in after you've closed?"

"They must be."

"What time do you close today?"

"Four o'clock on Saturdays."

It would be interesting to find out who was going in there. Margot pictured herself staying here all night, waiting in the wings for someone to turn up. But it wasn't even noon. She would be in for a long wait.

"Okay. Thanks for your help." She pulled a card from her pocket and asked him to call if anything else came to light.

"Of course," he winked. "It would be my pleasure."

Outside, Margot paused to reconsider. Whoever was collecting the mail could have been doing so in the middle of the night, and being a weekend, they might leave it until Sunday. What was she going to do – hang around all weekend? She looked up the train times back to Argents. The last train left at seven. After giving it a little more thought, she decided she would stay until six-thirty, but that was it.

With time to kill, Margot headed into the town centre. She spent an hour in the Museum of Art and History, perusing an exhibition of North African art, and afterwards bought a copy of *Femme Actuelle* and skimmed it over lunch in a bistro. Bored by three o'clock, she returned to the row of offices.

There was a café on the corner that gave a clear view of the whole street. Margot took a table by the window and kept her eyes peeled. The lights in the *Immobilier*'s window went out at four. At four-o'five, the staff departed. Five o'clock quickly came around, by which time Margot had read her magazine from cover to cover. By six, she'd drunk three glasses of wine and eaten a *croque-monsieur*. The waiter was starting to give her funny looks, and Margot began to feel a little foolish. In all probability, he wouldn't come until midnight, and she was sitting here wasting her time. If she left it much longer, she was going to miss her train, although she had to admit, the prospect of that happening did rather excite her. She'd done it before, in her youth – hopped on a train and rode it to the end of the line, deliberately got stranded to see how well she coped.

In the end, Margot chose to be sensible, and at twenty-nine minutes past six, she put some money on the table and left, fully intending to head back to the station.

———

But Margot didn't get anywhere near the station. The moment she stepped out of the café, her eyes were drawn across the street to a man who had just halted outside office number 5. He was a big man, easily six-two. 'Solidly-built,' Madame Janvier had described him. It could certainly be him, Monsieur Rémy Demis, though he looked a bit of an oddball. Despite the warm weather, he was wearing thick leather boots. He must have been sweltering inside his heavy combat jacket. After casting a glance over his shoulder, he took a key out of his pocket, unlocked the door, and went inside. Another two seconds and she would have missed him.

Margot immediately crossed over. She stood in front of the *Immobilier's* window, pretending to look at the properties for sale, while angling her eyes to the side to try and see what he was up to. He hadn't turned on the light. A couple of minutes went by and she was tempted to look in, but the door opened abruptly, catching her off-guard. Their eyes briefly met; he didn't seem suspicious. Margot flicked her gaze back to the *Immobilier's* window and sensed him locking the door. She resisted the urge to look round when he walked behind her back, and only went after him when he was halfway down the street. The only thing different about him was that he was now carrying a black leather briefcase.

He walked quickly without hurrying. The pavement was crowded, but he moved so efficiently, his gait was so precise, that Margot had to run short distances to keep up with him. He didn't look like the kind of man who normally carried a briefcase, and Margot couldn't help suspecting it was stuffed full of cash. The only time he paused was when a kid on an e-scooter shot out of a side street, almost clipping his toes.

They came to an island, the traffic nose-to-tail. Margot came close to catching up with him, but he spotted a gap and nipped over. Trailing a few seconds behind, she followed him through a small park and finally came to his side on the verge of another busy road. A number of pedestrians stood between them, but she was close enough to pick up the smell coming off him – a musty odour, mixed with cologne. The briefcase was easily within Margot's reach. She was tempted to grab it (what could he do – call the police?) but then a bus pulled up to let them cross and they were on the move again.

The next time he stopped was outside a video games store where he paused to check his phone, looking distracted. After glancing back briefly, he continued to the end of the street and turned right onto a wide avenue that Margot recognised as the road she had taken from the station. He crossed again, walked a short way down, and then disappeared into a small hotel.

Margot paused, considering her next move. She stood outside the hotel, looking up. It was a grim-looking place. An end terrace, three-storeys high; the kind of place that often came with a bad headline. Feeling apprehensive, she opened the door and stepped inside. Never judge a book... Inside was actually quite smart. Dark, classy wallpaper covered the walls, and an ornate bird-cage lift rose up from the centre of the lobby, wrapped in an equally delicate wrought-iron staircase. In the far corner, there was a cosy bar where two well-dressed people were relaxing in lounge chairs. Margot's eyes honed in on a man ascending the stairs, briefcase in one hand, keycard in the other. Monsieur Demis going up to his room.

A young woman appeared at the desk. "Bonjour, Madame."

"Bonjour," Margot smiled back, but then hesitated. She was flying by the seat of her pants and was unsure what to do next. If he was a guest here, this could take longer than she'd thought. Margot said the next thing that came into her head: "Do you have any vacancies?"

The receptionist consulted her computer. "A single or a double?"

"I don't mind."

"There's a standard double on the third floor. A hundred euros per night. Breakfast is nine euros extra."

A tingle of excitement passed down Margot's spine. This was just like old times.

"I'll take it."

The receptionist asked for her details. Had Margot been more on the ball, she would have come up with a false name, disguised her appearance in some small way, paid in cash, but her surveillance skills were a little rusty and she gave her real name and paid with her bank card instead. The receptionist's gaze lingered as she handed over a keycard. Margot suddenly realised she'd arrived without luggage and could only imagine what the young woman was thinking. After returning an awkward smile, she quickly walked away.

Margot stepped into the bird cage lift and pressed the large brass button with the number 3 on it. She was rewarded with a reassuring *ding*. The bell dinged again a few moments later as the doors opened on the second floor. Margot hoped to come face to face with the builder, but it was a younger man who squeezed in, tall and businesslike, zombified by his plastic white earbuds.

Arriving on the third floor, Margot located her room and had a quick look in. It was a little on the small side but not too bad – a comfy-looking bed, some characterful pieces of furniture, a window looking down on the street at the side of the hotel. She checked out the fire escape plan on the inside of the door. Six rooms on this floor; a similar layout on the floor below apart from an odd little annex that jutted out at the back. How could she find out which room he was in – set off the fire alarm and see which door he came out of? Or find some way of getting a look at the register.

Margot closed the door and returned to the lobby, this time taking the stairs. She browsed the rack of leaflets in the tourist information display while she planned her next move. The receptionist was on the phone, talking in English to someone. The street door opened and someone came in, then two people went out. The bar was now empty, and there was no sign of the bartender. Margot bided her time while the receptionist put down her phone, tapped something into her keyboard, and then answered another call. Two minutes later, she came off the phone again and this time disappeared into the back. Seizing her chance, Margot crossed the lobby.

She stretched over the counter and turned the monitor towards her. The register was already up on the screen, showing the list of guests. Margot scanned down, hardly expecting him to have used the same name, but there it was – Rémy Demis. Room 25. Margot stretched a little further to reach the mouse. According to the calendar, he'd been here all week and was due to check out tomorrow. A note had been made to say that he'd made a dinner reservation for eight o'clock. Requested a table for two. She was about to click back to his contact details when the door behind the counter opened. Margot immediately retracted her arm.

"Sorry, Madame. Was there something else?"

Margot smiled innocently. "Do you have a restaurant here?"

"Yes." The receptionist pointed to a double-sized opening off to the side. "It's through there."

"Could I book a table for dinner?"

"Of course. What time?"

"Eight o'clock, please."

3

Margot felt a pang of nostalgia as she took in the hotel room. Far from home, nothing but a bank card in her pocket and the clothes on her back. She had no idea what the coming hours might bring, and the uncertainty only added to the excitement. When she'd lived in Paris, she'd sometimes followed people for days, just to see what they got up to.

Realising she was unlikely to get home this weekend, Margot went to the Carrefour Express down the street to buy toiletries and a toothbrush. When she got back, she sent a message to her neighbour, Madame Barbier, asking if she could feed the cat. Afterwards, she washed her face, brushed her hair, flossed her teeth, and then sat on the edge of the bed, staring at her watch, watching the seconds tick by. Rémy Demis – Margot doubted it was his real name. She did a quick internet search, but little came up. What would she do if she did encounter him? She had no real evidence. He might be here on a job, conning one of the other guests. Better to just observe for now, she reasoned.

A noise outside prompted her to get up. Margot fought her way through the voile curtains and looked down on the street. Kids on bikes outside a kebab shop. It was five minutes to eight.

Bored of twiddling her thumbs, Margot grabbed her bag and headed down to the restaurant.

Taking the stairs, she slowed as she rounded the corner on the second-floor landing. A sign indicated rooms 25-27, and since no one was around, Margot decided to take a quick look. She entered a gloomy inner lobby, which, if her mental geography were correct, provided access to the oddly shaped annexe at the back of the hotel. She listened at all three doors, but each was as quiet as a church.

Dim lights and soft music welcomed her into the restaurant. A dozen tables had been set. The only diner presently in there was the solitary businessman she'd met in the lift, seated at a table in the far corner, still with his earbuds in. The sweet smell of seared beef whetted Margot's appetite.

A waitress showed her to a table. Realising she was being led into an alcove, however, Margot asked if she could have a table in the centre instead. It was laid for four, but would give her a much better view of the comings and goings. Happy to oblige, the waitress gathered up the superfluous cutlery and left her with a menu.

One by one, Margot watched her fellow diners arrive. First, a family of three: Mum, Dad, and a gangly teenage girl who looked like she would much rather be elsewhere. Next came two older couples, then another man on his own, happy to be denigrated to the alcove. The waitress brought some water to the table, and Margot gave her order, choosing artichoke soup followed by roast leg of lamb. Another few minutes went by without any sign of the builder. She began to suspect he'd seen her following him and had made the dinner reservation just to throw her off the scent. But finally, at twenty past eight, the big man appeared.

Margot tried not to react as he came in. He had taken off his combat jacket, but was still wearing a jumper and the thick leather boots. His eyes scanned the room as he moved, on the alert, taking everything in. Their eyes met as he passed Margot's table, but if he recognised her, he didn't show it. A young woman trailed in his wake. Shoulder-length black hair, bangs down to her eyebrows, a silky scarf worn like a tie around her neck, exactly how Madame Janvier had described. She also had a bad case of acne. She wore cheap tracksuit bottoms and a pink hoodie, and her tatty Dr Martens were covered in a floral design that looked as though she had painted it herself. Whatever they were stealing the money for, it wasn't to buy clothes.

Margot glanced casually over her shoulder as they went to their table, two rows back. They sat diagonally opposite each other rather than face to face, and didn't talk. Having an idea, Margot took her phone from her bag and activated the camera. By switching it to selfie mode, she could just about keep them in sight. Happy that no one had noticed, she pressed record.

They were easily the oddest couple in the room. The girl must have been half his size, no more than twenty, whereas he was mid-forties. They were close enough for Margot to hear them give their order: the builder going for steak; she chose gnocchi. They didn't order any wine. He stared into space, whereas she sat with her arms folded, examining her fellow diners with a slightly amused look on her face. At first glance, you might think they were ignoring each other after an argument, though Margot couldn't sense a bad atmosphere between them. Perhaps she'd guessed right and they were in the middle of a job, scamming one of the guests, although it was by no means clear what roles they might be playing.

Distracted by the arrival of her soup, Margot put down her phone. She shook out her napkin and ate quickly. As soon as her dish had been taken away, she resumed her surveillance.

The restaurant remained quiet. The family of three were the only ones talking, though the teenager sat moodily with her cheek on her fist, radiating ill-will towards the rest of the world. The businessman was already onto his main course, eating with gusto. Every now and then, the builder's companion fiddled with her scarf, careful to keep it pulled up. When their food arrived, there was little interaction between them. No smiles, nothing in the way of chat. Their manner towards each other was neither friendly nor unfriendly, yet there was clearly a bond between them. Margot wondered which of them was the brains of the outfit, though she suspected they were not working alone. If she bided her time, they might well lead her to a bigger fish.

Her lamb arrived. This time Margot turned off the camera and dropped the phone into her bag. She armed herself with a knife and a fork and turned her attention to the plate of food. She'd barely got started, however, when a noisy rattle of cutlery made her look round. The builder had dropped his fork and was reaching down to the floor to retrieve it. As he righted himself, he clutched his belly and groaned. The woman flicked him a curious glance.

"You okay?"

"I don't feel so good."

"What is it?"

He rubbed his stomach.

A suspicious look came over her. Whatever was happening, his companion wasn't in on it.

"I need some air."

"What about your food?"

"Just leave it."

He hauled himself up from his seat. His companion didn't seem very happy as she watched him walk away, but the builder didn't look back. After passing Margot's table, he strode straight out the door.

Margot was seized by a dilemma. Her instinct was to go after him, but the woman was sure to notice if she left now. But she couldn't let him get away. Margot forked the last piece of lamb into her mouth, chewed it for a while, and spent a moment dabbing her lips with a napkin. When the urge became too strong, she took her cigarettes from her bag and left the room as discreetly as she could.

He wasn't in the lobby. Margot immediately put away her cigarettes and headed for the door. Darkness was falling and the traffic had eased. Eyes searching the gaps, she spotted him, fifty metres away, heading in the direction of the station. His stomach ache seemed to have miraculously disappeared.

Margot took up pursuit. He moved stealthily, seeking out the shadows and the cover of parked cars. He paused at a junction and shot a glance back. Margot froze, caught in his direct line of sight, but either he was in too much of a hurry to notice her, or she wasn't the one he was worried might be following him. After turning down a side street, he stopped outside a bar. He waited a few minutes, anxiously checking his phone, and then a man came out of the bar. The builder drew him to one side and they fell into close conversation. Quickly reaching a conclusion, they set off down the street, shoulder to shoulder, thick as thieves.

Margot resumed her pursuit. They continued along a pavement bordered by a high stone wall, and then went through a set of tall iron gates. Realising they'd gone into the cemetery, Margot hung back, wondering if he was about to turn his hand to a spot of grave-robbery. But they were just using it as a shortcut and didn't stop until they'd emerged in the street on the far side. Eying up a row of tall stone houses, the man from the bar slid something out of his sleeve.

Margot followed them around the back. From the cover of a dead streetlight, she watched them go into a yard. Steps took them up to a back door where the builder knocked, quietly but firmly. The other man stood ready by his side. It quickly became clear that the thing he had slid from his sleeve was a cosh.

A half-dressed man came to the door. Surprised by who he found there, he took a step back and tried to shut them out, but the builder wedged the door with his foot. The man from the bar raised his cosh, but then, in a flash of movement that took everyone by surprise, the builder punched the man in the face, so hard and with such precision that he dropped in an instant.

He didn't get up. The two men stared down at him for a full ten seconds. When a noise came from inside, they were quick on their toes. They were halfway back to the cemetery by the time a woman came to the door, hands to her face in horror.

———

Stunned by what she'd witnessed, Margot hurried back to the hotel. In the lobby, she went straight to the bar and ordered a vodka martini. The bartender gave her a sympathetic look.

Perched on a bar stool, Margot felt sick in her stomach. She wasn't usually squeamish, but something about that punch had shocked her. The force of the blow, the lightning reaction, the crunch of breaking bone. She twisted to look at the door, expecting him to come in at any moment, but the door remained shut. She glanced at her wrist. Nine-thirty.

"Nice watch."

Margot turned sharply. She was surprised to find the builder's young companion seated at the end of the bar. She'd had her head down, reading a book, when Margot had come in.

"Thank you."

Margot shifted her gaze back to the watch, realising the diamonds had been catching the light. "A present from my husband," she explained. "Our tenth wedding anniversary."

"Cool."

She didn't wear it that often. It was actually a men's watch; Margot preferred the larger dials. It must have cost him an awful lot of money, dear Hugo, but the memories it came with were worth far more than diamonds. Not one to be flashy, Margot covered the watch with her sleeve. The woman had gone back to reading her book, though the comment still lingered in the air between them. There was something about the way she'd said it that was odd. Swift and to the point, delivered in a deadpan tone that made it clear she wasn't really interested in the timepiece. Margot was tempted to respond with a quip about building insurance, but just then the front door burst open. They both looked round to see the builder come in.

Face as dark as thunder, he scanned the lobby. Spotting his companion at the bar, he shot her an angry look, and then, without saying a word, he marched off up the stairs. The woman didn't seem like the type to jump at a man's beck and call, but she quickly finished her drink and went after him. She acted so fast that she left her book on the bar: *Pedagogy of the Oppressed* by Paulo Freire.

4

Woken by the sound of a van pulling up, Margot rolled wearily out of bed. Without turning on the light or putting on any clothes, she went to the open window and looked down on the street. A *boulanger*'s van was parked at the side of the hotel. Margot watched him carry his tray in through a side door, the smell of freshly baked bread making her stomach rumble.

She had a quick shower. Afterwards, she wrapped herself in a towel and sat on the edge of the bed, assailed by some early-morning doubts. She hadn't slept well. The mattress was too soft; the air-con too noisy. What she most wanted to do right now was go home and curl up in her nice comfy bed. Who was she kidding? She wasn't the same woman she'd been twenty years ago.

Nice watch.

What had she meant by that? Margot looked at the watch now as she fastened it around her wrist. She hadn't come back for her book. Margot had waited ten minutes and then handed it into reception. *Pedagogy of the Oppressed...* She'd read it herself at university. A controversial text in its day. If her memory served her correctly, it had been banned in a handful of countries on the grounds of promoting sedition. And that punch also continued to play on her mind. The last time she'd seen someone throw a punch like that had been in a boxing ring – raw, brutal, elemental. One human being using skin and bone to break the skin and bone of another.

Distant sounds came from the bowels of the building as the hotel started to come to life. Margot pushed aside her negative thoughts, and after putting on her clothes, went downstairs for a cigarette. She stood outside on the step for ten minutes, enjoying the Sunday morning vibe as the sun rose over the rooftops.

The solo businessman had just stepped out of the lift when she went back in. The breakfast buffet had been set up in the dining room, and being the first two there, they got to enjoy the spoils. Margot loaded her plate with two croissants, a thick slice of ham, a wedge of cheese, and a small piece of almond cake to go with her coffee. This time, she chose the table in the alcove.

The businessman took himself off to the far corner. A young couple she hadn't seen before came in next, followed by the family of three. Margot kept her eyes lowered when the builder and his friend arrived. When she did look up, the young woman briefly met her eye, though did nothing to suggest that their encounter last night meant anything to her. She was wearing the same pink hoodie and Dr Martens, while the builder had switched to jeans and a black sweatshirt. Margot studied them as they made their selections from the buffet. Their body language was different from last night. He seemed on edge, whereas she kept giving him curious glances like there was something about him she was seeing for the first time. Margot wondered what the exact nature of their relationship might be, how long they'd been together. She had evidently retrieved her book at some point because when they sat down, she placed it on the table next to her tray.

An idea popped into Margot's head. Without giving it a second thought, she left her table and went to the front desk. She rang the bell; a different receptionist appeared – a thin man, lost in his uniform. "Bonjour, Madame."

Margot feigned a look of distress. "This is very embarrassing. My husband's just gone out and taken the keycard with him. And I really need to use our bathroom." She scrunched up, clutching her stomach. "You couldn't give me a temporary keycard, could you? Room 25 – Monsieur Rémy Demis."

The man looked flustered. Margot did her best impression of someone who was about to leave a puddle on the floor, and he quickly got the message. He took a card from a drawer, activated it in his machine, and handed it over. Grimacing gratefully, Margot fled up the stairs.

She slowed as she reached the second-floor landing. There was no one around as she entered the inner lobby. She knocked on the door to room 25, waited ten seconds, and then went in.

It was a double room. The bed was unmade, but a blanket and a pillow had been spread out on the floor. Margot gave the bedding a sniff. Both sets were a little pungent, but she would guess it was the woman who had been sleeping on the floor. The wardrobe was empty; the drawers looked unused. Two fully packed rucksacks suggested they'd been living out of their bags. Margot poked her head into the bathroom, briefly spooked by the sight of her own reflection in the mirror. Basic toiletries, cheap plastic toothbrushes, a wet towel on the floor. Back in the bedroom, she searched for the briefcase. Her eyes settled on a dark blue messenger bag next to a chair. Kneeling down, Margot carefully undid the buckles. Inside, was a high-end camera, a couple of books, a bottle of Grey Goose tucked away at the bottom. The inner pouch contained an A4 folder. She pulled it out and opened it on the floor. Twenty or thirty pages of names and addresses, alongside columns of numbers. It looked like a tally of how much money they'd fleeced from each of their targets. Madame Janvier's name was there, along with all of her details, right down to her social security number. Margot did a rough count, gave up when she got to seventy-five thousand. If that was all in cash, she imagined it would easily fill a briefcase. She took some photos, and while she was down on the floor, looked under the bed. There was the briefcase, ripe for the taking. Together with the folder, it would make some useful evidence, but Margot left it untouched. Her instincts told her there was more going on here than just a scam operation.

Hearing what she thought was the elevator bell, Margot quickly snapped a few more photos. She then put the folder away, checked to ensure she hadn't disturbed anything else, and quietly slipped out.

———

After a quick freshen-up, she went back downstairs. There was no sign of the unlikely duo in the dining room. Assuming they had returned to their rooms to collect their things, Margot left her keycard on the desk and went outside to wait.

She watched from a bench across the street. Thirty minutes later, they emerged with their rucksacks on their backs. Margot shadowed them from the opposite side of the road. The builder was carrying the briefcase, while his companion had the blue messenger bag. He carried his load with ease, whereas she looked a little overburdened. Reaching the end of the street, he waited for her to catch up. They crossed the street together and went into the train station. Worried they were about to get on a train and disappear, Margot quickened her pace.

She entered the station a dozen steps behind. She followed them across the concourse and then out onto the platform. There were plenty of people around, despite it being Sunday morning. According to the information screens, the next train in was due in four minutes – a slow train to Nîmes, by the looks of it. Margot looked around uncertainly, once again in two minds. She couldn't just let them leave, not after what had happened last night, but how long was she going to keep following them? Go all the way to Nîmes and spend another night skulking around a hotel? The outline of a locomotive appeared in the distance, shimmering in a heat haze.

Making up her mind, Margot rushed back into the building. She bought a ticket from a machine and then returned to the platform just as the carriages squealed to a halt in front of her.

———

They boarded the second carriage. Margot followed suit, though she got on through the next door down. She spotted them working their way along the aisle, rucksacks swinging from their hands. Despite there being plenty of empty seats, they didn't stop until they were right at the front. Margot watched from the gangway as they slung their luggage up onto the overhead rack, except for the briefcase which the builder kept close to his side. They sat on opposite sides of the aisle, still not talking.

Margot swung herself into a seat several rows back. Peering through the jumble of headrests, she saw the woman resting her head against the window, looking as though she was about to have a nap. Maybe she hadn't slept well on the hotel room floor. Not very gallant of him to have taken the bed. It was odd that they hadn't splashed out on two rooms given all the cash they had. The fact they weren't spending the money they'd stolen only added to Margot's suspicion that a bigger fish was involved.

Once the train got moving, she looked up the route on her phone. It was a ninety-minute trip to Nîmes with a dozen stops on the way. With several trains back later in the day, she didn't have to worry about getting home. She toyed with the idea of confronting them. They would have no escape here, and if they turned nasty she would have plenty of allies. Margot scanned her fellow passengers for candidates: a tall young man watching football on his tablet; a mother and a toddler. When the ticket inspector came in, she realised she would be spoiled for choice, and while she was locating her ticket on her phone, Margot was sorely tempted to say something to him. But in the end, she did nothing but offer him a smile as he zapped her QR code. She wasn't done with these people yet.

Margot sent a text to Madame Barbier, asking her to check that everything was all right at home. Madame Barbier replied immediately to say that all was well. Then, as the train built up speed, Margot settled herself in for the wait.

———

Ten minutes later, the train suddenly slowed down. A few of the passengers lurched in their seats. As they came to a halt in a station, Margot looked down to the front of the carriage to see if they would get off. A couple of people alighted, but the builder and his companion remained in their seats. Precisely three minutes later, the train was moving again.

The scene was repeated at the next two stops, but then, around an hour into the journey, the builder got to his feet and reached up to the luggage rack. He passed one rucksack down to his companion, and then threw the other one onto his back, all the time guarding the briefcase between his feet. Fully loaded, the pair shuffled into the gangway to wait by the doors.

Margot peered curiously through the windows. They'd been moving through a landscape of scrub and low trees, with only a few isolated buildings to break the monotony. According to the timetable, they were still twenty minutes away from Nîmes. The next station they stopped at was tiny, somewhere in the back end of nowhere. An elderly man with a bicycle was the only one waiting on the platform.

Margot stayed seated. The doors hissed open, bringing in a draft of hot, dry air. She watched them get off and set off down the platform, walking with a purposeful stride like they still had a way to go. Margot found herself at another of those pivotal moments. To follow, or not to follow. She could stay on the train, give up the chase, convince herself that she'd done all that she could. Or, she could get out of her seat and go after them. It wasn't until the very last moment that she made up her mind, rushing for the doors a second before they closed.

They'd already made it to the end of the platform. Margot watched in surprise as they continued down a ramp that led directly onto the rails, wondering if they had a death wish. But it soon became apparent that the ramp led to a walkway across the track, and she watched them carry on up a slope of rough ground until they disappeared through a gap in the fence. Burning with curiosity, Margot went after them.

The gap turned out to be a gate. Margot stepped onto a quiet street lined with only a few small houses. Ten o'clock on a Sunday morning, no one was around. To the right, the road headed back to the station while to the left it curved gently downhill. It was anyone's guess which way they'd gone, so she tossed a coin in her head and went left.

The road led to a bridge. When Margot raised herself to look over a high brick wall, she found herself looking down at the thick steel rails of the railway line. Soon, her gaze fell upon two familiar figures, recognisable by their rucksacks, walking along an unmade road running parallel with the line. Backtracking, Margot found a gap in a hedge that she'd missed the first time, and pushed through some overhanging branches to set off after them.

She increased her speed and soon had them in her sights. They were moving at a steady but unhurried pace, looking like they knew exactly where they were going, even though nothing other than scrubland lay ahead of them. The railway embankment rose to their left, while to the right lay a dusty plain on the far side of which tiny vehicles were moving on a long, straight road. Pausing to consult the maps app on her phone, Margot realised the road was an autoroute. Beyond it was nothing but woods. The map also showed that the track they were on continued for several more kilometres before joining a network of smaller trails. Other than the village where the train had stopped, there was no habitation for miles around.

Margot put away her phone, having a bad feeling about all of this. The sun was making her head feel hot, and she was craving a drink of water. She allowed the gap to widen, and considered turning back. Whatever was going on here was out of her league. But for some reason, her legs wouldn't stop moving and on she went.

She lost them when the track entered a grove of small trees. She came to a fork, footprints in the sand indicating they had turned right, towards the autoroute. It was a few minutes before she spotted them again, heading for an underpass. It was a rather incongruous feature – high enough to drive a tractor through, yet there were no fields around. Cautiously proceeding, Margot looked up at the underside of the concrete, the traffic rumbling by just metres above her head.

Safely on the other side, she spotted her quarry tramping through some long grass towards the woods. They paused on the tree line where the builder unhooked what appeared to be a chain. He ushered his companion through and then carefully reattached it. Moments later, they'd both disappeared.

Margot batted a fly away from her face. After deliberating for a moment, she moved up to the tree line. The chain he had unhooked hung between two wooden posts, with a metal sign hanging from the centre: *CHASSE EN COURS* – Hunting in Progress. Margot cautiously peered in. The woods were dense. Other than a vague line of trampled undergrowth, there was nothing to indicate where they'd gone. The bad feeling she was having steadily grew stronger.

She checked her phone once again. The satellite imagery showed the woods extended for miles, although for some reason the images were pixelated. Zooming in only made it worse. She took a few photos. Checked over her shoulder. It would be folly to follow them in. She imagined them crouching in the bushes, waiting to jump out on her, kill her in the most gruesome of ways. But then, she'd come this far... Not one to give in to her fears easily, Margot reached out to unhook the chain. And in the very same moment, something whizzed past her ear.

Margot instinctively ducked. She turned her head quickly enough to catch sight of dust rising from where something had hit the dirt. Someone had fired a shot! And it had only just missed.

She spun back to the woods, her pulse racing. The trees stared innocently back at her, as if nothing had happened. This time, the fear won out, and Margot turned on her heels and ran, every fibre of her being telling her to flee for her life.

———

Dion waited until they were fully concealed by the trees before moving away from the path. Keeping a firm grip on the briefcase, he doubled back through the undergrowth, instinct and training allowing him to traverse the uneven ground with finesse, making no more noise than a deer would have made. He glanced back, unsurprised to see that Esmée, lost in a world of her own, hadn't even noticed he'd gone.

Locating a spot from where he could see the entrance to the woods, Dion hunkered down. The woman was still there, staring into the trees from the chain barrier. Tall, blonde, lithe... she'd been following them since they'd got on the train at Narbonne. He cursed himself for not having got rid of her sooner.

His hand moved to the butt of his knife, hidden at the back of his belt. He wouldn't hesitate to use it. A branch snapped, distracting him. He turned to see a man in military fatigues approaching clumsily, rifle in hand. Dion was annoyed to see that it was Golem.

"You were followed!" the moron whispered-shouted, dropping into a crouch beside him. "Who is she?"

Golem had the kind of face not even a mother could love. Dion sneered at him before turning back to his mystery pursuer. The hairs on the back of his neck spiked as he watched her taking photographs. If she came any closer, he would have to act. Things got worse when she reached for the chain. Sensing Golem raise his rifle, Dion grabbed the barrel, but not quickly enough to stop it from going off. The blast reverberated through the trees, making some birds take flight.

Now Esmée came crashing through the undergrowth, curiosity writ large on her face. She squatted beside them, and together they looked anxiously back at their pursuer. The shot had only just missed her. She seemed confused as she looked down at the ground, but then got the message. Dion breathed in relief as she high-tailed it back to the underpass.

He turned to Golem. "Idiot!" He snatched the gun from his hand, put the lock on the trigger, and then threw the weapon to the ground. "You could have killed her."

"Who was she?"

Dion ignored him. He retrieved the briefcase and went back to the path. The truth was he had no idea who she was, and that, perhaps, was what worried him most.

5

They'd only been walking for a few minutes and they were already swamped by trees. In every direction, spindly old oaks stretched into the distance, their trunks fading into darkness. Ancient and wizened, their branches gnarled and twisted – like old men who'd been in the world too long. Dion hadn't missed them. Outside, it had been a bright, sunny morning, but in here it was a Stygian gloom.

He pushed on, keeping his wits about him. You had to stay focussed. These woods covered hundreds of square kilometres, and if you let your mind wander, even for a second, you could lose your way, stay lost for days. Or worse – stumble into one of the man-traps. Prying eyes were not welcome here.

Dion glanced back. Esmée was struggling to keep up, tromping through the undergrowth so noisily a predator would have heard her from a mile off. This wasn't her natural environment. Golem, on the other hand, was very much a creature of the forest. Six-foot-four, round-shouldered, wiry as a twisted liana – he looked like someone had taken his teeth out and put them back in the wrong way. You could almost smell the glee coming off him as he goaded them on from the rear, like a hunter with his catch. The moment they got back to camp, he would go to Sébastien and snitch on them, like the good little pet that he was. And Sébastien would listen to him, like he did with all his people. Dion knew he would have to tread carefully.

The path had long since disappeared and all he had to follow were the markers carved into the trunks of certain trees, meaningless symbols to anyone else but a sure-fire way back to camp for those who knew what to look for. The woman continued to butt into his thoughts. He recognised her from the hotel, but it wasn't until she'd stepped off the train just now that he'd realised she was following them. He searched his memory, but was pretty sure he'd never seen her before.

"Hey, Dion – wait up."

Dion turned. Esmée had paused to take a drink from her water bottle. Golem stood guard, rifle at the ready, determined not to give up his catch. Dion unclipped his own water bottle and took a swig. The trees may have blotted out much of the light, but it was still humid. He remembered the first time he'd come this way, when Sébastien had accepted him into the group. Two of the brothers had collected him from the train station, way past midnight. They'd taken him down the track alongside the railway line and then up to the woods in pitch dark, no explanation as to where they were going. Sébastien had assured him he would be welcome in the group, but these weren't the kind of people you trusted without good cause. Dion had kept his wits about him as they'd gone into the woods by the light of their torches. One wrong word would have probably been his last. They'd shown him the symbols on the trees, and Dion had memorised every single one of them, just in case he ever needed to get out in a hurry.

Esmée pushed through the bushes to catch up with him, her cheeks flushed, her forehead shiny. She paused to draw breath. "How much farther?"

When she'd joined the group a few months ago, they'd collected her in one of the vans. She'd come in through the main gate and hadn't known about the route through the woods.

"Ten minutes," Dion replied.

He watched her to see if she had anything to say. Now that he came to think about it, he'd seen her with the mystery woman at the bar last night. She hadn't mentioned her when they'd gone up to the room, and he'd lied when she'd asked where he'd been. Esmée gave him a meaningful look in the eye, but if she had anything to say, she was keeping it to herself.

Golem stepped forward, attempting to goad them on. Dion sneered back at him but put away his water bottle.

Another ten minutes and they reached the perimeter fence. The vegetation was so dense you barely noticed it until you were almost upon it. *ZONE DANGEREUSE - ACCÈS INTERDITS*, the signs read. Keep out, for your own good, though the coils of razor wire attached to the top probably sent a stronger message. Dion leapt over a small stream, climbed a bank to get onto the access road, and then walked the short distance to the gate. He opened the metal box fixed to the gatepost and pulled out the telephone receiver.

"Open up. We're back."

High in one of the trees, a camera moved. Dion stared into the lens, picturing how he would look on a monitor in the Command Centre. After a short delay, the gates opened with a quiet whir.

It was still a trek to the nearest building. Dion estimated the base covered over two hundred hectares, most of it woodland. Not a single light guided their way as they followed the road around a clearing and then back into the trees. A dozen buildings made up the heart of the complex, but they were so dark you could easily miss them even if you knew they were there. Mounds of soil and rubble had been pushed against many of the walls, and the few remaining windows had been shuttered and boarded up. It seemed that whoever had been using the base before them had tried to bury it, quite literally.

There was only one way in or out: a sandbagged alley that cut through the only mound that had been cleared. It led to an anonymous grey door, but before they could reach it, two dogs appeared from behind and came bounding down the sandbagged alley towards them. Dion tensed, reaching for his knife. It was wise to be wary of them – several were Boerboel mongrels and were kept deliberately underfed – but they were also well trained, and two sharp whistles from their handler were enough to bring them to heel.

A beard emerged from the anonymous grey door. "Welcome back, brothers." They exchanged fist bumps. "How was the trip?"

Dion held up the briefcase, exaggerating its weight. "I think you can call that fruitful."

The beard grinned, but raised a hand to stop them going in. "Phones off?"

Dion handed his over. Arriving at his side, Esmée did the same. The beard checked to make sure they were both switched off and then put them into a Faraday bag.

Dion felt his heart sink as they went inside. A short dark corridor led to a gloomy open room that was as dank as it was dark. After six weeks on the outside, it felt like going back to a tomb.

They were shouldering off their rucksacks when Sébastien and Tik came in, along with a small group of others. Their leader was a slightly built man with blond hair and glasses, only twenty-three years of age. He had the baby white face and piercing blue eyes of a Nazi. Tik was the IT guru – the beard in chief, as Dion liked to think of him.

"Good to see you back, brothers." Sébastien shook him

warmly by the hand. "All went well, I take it?" He glanced at the briefcase.

Dion knew his question had little to do with the money, however. He would be more concerned that they had not been led astray. No one kept track of them when they were out in the field. The group operated on trust.

"Esmée has all the figures," Dion said, and after a nod from Sébastien, she took out her folders and set up on the nearest desk.

"The car parking scam worked well," she began. "Of the twenty-one targets originally identified, we scored on sixteen." She unlocked several pages from her folder and handed them out. Sébastien and Tik scrutinised every detail, keen to know exactly what had transpired. Tik had compiled the list of targets before they'd left, but Esmée had done lots of additional research while they'd been out on the road. Many long nights she'd sat at her laptop. She wasn't part of the IT crew, but she'd seemed to know what she was doing. By the time they'd finished, Sébastien was clearly impressed. Tik also nodded his appreciation.

"That's a much higher success rate than we were expecting," Sébastien said. "You've done well. And is this the final total?"

His fingertip was on the last page, but Esmée pointed to the briefcase instead. "There's a hundred and seventy-five thousand in there."

Everyone in the room turned to look at the briefcase, hanging innocuously from Dion's left hand. Dion kept them in suspense for a few moments before lifting it up onto the desk. He raised the lid and watched dollar signs light up their eyes. All except Sébastien, for whom the cash was just bundles of paper, a means to an end. Their leader gave them both an appreciative look.

"Good work, brothers. Your contribution will not go unacknowledged." Sébastien closed the briefcase and handed it to one of the beards. "Now it's time to eat. You must be hungry."

They made a move to leave, but Golem chose that moment to push his way to the fore. "They were followed," he blurted out. "Someone saw them come into the woods."

Dion shot him a look of contempt. Golem was the kind of person who would snitch on his own grandmother if he thought it would win favour with their leader. Sébastien turned to give them a curious look. "What's this?"

Dion avoided meeting his eye. Sébastien's paranoia was an unpredictable beast. He could fly off the handle with no warning at all.

"It was nothing," Dion replied calmly. "It looked like someone followed us from the train, but she didn't come into the woods."

"She took pictures!" Golem protested. "She came right up to the sign."

"Yes, and some idiot took a potshot at her," Dion snapped back. "Imagine if he'd hit her."

Golem squared up to him, ready to retaliate. Dion balled his fists... Oh, how he would love to punch that ugly face of his. Sébastien raised a pacifying hand.

"All right, brothers. Let's deal with this calmly."

Golem backed down. After a moment, Sébastien returned his attention to Dion. "Who was she?"

"I've no idea. I'd never seen her before."

"How long had she been following you?"

"Only from the station."

Sébastien remained puzzled. "Nothing went wrong? On any of the hits?"

Dion shook his head. "Nothing went wrong. We had no problems at all," he said, and avoided looking at Esmée. He should have anticipated this moment and spoken to her on the train, made sure she was prepared to back him up. But he hadn't been thinking clearly for days. The lack of sleep was catching up with him; he was making too many mistakes.

After a pause, Sébastien switched his attention to Esmée. "What about you? Have you any idea who she was?"

Another pause formed. Dion kept his eyes down, his pulse quickening, not sure how he would handle it if she gave him away. As the pause grew longer, his hand twitched, tempted to reach for his knife. Worst-case scenario, he could take any man in this room, but outside, with the dogs on the loose, he didn't rate his chances.

"No idea at all," Esmée replied at last. "I did notice someone walking behind us, but I think it was just a coincidence. She looked a bit lost."

Dion flicked her a look of gratitude.

Sébastien remained silent for a little while. He divided his attention between the two of them, as if not sure whether to believe them. Dion knew this would not sit well with him. But finally, their leader conceded a small nod.

"Ask the guard to double the patrol on the perimeter tonight, please," he said to Golem. "We don't want to take any chances."

Defeated, Golem retreated to whichever rock-pool he'd crawled out of.

———

Noon, and the mess hall was bustling. Two very long tables ran down the centre, with enough seating for eighty or ninety people. They all ate together. Mealtimes were one of the few constants about life in the group: seven, noon, seven. Dion liked the regularity. Except for those who were on guard duty, everyone would gather in the mess hall at mealtimes, even the geeks who normally hated to tear themselves away from their computer screens.

The food was good, no one ever went hungry. Sébastien insisted the kitchen always be well stocked. Their cooks were ex-military, used to serving up hearty and tasty meals en masse. Dion took a tray from the stack and cast his eyes over the various dishes as he moved along the counter: meat, fruit, bread, pastries. They wanted for nothing, except for alcohol, which was strictly forbidden. Dion asked one of the servers for scrambled eggs and *pain grillé* and took a seat on his own, not in the mood for talking.

A dozen men were already seated, more were coming in every second. The mess hall was the one place in the base that was always full of chatter. The brothers' appetite for the food was matched by their keenness for debate, and passionate discussions would often break out. Politics, history, economics. The exchanges would sometimes get heated. But Sébastien insisted that everyone was listened to, that their opinions were heard. There were no hierarchies here.

They were a motley crew, left-wing in the main, quite a few communists, but there was also a small group of anarchists. Dion knew most of them by name, though he didn't consider any of them friends. Nearly all of them were men, ranging in age from a precocious seventeen-year-old to a couple in their sixties. They came from all walks of life: plumbers and electricians; a couple of doctors; lawyers and academics. Sébastien's was a broad church. Some were waifs and strays, people who'd never managed to find their place in society. Then there were the troubled and the malcontents, some of whom really should have been in an institution. Others had more intellectual axes to grind – bearded academics who'd given up good careers to be here. All of them were angry with the world. Or just felt let down by it.

If there was one other thing they had in common, it was distrust of the government. The idea that the powers that be were actively manipulating the populace was never in doubt. Whether it was through putting fluoride in the water or broadcasting subliminal messages on TV, the evidence was undeniable, they claimed. The world was run by powerful elites who controlled the media and used it to brainwash the public, and governments were their puppets, manipulated to ensure the billionaires remained untouchable. The system was corrupt, and something had to be done about it.

Mostly, Dion just listened. "Is France ready for the Sixth Republic?" the man to his left was saying. They'd been discussing the mistakes Charles de Gaulle had apparently made in founding the Fifth Republic by putting too much power in the hands of the executive. Many of these men bore grievances dating back decades. Another group was talking about election fraud. "It's why they only allow you to use pencils in polling stations," one man said. "Pencil lead can be erased." "Sheeple," he heard someone else comment.

On it went. Dion had heard the arguments many times before.

"The people who gain from the system are never going to change it," Sébastien piped up at one point. Dion observed how quickly the room quietened down. Their leader, seated at the head of the table, was a good orator. People were always keen to hear what he had to say. "They pretend to listen, but they don't care about us, the little people. They make promises to bring about change, but then break those promises as soon as they get into power. How do we get through to people who won't listen?"

"We make them listen," someone called out.

"They need teaching a lesson," a young man responded.

"This country belongs to us," an older man cried out. "We are the men and women who make it function. We are the ones who fix the roads, and farm the land, and produce the food – not them."

One of the beards stood up. "This president acts like a monarch. He's been given way too much power and he needs to be taken down a peg or two."

Several men banged their fists on the table, loudly proclaiming their agreement. The room filled with noise once more.

"It's time to draw a line in the sand," Sébastien put in, raising his voice over the hubbub. "You've pushed us this far, now no more. Our day is coming, brothers. You mark my words."

Dion looked around the table as the others joined in, banging their cutlery in hearty agreement. They all had dreams of building a better world, and he admired that. Problem was, with this group, dreaming wasn't going to be enough.

First thing on Monday morning, Margot put on her swimsuit and went down to the cove. She stripped off down to her Speedo, tucked her clothes away in her swim bag, and then picked her way to the water's edge. After wading in ten metres, she flung herself onto the waves.

She headed for the rising sun, blazing on the horizon. Swim as hard as you liked, you were never going to reach it. Drained after half an hour, she swam back to the beach and plonked herself down on a rock. It had been a whole day since she'd got back from Nîmes and she was still unsettled. It wasn't every day you got shot at. Half a metre to the left and that bullet would have hit her, Margot had no doubt about that. She pulled her towel from her bag and wiped sand from between her toes, thinking she was lucky to still be alive. It had probably been hunters, she'd told herself. A stray bullet – it wouldn't have been the first time it had happened. But then, how come it had happened so soon after they'd gone into the woods? It couldn't be a coincidence.

Margot was home by seven. Having not had time to shop at the weekend, her store cupboard was depressingly bare. She leaned against her open fridge door while she contemplated how she was going to concoct a breakfast from three old eggs, a small packet of cheese, and a drawer full of sorry-looking salad vegetables. A weaker-willed Margot would have escaped to the boulangerie, treated herself to a croissant and a cake, but she made do with the cheese, sliced and toasted a stale baguette, and brewed a strong pot of coffee.

Margot took her tray and her laptop out to the yard and sat in the sun. Munching her way through the toast, she checked her emails and caught up on some correspondence. Afterwards, she went to the site of the École Nationale de la Magistrature and retrieved her draft application form. Several minutes passed while she stared at the screen, coffee cup to her lips, feeling rather unsure. So far, she'd filled in her personal details and the section on qualifications and work experience, but she was a long way from clicking on 'Send'. Célia had been right – according to the guidance notes, Margot's time working as an *avocat* in Paris meant that she would only need to do the twelve-month course and, once qualified, would be able to start working as a *magistrat*. Less appealing was the fact that the school was in Bordeaux, and Margot was still trying to get her head around the logistics. It was a five-hour train ride from Argents to Bordeaux. Too far to commute. The alternative was to find a bolt-hole over there and come home at the weekends, but did she really want all that toing and froing at her time of life? The website was full of images of bright young things, full of energy and ambition, which made her even more unsure. Everyone in her class would be half her age. She wasn't quite sure how she would feel about that.

Margot was drawn away from the screen by a movement in her peripheral vision. The cat had jumped down from the wall and was padding towards her, a purposeful look on his face. Reaching her feet, he looked up, let out a curious *meow*, and then disappeared under her chair. Glad of the distraction, Margot closed the laptop and craned her head downwards.

"Good morning, Buster. Nice of you to drop by."

The cat rubbed his right cheek against her calf, then did the same with his left. *You belong to me now, woman. Don't ever forget that.*

"Does this mean you've missed me? You couldn't wait to come over and show me some affection, is that it?"

More likely he was hungry and hadn't been given the food he wanted from Madame Barbier.

Having duly claimed her with his scent, the cat parked his bottom on the flagstones and stared at the kitchen door. A few seconds later, he turned his head and stared at Margot. When Margot didn't respond, he did it again, astounded that she hadn't yet got the message. *Come on, woman. How hard can it be?*

Although he'd become a regular visitor, Margot wasn't entirely convinced they'd become friends. He divided his time between her house and Madame Barbier's at the end of the row, who, it turned out, was just as big a sucker as herself. Often, she wouldn't see him for days – particularly if Madame Barbier had roasted a chicken – and then, presumably tiring of that, would return to see if Margot could offer him anything better. Not since the days of the Ancient Egyptians had a feline been pampered on such a grand scale.

Orders received, Margot went to the kitchen and sorted him out a packet of duck meat, gizzard and liver. Then she went upstairs to get ready for work.

———

At noon, Margot left her desk at the *Palais de Justice* and walked along Rue Garenne to the Gendarmerie. The front door was wide open, and inside, she found the front desk unmanned. The place seemed deserted until she heard the sounds of heaving and straining coming from behind the counter. Quietly approaching the Perspex screen, Margot raised herself on tiptoe. Lieutenant Martel was down on the floor, doing some energetic push-ups.

"Having fun?"

Surprised, the lieutenant twisted his neck. He quickly put his knee to the ground and got up, a rare look of embarrassment on his face. "Sorry, Madame. I didn't hear you come in."

Margot smiled. "I didn't mean to startle you."

"Not at all." The lieutenant reached for a towel. "I was just working on my upper body strength."

"Don't you get enough exercise already?"

"I'm training for the Argents triathlon."

"Oh, really? I've heard that's quite tough."

"It is. It's an Ironman triathlon." Having dried his face, the lieutenant began tousling his hair. "A three-point-eight-kilometre swim, one hundred and eighty k on the bike, and then a forty-two k run."

"Wow. Sounds exhausting," Margot said. Then, after giving it some thought: "I could probably manage the swim, but after that I would definitely need a lie down."

The impish grin returned to the lieutenant's face. "To what do we owe the pleasure?"

"Is the captain in?"

"Come through."

The lieutenant unlocked the interconnecting door and left her to find her own way down the corridor.

Captain Bouchard was alone in his office, eyes down, engrossed in a pile of paperwork. Margot knocked on the open door, then greeted him with a smile when he looked up. "Sorry to bother you at lunchtime," she said. "I seem to be making a habit of it, don't I?"

The captain twitched his lips. He didn't seem entirely displeased. "It's no bother, Madame. How can I help?"

"I was wondering if I might get your advice."

He raised an eyebrow, intrigued. He closed the file he'd been working on and indicated the chair facing him. After making herself comfortable, Margot told her tale, starting with her chat with Madame Janvier and ending with her trip to the woods.

"I probably should have called you sooner, but I was hoping they might lead me to a bigger fish. Or an address where they were operating from."

"You've certainly had an eventful weekend," the captain said, leaning back in his seat. He pondered for a moment. "How did they pay the rent on the office?"

"With cash, I presume. I can check with the *Immobilier*, but I doubt they'll have left a paper trail. They knew what they were doing."

"And the permits he had for the car park?"

"All fake. The piece of land doesn't even exist."

"You said you got a good look at them."

"Yes. I took some photos." Margot took out her phone and swiped through until she found a good one from the restaurant. She turned the screen around to show him. The captain nodded, seemingly pleased with her efforts.

"Send it to me and I'll put out an alert."

"And this is a file I found in their room." She flicked through to the next series of images. "I'm assuming these are the details of other people they've conned."

The captain leaned across the desk to look more closely. He seemed genuinely impressed. "Excellent work. Send that across too. We'll see if we can track some of them down."

"Could we also check Madame Janvier's phone records? The woman posing as the insurance agent called her several times."

"I'll make some enquiries. And I'll talk to our *Policier Munic-*

ipal; ask him to spread the word. It's the classic tactic of the con artist, of course – gain the victim's trust by doing them a favour and then reel them in. But we don't want anyone else falling into the same trap."

"That's a good idea."

"Other than that…" The captain opened his hands. "There's probably little else I can do."

Margot nodded in acknowledgment. She hadn't really expected anything more. The only regret she had was not doing more herself. "I wish I'd challenged him now. I'm sure that briefcase was full of cash."

"That would not have been a wise idea. Confronting them would only have antagonised them. You did the right thing bringing this to my attention, Madame."

A knowing look passed between them. They'd clashed in the past about her unofficial involvement in police investigations. It seemed Margot had learned her lesson.

"There is one other thing," Margot went on.

The captain raised an eyebrow.

"Just after they went into the woods, there was a gunshot. The bullet missed me by just a few metres."

The captain's eyes widened. "They *shot* at you?"

Margot nodded. "Well, somebody did. The hunting signs were up. It could have been a stray bullet, I suppose."

Captain Bouchard emphatically shook his head. "The hunting season doesn't start until September, Madame."

"Of course," Margot mused aloud. Why hadn't she thought of that?

"Could you tell what kind of firearm it was?"

Margot shrugged. "A shotgun. Maybe a rifle. Although, if it was a rifle, it couldn't have been either of them who'd fired it. They certainly weren't carrying one on the train."

The captain nodded sagely.

"Another odd thing," Margot went on. "The satellite imagery on my phone was all blurred. I assumed it was just a bad signal, but when I got home, I checked it on my laptop and it was just the same. That entire area of woodland was obscured."

The captain frowned. He picked up a pen and turned his notepad to a clean sheet. "Give me the exact location and I'll look into it."

———

With an hour to kill before she needed to be back at work, Margot went down to the seafront. Finding Madame Janvier's bookshop closed, she shielded her eyes with her palm and peered in through the glass. Seeing a light on at the back, Margot tapped lightly on the door. Madame Janvier's face appeared, and realising who it was, she came to the door.

"Bonjour, Margot. How lovely to see you again. Do come in."

Margot followed the shopkeeper through to the back. At the counter, Madame Janvier turned to give her a hopeful look. "Any news?"

Margot pulled an unhappy face. "Yes, but I'm afraid it's not good."

"Oh." Her face dropped.

"I went to that office in Narbonne. I waited outside for a few hours, and the man you described came along."

"Did he now?" Madame Janvier's face brightened. "And what did he have to say for himself?"

"I didn't actually speak to him. I followed him, and found the pair of them staying in a hotel. On Sunday morning they took a train to a small town near Nîmes. But then I lost them on the edge of some woods."

"You went all the way to Nîmes?" She sounded surprised.

Margot nodded keenly.

"But you still didn't find out what they'd done with my money?"

Margot stiffened, not quite the reaction she'd expected. She cleared her throat. "I was guessing they had a hideaway somewhere. Or were working with someone else. People like that often operate in groups."

Madame Janvier turned away, failing to hide her disappointment. She retreated behind the counter and started tidying a display of gift bags. "Well, at least you tried."

"I did my best," Margot insisted.

"I'm sure you did."

And I did get shot at, Margot was tempted to add, peevishly. But she bit her tongue, not wanting to exaggerate the danger she'd been in. She continued:

"I thought it best to inform the Gendarmerie, so I went there this morning and told Captain Bouchard. He said he would circulate a description. We've also got the details of some of the other people they've targeted, so he's going to try and get in contact."

Madame Janvier nodded, though not in an appreciative way. She stopped tidying the gift bags and cheered up. "Anyway, I spoke to my granddaughter last night. I had been putting it off, knowing how she would react, but she's coming down as soon as she can. Trust me, sparks will fly when Natalie gets here."

Margot frowned. "I can't see there's anything more she can do."

Madame Janvier smiled wryly. "You don't know Natalie. She's very determined."

"Yes, but... I stuck with them for the best part of the weekend. They weren't amateurs."

"I know. I am grateful for your help, Margot. Truly, I am. But Natalie's young and full of energy. She won't take no for an answer."

Margot narrowed her eyes. It probably wasn't the shopkeeper's intention, but Margot couldn't help feeling she'd failed in some way.

"So, if you could let me have that business card back, please." Madame Janvier held out her hand.

Reluctantly, Margot opened her bag. "These people could be dangerous," she warned. "I think there's more going on here than a simple con trick."

"Don't worry. Natalie knows how to take care of herself."

Margot looked down at Madame Janvier's waiting palm. Her gut told her she was making a mistake, but she didn't really have much choice. Finally, with a shrug of the shoulders, she handed over the card.

Madame Janvier tucked it into her pocket. "I'll give this to Natalie. See what she can come up with."

She may as well have slapped Margot's face with a glove.

7

Sometimes the gloom got to him. Even on sunny days, it could feel dark inside the base. The electricians in the group had restored power to a number of key areas, but with the doors barricaded and the windows boarded up, most of the buildings were permanently in the dark. One stray chink of light could be enough to give them away, Sébastien constantly reminded them. To Dion, it seemed unlikely.

At least at night it wasn't so bad. When the rest of the country was also facing the void of space, he didn't feel he was missing out so much. Golem had been shadowing him most of the day, reluctant to let go of his suspicions, but at eleven o'clock Dion had had enough. He switched off his torch, ran down a completely dark corridor, and then hid around a corner. A torch beam appeared in the corridor behind him, but quickly moved on. Dion shook his head in disbelief. Outwitting a slug would have been more challenging.

He switched his torch back on. He took a rambling route back to the Command Centre and paused when he got to the hub, the place where the four main wings of the building intersected. The original entrance to C-wing had long since collapsed, but someone had bypassed it by cutting a hole in the wall. After ducking through the hole, Dion passed through a small room and emerged in the main corridor.

C-wing looked like a bomb had gone off. Or at least, it had suffered a very bad fire. The walls were blackened, the floors covered in rubble. Most of the doors had been blown off their hinges, or kicked down, or bashed with hammers. Who could tell? At the end of the main corridor, he approached the door marked C-5, one of the few that was still intact. He'd secured it with a padlock, just in case anyone came looking, and always kept the key in his pocket. He checked again to ensure he hadn't been followed, then went inside and locked the door behind him.

Going into the old gymnasium always made him happy. It looked like it had once been well-equipped, but its most notable feature now was the hole in the roof, his link with the outside. Part of his escape plan should things ever turn ugly. He'd found it over a year ago. In the weeks that followed, he'd improvised a grappling hook and used it to secure a rope. Over time, he'd turned the rope into a rope ladder, fashioning treads from a desk he'd cut up. Now he could be up on the roof in eight seconds flat.

Dion climbed the ladder as quietly as a mouse. Up on the roof, the moon cast an eerie white glow. On nights like this, the base looked like a ghost ship, lost in a sea of woods. Not a breath of wind was blowing as he moved to the verge, choosing his footsteps carefully. The roofing sheets were brittle – one wrong step could lead to a deadly fall. Safely at the verge, he looked down at the mound of earth piled against the side of the building. The bulldozer that must have been used to put it there sat just a few metres away, its cab door wide open, the key still in the ignition. Like everything else in the base, it looked like it had been abandoned in a hurry.

Dion dropped to the mound, hunkered down to check that the dogs hadn't picked up his scent, and then scrambled to the ground. A twenty-metre sprint took him to the fence, then an inner gate, and finally to an avenue through the trees where he knew he could relax, confident he couldn't be seen.

The avenue led to an outlying part of the base that seemed straight out of 1950s science fiction. A large clearing was filled with an array of oddly shaped antennas. Dion had a good knowledge of science, but some of this stuff was completely unknown to him. What interested him most, however, was the optical observatory, swamped in the trees to one side, its verdigris dome poking up through the canopy.

Dion navigated through a sea of dense undergrowth. Like everything else around here, the observatory was slowly being consumed by the forest. He entered via a service door in the base of the structure and switched on his torch. When he'd first come in here, it had looked like an animal had been using it as a den. He'd cleared it out and repaired as much as he could. Shining his torch up through the tangle of steelwork that supported the telescope brought a boyish grin to his face. He'd always wanted to be an astronomer. As a boy, he'd spent many long nights on the farm, lying on his back in a field, gazing up at the night sky. Later, he'd managed to pick up a small telescope from the local *brocante*. Setting foot in an observatory like this had been the stuff of dreams.

He climbed the spiral staircase to the circular gantry, tracing his light across the smooth, clean lines. It was a remarkable instrument – a twenty-four-inch refractor. Other than a little fungus on the main lens, it was in remarkably good condition. Most of the equipment on the control desk looked like it had been installed in the 1980s, but the telescope itself had probably been built in the 1950s. German lenses, precision mechanical control gear. The only problem was, the mechanism to rotate the dome was jammed, meaning the view was restricted to a long, narrow rectangle. A crying shame it had gone to waste.

Dion removed the lens cap and cleaned the lens with a cloth. When he lowered his eye to the eyepiece, the moon was edging into view. He turned the knob to adjust focus, and watched as the ridges and craters popped out, seas full of dry moon dust, pin-sharp in detail. He often imagined what it would be like to walk on its surface and look back at the Earth. Billions of people had looked up at the moon yet only a privileged few had ever seen the Earth rise.

Dion closed his eyes as a wave of emotion swept over him. The night before he'd come to the base, he and his wife had made a pact: if the moon was out at midnight, they would look at it and think of each other. Dion had stuck to his side of the agreement. Yvette was his soulmate, the only person he'd ever really opened up to. He'd told her things about his childhood he would never have dreamed of telling anyone else. After three dates, he'd known he'd wanted to marry her, and in the years that followed, his love had only grown stronger. It had been unthinkable that they would ever split up, yet here they were, on the brink of it happening. Joining the group was always going to put a strain on their relationship. He'd assured her it wouldn't be for long. Six months at most. A year down the line, he'd promised they wouldn't be apart for much longer. In truth, there had never been an end date in sight.

By eleven-thirty, clouds had come in and covered the moon. By midnight, there was nothing to see other than dark, amorphous shapes moving across the sky. Dion replaced the lens cap, disappointed, though it hardly mattered. After all this time, he doubted she was even bothering to look.

———

Dion paused after locking the gymnasium door, checking that no one had seen him come out. You never knew who might be lurking, even in C-wing. He took his time walking back to the Command Centre, shining his light into the nooks and crannies, expecting Golem to crawl out from every dark crevice. But it was well after midnight. The place was as quiet as a graveyard.

Back at the hub, he spotted a light down the corridor to B-wing. Curious, he went to take a look. B-wing had once been home to the classroom block, and was a long, single-storey structure with a low, flat roof. The light was coming from under a door. Dion waited outside, listening in. Hearing no sound, he reached out and quietly turned the handle. Inside, Esmée was sitting on the floor, knees up, reading a book by the light of her torch.

She was so engrossed she hadn't noticed him come in. Dion held his breath while he watched her turn a page. Despite all that time on the road together, they hadn't bonded. He was curious to know why she had backed him up. Finally, something alerted her to his presence and she turned her head, though she didn't seem surprised to see him. "Sneaking up on people again?" she said.

Old habits die hard.

There was a pause while they assessed each other's reactions. After a few moments, Esmée put the page holder into her book. "Everything all right?"

Dion shrugged. He cast his eyes around the room. It was pretty much the same as every other small room on the base: cold bare walls; crumbling ceiling; a smell like someone had died. She didn't get up off the floor. Whenever they'd shared a hotel room, he'd offered her the bed, but she'd always preferred to sleep on the ground. Dion bent his neck to look at the title of the book she was reading. "*Pedagogy of the Oppressed* by Paulo Freire," he read out loud. "Sounds riveting."

"If I read it very slowly it helps send me to sleep."

"Does it?" Dion wasn't sure if she was joking. He'd always been wary of intellectuals. They often looked at you in a supercilious way, and in his experience, it was rarely justified. He may have been a farm boy, but he was as smart as many of them.

"It's actually quite interesting," Esmée said. "It's about how the ruling classes have used the education system to keep people in their place. Students are just passive recipients of the information poured into them. The system indoctrinates them to keep them oppressed."

Dion nodded in acknowledgment.

"You should read it."

"Maybe I will."

"I've never understood why people who live in dictatorships put up with it," Esmée went on. "I mean, why don't they just overthrow them?"

"Overthrow a dictator?"

"Why not?"

Dion thought about it. "Because... dictators have armies to protect them."

"But people outnumber them a hundred to one."

"A lot of people would still get killed. Would you be willing to stand up to a tank?"

"Maybe," Esmée replied.

Dion conceded the point. Given what he already knew of her, he should have known better than to ask.

"The other reason," Esmée went on, closing the book, "is that I'm trying to keep up with my coursework."

"Really?" Dion scoffed. "You hoping they'll have you back?"

She looked offended. After what had happened in Monaco, she'd been thrown out of college. The story hadn't been big enough to make it into the national newspapers, but it had garnered a few headlines in the local press. 'Student throws paint in Monaco's Dior,' was probably not the image her college had wanted to project. Sébastien had been impressed, however. He'd interviewed her for an article in *La Vérité*. Despite her young age, she'd had a lot to say for herself. He'd invited her to join the group, and apparently Esmée had jumped at the chance. Angry young people with something to say were usually a good fit.

"You got anyone on the outside?" he asked, completing a slow circuit of the room.

"Mom, Dad. Little sister."

"You miss them?"

Contact with those on the outside was forbidden. Everyone signed the pact. Once you were in, you were in.

"I miss my sister," Esmée said. "We were inseparable growing up. I wanted her to go to Monaco with me, but she backed out at the last minute."

"You're a bad influence, then?"

"That's what my parents like to tell me."

Dion had to smile. "They still around?"

"Oh yeah. Don't get me wrong, I do love them, but they're just so *ordinary*. Every morning they get out of their ordinary beds, put on their ordinary clothes, go to work in their ordinary car. They spend the day doing their ordinary jobs until it's time to go home, back to their ordinary house."

From what he could remember, her family hailed from Arras. Her father worked in a factory, her mother in a shop. Dion got the impression they didn't have much money.

"There's nothing wrong with being ordinary."

"I didn't say there was. I just wanted to be different, that's all. I left home at fifteen. Wanted to see more of the world."

"And did you?"

"I saw quite a lot of it, yeah. I hitchhiked around Europe for a year. Slept on park benches for a while. Worked in champagne fields in the summer. Then, when I'd had enough of doing that, I went back home to my parents."

"Good of them to have you back."

"I suppose it was, though there was never any hard feelings. They were never mean to me. My feeling was, what's the point of living if you don't make some kind of mark?"

Dion had no answer to that. Esmée fiddled with the collar of her shirt, then folded her arms. "What about you? You got anyone?"

Dion lowered his eyes. "A wife."

"No kids?"

He shook his head. He'd been keen to start a family. Yvette had told him she didn't want to have kids. He'd said it didn't matter.

"I suppose it's best not to think about the outside," Esmée said, gazing around distractedly. "Easier to block things out."

She was probably right.

They were quiet for a few moments. Then Dion said: "By the way, thanks for backing me up earlier."

"No problem. Who was she?"

He shrugged. "Like I said – I have no idea."

Esmée frowned. "But you knew she was staying at the hotel?"

Dion looked at her more closely. "So what if I did?"

"And she followed you out of the restaurant."

"What?"

"When you said you were feeling unwell. You got up and left, then a few seconds later she followed you out."

Dion's mind reeled. "How do you know she followed me?"

"I just assumed. She was watching us with the camera on her phone. You had your back to her so maybe you didn't notice, but she was definitely keeping an eye on us."

A pause grew. Dion watched her steadily, unsure if she was

accusing him of something or just being curious. "If there's something bothering you, come out and say it."

"It seemed a bit of a coincidence, that's all."

"Well, that's all it was – a coincidence."

"Okay."

"You were sat at the bar with her," he accused.

"I know. When I found you hadn't gone up to the room, I waited at the bar. She didn't have much to say. I teased her about her watch. She didn't take it well."

Dion blinked, surprised she'd suddenly turned on him. If she repeated any of this to Sébastien, his days would be numbered. He fixed her with a harder look.

"I was meeting a friend. It's none of your business. Okay?"

Esmée held his eye for a moment, but then said: "Okay."

Dion left without another word.

He headed back to the Command Centre. Too much was going on in his head for any chance of sleep. He went upstairs to the old radio room where a light was still on and found Tik and Tak still at their terminals. Seasoned hackers, both in their fifties, teenagers who had never grown up. After all those hours staring at screens, Dion was surprised their eyes still worked. He approached Tik's booth and said hi. Tik jutted his chin. "How's it going, brother?"

"Not bad."

Most of the old radio equipment had been stripped out and a dozen state-of-the-art workstations installed in its place. The technology this room now boasted was light years ahead of what had been here before. The room had its own power supply, a backup generator, and a river of wires running up to a dish on the roof. Online subterfuge was a key weapon in the group's arsenal.

Dion pulled up a chair. His interest was drawn to a video clip on Tik's screen. A prominent figure in the upcoming presidential election was discussing immigration policy with a well-known TV reporter. "Our towns and cities are being ravaged by migrants committing crimes," the politician was saying. "We need to stop this invasion. Close the borders. Send them back." The words coming out of his mouth were completely at odds with everything he'd previously said on the subject. Dion quickly cottoned on. "You made this?"

Tik nodded. "He's speaking at the G7 on Friday. With any luck we can get this viral by the end of the week."

He'd done an incredible job. The lips had been perfectly animated, the sound mastered. Only an expert would have been able to tell it was deepfake. It was scary what these guys could do, literally putting words into people's mouths, making puppets of anyone. Deepfake was their latest toy, but their bread-and-butter tactics were just as effective. At any one time, they had hundreds of fake social media accounts on the go, ready to join in social media pile-ons and help spread fake news. Their biggest fake profile had three million followers; every piece of clickbait 'she' posted got a tonne of reactions. All they needed to do was sow a seed in people's minds; watch it grow; let prejudice do the rest. Flash mobs were a particular favourite of Tik's. Dion had been in the room one time when a particularly successful mob had been summoned. In the space of ten minutes, a fake post about an alleged paedophile working at a school in Marseille had sparked online hysteria, prompting a mob of over a hundred to descend on the school. Riots had broken out; the violence had spread to other schools in the area. Spontaneity was the key – acting so fast they didn't appear on the security force's radar until it was too late. It was a difficult tactic to fight. Watching the news unfold, Dion had been unable to deny what an exciting experience it had been, a reminder of how fragile civilisation was. And now that they had AI to help, who knew what was on the horizon.

Tik sat back from his screen and stretched out his arms. "I think I'll call it a night." He looked at Dion as if he expected him to leave. They didn't like anyone hanging around when they weren't there. Dion got up, but looked across to the corner. "I'll just see what Tak's been up to while I've been away, if that's okay?"

Tik nodded his approval.

Dion headed for Tak's desk, but as soon as Tik left, he ducked into an empty cubicle. Headphones on, Tak remained oblivious.

Dion took a USB stick out of his pocket and plugged it into the computer. The only file it contained was his secure messaging app. He double-clicked on Yvette's avatar and a simple black window popped up. Dion typed:

You there?

The little green dot on her avatar showed she was online, but she didn't reply immediately. Dion waited anxiously. It was two in the morning, but she would know he was there. He'd configured her smartwatch to deliver a notification whenever he logged on. Finally, after five minutes of waiting, two words came up:

I'm here.

You okay?

I'm okay.

Did you not get the notification?

I disabled it. It was annoying me going off in the middle of the night.

In the early days they'd chatted for hours. Recently, her messages had become more and more succinct.

Sorry to be annoying.

I spoke to Thierry today. He said you turned up on his doorstep on Saturday night.

Dion hesitated before typing a reply. He'd rehearsed this conversation in his head countless times, but words now eluded him.

I was in the area.

Why did you punch him.

I heard the two of you had been getting friendly.

We've always been friends. He's YOUR best friend.

Not anymore.

This time, she was the one who paused. Dion went on:

I heard you've been sleeping with him.

What if I was.

I'm your husband god dammit!

You've been gone a long time.

So what? We made a vow. Remember?

You haven't even asked how he is.

Could he admit he didn't even care? Another message came through while he was thinking:

FYI, you broke his nose. He spent the night in hospital. They say he has concussion.

Dion still felt no sympathy. If there was one thing he had in common with Sébastien it was a belief in loyalty. If you couldn't keep a promise you were the lowest of the low. His mind racing, he tried something different.

Remember when we went canoeing? We camped out on that beach on the river.

It had been truly idyllic. Three days exploring the Ardèche. They'd camped out on a beach on a big, wide bend in the river. The skies had been so dark they could see the Milky Way. One day it had been so hot they'd walked naked through the woods, nothing but the sound of rushing water for company.

Nothing came back.

That squirrel that kept watching us. Dion prompted.

It still made him smile. The same squirrel had appeared to follow them downriver, popping up every time they made camp. They'd nicknamed him Dingu – he always seemed to go crazy after munching on nuts. Finally, a reply came back:

Things change, Dion. People change.

I haven't changed.

You know that's not true.

Dion's smile faded. A profound sense of emptiness washed over him. Shared memories were all they had to connect them. When they were gone, what was left?

Can't we start over? I love you as much now as the day we first met.

I have to go. It's work tomorrow.

Don't go. Just tell me you still love me.

Goodnight Dion.

Don't go, he quickly typed.

But the little green dot on her avatar went out.

———

Dion stared at the screen for a very long time. When the numbness finally began to wear off, he opened a second chat window. Seeing that AL was on-line, he typed another message:

Someone followed us. A tall blonde woman. She was at the hotel in Narbonne on Saturday night. Find out who she is. And deal with her.

8

"Have you seen the forensic report on the Bernstein file?" Florian asked, sifting through the papers on his desk in an increasingly agitated state.

Seated across the office, Margot sighed. She got up from her desk and went to his aid. So many files and books and folders were cluttering up the space around Florian's three giant monitors that it was a miracle he managed to find anything at all. After several fruitless minutes turning over pieces of paper, Margot sighed again. "Are you sure it was here?"

"Yes," Florian insisted. "I put it down right here." He indicated a wire tray to his left, which itself was overflowing with papers. Despite the complete lack of order, he claimed to know the location of every single paperclip in the office. Margot had a sudden thought, followed by a pang of guilt.

"Ah."

Florian gave her an enquiring stare. "What?"

"Did you say the Bernstein file?"

"Yes. The forensic report. It came in yesterday afternoon, remember?"

Margot smiled to soften the blow. "Now that you come to mention it, I think I may have put it in Célia's office. Sorry. Force of habit. I'll nip in and get it." She backed to the door, turning on her heel before Florian could get another word out.

Again from habit, Margot knocked on Célia's door before entering, fully aware that her boss wasn't inside. Having completed her latest round of cancer treatment, Célia had gone to the Italian Lakes to recuperate and had been holed up in a villa on the shores of Lake Garda for the past two weeks. The radiotherapy appeared to have been successful, but it had taken its toll. Their boss had looked pale and exhausted when they'd waved her goodbye.

Margot moved to the desk, her footsteps silenced by the thick pile carpet. Even when it was occupied there was always a hush about the room, yet now it seemed even quieter. The eyes of the figures in the oil portraits seemed to track her every movement, like dusty old guardians in a museum. Margot recalled the first time she'd been summoned to this office when Captain Bouchard had come down to the marina to collect her. He'd escorted her back to the *Palais*, annoyed by her meddling in one of his investigations. Despite giving her a reprimand, Célia had had a twinkle in her eye, a twinkle that had blossomed into a very good friendship.

Margot stared at Célia's empty chair. Could she see herself sitting there one day, spending her days in an office like this, scrutinising file after file? Reviewing the cold case files had proved an interesting job, but the role of a JI was far more involving, and predominantly office-based. Margot moved around the desk and tried the seat for size, careful not to make the leather squeak. She passed a hand over the thick slab of mahogany, imagining all the case files that had crossed its smooth surface. All the misery, and the ruined lives. These days, a *juge d'instruction* handled only the most serious of cases, but even sleepy towns like Argents-sur-Mer saw their share of villainy. And she would also have to deal with the *procureurs* of this world. People like Cousineau, whom she detested, and who, though technically Célia's equal, wielded the most power in the *Palais*. In his role as senior *procureur,* he was responsible for defining the parameters of an *instruction* and even got to decide whether to open one at all. And of course, there was no guarantee she would get a posting anywhere local. She could end up anywhere in the country, shut away in a dull office block, barely getting a glimpse of the sun. Maybe she should forget the whole idea.

She returned distractedly to Florian's office, and found her colleague looking up, expectantly.

"Any luck?"

Margot returned a blank look. "Sorry?"

"The forensic report..." Florian seemed baffled.

Margot flushed. "Oh yes. Of course. The forensic report." She turned on her heel and went straight back.

———

Lunch at La Lune Bleue was becoming a habit. Raymond had reserved her favourite spot – a table for two at the end of the terrace, away from the hustle and bustle, and just a stone's throw from the sea. A bottle of white wine was already on ice.

"I've been meaning to ask," Margot said as she pulled up a chair. "How did this place get its name?"

Raymond handed her the *menu du jour*, looking pleased to have been asked the question.

"It's to do with the stone they used to build the wall." He indicated the giant defensive wall, a hundred feet high, that loomed over them. It formed part of the old fortifications and was one of the most photographed features of the town. Built hundreds of years ago to defend the town from attacks by pirates, it was now more likely to be besieged by tourists. "It contains an unusual mineral," Raymond went on. "Whenever there's a full moon, the whole wall glows blue."

"Really?"

"I've not yet seen it myself, but they say it's quite a sight." (He had only been working there for a few months.) "Apparently, there's going to be a supermoon in a few weeks' time. The owner's planning a party."

"I shall have to come."

"I'll put your name down."

"Please do."

They were interrupted by Rogier, Raymond's older brother, who approached along the terrace, a troubled look about him. He shot Margot a nervous smile, ran a hand through his quiff of black hair, and then tapped his brother's elbow. "Can we talk?"

Raymond glanced around conspiratorially, even though only a handful of customers were in. "I can spare five minutes."

"Okay."

"Over here."

Intrigued, Margot stopped them before they could go off in a huddle. "All right, you two. What are you plotting now?"

At twenty-three, Rogier was the more dashing of the two. Baby-faced and stylishly dressed, his only failing was that he was painfully shy. His girlfriend, Cerise, worked behind the bar, although ever since Raymond had started working here, the two of them always seemed to be in cahoots. Rogier gave Margot a despondent look. "It's about Cerise."

"What about her?"

"I…"

"He wants to ask her to marry him but can't pluck up the courage," Raymond interrupted.

Rogier glared, then punched his brother in the arm. "Yeah, right – said the guy who's never even had a girlfriend."

"Says who?"

"Says me."

"Oh, yeah. And what ab – "

"Boys, boys," Margot butted in this time. "Let's have a little decorum, shall we?"

They settled down. Underneath the table, Margot shoved the other chair out with her foot. "Sit down, Rogier."

He sat.

"Talk to me."

Rogier pulled a packet of cigarettes from his pocket and tapped one out. He offered one to Margot, but she declined, not wanting to encourage him. She hated to think what smoking was going to do to that beautifully smooth skin of his.

"I want to ask Cerise to marry me."

"So what's the problem?"

"I've wanted to ask her for ages, but every time I get the chance, I freeze up. This little voice comes into my head and tells me she'll say no. Or worse, laugh at me and I'll look like a fool."

Margot tutted. "What makes you think she'll say no?"

He shrugged while he was lighting his cigarette. "She wants to be married, she often talks about starting a family, but I'm not sure she means with me."

"How long have you been dating?"

"Twenty-eight months."

"And do you really think that after all that time you're not the one she wants to be with?"

He shrugged again.

"Do you love her?"

"Of course I do!"

"Does she love you?"

He looked unsure. "I think so."

"Then you've got nothing to worry about. Pick the right moment and pop the question."

"But there never seems to be the right moment," he moaned. "Something always crops up."

"Then take her out to dinner and ask her then."

Rogier shook his head. "It has to be something special. An occasion she'll never forget."

"All right," Margot reconsidered. "What about a weekend away?"

Rogier shook his head once more. "More special than that. My friend at work did that scene from *Crazy Rich Asians*, you know, the one where he goes down on one knee and proposes in front of the whole plane. He bought first-class tickets and everything."

"I know someone who hired a mega-yacht," Raymond chipped in. "For his bachelor party, he got VIP tickets to a Scorpions concert. They had front-row seats and backstage passes. It was awesome."

Margot rolled her eyes. When had getting married become a competitive sport? "It doesn't have to be showy," she said. "Just come from the heart."

"I could bake a cake," Raymond suggested. "Write: 'Will You Marry Me' in chocolate piping on top."

But Rogier still wasn't convinced. He tapped the ash from his cigarette into the ashtray. "It has to be something big, or I'll never live it down."

They considered it some more.

"I could bake the cake," Raymond tried again, "and we could get someone famous to deliver it."

"We don't know anyone famous."

"What about that Amy Winehouse cover band you know?"

Rogier's face lit up. "Rock 'n' Roll Rehab?" Suddenly he was excited. "We could get them to do a special performance."

"Rent a whole club."

"Put on a fireworks display."

"Hire a skywriter to write 'Marry me' in the sky."

"And a limo! We have to have a limo."

Their enthusiasm overflowed.

"Or," Margot chipped in, feeling mischievous. "You could get a paratrooper to deliver it. Have him jump out of a plane from two thousand feet, abseil down the wall, deliver it with a box of chocolates tied in a pink ribbon." She had only been joking, but worryingly, they both seemed to take her suggestion seriously. Seeing that Cerise had just come out onto the terrace, Margot leaned in. "Here's another idea – ask her now." She pointed with her head.

The boys looked over their shoulders to where Cerise was wiping down some tables. Spooked, Rogier quickly wound his neck in.

"I can't ask her now! I have to get back to work."

Margot exhaled in frustration. "All right then. Do it tonight. Bring her a red rose."

Rogier looked about as enthusiastic as someone who'd just been asked to clean the toilets after a men's soccer match. But finally, after a considerable amount of grumbling, he agreed.

———

Captain Bouchard called on her way back to the *Palais*. After unpocketing her phone, Margot stepped into a side street. "Any news?"

"We've managed to get hold of Madame Janvier's phone records," the captain replied. "We think we've identified the number the insurance agent was calling from, but it was a pay-as-you-go phone."

"Anything on the office in Narbonne?"

"No. As you suspected, they left no trail. I've also been looking into that area of forest you mentioned."

"Oh yes."

"There's certainly something odd about it." She heard him strain as if reaching for a paper. "I've checked every available resource but couldn't find out who owns it. It's not listed as a public forest, or used by any of the local hunting groups. The lack of any official records is, in itself, noteworthy, given what French bureaucracy is like."

Margot smiled wryly. She was reminded of the old joke about the difference between Heaven and Hell: in Heaven, the cooks are French, the police are English, the engineers are German, the lovers are Italian, and the bureaucrats are Swiss. In Hell, the cooks are English, the police are German, the engineers are Italian, the lovers are Swiss, and the French are the bureaucrats.

"The fact that the satellite imagery is blurred would suggest it's a sensitive site," the captain went on. "It's most probably military, although I've never heard of any army bases out there. I'll put out a few more feelers, but if it is hush-hush, I don't imagine I'll hear anything back."

"Okay. Well, thanks for trying."

———

Eight hours later, Margot was back at La Lune Bleue. It was a busy night; all of the outside tables were taken and Raymond had his hands full serving customers. Seeing no sign of Rogier, Margot squeezed through the crowd to get inside and, spotting a gap, pulled up a stool at the bar. She hoped she hadn't missed the show.

"What can I get you, Margot?" Cerise asked when things had quietened down a little.

Feeling adventurous, Margot asked for a Jungle Bird cocktail. To fill her empty stomach, she ordered salmon rillettes, fig and goat's cheese parcels, and a bowl of panellets from the tapas menu. She glanced around, but there was still no sign of the reluctant Romeo.

"Damn!" Cerise exclaimed.

Margot glanced across the counter. Cerise had mistakenly put lemon juice in the glass instead of lime.

"Never mind," Margot smiled. "We can invent a new one."

Creating cocktails had to be one of the most fun jobs in the world. Not just with the alcohol combos but with coming up with the names: the Pornstar Martini, a Hanky Panky, a Slippery Nipple, and the good old Harvey Wallbanger.

But Cerise remained annoyed with herself. She poured the contents of the glass down the sink and started again. Margot gave her a closer look. She didn't seem her usual cheerful self this evening, and that didn't bode well for Rogier.

"So, how are things with you?"

Cerise heaved a sigh. "I'm tired, that's all. My sister's on nights this week, and my mum and dad are still looking after my brother's boys. I'm lucky if I get three hours sleep a night."

"Sounds like a crowded house."

"Tell me about it." Cocktail remade, she garnished the glass with a wedge of pineapple and placed it on the counter. "Six of us, living in a two-bedroom house. It's not easy."

Margot took a slurp through the straw, pleasantly surprised. The bitterness of the Campari was beautifully complemented by the sweetness of the pineapple. "Have you and Rogier not thought about getting a place of your own?"

Cerise rolled her eyes. "We'd love to, but have you seen the price of property in this town? They're asking crazy money, just for a one-bed."

Margot sympathised. Her little cottage down by the harbour

was probably worth double what they'd paid for it six years ago. They'd been lucky to find it. Hugo had heard about it through a friend of a friend, and they'd snapped it up before it had even come on the market. It was a familiar story – wealthy outsiders looking for their perfect place by the sea, pushing up prices. She could only imagine how hard it must be for young people trying to get a foot on the ladder.

"I can ask around," Margot said. "Let you know if I hear anything."

"Thanks," Cerise said. "Rogier's been looking at that new block they're building on the other side of the harbour."

Margot nodded. "I can see the cranes from my window. It's a lovely spot."

"It is a lovely spot, but there's no way we can afford it. He keeps drooling over the pictures in the brochure. Last night he was even planning where to put the furniture, not that we have any decent furniture."

Rogier worked for a mobile phone company and was probably on minimum wage, and Cerise was unlikely to earn much working at the bar. Neither of them appeared to have family who might help.

Cerise raised her head, her attention drawn elsewhere. Margot looked round and found Rogier staring back at them from the doorway. He was dressed in a smart white shirt and a tie, and appeared to be hiding something behind his back. Realising what was afoot, Margot gave him a nod of encouragement.

"What's got into him?" Cerise muttered, looking puzzled.

"Call him over," Margot prompted. "See what he has to say."

Just as Margot thought she'd secured a front-row seat, however, a noisy group of customers came in. They hustled Rogier out of the way as they barged through the door and promptly laid claim to the bar. Looking back through the tangle of limbs, Margot spotted a single red rose trampled on the cobbles. Her heart sank as she glimpsed Rogier marching away. Poor boy.

Cerise had her hands full dealing with the new arrivals, so as soon as she'd finished her food, Margot left. It was only ten o'clock, too early to go home, so she went for a stroll along the promenade. She found a quiet bench and sat down. Craving a cigarette, she reached into her bag.

Margot cast her thoughts out to the waves and hauled in the memory of the day Hugo had proposed. They had only known each other for two weeks, and spurred on by her impending return to England, he'd popped the question on the platform of the Gare du Nord. Despite a few doubts, Margot had said yes. To celebrate, he'd suggested an impromptu weekend in the country, and everything that could have gone wrong did. It had been dark by the time they'd got out of Paris; the car had broken down in the middle of nowhere; in pouring rain they'd trekked along dark country lanes to a village that resembled a ghost town. The owner of the local auberge had answered their knock at the door, but the only food he had on offer was stale bread and cheese. The heating wasn't on and the water was cold, but they'd muddled through. Cuddled up in front of the fire, she'd known with all her heart that she had made the right decision.

Margot brought her thoughts back to the present. She looked at the worn wooden slats of the bench, the wrought iron streetlights, the smooth, weather-beaten cobbles. A seagull, up past its bedtime, came waddling towards her, looking like it was up for a fight. She'd been much more impulsive back then, and had often done things just for the thrill of it. Twenty years ago, she would have happily curled up on this bench and stayed out here all night, nothing for company but the sound of the waves. These days, the armchair in her living room seemed more and more appealing.

The seagull was far less intimidating than he imagined

himself to be, and Margot easily shooed him off. She lifted her feet off the ground and lay down on the bench, turning the world onto its side. She took the cigarette from her mouth and smiled contentedly. She might not be able to stay out here all night, but she could stay for a while. She wasn't ready to be old. Not yet.

9

He was probably imagining it, but the trees seemed to get closer every time he looked. Patrolling the perimeter fence, rifle in hand, Dion pictured them advancing, leaf by leaf, root by root, creeping towards them in such tiny increments that no one would notice until it was too late. One day, someone would come out here and find that the fence had been breached and the base invaded, a swarm of angry oaks surrounding them. Not that you could blame them: humans were the intruders here. *Someday, we'll reclaim what's rightfully ours,* he imagined them thinking. Nature was patient. It knew it would win in the end.

Dion shared a smile with himself as he moved on. He'd been in here too long if he was speculating about what the trees were thinking.

Guard duty was a tedious job, but he didn't really mind it. Out in the fresh air, with an occasional glimpse of the sun, it was easy to let your mind wander. Other than the odd movement in the bushes (usually a deer) or a small plane passing overhead (he was often tempted to wave, like the sole survivor on a desert island), nothing much happened. Most jobs in the camp were shared, even the technical trades like plumbing and electrics.

Sébastien expected everyone to muck in, himself included. "How can you know how hard someone works unless you spend a week in their shoes?" was one of his mantras. Every job, and every brother, mattered.

He continued down to the southern boundary, careful where he stepped. In places, Sébastien had gone overboard with the man-traps. The sense of isolation was even more pronounced down here – the trees were bigger, the gaps between them tighter – though it was better in winter when the bare branches let in more light. Here and there, a bough had pushed through the fence, twisted wooden fingers searching for a weakness. The fence followed every undulation, doing its best to keep them at bay. It must have been quite a feat of engineering enclosing two hundred hectares of land. You couldn't beat military efficiency. A little bird chirped as it flew by, then looked back from a branch. Catch me if you can.

The ground sloped down to a clearing, pockmarked by craters. It had probably been a firing range when the army had been here. He strode to the edge of one of the craters and, checking that none of the dogs were around, jumped down into the hollow. He unclipped his rifle and lay on his back, then stared up at the sky, freeing his mind to the wild blue yonder. What day was it today... Tuesday? Wednesday? It was easy to lose track. He wondered what Yvette was doing right now. She worked in an office, selling insurance. Three years ago, she'd won a promotion and had wanted to move house, get something bigger and better. She'd chosen a place close to Toulouse. Toulouse was where Thierry had been living at the time. Maybe Dion should have seen it coming. There had always been a twinkle in her eye whenever she was around him, and she was always commenting on how good he looked. Thierry and his wife used to come round for barbecues. (Did his wife know? More deceit. More broken promises.) Thierry was the outgoing one, the guy with all the banter. Dion had been best man at all three of his weddings. Always clean-shaven and smartly dressed... he hadn't looked so smart when he'd been lying on the ground the other night.

As Dion had stood on that doorstep, he'd seen the betrayal in his former friend's eyes. He hadn't gone there with the intention of hitting him, but something inside him had snapped. How could you not react on a visceral level when the givens in life were taken from you? When the things you'd thought were unbreakable had apparently been built on nothing but sand. Seventeen years of marriage apparently meant nothing. The only thing Dion regretted was letting him get up.

A crackle came over the walkie-talkie. "Warehouse here. Van's back. Copy."

Dion kept his eyes on the sky, reluctant to let go. Wouldn't it be nice if you could escape up there, let your mind roam free?

"Dion, confirm. Over."

Dion raised his left arm to look at his wristwatch. He lazily sat up and pushed the button on his walkie-talkie. "Dion here. Affirmative."

———

Every few weeks a group of brothers went off to collect supplies. Sébastien had contacts all over the place: patriots working in food factories, army stores, fuel depots, each willing to look the other way. Whenever supplies were needed, contact would be made and a van would go out. They rarely went short of anything.

Two Mercedes Sprinters were parked in front of the warehouse. A dozen brothers were already busily offloading, so Dion rolled up his sleeves and quickly joined in. He enjoyed this aspect of life in the camp – the camaraderie, everyone helping out. A chain gang was formed. Boxes were passed from brother to brother, then piled in the warehouse, ready to be taken to the stores. There were bags of medical supplies, boxes of tools and fittings, vacuum-packed clothes and bedding. At one point, the forklift came in and unloaded some drums of kerosene. They'd clearly had a good haul. Dion wasn't surprised to see Sébastien there, his face red and sweaty as he struggled with heavy boxes. Solidarity formed strong bonds, he said. Humanity was strongest when people worked together for a common cause. A less welcome sight was Golem, whose eyes rarely left Dion. Dion shot him a contemptuous look in return. Maybe one of these days someone might pull out those mangy teeth of his and put them back in the right way.

It didn't take long to empty both vans. Afterwards, the brothers hung around, taking a break. Someone opened a box of fruit drinks and handed out cartons. Sébastien stayed busy compiling an inventory, seemingly pleased with the haul. Enough food to keep them going for at least three months, he estimated. And more than enough kerosene to see them through another winter. It would all be shared equally, and none of it would go to waste. The Earth had given up its resources for them, and everything they took was treated with respect. Although, as Dion sat watching from the sill of one of the van doors, he was reminded of the darker side of their leader's nature. Another time, on a day just like this...

They'd been having problems with a new recruit, a woman who'd thought she was a medium. She'd claimed the base was haunted, said she could hear people screaming in the night, both in the corridors and out in the woods. She'd told Sébastien she wanted out; Sébastien had said it wasn't that simple. A few days later, when the vans came back from an outing, someone mistakenly left the gate open, and while everyone was busy unloading, the woman had made a run for it. Sébastien, along with a group of men including Dion, had raced after her. Several anxious minutes had gone by before a piercing scream rang out. When the men honed in on it, they found the woman lying on the forest floor in agony, her leg caught in the jaws of a man-trap. A couple of brothers had immediately tried to free her, delicately feeding their fingers into the jagged steel jaws. But Sébastien had told them to move aside. He'd aimed his rifle and pulled the trigger without even blinking. A single bullet in the forehead. "Better to put her out of her misery," he'd explained later. He'd claimed she'd lost too much blood, wouldn't have survived even if they'd freed her. Most of the brothers had voiced their agreement. He may have been right, although Dion suspected Sébastien's motives had more to do with retribution than a desire to put an end to her suffering.

Break over, the brothers dispersed. Most of them went back to the main complex, but Dion stayed behind to help re-load the van. Tomorrow they would be spreading the word, handing out copies of *La Vérité* – the group's mouthpiece – in Montpellier and Nîmes. Two large trolleys, laden with bundled-up magazines, were wheeled out of the warehouse.

"We're two brothers down this week," Sébastien said, coming to his side. "Would you be willing to help out tomorrow?"

Dion looked at him in surprise. Another trip out so soon was unusual. "Of course. Where?"

"Montpellier. I've already asked Esmée. You two seem to work well together."

Dion nodded slowly, not sure he agreed. But then there wasn't really much to consider. Any opportunity to get out of the base was worth taking.

They set off before dawn, six of them, sitting on benches in the back of the van. Seated directly opposite, Dion avoided Esmée's eyes, still unsure whether to trust her. He gazed down at the bundles of *La Vérité* between their feet. On the front cover, a caricature of a well-known politician, wrestling sumo-style with the Russian President, made Dion smile. Sébastien had been producing the magazine for years. An issue every month, a print run of five thousand; the content was generally quite salty. Most of it was produced in-house, but submissions came in from all over the world, everything from serious pieces by a regular cohort of writers to the deranged ramblings of the clinically deluded. Sébastien was a discerning editor. He chose only those stories that had a serious point to make, and often penned two or three pieces himself. He wrote well; for such a young man he was politically astute. His articles were both erudite and thoughtful, and he somehow managed to pull off the trick of appealing to both the far left and the far right. The back page was always reserved for *Les théories du complot* – a light-hearted piece on whatever conspiracy theory was doing the rounds.

After a ninety-minute drive, the driver pulled up on the edge of a supermarket car park. Bright sunshine greeted them as he opened the back doors. A woman pushing a shopping trolley gave them a suspicious look as they climbed down from the back of the van. The driver cut the bindings on the magazines while they each grabbed a blue IKEA bag and began loading up.

"We'll meet back here at three," the driver said, handing out photocopied street plans. "Don't be late."

The city had been divided into three equal sectors, and they would go out in pairs, one per sector. The others had already paired up, so when the van drove off a few minutes later, it was only Dion and Esmée left. A few awkward moments of silence passed.

"I guess it's you and me then," Esmée said.

"Looks that way."

The dorks not picked for the team. Dion didn't mind. He'd never been a team player.

"Okay." Esmée turned her attention to the map. "Where do we start?"

Dion only glanced at the street plan. He knew the city well. He and his wife often used to go shopping there. Newlyweds, looking for furniture.

"We'll start by the old university. Then work our way into the centre."

"Who are we targeting?"

"Anyone who looks like they've got a grievance. Loners. People on the margins." Dion looked through the flaps of her pink hoodie to the slogan on her T-shirt: *WE ARE THE 99%.* "Don't worry," he smiled. "With that T-shirt you've got on, you'll attract the right crowd."

Esmée smiled back, catching his drift.

They walked without talking. Dion remembered the first recruitment drive he'd been on, a few months after arriving in the camp. He and five others had been let loose on the streets of Nîmes, a sack full of magazines over their shoulders. After being deprived of natural light for so long, his brain had become a monotone, and his eyes had eagerly sought colour: a bright red car, a woman in a blue dress, a splash of orange on a billboard. He'd been amazed that something as simple as a jazzy yellow logo could have made him feel alive.

They hopped on a tram in Saint Lazare. Someone had once described Montpellier's tramway as the sexiest in Europe, and Dion could see why. Some of the carriages had been designed by Christian Lacroix; in places, the trams glided along avenues of neatly trimmed grass. Leafy suburbs passed by through the windows, and you could be forgiven for thinking that here was just another sleepy old city in the south of France. Well-off people, languishing in the heat – hardly a fertile breeding ground of radical malcontents. But if you scratched the surface, you would find it. Ask the right questions, push the right buttons: can you honestly say you are happy with your life? Is this the way you think things should be? It was a thin veneer that separated order from chaos.

They got off the tram at Le Corum, then headed along Boulevard Louis Blanc. At the turning to Rue de l'Université, they passed under an ancient stone arch into a bohemian part of the city, brimming with life and full of chic little bars and cafés. The sounds of a violinist busking on the steps to the Agora Theatre accompanied them all the way down to the corner of Rue du Four Saint-Eloi where Dion halted, just down from the Faculty of Law and Political Science. "You start here," he said. "I'll try a little further up."

Esmée eyed up her surroundings and then gave him a nod. Dion left her to it, but he didn't go far, feeling the need to keep an eye on her. Some people took exception to the things they had to say, and there was often an argumentative type wanting to cause trouble.

But Esmée jumped right in. Dion had barely taken up position when he saw her approach a group of young men and women. She quickly captured their attention, and soon had them laughing and joking. A couple of them looked genuinely interested in the magazine, and by the time she'd finished, three or four copies had changed hands. Catching Dion's eye, Esmée gave him a sneaky thumbs-up. Wasting no time, she moved onto her next target: an earnest young man wheeling a bicycle. He didn't say much, but willingly accepted a copy. Next, she moved on to one of the cafés and began circulating the tables, clearly a natural.

Dion felt clumsy in comparison. He held up a copy of the magazine, inviting people to approach him. A few seemed to find the cover amusing, and one or two took a copy, but most walked by. After about twenty minutes, a waiter at the nearby café noticed what they were doing and got irritated. Dion gave Esmée a signal and they moved on.

They used the side streets to return to Le Corum. Dion looked the other way as they passed a gendarme, as had become habit. The *Jardin l'Hôtel de Sully* was a brief oasis of shade, and then they were back in the sun for the short walk down to the esplanade Charles de Gaulle where a wide leafy park opened up to them. They split up again. Dion decided to try a different tactic and target the older generation. They were often more passionate than the young and eager to talk, drawn by the provocative headlines and wanting to know more. He honed in on two old guys playing chess at a table and showed them the cover of *La Vérité*. "Is the country moving towards or away from the kind of society you want?" he asked, using one of the stock questions Sébastien had prepared for them. Dion stood waiting for an answer. After a lifetime of building up prejudice, people of their generation were usually more than happy to air their (usually racist) views, but these two were reluctant to engage. Their weatherbeaten faces looked at him like he was a weirdo; a look Dion had grown accustomed to. "Show some respect," one of them finally piped up, jabbing a finger at the caricature on the cover. "That man has done more for this country than any of your lot." Dion wondered who 'his lot' was, and what, exactly, the man in the caricature had done for the country other than breed hate. *Don't bother challenging them*, Sébastien always cautioned. *It never pays off.* Dion left them to their game of chess.

The pickings in the rest of the park were equally fruitless, and when they met up at the fountain an hour later, Esmée said, "How'd I do?" and showed him her nearly empty sack. Dion's was still half full. It wasn't a competition, but he let her choose where they ate lunch. After they'd scouted around for a while, Esmée chose a burger bar.

Eschewing the self-service terminals, they went to the counter to order. Sébastien only provided them with cash; plastic left a trace. After a ten-minute wait, they collected their trays and took stools by the window. Dion opened his burger carton and tipped his fries into the lid. Both hungry, they ate in silence for a while; almost companionably, Dion thought, although he hesitated to believe they had become friends.

Esmée took a copy of *La Vérité* out of her sack and flipped it to the back cover, then read *Les théories du complot* while she carried on eating her wrap. "Get this," she said, suppressing a smirk. "The American government is now *weaponising* the weather. Last year they created a hurricane to wipe out voters in opposition states, and they're using artificial rainmaking to create flash floods. Apparently, the freak weather has nothing to do with climate change, it's all black ops."

Dion kept a straight face. "You mean you don't believe that?"

The humour faded from Esmée's eyes. Dion had been trying to tease her, but Esmée still didn't seem to know how to read him yet. He put down his burger and wiped his fingers on a serviette, then smiled to let her know he was pulling her leg.

"Sébastien doesn't believe any of that," he said. "He sees it as a good way of getting into people's heads." Anything that eroded trust in the establishment was good for the cause.

"But some of this is just garbage," Esmée scoffed, reading on. "A guy here thinks that aeroplane contrails are produced by mind control drugs. The government is secretly adding harmful chemicals to the air to control its populous. But get this: the harmful chemicals can be neutralised if you spray your airspace with distilled vinegar." She laughed. "Who in their right mind would believe that?"

"Golem."

"You could tell Golem the government was incubating babies on the moon and he would believe it."

Dion smiled. "People believe in conspiracy theories because they're suspicious of the government. If the government isn't honest with them, can you blame them for being sceptical?"

"Not really."

"And most people who believe in one conspiracy theory tend to believe them all. It's like disappearing down a rabbit hole. Before you know it, you're living an alternative reality."

Dion went back to his meal and took another big bite out of his burger. On the other side of the glass, people walked by in the street, many of them transfixed by their phones. Was this the Brave New World they had to look forward to: people trapped in their own narratives, denouncing all others? Having finished her wrap, Esmée unwrapped her donut.

"So what's Sébastien's grand plan?" she asked.

There was a pause while Dion swallowed his food. He picked up a serviette and wiped some sauce from his chin. "What did he tell you when you signed up?"

"He said I'd be joining a group of like-minded people committed to making a change. He didn't go into detail. But I expected it would be more than handing out free magazines."

It was unlikely anyone knew exactly what was going on in Sébastien's head, but if only half the things he talked about came to fruition, the country was in for a shake-up. Dion took a slurp from his coffee to wash down his mouthful.

"Sébastien believes people work best on an equal footing. As soon as you give one person power over another things start to go wrong."

"So he's an anarchist communist then."

Dion watched her take a bite out of her donut. Blood-red jam squirted out and almost hit her in the eye. He passed her a serviette. *Anarchist communist*, he repeated thoughtfully to himself. It was the kind of term the intellectuals in the group often used, and Dion didn't really know what it meant. He didn't like labels. Some people liked to slap a label on everyone, but in Dion's eyes it was a lazy way of thinking. Putting someone in a box didn't mean you knew all about them. Real people were more complex.

"I suppose he just wants to make the world a better place," Dion replied.

"By starting a popular uprising?"

He looked her in the eye. "If he were, would you be on board with that?"

Esmée shrugged. "There are a lot of angry people out there. Something has to change."

Sébastien was in contact with other groups around the country, and most were growing impatient. If you believed the historians, another revolution was long overdue. When people felt they weren't being listened to, they could only be ignored for so long. In isolation, they were nothing to be worried about. A lonely malcontent stewing in a bedsit could only do a limited amount of harm. Organised in a group like Sébastien's, however, they posed a serious threat.

"What about you?" Esmée asked. "Would you be on board with that?"

Dion looked away. Outside the window, two kids were looking at a banner pasted to the glass. They didn't seem to see him just a few inches away. He could have been invisible.

"I had an uncle who was there in May '68."

"Paris?"

"Bordeaux."

"One of the students?"

Dion nodded. "He manned one of the barricades in Rue Paul Bert. I found his journal a while back. He'd been shunned by the rest of the family, but he was proud to have taken part."

May '68 – the last time France had come close to a full-blown revolution. Seven weeks of unrest had brought the country to its knees. Angered by what they saw as an authoritarian regime, forty thousand students had marched through the streets of Paris. When the police responded with violence, the public became outraged, and a general strike soon followed during which ten million workers walked off the job. With the country in danger of collapse, President Charles de Gaulle fled to West Germany. In some parts, the police showed solidarity and joined in with the protests.

A black BMW rolled by the window, looking for somewhere to pull in. All the regular parking bays were taken, so it reversed and parked in a blue-badge spot. A guy with a ponytail got out, a poncy man-bag slung across his chest. He didn't appear to be affected by any kind of disability as he skipped across the pavement and pushed through the plate glass door. "Asshole," Esmée commented under her breath.

Realising what had irked her, Dion smiled to himself. He peeled back the lid of his tub of mayonnaise and dipped in a fry. He scooped out a dollop and popped the whole thing into his mouth.

"So, why did you throw paint in Dior?"

"Because I prefer the dresses in Prada."

Stifling a laugh, the mayonnaise almost came back down his nose. "Come on, seriously," he coughed. "Why did you do it? And why Monaco? They must have more cameras there than anywhere."

"They also have a pretty nice jail."

That was true. It was no secret that Monaco's prison was one of the most luxurious in Europe. Located right on the seafront, many of the cells had sea views. There was steak for dinner, a doctor visited three times a week, and the inmates had access to a psychiatrist, although, by all accounts, conditions weren't quite so favourable for inmates who hailed from countries other than Monaco or France.

"I mean," Dion persisted, "considering it got you thrown out of college, was it worth it?"

"Did your uncle think it was worth it?"

He shrugged. From what he'd written in his journal, he'd had no regrets, though looking back, many would argue the protests had achieved nothing.

Esmée jabbed a straw into her milkshake and gave it a stir. Eyes lowered, she mulled something over for a while.

"Did you know that residents of Monaco pay no income tax?" she said. "There's no wealth tax, no property tax, no capital gains tax."

"That's what you'd expect in a tax haven, isn't it?"

"Instead of taxing its residents," she went on, "the government chooses to get its money from tourists and gamblers. The people who go there to gawp don't seem to realise that they're the ones who're actually paying for the thing they're gawping at."

"It's hardly unique."

"It's hardly fair. Why should billionaires pay a lower rate of tax than everyone else? Just because they're allowed to funnel their income through offshore tax havens."

Dion shrugged. "It's the way things work."

"But it doesn't *have* to work that way, does it?" She moved her milkshake to one side and faced him. "It's not written in stone. If farmers were in charge instead of lawyers and bankers, things would work differently."

"I thought the free market decided these kinds of things."

"The free market?" Esmée scoffed. She gave him a wide-eyed look of amazement. Now that she had come out of her shell, a zeal shone in her eyes. "There's no such thing as a free market. If there was, every job in the Western world would be taken over by someone in Asia. Governments control all sorts of things from immigration to tariffs. The free market is a myth, pedalled by capitalists whenever the government interferes in a way they don't like."

"So what's the answer?"

"The answer is, if the state can intervene in one way, then it can intervene in a different way. Create a market that benefits everyone, not just the select few."

Dion took her point. He'd known plenty of people who'd worked hard, put in long hours and made sacrifices, yet still struggled to make ends meet. And others who were lazy, often corrupt, yet made enough to afford holiday homes in the Alps simply because their talents were valued more favourably.

They were distracted by the sound of raised voices. Over at the counter, ponytail guy was creating a ruckus. It seemed he wasn't happy with the food he'd been given and was demanding to speak to a manager. Losing his temper, he threw his packet of fries across the counter and swore at one of the servers. Esmée tutted as they turned back to the window.

"Okay," Dion said. "So how does throwing paint over Dior help change the world?"

Esmée retrieved her smoothie and took a slurp. "It sends a message."

"To whom?"

"To the people in charge. It says: 'Hey, rich guys. Stop beating us down, or maybe one day we'll fight back.'"

Dion wasn't convinced. "But why attack luxury brands? They're aspirational, aren't they? Having nice things encourages people to work harder."

"Yeah, right," Esmée responded immediately, the fiery look returning to her eyes. "You fall for that one, do you? Like, someone who can barely afford to pay their electricity bill might somehow find the spare cash to buy a two-thousand-euro handbag *if only they worked a little harder*. Or a single mum, struggling to raise two kids, might somehow put enough money aside to buy a forty-million-euro yacht when they retire *if only they put in a little more effort*." She shook her head in dismay. "It's not a divide, it's a canyon, and it's growing wider every day. The haves have it and they don't want to share it."

"The dream of socialism."

"It's not a dirty word."

"Doesn't anti-rich boil down to envy?"

Esmée shook her head again while she sucked another mouthful of thick banana smoothie through her straw. She took a while to swallow it, then wiped the foam from her top lip. "It's not about envy," she said. "I don't want what they have got. I just don't want them to have got it at my expense."

Dion thought about that for a while. If he was one of the haves he would want to protect what he'd got, but he would also want to believe he'd earned it fairly. Where was the joy in hiding behind electric gates and intruder alarms, knowing people resented you? He crumpled up his rubbish and stuffed it into the brown paper bag, then took the lid off his coffee. He gazed through the window for a while, watching the world go by. Rich and poor. Old and young. Did someone put a barcode on you when you were born? This one's going to have nothing, this one's going to be a millionaire. This one's going to live to a hundred, this one won't even see their twenty-first birthday. He sensed Esmée lean into his arm.

"What's the difference between a capitalist, a communist and a socialist?"

Dion turned his head. "Is this the start of a joke?"

Esmée pushed aside her empty food cartons, then folded her arms on the counter. "A guy is wheeling a cart along a bumpy road. The cart's loaded with rocks so he's struggling to shift it. The capitalist looks on from the end of the street, and after seeing the guy, he rubs his hands together in glee and thinks: Great. How can I make a profit out of this sucker?

"Further down the road, the guy encounters the communist. He is full of sympathy, but he's not that smart. He goes off to fetch his own cart, fills it full of rocks, and then toils alongside his comrade."

"And the socialist?" Dion interrupted. "What happens when he gets to your guy?"

Esmée gave him a meaningful look in the eye. "The socialist is also full of sympathy. But unlike the communist, he goes up to the guy, puts a hand on his shoulder, and says: 'You appear to be struggling, my friend. How can I help?'"

Dion looked back at her, long and hard, then nodded appreciatively. A wise head on a young pair of shoulders.

———

Cup aloft, Dion teased the last few dregs of coffee foam into his mouth. He looked at his watch: one o'clock. Two hours to go until they had to be back at the van. He gathered up the handles of the IKEA bag and lifted it down from the counter.

"How many you got left?" Esmée asked.

Dion did a rough count. "Twenty-five. I thought we might try Rue Foch. Take in the park. There's usually something going on around there."

"Lead on, MacDuff."

They gathered their rubbish and fed it into the recycling bins. On their way out, they passed ponytail guy, now seated at a table, tucking into his salad. He gave them a slightly confused look as they walked by, perhaps sensing what Esmée was thinking about him.

Outside, Dion pointed to their right, indicating the way they needed to go, but Esmée halted, looking like she still had something on her mind. Dion gave her a puzzled look. "What is it?"

"Won't be a second."

"Where are you going?"

He watched her walk back to the BMW parked in the blue-badge spot. When she took a penknife out of her pocket, Dion had an idea of what was coming. A look of determination came over her as she stared at the burger bar window. Then she opened the penknife, dug the blade into the BMW's paintwork, and dragged it all the way to the fender.

———

"Run!"

Esmée ran past him like a cat with its tail on fire. Briefly stunned, Dion stood watching as ponytail guy burst out of the burger bar, horrified to see what had been done to his car. He spotted Esmée running away and immediately ran after her. A split-second later, Dion turned on his heel and joined in the fun.

Esmée was fifty metres up the street, running with her arms pumping. She ran across the busy road, veered towards a stationary tram, and hopped on board. "Come on!" she cried, beckoning him from the door.

Dion ran as fast as he could and didn't look back. He jumped aboard and willed the tram doors to close behind him, but it didn't matter – ponytail guy had already given up the chase. The last they saw of him, he was heaving for breath at the side of the road, hands on his knees, man-bag dangling pathetically around his neck.

"We're meant to be keeping a low profile." Dion grinned excitedly as the tram got moving.

"Sorry," Esmée grinned back. "Just couldn't resist."

Dion hadn't had such fun in years. He felt twelve years old

again, although he quickly composed himself. They were here to do a job, not have fun.

Not sure which tram they'd got on, he scanned through the windows as they moved along. A few minutes later, he spotted the Pathé Comédie and decided to get off.

They headed into the old town along Rue de la Loge, church bells ringing in the distance. This was one of the more fashionable parts of the city, full of big-name brands and luxury goods. Eying up one of the designer boutiques, Dion turned to Esmée to make a quip, only to find she wasn't there. He halted and looked back. She'd stopped outside a clothes shop and was perusing an outdoor rack. Dion gave her a moment. He wondered how other people saw her – denim cutoffs, thin white legs, pink hoodie tied around her waist. She might have been pretty if it weren't for her acne. But her clothes were shabby, her hair a mess. Cheap white trash, to those who liked to put a label on things.

But for a few brief moments she looked happy, doing a bit of shopping, enjoying the things that other people enjoyed. Normal people. Then her face turned serious again and she gave up looking at the clothes. It hit you sometimes, the sacrifices you made being part of a group like this. No more weekend jaunts into town, or late nights out with friends. It must have been hard, especially for the younger ones, knowing you weren't destined for a normal life. She gave him a curious look as she caught up, perhaps wondering what he'd been thinking.

They arrived on Rue Foch, one of the city's great thoroughfares. Its grand old buildings with their extravagant corbels and black iron balconies could have rivalled many in Paris. They walked under the Arc de Triomphe (a third the size of its more famous cousin on the Champs-Élysées, but an arresting sight nonetheless) and continued into the Promenade du Peyrou – the Place Royale – where a statue of Louis XIV, majestically cavorting on horseback, took pride of place. It must have been the day of the summer school trip because hordes of kids were out and about. One group was sitting on the cobbles, busily sketching the arch; another group was listening to their teacher talk about the history of the site. They'd certainly picked a good day for it. A tricolour flew at the top of the arch; red-white-and-blue. The sky was so blue you could swim in it. A perfect day in a perfect French city.

They carried on down to the water tower, a domineering building adorned with Corinthian columns and arches. On the far side, the Arceaux Aqueduct was an equally impressive structure, built in the 18th century to bring water in from a nearby spring. Its double layer of arches was inspired by the Pont du Gard, and at fourteen kilometres long, it was an unmissable part of the city. Spotting a gang of scaffolders setting up beneath one of the arches, Dion tackled them one by one and managed to hand out another half dozen copies of *La Vérité*. They continued down a car park, and caught people as they were coming and going. With Esmée's help, he'd emptied his sack in less than half an hour.

With time to kill before they needed to be back at the van, they strolled back to the Promenade du Peyrou. Most people had chosen benches in the shade, but Dion and Esmée picked one in full sun. He noticed that everyone else was wearing sandals, while he and Esmée were in heavy boots. Arms folded, Dion watched them pass by, carefree and relaxed, soporific in the heat. When looked at like this, the world didn't seem such a bad place. If you were one of the lucky ones, one of the ones who fit in. People who'd found their groove in life and were content with what it gave them. Why would you want to start a revolution? It seemed an awful lot of effort with no guarantee things would get better.

"Can you imagine what it would be like if there was another

revolution?" Dion said. He pictured the streets full of chaos. Cars on fire, looting. There would be carnage and bloodshed on every corner. Neighbour turned against neighbour. The police were all that protected them from anarchy, but get them on your side and imagine what would happen. Even just a few of them could be enough to turn the tide.

Realising Esmée hadn't responded, Dion turned to find her curled up on the seat beside him, eyes closed, using her hoodie as a pillow. She probably wanted to catch up on some sleep, but a few moments later, she opened her eyes and sat up. "*Vive la Sixième République,*" she said sleepily. Clearly she had been listening.

"You think it will happen?"

She joined him in contemplating the view. A group of the school kids trooped by, heading towards the aqueduct, armed with their lunch bags and sketchbooks. What kind of world would they be growing up in?

"Don't see why not," Esmée said. "It's happened before, it can happen again."

"Innocent people would die," he said. "How can you justify that?"

"Innocent people die now," Esmée responded. "How can you justify that?"

She turned to look him in the eye. For someone so young, she was remarkably sure of herself. Dion tried to remember what he'd been like at that age, but much of his early life was a blur. They were quiet for a few moments.

"Which of the Republics do you think was the best?" Dion asked.

Esmée gave it some thought. "Either the First because it abolished the monarchy, or the Third because it lasted the longest."

"I heard someone in the group say that the best Republic is always the next one."

"Good answer. Change doesn't happen easily. Politely asking people to think a different way isn't going to work. 'Without virtue, terror is destructive; without terror, virtue is impotent.'"

"Who said that?"

"Robespierre."

Dion smiled. He'd often thought Sébastien modelled himself on the great revolutionary. "The great incorruptible – wasn't that what they called him?"

Esmée nodded. "Despite all the bloodshed, a lot of people still see him as a hero. He championed the poor, fought against slavery. And he had no interest in personal gain. Name me a politician today who can claim that."

"Pass."

"Before the Revolution, the clergy and the nobility owned most of the land, yet paid next to nothing in tax. The Third Estate did all of the work and paid virtually all of the tax. Robespierre fought against that. So what if he got a bloody reputation?"

"I read somewhere that he executed so many people they had to move the guillotine. All the blood was polluting the water supply."

"They called it his Red Summer. Over a thousand people executed in forty-seven days. Even his friends and former allies got the chop."

"Not his finest hour, then?"

Esmée shrugged. "He had high standards. Problem was, anyone who didn't live up to them wasn't worthy of his loyalty. In his eyes, they deserved a trip to the national razor."

Dion thought about that for a while. The similarities with Sébastien were uncomfortably apt at times.

He stretched out his legs and made himself more comfortable, face toasting in the sun. It was far too nice a day to be thinking about such things. "Let's hope history doesn't entirely repeat itself," he said before losing himself in a daydream.

———

The sun was so intense it felt like his face was melting. Blissfully unconcerned, Dion could have stayed out there all day, lost in imaginary worlds.

"Come on," Esmée said, giving him a nudge. "The van'll be waiting."

Dion opened his eyes. Esmée stood over him, silhouetted against the sky, her tousled hair making her look like an album cover. Realising he'd been dozing, Dion quickly righted himself. He looked at his watch: two-forty-five. The prospect of going back to the base left him cold, and for a few moments he contemplated jacking it all in. Sometimes, the reality of what he'd let himself in for was frightening.

They folded up their IKEA bags. Esmée reckoned she'd found a shorter route back to the rendezvous point and took them down a series of narrow side streets. Partway down an alley, she halted next to a homeless guy curled up in a doorway. Two small round eyes looked up at them from a grizzled grey face. An old man, frightened and alone. A collection of stuffed white carrier bags likely contained his worldly possessions. A few coins lay in a hat beside him. Just around the corner were the shops where people spent hundreds on a handbag.

"We got any money left?" Esmée asked.

Dion dug into his pocket. He counted it all out – twenty-six euros and fifty-one cents. Esmée took the money from his palm, leaned down, and placed it in the man's hat.

10

Arriving home at noon, Margot was pleased to see Raymond's scooter parked by her gate. She went through the passageway to her rear courtyard where she found her back door wide open and the young man busily at work in her kitchen. Tomorrow was Rogier and Cerise's two-year anniversary, and the brothers' latest idea was that Rogier would present her with the proposal cake at La Lune Bleue and pop the question when she came in to work. Margot had offered up the use of her kitchen so that the cake could be made in secret and then snuck into the restaurant before Cerise arrived. It had seemed a good idea at the time, although when Margot looked in from the threshold and saw the mess he'd made of her kitchen, she began to have second thoughts. Every flat surface was covered in something or other, and the sink was piled high with bowls and tins.

"Bonjour, Margot. Sorry about the mess. Don't worry, I'll clean it all up when I'm finished. I promise."

Going in, Margot replaced the lid on an open carton of milk only to have her attention swiftly drawn to the table. Buster was sitting there, taking a keen interest in what was going on. Margot blinked in astonishment. "I see you've made a new friend."

"Oh, the cat, you mean?" Raymond wiped his hands on his apron and joined her at the table. "He showed up just after I got here. Is he yours?"

Margot folded her arms. "The jury's still out on that one."

"He's adorable. What's his name?"

Margot watched in amazement as Raymond started to fuss him. To her utter astonishment, the cat rolled onto his back, stretched out all four of his limbs and allowed Raymond to run his fingers through the thick white fur on his belly, purring in delight. What miracle was this?

"I've been calling him Buster, but he never lets me do that."

Yes, woman, that's because you don't do it right. My new slave, Raymond here, knows just how to reach the right spot. He gets his fingers right into that itchy patch just behind my left ear and scratches and scratches until... oh yes, right there, Raymond. Yes! Do it some more, my good fellow, and a little bit more, and, oh yes... Heavens have mercy!

"I've always been good with animals," Raymond explained. "We used to have a cat when I was a kid. I miss having one around." After bringing the cat to a state of near ecstasy, he went back to the sink and washed his hands, then returned to his mixing bowl.

Buster promptly righted himself. He wetted a paw and began washing his face. Margot was surprised he didn't light a cigarette. She gave him a cool stare. *Tart.*

The cat gave her a cool stare back. *So?*

Ignoring the impudent feline, Margot moved to the counter. She lowered her head to the mixing bowl and inhaled deeply. "Mmm. Is that beetroot?"

"Yes. It keeps the sponge nice and moist."

"It's a wonderful colour. Can I lick the spoon when you're done?"

"You can try it now, if you like."

He added a little more cocoa powder and then gave it a good stir. Margot dipped a finger into the bowl and popped it into her mouth, closing her eyes blissfully. There was something about the taste of raw cake mixture that brought out the seven-year-old in her.

"This is what it'll look like when it's done." Raymond showed her a picture on his phone. It was wonderfully elaborate, with multiple layers and decorations. She had no idea how he was going to manage to do it all in time, but good on him for trying.

"Did you learn this at college?"

"We've not got onto baking yet. I've been practising this one at home."

He'd been doing a course at the *Lycée Hôtelier* and seemed to be enjoying it. The chef at La Lune Bleue had also been letting him cook a few dishes at the restaurant, and from what Margot had sampled so far, the boy had talent.

Having completely lost interest in the cake-making (or because he was miffed with Margot for playing gooseberry), the cat jumped down from the table and mooched off elsewhere. Margot made a pot of tea while Raymond poured the cake mixture into the baking tins. Then, once the tins were in the oven, she removed his crash helmet from one of the chairs and cleared some space on the table. She retrieved her tin of biscuits from the top shelf and they sat down.

"So, is everything set for tonight?" Margot offered him a biscuit. Raymond reached in and took out a small handful.

"I think so. The band are up in Troyes at the moment, but they said they could make it."

"Let's hope he goes through with it this time."

"I'm not making him another cake if he doesn't," Raymond said emphatically, mouth full of biscuit.

"I don't see why he's so reticent. They make a lovely couple."

"He's always been shy around girls."

"It's such a shame."

"There were plenty at school who fancied him, but he always liked ones who showed no interest in him." He leaned in. "Don't tell him I said this, but there was one girl he was really keen on. He pined over her for months, even said he was in love with her. But when he finally plucked up the courage to ask her out, she turned him down."

"Oh dear."

"Not only that, she told half the class about it. They laughed at him when he went in next day."

Margot sighed in sympathy. Teenage girls could be pretty cruel when they wanted to be.

"And you've seen Cerise," Raymond went on. "Perhaps I shouldn't say this about my future sister-in-law, but she's hot. He thinks she's out of his league, and that's why he's so keen to impress her."

"Well, let's hope your cake does the trick."

Some wonderful smells were coming from the oven. Tea break over, Raymond got up to check on it. He reckoned another twenty minutes would do it. "I'll have to come back later to do the decorations."

"No problem."

"While we're waiting, I could make us some lunch, if you like." He looked in the fridge. "I've got some beetroot left over, and there's some goat's cheese that needs eating. I could make a beetroot and blackberry salad, if that sounds okay?"

He seemed keen to gain her approval. Margot folded her arms, pretending to mull it over. Clearly, she'd done the right thing encouraging him to catering college.

"Oh, go on, then," she said. "If you insist."

———

Stuffed full of food, Margot walked slowly back to work. She was on the cascading steps at the front of the *Palais* when her phone buzzed. Captain Bouchard asked her to call in at the Gendarmerie, so Margot turned through ninety degrees and set off down Rue Garenne.

For the second time this week, the reception appeared to be empty. Margot looked through the screen to check that Lieutenant Martel wasn't on the floor, attempting to break the world record for sit-ups, and then pushed the buzzer on the counter. Less than ten seconds passed before Captain Bouchard appeared, looking like he'd been waiting for her.

"Madame Renard – please come through." He unlocked the interconnecting door and showed her down to his office. Once they were both inside, he quietly closed the door behind them. The expression on his face was even more serious than usual.

"Take a seat."

Margot sat. Ever since she'd first been summoned to this office, she'd been unable to escape the feeling that she was here because she'd done something wrong. Perched on the edge of the chair, she gave him a curious look. "Has something happened?"

The captain didn't answer directly. Instead, he walked to his side of his desk and sat down in the chair, lacing his fingers together as he often did when questioning a suspect. "I wanted to talk to you about what happened at the weekend."

"Okay."

"Could you tell me again how you came to be following those two people?"

Margot took a breath, then recounted her story, starting with her visit to Madame Janvier's bookshop and ending with the incident on the edge of the woods. She took her time, carefully checking her memory to make sure she hadn't left anything out.

"Other than myself, is there anyone else you've told about this?"

Margot thought back, then shook her head. "I gave Madame Janvier the gist of what happened, but I've not mentioned it to anyone else."

"Those photographs you took."

"Yes?"

"Could I see them again?"

Margot reached for her phone, but then paused, feeling uneasy. She wondered where this was going. "I'm more than happy to oblige, Captain, but why the sudden interest?"

Captain Bouchard removed his arms from the desk and leaned back in his chair. "Earlier today, I received a telephone call from our Brigade Commander. He instructed me to cease our investigation and advise you in the strongest possible terms to take no further action in this matter. I am to confiscate any information you've collected and hand it over to the GIGN."

The skin on Margot's forearms prickled. "Gendarmerie Special Operations?"

He nodded.

Margot stared at him, baffled. "Why would the GIGN be interested in a shopkeeper being conned out of her savings?"

"I lack the security clearance to be trusted with that information," the captain smiled ironically. "All I can do is pass on orders."

"But aren't they involved in counterterrorism?"

"Counterterrorism is one of their responsibilities. They're also involved in hostage rescue, protection of VIPs, and surveillance. These days, they work closely with RAID – the *Police Nationale*'s elite force."

Margot still couldn't understand their involvement. "They didn't give any hint at all?"

"Not as such." The captain lowered his voice. "But they did leave one small clue: the email address they told me to use was for division 51. I'm pretty sure that division is involved in undercover operations."

Margot gave him a closer look. "You mean one of them was an undercover cop?"

"It's a possibility."

"But how did they know I was following them?"

"Someone must have seen you. The Commander mentioned you by name."

"He did?"

The captain nodded. "When you checked into the hotel, did you use a credit card?"

Margot flushed, cursing her stupidity. Reluctantly, she nodded.

"That would have been enough for them to trace you. They would have had access to your emails, every purchase you've made with your cards, every website you've viewed."

"They're not allowed to do that. Not without good reason."

"When it comes to national security, Madame, they can do pretty much anything they like. Did you back up the photos to any cloud-based resource?"

"No."

"Then if you let me have your phone, that will hopefully be an end to it." He opened his hand.

Margot hesitated, considering her options. She hated the way she was being treated like a criminal when she hadn't done anything wrong. It stank of Deep State, and that frightened and appalled her in equal measure. Realising she had little choice but to cooperate, however, she reached into her pocket and took out her phone. She swiped back to the first of the photos she'd taken in Narbonne and then handed it over. Captain Bouchard took his time looking through. At one point he activated the video she'd taken in the restaurant. The sounds coming from her phone transported her back: the soft music, the hushed conversations, the clink of cutlery. Finally, when he was satisfied, he took a plastic evidence bag from a drawer and dropped the phone into it. It was a wonder he didn't take her mugshot, too.

"When will I get it back?"

"I promise we'll be as quick as we can. In the meantime, I strongly advise you to leave well alone. These people don't play games."

"Of course."

"And that includes Madame Janvier. It's probably best if you have no further contact with her."

"That's a shame. I rather like going to her bookshop."

"My advice is to forget everything you saw."

If only it were that easy. Margot's thoughts were already galloping ahead. They must have been onto her from the start, either when she'd arrived at the hotel or later when she'd followed the builder and his accomplice. She should have been more cautious.

The captain stood up and moved to the door, ready to show her out. "Enjoy the rest of your day, Madame."

Still pondering, Margot was slow to leave. "I'll try," she said and then halted just after she'd passed him. "Which one was it, I wonder? Him or her?"

Captain Bouchard gave a light shrug of his shoulders. "I'm as much in the dark as you."

———

True to his word, Raymond had cleared up by the time Margot got home. He'd washed and put away every bowl and utensil, wiped down all the work surfaces, and returned every packet of ingredients to its rightful place. He'd even baked a smaller version of the proposal cake and left it on the table with a note: *Thanks for letting me use your kitchen.* How sweet.

Margot pottered around the house for an hour, feeling lost without her phone. She had managed to blag a temporary one from work but was wary of using it, wondering who might be listening in. *Forget everything you saw*, the captain had said, yet his warning had done just the opposite. Hoping to distract herself, Margot switched on the TV, but still couldn't settle. All she could think about was the force of that punch; the young woman with the neck scarf. *Nice watch.* The pair of them disappearing into those mysterious woods.

Stéphane had been making a habit of calling her after work. Now divorced, he'd moved out of the family home in Strasbourg and into an apartment close by. He seemed to need someone to talk to, and Margot had grown rather fond of their late evening chats. She texted him her temporary number, put the phone down on the table, then flinched when it buzzed immediately. She picked it straight back up again. "Hello."

"What's with the new number?"

Margot switched off the TV. She was all set to tell him about her weekend adventures, but quickly stopped herself, remembering the captain's warning.

"Mine needs a new battery," she lied, then promptly changed the subject. "How's your mother getting on?"

A small sigh came down the line. "Oh, she's okay, I suppose. She's staying in a beautiful villa, right on the edge of the lake. She has her own private swimming pool. You'd love it there."

"Sounds heavenly."

"It is, but something's not right. She normally hates going on holiday and can't wait to get back to work, but last week, when I stayed with her, she didn't seem interested at all. She's been going on long walks, spending time alone."

"She needs to recuperate."

"I know, but it's not like her. Do you know what she said to me when I was there?"

"What?"

"She asked me to look into setting up a foundation for her. She's planning on giving away all of her money."

"That's very noble of her."

"I agree, and I'm not being selfish. I honestly couldn't care less about the money. What bothers me is why she's started talking about it now."

Margot kicked off her shoes and put her feet up on the sofa. Perhaps it wasn't that surprising. Once you've had a glimpse of your own mortality, you start to see things differently, think more about the days you have left than the ones that have gone by. If Margot ever came into a fortune, she liked to think she would enjoy giving it all away.

"What has her doctor said?"

"He seemed to think everything is all right, but I'm not sure I believe him."

"I'm sure he would say if something was wrong."

"It was the first time I've looked at her and thought of her as being old. People are usually surprised when she tells them she's seventy-two."

Margot didn't know what to say to him. It was no fun watching a loved one grow old. Time flies by, and there's not a damn thing you can do about it.

"Well, I hope she's feeling better soon. We're certainly missing her. The *Palais*'s not the same without her."

Another deep sigh came down the line. "Thank you, Margot. I'll tell her that." He went on: "Anyway. What have you been up to lately?"

"Nothing much. You know me, anything for a quiet life."

She heard him scoff. "I find that hard to believe."

"What would you say if I told you I was moving to Bordeaux?"

"I would say: 'Why on earth are you moving to Bordeaux?'"

"It was your mother's idea."

"Really? My mother likes you; why would she want to banish you to the Atlantic?"

"Because that's where the magistrates' school is."

A pause. "You want to become a *magistrat*?"

"Don't sound so surprised."

"I thought you liked it in Argents."

"I do. I love it here. It's just..." If her telephone had had a cord, Margot would have been twirling it around her fingers right now. "Oh, I don't know. Perhaps I feel there's more I should be doing with my life."

"That's understandable."

"And with my experience, I would only need to do the twelve-month course."

"Direct integration?"

"That was what they called it. My only worry is I'd probably be the oldest student in the class. How would I cope, surrounded by all those thrusting young men?"

Stéphane made a point of clearing his throat. "Correct me if I'm wrong, Margot, but don't all direct integration candidates have to be at least thirty-five years of age?"

"Do they? Damn. You've burst my bubble."

"I won't pretend to be sorry. And many of them will be women, of course."

"Blasted women's liberation," Margot joked. It was fun teasing him.

"So you're seriously thinking of applying?"

"I've started filling in the application form."

"And then what? Once you've qualified, where would you go?"

A note of caution had crept into his voice. Was he worried about the logistics of how they might see each other?

"Wherever there was a vacancy, I suppose."

"Strasbourg?" he suggested hopefully.

Margot smiled, then put a lid on it. "Oh no, definitely not Strasbourg. Not with all those human rights lawyers around."

There was a pause while Margot waited for his comeback. Fearing she'd pushed a little too far, she pedalled back. "All right, if an opportunity arises in Strasbourg, I'll go willingly. The weather's always nice up there, isn't it?"

"Oh yes. Hot and sunny every day."

"Hmm. I hope you don't lie so easily at work, Stéphane."

"You know us lawyers: the truth, a lie... they're just words expressed in different ways."

A *yowl* came from the direction of the kitchen. Margot rolled her eyes. "Oh, here we go."

"What's that? No, don't tell me – his Royal Fluffiness has just put in an appearance."

"How did you guess? You wouldn't believe what I found him doing at lunchtime."

"Amaze me."

"He was only spreadeagled on my kitchen table, letting Raymond rub his belly."

"The hussy!"

"Exactly what I thought. And now here he comes, bold as brass, acting like nothing has happened. Yes, you, young man. I'm talking to you."

Buster strolled up to the sofa and parked his backside twenty centimetres from Margot's right foot. His furry little face looked up at her, not giving the slightest damn.

"And yet, Margot, you'll still give in to him. Pander to his every need, feed him the finest cat food on the planet."

"I'm such a patsy, aren't I?"

"You are. But all I can say is, animals know how to pick out the good guys."

A lump formed in Margot's throat. What a lovely thing to say.

11

A buzz of excitement filled the room as two large TVs were wheeled in. Probably ninety per cent of the group's members were crowded into the mess hall, and others were on their way. Eager volunteers helped set up the equipment, routing cables and plugging things in. At the front of the crowd, Sébastien looked on anxiously, biting the skin on the inside of his thumbnail.

A small cheer went up when the TVs came to life. Each one was tuned to a different news channel, but the message was the same on both: BOMB ATTACKS ROCK GERMANY. Munich had been the first city to be targeted, closely followed by Cologne and Hamburg. According to the captions on the screen, the latest and biggest of the bombs had just gone off in Berlin. The room went quiet as images of burning buildings appeared, chaotic footage of people running for their lives, faces streaked with blood, like something out of a war zone. The Berlin bomb appeared to have gone off in a nightclub, ten minutes after midnight. The place would have been crowded with partygoers.

Dion pulled out a chair, turned it around and sat with his elbows on the backrest. Many of the people around him were only half dressed, looking like they'd come straight from their beds. Once the news had broken, word had spread quickly and excitement had mounted as they'd made their way down the corridors to the mess hall. It had clearly been a coordinated attack. Sébastien had been promising that something like this was coming, though the timing seemed to have taken them by surprise. Dion had sensed excitement, fear, and trepidation as the group had assembled in the mess hall, wondering what this would mean for them all.

The news switched to a reporter broadcasting live from the scene in Munich. Some mobile phone footage had been sent in showing the exact moment the bomb had gone off – a pretty big one judging by the sound of the accompanying boom. It appeared to have gone off in a shopping mall, and the fire had spread to the cinema next door. The newsfeed cut back to a female newscaster who looked gravely into the camera to announce that three people had been confirmed dead. If the number of ambulances were anything to go by, it was a number that was sure to increase.

Dion divided his attention between the screens and their leader. Sébastien stood in a huddle with Tik and Monika. They probably knew who was behind the attacks, though it was unlikely they had been given an advance warning. Attacks like this were a closely guarded secret, known only to the people involved.

Recording equipment was set up, a few people started taking notes. Debates were already breaking out about what would happen next. It looked like they were in for a long night. Dion remembered the last time an attack of this scale had happened when a car bomb had rocked London. Sébastien had wanted a full report compiling in the course of which hundreds of hours of footage had been recorded. They'd analysed key scenes from every angle, studied how events had unfolded and how the security forces had responded. If (or more likely when) their own moment of glory came, Sébastien wanted them to be fully prepared.

The number of casualties soon began to rise. Another seven had just been reported in Berlin: four men and three women, including a twelve-year-old girl. Dion shifted uncomfortably on his seat. He scanned the room, observing the reactions of those around him. Even if you allied yourself with the ideology, how did you deal with the fact that an innocent twelve-year-old had just died? He was genuinely interested to know. Some looked sad; most remained impassive. One of the skinheads appeared to be smirking as the screen filled with images of what had to be dead bodies lying amongst the rubble. It wasn't surprising Sébastien looked worried. This would put pressure on him to act. He needed his followers to believe that the sacrifices they'd made were worth it, that something was actually going to be achieved. They'd spent long enough talking; soon it would be time for action.

Dion was distracted by a tap on his shoulder. He looked round to see Esmée crouching beside him.

"What's the latest?"

Dion filled her in. Esmée's face stayed blank when he told her about the fatalities, though her eyes narrowed a little when he mentioned the young girl. He wondered if she really was as hardcore as she tried to make out, or if there was someone more vulnerable inside. They turned back to the screens and watched a little more of the coverage, but the newscasters soon started repeating themselves and the video clips began playing on loop. He looked at his watch. Almost two in the morning. Esmée leaned into him. "Fancy a drink?" she whispered.

Dion gave her a surprised look. "You know a bar that's open?"

She stood up, tilted her head conspiratorially, then headed

for the exit. Intrigued, Dion checked that no one was looking, then followed her out.

She led him down to the barrack block. There was no segregation in the bunkhouse, but most of the women chose to sleep close to the doors in bunkhouse B (more to avoid the smell (reminiscent of a cattle-shed) than out of concerns for their safety). They passed rows and rows of metal bunkbeds, crammed into a hot, dark space, until Esmée stopped next to a bed in the corner. She reached under the mattress and pulled out her messenger bag. Dion looked at her in surprise as she produced a bottle of Grey Goose.

"Where'd you get that?"

"Narbonne."

She hadn't spent the entire time reading her book, then.

Dion checked over his shoulder. The bunkhouse was empty, but it was still too risky. "Not here," he said.

"Then where?"

"I know a place."

This time Dion led the way. They passed through the hub, the sound of the TVs drifting down from the mess hall, then went into D-wing. Dion activated his torch in a long, straight corridor. D-wing was the most solidly built part of the base. Its walls were so thick that it could probably withstand a nuclear blast. They came to a circular steel door, which, though unlocked, caused Dion to pause. Most people who'd ventured beyond it rarely went back for a second visit. Sensing his hesitancy, Esmée swung her torch towards his face.

"What's in there?"

"You've not been down here before?"

"Nope."

A smooth steel wheel turned the locks, the kind of thing you might find on an airlock. Despite its weight, the door swung easily on its hinges. A short narrow corridor led to an opaque,

PVC strip curtain which Dion approached with caution. He lowered his head to push through, then used his elbow to hold it aside so that Esmée could slip through. They arrived on the edge of a room that was cold and dingy, the boundaries of which could only be guessed.

"Don't touch anything with your bare hands," Dion cautioned.

Their torch-beams roved over a dozen gurneys lined up along the longest wall. At first sight you might think it was a hospital ward, but it made no sense to have an infirmary down here when there was a well-equipped, fifty-bed facility in A-wing. The equipment looked like something out of the dark ages – stainless steel trays loaded with cleavers and saws, syringes and scissors.

"Why are there bars on the windows?"

Esmée shone her light onto the row of small windows right up at the top of the wall. Bars on the inside, shutters on the outside. The concrete on the reveals must have been a metre thick.

"Come and see this."

Broken glass crunching under his feet, Dion set off across the room. An opening led to a space that resembled a laboratory. Most of the equipment had been stripped or smashed: drawers emptied, cabinets overturned. A rack of test tubes and a few glass beakers were one of the few things that remained intact. A strong smell of chemicals hung in the air. This place had served a very different purpose to serving the sick and injured.

Another pair of doors led to a short, blank corridor where the walls were blackened with fire damage. Puddles on the floor suggested the sprinkler system had gone off. Dion steeled himself as he entered the next room – a simple room, five metres by five, containing nothing but a high-back armchair. Thick leather straps with strong metal buckles were fixed to the arms of the chair, while a head restraint was attached to the back. Dion had stood on this spot at least a dozen times before, but the sight of that chair still sent shivers down his spine. The ceramic white tiles gave the room a clinical feel, but even down here nature had invaded. The walls were stained with green algae, and a tendril of ivy had managed to creep in from somewhere. If ghosts really were haunting the base, this was where they would want to hang out.

Dion gave Esmée time to take it all in. It was so quiet he could hear the sound of her breathing – in and out, in and out. Finally, she turned her torch towards him.

"What the hell were they doing in here?"

He gestured towards an inner room. Used syringes littered the floor. Two large pinboards covered the walls, and both had been cleared apart from a couple of Polaroids that still hung from one corner. Dion unpinned them and handed them to Esmée. The photos had been taken in the room with the chair. In one, a man in a hospital gown was strapped to the chair, looking terrified out of his mind. In the other, a naked black man was cowering in a corner, being hosed down by men in rubber suits.

"What the hell...?"

"There's more in here."

Dion opened a drawer in one of the cabinets. Inside were dozens more Polaroids, all in a similar vein, presumably overlooked by whoever had cleaned the place out. Esmée pulled out a stool and sat down. She spread the Polaroids across a desk, both appalled and fascinated by what she was seeing. The subject in the chair was different each time, but they all shared that same spaced-out look. They were either being injected or beaten or humiliated in some way. Dion reckoned he'd counted over twenty different faces, though it was difficult to be certain, as many of them looked the same with the bright lights illuminating their saucer-like eyes.

"How old are these?"

"The first Polaroid camera came out just after the war," he said. "These look more recent; I'd say 1960s."

"Who was doing this – the army?"

Dion shook his head. He couldn't believe anyone in the army had sanctioned this, at least, not officially. More likely it had been done by some rogue element, probably in the intelligence service. They'd been involved in some pretty bizarre operations back then. Similar secret programmes had gone on in the US at that time, though he couldn't believe it had been that extensive, not here in France.

"Does Sébastien know about this?"

"I presume so."

Esmée pored over the pictures for a little while longer, but then suddenly sat back, looking like she'd seen enough. Dion wasn't surprised. Once the ghoulishness had been sated, it was hard not to feel disgusted. He gathered up the pictures and returned them to the drawer, then nodded his head, indicating that she should follow him out.

Crossing the corridor, they found a room that was a little more hospitable – a mess room with half a dozen easy chairs and a tan leather sofa. An armoire, which appeared to have once been used as a drinks cabinet, still housed a few pieces of cut glassware. It was bizarre to think that people had once sat relaxing in here, enjoying their nibbles and drinks, while that horror show had been going on down the hall. Dion converted his Maglite to candle mode and then set it on a shelf.

"It's not the most cheerful of places," he said. "But at least we won't be disturbed."

He took two tumblers from the armoire while Esmée retrieved the bottle of Grey Goose from her messenger bag. She half-filled the tumblers and then settled into one of the easy chairs. Dion lay down on the sofa. They drank in silence for a while. In some ways, Dion liked it down here. He could hear himself think. The walls were so thick they shut everything out.

"So what's your story?" Esmée said at last. "How did you end up here?"

Dion rolled his head to the side to look at her. Her face was a mass of dark shadow. "Let's just say, I was unhappy with the world."

"Where did you work?"

"I worked on a farm," he said, and took another sip of the vodka. He felt uncomfortable lying to her, but didn't really have much choice. "It was a hard life. The government was always bringing in new regulations, putting up costs, but food prices never increased to make up for it. I joined a local protest group, went on a few marches. Then someone suggested we drive a tractor into the centre of Paris and dump a load of horseshit on the Champs-Élysées."

"I bet that caused a stink."

"You could say that."

They shared a friendly smile. Dion went on,

"A friend of a friend knew someone in Sebastian's group. We met up. I liked what he had to say and it went from there." That, at least, wasn't too far from the truth.

"How long have you been in here?"

"Eighteen months."

"You got anyone on the outside? You mentioned a wife."

Dion tensed. "That's right."

"You missing her?"

Dion swirled the vodka in his glass. He moved his face out of the light as emotion caught hold of him. How could he explain how much he missed Yvette? Brutes like him weren't meant to have those kinds of feelings. He felt like he'd been cut down the middle and had one half taken away, but he was never going to say that. Not to Esmée, not to anyone.

"That night at the hotel in Narbonne," he said. "I lied."

"I kind of suspected that."

"I wasn't feeling unwell. There was someone I needed to see."

"Okay."

"A few weeks back, I found out my wife had been having an affair. I'd known the guy for years. I got a message to say he was staying with his sister in Narbonne. Since we were in the area, I went to see him."

"And made your feelings known?"

"Apparently I broke his nose."

He expected her to smile, but Esmée was sharper than that. "You've spoken to her?" she said in surprise.

Dion froze, realising his mistake. They'd talked more in the past couple of days than in the whole of those six weeks out on the road. It was the first time in ages that he felt he had someone to confide in, but he needed to be careful. He drained his glass and then sat up and reached for the bottle.

"We've been married for seventeen years. I don't understand how someone can stand up and make a vow, then, as soon as your back is turned, go off with somebody else."

"People are inherently selfish."

Wasn't that the truth.

Dion filled his glass. Esmée threw back her head to empty hers. As she leaned forward for a refill, her neck scarf came loose, exposing her scar to the light.

"How did you get that?" Dion pointed to her neck. "If you don't mind me asking."

Reflexively, Esmée pulled the scarf back into place. She sat back in her chair, raising her legs over the armrest. "Happened when I was a kid. A branch fell from a burning tree."

"Ouch. That must have hurt."

"It was my own fault really, since I was the one who set fire to it."

"What happened?"

"The tree was in our neighbour's garden. Me and the girl next door used to play together, when we were eight or nine or something. We were quite pally for a while. Our dads worked in the same factory, but it wasn't until about a year after we moved in that we realised that her dad was my actually my dad's boss. He was quite high up in the firm, whereas my dad was a nobody on the shop floor. It suddenly dawned on me why they had such a big garden, and why her mum was at home all day when my mum was at work. As soon as my so-called friend realised that her position in society was rather higher than mine, everything changed. She started looking down on me, kept making insidious comments about how we couldn't afford things."

"That's not nice."

"Anyway, one day we fell out about something. I can't remember what it was, but I got the blame for it. She said that if I didn't back down, she would go to her dad and tell him to give my dad the sack."

"What a bitch."

"Totally."

"So what did you do?"

There was a pause while she took a drink. Dion watched her swallow her mouthful.

"Burned down her treehouse."

He laughed.

"It was this big, fancy thing at the bottom of their garden. It must have cost thousands to have it built. I splashed some petrol on the bottom of the ladder and set light to it."

"Firebrand."

"But I must have put too much on because the flames shot

up the ladder. Then the whole thing went up, the curtains were ablaze, the roof was on fire. I was so surprised I just stood there and watched. And that was when this burning branch fell down on me."

"I'm guessing it was a pretty bad burn."

"I had to spend a week in hospital. They tried to do a skin graft, but it didn't go well."

"And the girl next door?"

"Never spoke to me again. The following year, they sold up and moved away. Probably to a better neighbourhood."

Dion looked at her with a newfound admiration. In his book, kids who stood up for themselves were special kinds of heroes. "You've always been a rebel, then?"

"If that's what you want to call it. I could never understand why my parents were so passive. They both worked hard, yet compared to the people next door we had nothing. And they didn't seem to notice how unfair it was, or if they did, couldn't be bothered to do anything about it. Like it was their lot in life and they just had to accept it. And it wasn't like her dad was smart or worked hard or anything. He seemed to spend most of his time playing golf."

"Will your parents be worried about you?"

"Dunno," Esmée shrugged. "They probably still think I'm at uni."

She got up and walked to the door. She shone her light into the corridor, looking curious. "What else is down here?"

"Nothing much. A few more rooms along the hall."

The light from her torch faded as she went off to explore.

Dion leaned back on the sofa. He was in the mood to get blind stinking drunk; couldn't remember the last time he'd done so. He moved his torch around the confines of the room, tracing a line along the ceiling, down one wall, and onto the floor. It was an old saying, but if walls could talk...

A loud clattering sound came from down the hall. Dion pricked up his ears. "You okay?"

"Oops!"

Dion got up. He followed the light to the end of the corridor where he found Esmée inside one of the storerooms. The top drawer of a tall metal filing cabinet lay at her feet.

"The drawer was stuck so I gave it a tug," she explained. "I think something was jamming it."

Esmée shone her light into the space where the drawer had been. She reached in, and when her hand came out, she was holding a bulging file, bent and creased from where it had got jammed. Dion's eyes lit up when he spotted the bold red lettering stamped on the front: *TRÈS SECRET.*

"Let me see that."

He took the file from her. It was stuffed full of loose papers, many of them stamped with the *Ministère de la Défense* logo. He flipped the fallen drawer onto its side and laid the file on top. The papers were all jumbled up: letters, charts, pages of statistics, chemical equations and structural formulas. There was a whole tranche of official correspondence between various departments of the army, including, he was dismayed to notice, the *Gendarmerie Nationale.* All typed, except for a few hand-written notes in margins. A smaller bundle fell out in his eager-ness to leaf through. Crouching beside them, Esmée picked them up. Pages and pages of photocopied images, similar to the ones they'd found next door. Men with gaunt faces, dead behind the eyes, being treated in the most despicable of ways.

"Some of these are less than forty years old," Esmée said, pointing out the dates. She pored over the pages of statistics. "This looks like test data to me. Some kind of drug trial, I reckon."

She turned to look him in the eye. Dion stared back at her, beginning to understand what might have been going on here.

The syringes, the charts on the walls, the smell of chemicals. He was keen to see what else the papers had to reveal, but his instincts told him they shouldn't even be looking. He snatched the papers from Esmée's hand and stuffed everything back into the file.

"Come on," he said. "Let's get out of here."

12

Margot was in the lobby of the *Palais de Justice,* heading for the grand marble staircase, when she noticed the receptionist trying to attract her attention. Smiling, she detoured to the desk. "Looking for me?"

"Yes," the receptionist replied. "Someone was asking for you just now. A youngish woman, tall, blonde, said her name was…" she consulted a note, "Natalie Belmont."

Margot repeated the name to herself, but it didn't mean anything to her. She shook her head. "Did she say what it was about?"

"No, but she was very insistent. She wanted to wait in your office, but I told her she couldn't. She's only just left."

Thinking about it, Margot recalled passing a tall blonde on the steps outside. She had seemed in a hurry.

"Never mind. If she comes back give me a call."

"I will."

Margot put it out of her mind until, arriving at the top of the sweeping staircase, she spotted what appeared to be the very same woman stationed outside Florian's office. Their eyes connected from a distance, and Margot paused, unable to shake the feeling they'd somehow been destined to meet.

"Are you Margot Renard?" the woman asked as Margot drew near. She said it in a combative way, more challenge than question, like a would-be dueller throwing down a gauntlet. Margot remained on her guard.

"I am."

"I've been calling you. You didn't answer your phone."

"I've been having some problems with it," Margot replied defensively. She frowned. "I'm sorry, can you remind me who you are?"

The younger woman rolled her eyes. "My name's Natalie Belmont. My grandmother said I could find you here."

"Ah." The penny dropped: "You're Madame Janvier's granddaughter."

"That's right."

Margot still hadn't shaken off her confusion, however. "But didn't I see you leaving just a minute ago?"

"Possibly."

"Then how did you get up here so quickly?"

Another condescending roll of the eyes. "The back door was open. One of the catering staff let me use the service elevator. It wasn't that hard."

How very resourceful.

Margot gave her an up-and-down look. She was quite a striking woman. Early thirties; smartly turned out in a fashionable grey blazer and matching loose shorts. Now that she came to think about it, Margot used to have an outfit just like it. She was probably an inch taller than Margot, even in low heels. She had the dimensions of a catwalk model and a face that could have graced the cover of a glossy magazine. Margot couldn't quite put her finger on it, but there was something about this younger woman that was making her uncomfortable.

Margot tried again, producing a smile. "We haven't got off to the best of starts, have we? Tell me – what can I do for you?"

"My grandmother said you'd promised to help."

"I said I would do what I could."

"So what have you achieved?"

Margot kept her cool. "I went to see the police. I told them what had happened."

"And?"

"They said they would look into it. But I doubt there's much they can do."

"What about the office this supposed builder was renting?"

"A dead end."

"And those woods... My grandmother said you followed them to the edge of a forest somewhere."

Someone walked by, close enough to overhear. Margot smiled awkwardly and then gently touched Natalie's arm. "Let's talk in here, shall we?"

She indicated an alcove around the corner. It was a cosy nook with two formal armchairs, but Natalie showed no inclination to be seated. Margot tried a third time.

"Look, Natalie. I'm very sorry for what happened to your grandmother. Truly, I am, but there's nothing more I can do. We must leave it to the police."

"Fat chance of them doing anything," Natalie huffed.

"The people behind this are very professional. You're not going to find them."

"But these woods you talked about... If that's the last place they were seen, then someone should be out there searching for them."

Margot shifted uncomfortably. Had their roles been reversed, these were exactly the same questions she would have been asking, and she found it difficult to know how to respond.

It was like arguing with a younger version of herself. But it was imperative she throw her off the scent.

"I understand your frustration, really I do, but it's out of my hands."

"Then I'll speak to the police myself."

"There's no point. I've already told you what they said."

"Then I'll go to the mayor," Natalie announced pompously. "Tell him what's been going on in this town."

Good luck with that, Margot thought, given her recent experience with the mayor of Argents. She placed a conciliatory hand on Natalie's arm, but the younger woman recoiled. Margot persisted:

"I suggest you go home and comfort your grandmother. If the police come up with anything, I'll be sure to let you know, but in the meantime, take my advice and let it go."

"Don't patronise me!" Natalie's eyes flared with anger. "They can't be allowed to get away with this, just because the police think it might be difficult to trace them. It's outrageous!"

Other than a rather weak smile, Margot had nothing left to give. Natalie continued to glare. "Don't think this is the end of the matter. Not by any means."

She promptly walked away, but Margot had no doubt she hadn't seen the last of her.

———

Margot retreated to the office and attempted to get on with some work, but her mind wouldn't settle. She turned to the window and craned her neck to look down on Place Jeanne d'Arc. She had a good view of the square and of the *mairie* opposite, but she couldn't quite see Rue Garenne. If Natalie carried out her threat and went to see the captain, it would likely land Margot in even more hot water.

Yet Margot knew full well that if she were in the younger woman's shoes, she would be doing exactly the same thing. She looked across the office at Florian. "Mind if I nip out for a few minutes?"

Florian surfaced from behind his triptych of screens. He was so engrossed in his work that Margot often wondered whether he noticed she were there at all.

"Sorry?" he said, like a mole that had just remembered it wasn't alone in the world.

Margot grabbed her bag. "I need a quick word with Captain Bouchard. Won't be long."

Lieutenant Martel greeted her from behind the Perspex screen. "Madame Renard – to what do we owe this pleasure?"

"Has a woman just been in? Blonde hair, tall, wearing a designer blazer and shorts."

The lieutenant gave it some thought, but Margot took that as a no. If someone as striking as Natalie had just walked into the Gendarmerie, the chances of Martel not having noticed were somewhere between nil and zero.

"I don't recall seeing such a person, no."

Margot smiled. "No problem. Could I have a quick word with the captain, please?"

"Of course. Come through."

She found him in the detectives' office, conferring with a small group of men. Rather than interrupt, Margot waited at the door, and half a minute later he joined her.

"Madame."

"Have you finished with my phone?"

"Yes, I think it's come back." He signalled across the room to one of the men. A young gendarme promptly came over and handed him a plastic evidence bag. The captain opened it up, reached inside, and took out her mobile phone.

"I'm sorry it took so long."

"That's all right."

He tilted his head to suggest they go into his office. Once inside, he closed the door behind them.

"The images have been deleted," he said. "But I gave strict instructions that no other data was to be accessed. I trust everything is in order."

He waited while Margot checked. As soon as the phone came on, she had a quick swipe through. Everything apart from the photos she'd taken at the weekend appeared to still be there. She gave him a nod and then slipped the phone into her back pocket.

"Any news from the GIGN?"

The captain shook his head. "I filed my report and assured them you had fully cooperated. I wouldn't expect to hear back from them unless there was a problem."

Margot pulled a face. "Actually, there is one small problem," she confessed.

The captain stiffened. "Oh yes?"

"Madame Janvier's granddaughter just turned up at the *Palais*. She said she was going to come and see you."

"What did you tell her?"

"Nothing. I warned her off. At least, I think I did."

"How much does she know?"

"Only what I'd already told her grandmother. But she seems very determined."

The captain moved slowly around his desk. "Thanks for the heads up. I'll deflect her if she comes in."

Margot was relieved to hear that, though she couldn't help fearing that a rebuttal from Captain Bouchard was only likely to add fuel to the fire where Natalie was concerned. She continued:

"Given that this is an official operation, is there any chance Madame Janvier might be entitled to some form of compensation?"

"From the government?" The captain sounded surprised.

"I was thinking of the Victims Compensation Fund."

He gave her a doubtful look. "I wouldn't hold my breath."

"But surely an undercover officer can't go around committing crimes? There must be rules."

"Of course there are rules, but in real-life situations the lines often get blurred. Maintaining cover is imperative."

"But at what cost? How far are they allowed to go?"

"The parameters of an operation would be defined from the outset. If the officer involved is from GIGN, I can assure you that he or she will be very well trained."

"Does that include stealing from people? Or assaulting someone?" The force of that punch. A blow like that could have killed a man.

Captain Bouchard firmly shook his head. "Crimes of violence would never be sanctioned. But if, for example, an officer had infiltrated a drug cartel, you would expect them to take part in dealing drugs."

Margot sighed, still unable to get her head around it.

"Do not underestimate the dangers they face, Madame," the captain went on. "Undercover officers put themselves and their families at great risk. Having their identity exposed could mean death, hence the need for stringent precautions." He indicated her phone.

But Margot remained unconvinced. In her book, justifying law-breaking, however worthy the cause, was the start of a slippery slope.

———

At five-thirty that evening, Rogier came to collect the proposal cake. He already looked stressed when he hurried across the courtyard and into Margot's kitchen. He dumped his things on the table, puffing out his cheeks in annoyance. "Could this day get any worse?"

"It's your anniversary," Margot replied. "You're meant to be happy."

"Happy? Oh, yes... I think I can remember what that means." A heavy cloud of doom hung over him as he sat down.

Margot sighed. "What's happened now?"

"You know the band that's meant to be playing tonight?"

"The Amy Winehouse cover band."

"They just called. Their car's broken down. They won't be able to make it."

"Couldn't you get someone to collect them?"

"They're two hundred miles away!"

"Oh."

Rogier clamped a palm to his brow. "The whole thing's ruined. I knew it would be a disaster." He looked like he was about to burst into tears.

Margot placed a hand on his head and pulled him close. "Now don't be silly. It's not going to be a disaster. Let's carry on as planned; get the cake down to the restaurant, and everything will be fine. You'll see."

The three of them had been up half the night, putting the final touches to the grand plan. They were on a tight schedule – Raymond's boss at La Lune Bleue had told them they needed to be finished and have everything cleared away before the restaurant opened at seven, but they weren't allowed to set anything up until after five when the afternoon service ended. To complicate matters further, Cerise rarely got into work before six-forty-five, meaning that Margot had had to call her at lunchtime and come up with a reason for her to come in early. The plan was so complicated that something was bound to go wrong, but Margot kept her doubts to herself.

Rogier pulled himself together. "Thanks, Margot. We'd better go."

Margot retrieved the cake from the fridge. Raymond had done an excellent job on the decorations, covering it with edible flowers and piping the lettering to perfection. Rogier opened the lid on the cake box and carefully transferred the cake to the box, but in doing so, his elbow caught the back of a chair. For one heart-stopping moment, the cake slipped on its base and looked like it was going to drop. Margot's hand came to the rescue. "Careful. Your brother spent hours making that."

They both let out a sigh of relief.

Cake safely stowed, they set out, but only made it as far as the door where Rogier turned back, still looking worried.

"She will say yes, won't she?"

Margot exhaled. Any more dithering and she was going to slap him. "After all this, she better had," she said, and ushered him on.

From the harbour, they crossed the footbridge to the ramparts and then walked quickly down the zigzagging path to La Lune Bleue. Along the way, Margot cast a worried look up at the sky. The weather forecast had been useless. Instead of the promised late-evening sunshine, some dark clouds had come in. It didn't look promising.

Raymond was busy on the terrace, putting the final touches to his tableau. He'd moved two tables together and covered them with a clean white cloth. He'd made an elegant stand for the cake using dinner plates and a champagne glass, and was now attempting to light some candles in a fancy brass candelabra, though a keen onshore wind wasn't helping.

"Have you got it?" he asked anxiously.

Margot took charge of the cake box and carefully set it down on the table. "Right here."

"What about the sparklers?" Rogier suddenly announced. "We were going to have sparklers."

"Behind the bar," Raymond said. "Next to the champagne."

Rogier hurried inside to fetch them. Meanwhile, Margot helped Raymond set up the cake. They took it out of the box and arranged it on the homemade stand. He'd used starch to glue the plate to the champagne glass, but it was still a bit wobbly. After three attempts (and a dozen curses), they finally got it to balance. A brief pause to stand back and admire their handiwork (pats on backs, it did look rather good), but then Margot anxiously checked the time: six-thirty-five. Cerise was due any minute.

"Come on, boys. We need to get a wiggle on."

Rogier reappeared with a handful of sparklers and a bucket of champagne, but promptly stopped short of the table, face turned to the sky. "You have got to be kidding me."

But it was no joke. Cold, wet spots of rain began hitting Margot's bare forearms. The three of them looked at each other in stunned disbelief. The Gods were not smiling on them.

"Quick!" Raymond snapped, breaking the spell that had been cast. "Let's get everything inside."

Margot ran in to clear some space while the boys took charge of the table. They each grabbed an end, intending to carry it in fully loaded, but in all the confusion they seemed to have forgotten that it was two tables made into one. As soon as they lifted, the two ends went up, the middle stayed put, and the entire tableau collapsed. The wine glasses rolled to the ground, the candelabra fell over, and the champagne bucket dropped like a weight, bombarding their feet with ice cubes. It was almost comical to watch the cake slide off its stand, flip through one hundred and eighty degrees, and land with a splat on the cobbles. For the second time in under a minute, their jaws hit the floor.

To add insult to injury, Raymond's boss chose that very moment to come out from the kitchen. Venturing no further than the threshold, he gave them a weary shake of his head. He gave them five minutes to clear up the mess.

13

The day after the news of the Germany bombings broke, excitement buzzed through the camp. The brothers went about their tasks with a spring in their step, an added sense of purpose to whatever chore they happened to be doing. Something was coming. Everyone could feel it. It was only a matter of time before Sébastien told them what it would be.

At noon, the speakers on the old tannoy system squealed to life. Everyone in the base immediately stopped what they were doing. No one made a sound as Sébastien's voice came over the speakers to announce that he was calling a special meeting of the Strategy Committee. Looks of surprise passed from face to face when he went on to add that it was to be an open meeting and that everyone was urged to attend. The group had dozens of committees, each one overseeing a particular aspect of the group's agenda, but it was the Strategy Committee that made the important decisions. Few beyond Sébastien's inner circle were usually invited.

The day passed in a flash. At three-thirty, Dion joined the queue of brothers making their way along the corridor to the former classroom block. By the time he got to the lecture room, the place was packed and it was standing room only. He finally found a space at the back and scanned around for Esmée. She was down at the front, amongst a group of beards.

Cheers broke out when Sébastien entered the room, flanked by his entourage. A podium and a row of chairs had been set up at the front, but nobody sat down. Sébastien raised his hands, calling for hush, but the noise carried on. It wasn't until he banged the podium with a gavel that the room finally quietened down. Passions were running high. Clearly there was a lot people wanted to say.

"My fellow patriots," their leader began, gazing out at the assembled crowd. "Thank you all for coming. It's good to see so many faces. I apologise for the short notice, but I think many of you may be able to guess why I've asked you here today."

"*Vive la révolution!*" someone called out from the back. It sparked a rumble of laughter that quickly died out.

"*La révolution* is coming, brothers – have no fear about that. We'll get there one step at a time. Sometimes that step is a small one, and sometimes it's a big one. Yesterday, in Berlin and Munich, we saw one giant leap. Our comrades in Germany have acted. Now it's time for us to decide: do we sit on the sidelines and watch, or do we follow their lead?"

A chorus of approval went up, along with a few loud voices of objection. Sébastien quietened them with a bang of his gavel.

"Every decision we make in this group is democratic. You all know that. Every one of you has a vote, and the Strategy Committee listens to all of your opinions. Today we are going to put forward two choices. We can either continue with our peaceful protests, spread the word via *La* Vérité, do what we can to influence the online community. Or, we can switch to a different tactic: a campaign of direct action. We've talked about it many times before. We've weighed up the pros and cons. Now is the time to ask ourselves: is this the right moment? Is this the right moment to take our campaign to the next level? Is this the time to make our voices heard on a bigger stage? I, for one, say yes."

A volley of voices rang out, each one demanding to be heard. After a few moments, Sébastien quelled them with further bangs of his gavel. "One at a time, brothers. Raise your hand if there's something you wish to say."

Dozens of hands went up. Sébastien pointed to a man by the door. "What do you have to say, brother?"

"When you say direct action, are you talking about bombs?"

There were a few isolated grumbles of disconnect. Whenever they'd had these discussions before, a hardcore had always opposed the use of violence.

"If those who wield power won't listen to us, brothers, then we have to speak with a louder voice. We have to be prepared to use whatever means necessary. The people behind the attacks in Germany are just like you and me. They share our anger. And they have nothing to apologise for. We have nothing to fear about the methods they've used."

Sébastien pointed to another man. "Yes, brother."

"What would be the targets?"

"The targets are either infrastructure or the streets. Attacking infrastructure will force the government to take notice; attacking the streets might shake people out of their complacency, but comes with a greater risk. Monika has been working on a number of strategies."

Sébastien stood aside to make way for Monika, the group's chief strategist. Long grey hair, a worn leathery face, she was a formidable woman despite her short stature. She spoke French with an American accent.

"Option one: infrastructure," she began, opening a thick folder. "The list of potential targets here is almost endless. We've looked at road and railway bridges, chemical plants, the water supply, the electricity grid... An easy option is to sabotage unguarded sections of the rail network. It's a tried and tested tactic that's been used before, as many of you know. Another easy target is the electricity grid. I've calculated that a coordinated attack on a small number of key substations would be enough to bring the country to its knees within days. That's how weak your government has left you, brothers."

"They take our taxes and give us second-class infrastructure in return," someone chimed in.

"How are you planning on blowing them up?" asked a sceptical voice. "They've beefed up security in the past few years."

"Not nearly enough," Monika responded. "They're still far too vulnerable. We can use drones to deliver a small, highly targeted incendiary device. It doesn't take much to knock one out."

"How many substations are you talking about?"

"In the model I was working on we assumed six."

"That won't bring the country to a standstill," another man put in, adding to the chorus of skeptical voices. "They'll have them rebuilt in under a week. Mesny's men are much too efficient."

A few of the men around him laughed. Mesny had been in the group for longer than most and had formerly been a manager for RTE, the government agency responsible for maintaining the electricity network. He was often heard bragging about the efficiency of his team.

"Things have gone downhill since I left," the man in question responded. "They want too many holidays these days."

The laughter rumbled on for a little while and then died down.

"Why not coordinate it with a general strike?" someone else suggested. "That will delay the repairs."

There were murmurs of approval around the room, though the first man who'd spoken stuck to his guns. "A general strike is not going to work. People aren't motivated enough these days. Even if they were, the government would step in with bribes and incentives. We would lose support in no time."

"Do we even have the means to do this?" asked someone else. "If you're talking about blowing up road and railway bridges, you're going to need an awful lot of explosives."

"That won't be a problem," Sébastien said, stepping back to the podium. "As some of you already know, we've been sourcing explosives for the past twelve months. There's enough material stockpiled for an extensive bombing campaign throughout the summer."

His revelation didn't go down well with those who had been objecting, but it came as no surprise to Dion. He'd seen the vans unloading. All those unmarked crates in the warehouse, locked away in shipping containers. And Monika had at least two explosives experts at her disposal, one of whom used to work in mining. Expertise was never going to be in short supply.

"You said there were two options," a different voice asked. "What's the second choice?"

Monika retook the podium. "The second option is to target more high-profile locations: shopping malls, busy thorough-fares, office buildings. Again, the execution couldn't be more simple: a single operative, working alone, carrying a bomb in a backpack. He or she walks into a crowded place, leaves the back-pack next to a bin, and then detonates it with a mobile phone. Boom – we're on the six o'clock news."

Her levity sparked a longer outbreak of grumbling. Monika was not popular with all factions of the group.

"You're talking about killing people!" a woman cried out.

"We are fighting a war!" someone else countered. "There's always going to be casualties."

"All deaths are regrettable," Monika put in when the shouting had died down a little. "But that shouldn't stop us from doing what we know is right. When armies go to war and civilians get killed, the government calls it collateral damage. What we're proposing is no different."

The grumbling men still didn't seem happy, but they offered no comeback. Sébastien pointed to another man. "Yes, brother – what do you have to say?"

"Couldn't there be a third option? Blowing up substations is not going to cause enough disruption, your second option means killing people... so why not attack a more high-profile target – like an airport?"

"Blow up the runway at Charles de Gaulle," someone called out from the back.

His comment went down well. An animated discussion broke out amongst his companions, and several others joined in. The discussion rumbled on, but Sébastien was shaking his head.

"We've discussed this at length before, brothers. There's too much security at airports. We wouldn't get within five kilometres of the runway at Charles de Gaulle." He pointed to a different man, who stood close to Dion's side. "Yes, brother?"

"Whichever option we choose there are going to be casualties. I helped Monika compile those reports. If the grid stays down for five days that's going to affect hospitals and schools. The emergency services won't be able to cope. People are going to die in fires and waiting for cancelled operations. Killing innocent people is only going to turn public opinion against us. I've said this till I'm blue in the face."

A prolonged period of chatter broke out. Whenever they had debated this before, opinions were split, pretty much fifty-fifty. Ironically, perhaps, it was the intellectuals in the group who usually argued in favour of direct action. Put some of them in charge, and Robespierre's Reign of Terror would look like a kids' day out. It seemed years of buttoned-up academia had left them with a lust for blood.

Sébastien let them talk amongst themselves for a while. After two or three minutes, he called for order.

"Brothers," he said, banging his gavel repeatedly. The room quietened down and every face turned to him. "Let me ask you a different question – why are we all here?"

His question took them by surprise. Everyone paused to reflect. A woman at the front was the first to put her hand in the air. "Because we want change," she said, and Sébastien's eyes lit up.

"That's absolutely right, brother. We're here because we want change. We've had enough of the way things are and we want to move on. We *demand* to move on. We demand a fairer system, a system that benefits everyone, not just the lucky few. That's what our forebears were striving for when they laid down their lives. But if history tells us one thing, brothers, it's that change doesn't happen unless people make it happen. If the government won't listen, if they try to make us invisible, then we have to stand up and make a louder noise. We've all made sacrifices to be here; I don't want them to have been made in vain. A time must come to reap the rewards. And I tell you this, my fellow patriots – that time is now."

An upsurge in high spirits had more people cheering, but Sébastien didn't appear to have finished. He quelled them again.

"I told each and every one of you when you signed up that difficult choices would have to be made. So let's put it to the vote. I want a show of hands – all those in favour of continuing with non-violent methods, raise your hand now."

A number of hands shot up. Sébastien and Monika counted them up, then made a note.

"And those in favour of a bombing campaign?"

Another collection of hands were raised, some straight away, others with a degree of reluctance. Through the tangle of limbs, Dion saw that Esmée's hand was in the air. A few seconds later, he found himself adding his arm to the vote.

It was close. Sixty-two to fifty-one. But Sébastien declared a winner: bombs it would be.

14

After the meeting had ended, the brothers slowly dispersed, continuing the debate in smaller groups. Dion loitered at the back and then went out with the stragglers, avoiding having to talk to anyone. At the hub, he stepped into an unlit side corridor and waited for everyone to move on. Once it was quiet, he made his way to C-wing.

The evening sun beat down on his head as he climbed up through the hole in the roof. There was barely a breath of wind to move the trees. Satisfied no dogs were around, Dion dropped to the mound, scrambled down the side, and then ran for the avenue of trees.

Safely inside the observatory, he climbed the steps to the gantry. The platform widened on one side to make room for a bank of control equipment and an integrated desk. Dion sat on a stool and opened a small metal drawer. *TRÈS SECRET* looked up at him from the file they had taken from the lab. The words were like a double-edged sword: on the one hand, he knew he was forbidden to look; his training had drummed that into him. But every fibre of his being told him that he needed to know.

He spent a few moments putting the pages into some kind of

order. They looked like they'd been taken out of the folder and shoved back in again without care or consideration. Much of the text was densely worded – typed-up reports full of facts and figures that made no immediate sense to him. Dion paused when he came to the images. Several pages of photocopied polaroids showed the room with the chair, a different subject in each. Most of the men were skinny young men, but he was disturbed to see a woman, barely more than a teenager, among them. A sequence of time-lapse images showed her strapped to a gurney while men in white coats watched on, clipboards in hand. In another short series, the black guy was on the floor, being beaten with a length of hose. There was a close-up of his face: dead behind the eyes, looking like death would be a relief. Dion felt sick in his stomach.

He leafed on.

Little by little, he began to make sense of it. As Esmée had surmised, the statistics were test data. If he was reading it correctly, they thought they'd created some kind of wonder drug that would eliminate the need for sleep. Initially, they'd been planning to use it as an interrogation technique, but then, bizarrely, the focus had shifted to creating some kind of super-soldier. They had kept people awake for days, monitoring their performance. If the test results were anything to go by, all they'd succeeded in doing was creating a bunch of zombies. One report described how they'd managed to keep a man awake for 96 hours – the side-effects had ranged from hallucinations to hyper-arousal. There were scant details about the identities of the test subjects. No names or addresses – just vital statistics. With MKUltra (the secret programme that had gone on in the US in the 1960s), most of the experimentation had been done on hospital patients and prisoners, often without their consent. Dion recalled one particular CIA project that had used govern-ment-employed prostitutes to lure unsuspecting men to 'safe houses' where they'd been plied with drugs while the men-in-black watched from behind two-way mirrors. But in those cases, the operations had been conducted by rogue agents with little oversight by the upper echelons, whereas several of the papers Dion was examining had been signed off by the DGSE, France's secret service. The head of the army had also been copied into the correspondence, and Dion was particularly disturbed to read a report of how, in one instance, the *Gendarmerie Nationale* had helped procure test subjects from a local mental institution when it had closed down. There were references to other programmes being conducted in facilities across the country. What had been going on here was clearly part of a much larger programme of psychological warfare. And the dates... some of the papers were dated in the 1980s. Dion could hardly believe what he was reading. Part of him had been holding on to the possibility that it was the work of some rogue outfit, but this blew that hope out of the water.

A bat flew into the observatory. Dion looked up and watched it swoop low over his head, then circle the dome and fly back out. Somehow, it had got dark. He checked the time; surprised to find it was close to midnight. He put everything back in the folder and then locked it in the drawer.

————

Despite all the excitement of the past few days, the base was quiet. At the hub, Dion smelled food in the air and realised he'd missed dinner. He had no appetite. He moved soundlessly along the corridors, keeping his wits about him, and opened the big sliding door into the Command Centre. Two beards passed him on their way out, too busy chatting to give him a second look. Dion watched them leave, and then padded up the stairs to the radio room.

Tik was the only one in there. Dion hid in a nook and watched him from the shadows. He didn't really know much about the beard in chief. Without the facial hair, he would probably look a lot younger, college age maybe. He could certainly have had a successful career in IT or the gaming industry. Dion wondered what had prompted him to offer his talents to the cause.

Luckily, he didn't stay long. After another few minutes, Tik shut down his computer and packed up his messenger bag. When he left, he walked straight past the nook where Dion was hiding without even noticing he was there. After he'd gone, Dion gave it an extra minute, just to be sure.

He chose a different computer to last time. When it came to security, his messenger app was state-of-the-art, but Tik and his cohorts were smart. One wrong click and they would inevitably be onto him. He chose a cubicle from where he could keep an eye on the door, and inserted his flash drive. A window popped up.

You there? he typed immediately.

The green light on her avatar was on. It was thirty-two minutes past midnight. Dion imagined her lying in bed, staring at those two words on her phone. The minutes ticked by. He picked up a pencil and rolled it anxiously between his fingers until finally:

I'm here.

Relief surged through him. He leaned over the keyboard, ready to type a reply. He had rehearsed his words a hundred times, but now that his chance had arrived, his mind went blank. He typed a quick reply:

You okay?

I'm ok.

How's Thierry?

Do you care?

Not in the slightest, Dion thought. A man who slept with another man's wife was the lowest of the low as far as he was concerned, and he hoped the scumbag would rot in hell. He couldn't believe they'd ever become friends. But he didn't put any of that in his message. Instead, he typed:

Did you think about what I said?

I did.

And?

Like I said you've been gone a long time. Things change.

How long have you been seeing him?

Let's not go there.

Was it before I came in here?

A longer pause. Dion blinked, hardly able to believe it.

I take it that's a yes?

Does it matter?

Of course it matters? Is he there now? Are you doing it in our bed?

Grow up.

Do you love him?

Another long pause. Finally, she replied:

Talking like this isn't going to help. We'll discuss it when you get out.

A second chat box popped up. AL's avatar came online: *Anything to report?* Dion impatiently clicked back to the first window.

What if I get out tomorrow?

Is that a possibility?

What if I never get out?

Stop playing games.

Do you want me to come home?

Why are you talking like this? Has something happened?

Lots of things have happened.

Ok. Well, you're not really making much sense. I may as well go.

Dion started to type his reply, but too late... the little green light on her avatar went out. He threw himself back in his seat in frustration.

A few moments later, he closed the chat box. AL's message continued to stare back at him from the second window. *Anything to report?* Yes, Dion had lots to report, but he doubted AL would want to hear it. He stared at the message. Type the right reply and all this could be over. He could be on his way out of here in less than twenty-four hours. Instead, he closed the window without leaving a reply.

15

Margot was in Cave St Joan, browsing a selection of new wines they'd had in, when her phone buzzed in her pocket. No name came up on the screen, but she recognised the number of Madame Janvier's bookshop. She swiped to answer, then stepped outside.

"Hello?"

"Margot, I'm so sorry to bother you, but could you come here right away?" Madame Janvier's voice carried a note of desperation.

"Of course. Has something happened?"

"It's Natalie. She wants to go looking for those woods you told me about. I was hoping you could try and talk some sense into her."

An alarm went off in Margot's head. She felt like she was standing on quicksand.

"I'll be right there."

"Thank you."

She took one of the alleys off Rue Voltaire and arrived at the bookshop in under five minutes. The shop was closed, but soon after Margot put her face to the glass, Madame Janvier appeared at the door.

"Thank you for coming so quickly." She ushered Margot inside, closing the door behind her. "She's so het up."

"Where is she?"

"Upstairs, packing a bag. I asked her to wait, but she just won't listen."

"She can't go into those woods," Margot stressed.

"I've tried talking to her, but once she's got an idea into her head there's no stopping her."

They turned at the sound of heavy footsteps descending the stairs. The door to the back room opened and Natalie appeared, a hold-all slung over her shoulder. Initially surprised at the sight of Margot, her face tightened. Then she dropped her bag and approached, the head of steam she'd been building up since their meeting at the *Palais* clearly undiminished.

"Are you here to help?"

"Your grandmother asked me to come."

"I went to the police," Natalie continued combatively. "I spent all day waiting for that Captain Bouchard to see me, and guess what happened? When he finally deigned to come out of his office, all he did was fob me off."

Put on the back foot, Margot struggled to find her words. There was something about this woman that she continued to find unsettling. Had she been that stubborn at her age?

"What exactly did he say?"

"Everything you said he would say: they were looking into it, but there wasn't much chance of finding the people involved."

Margot lightly shrugged her shoulders. What more did she want?

"It's not good enough," Natalie went on as if reading her thoughts. "If he thinks I'm going to sit around twiddling my thumbs, he can think again."

"You really need to stay out of this."

"They stole my grandmother's money!"

"I know they did, but unfortunately there's nothing you can do about it."

Natalie's face turned to the consistency of rock. It was like flicking peas at a block of granite.

"Will you show me those woods?"

"No."

"Then at least tell me which station they got off at."

"There's no point. They'll be long gone by now."

"It's somewhere to start. They left a trail, and we can follow it."

Margot shook her head. "They won't have left a trail. People like that know how to disappear."

"People like that..." Natalie repeated immediately, giving her a probing look. Margot cursed her mistake. "What's that supposed to mean?"

"Nothing."

Natalie turned the screw. "Is there something you're not telling me?"

"No."

"Then show me those woods."

Margot gritted her teeth. "I am *not* showing you those woods. Okay!"

"Why not? Are you afraid?"

"Don't be ridiculous."

"So who are the 'people like them'?"

Margot despaired. How had she let herself get backed into this corner? "Will you just let this drop?"

"No, I won't. You can at least show me on a map." Natalie went over to the stand of IGN maps by the counter and started to search through. Margot watched helplessly as the stubborn little fox pulled out a map and began to unfold it. "You told *mamie* you got off the train just outside Nîmes. Was it this one?"

She held the map open for Margot to see, her fingertip aimed at a specific spot, but Margot didn't look. Part of her wanted to drop the charade, tell her the whole story, and go back to those woods – despite the danger, she couldn't deny that she had been itching to return. But another, more sensible part, told her to dig in her heels. Margot turned briefly to Madame Janvier, who had been observing silently with interest. She gave her a thin smile before returning to tackle her grand-daughter.

"Look, Natalie. I've helped you as much as I can. I am not showing you those woods, and that's the end of the matter."

There was a moment when it looked like the younger woman might relent, but a moment was all it was. The anger finally burst from her eyes. "Fine! I'll find it myself."

With that, she clumsily put away the map, horribly creasing it when she messed up the pattern of folding. Giving up, she shoved it into the side pocket of her holdall and then came to give her grandmother a peck on the cheek. In the space of five seconds, she'd grabbed her bag and stormed out the back door.

Madame Janvier started to panic. "I can't let her go off on her own." She looked around the shop in a state of bewilderment. "I'll have to close up and go with her."

She moved to the door, but Margot held her arm. "It's all right, Madame Janvier. I'll go after her."

"Are you sure?"

Margot nodded. One way or another, this woman had to be stopped.

The back gate was open. It led to a narrow street from where Margot caught a glimpse of the fleeing figure turning right at the end. She ran after her, and a short way down the next street, saw Natalie turn right again. One final turn brought her to a small square at the back of the shops, hemmed in by buildings. A dozen cars were crammed into a makeshift car park.

"Natalie – wait!"

Natalie turned her head but didn't slow down. She weaved her way through the jumble of parked cars and got into a sleek bronze saloon. Before she had time to pull shut the door, however, Margot lurched. With her arm outstretched, she managed to catch hold of the edge of the door. Natalie glared back from behind the wheel. "Let go of my door."

"You're making a big mistake."

"So are you if you don't let go."

She pulled the door, but Margot pulled back. Natalie pulled again, and so did Margot, turning it into a tug-of-war. Losing patience, Margot bared her teeth.

"Now you listen to me. Charging off like this won't help anyone. Least of all your grandmother."

"I'll be the judge of that."

"You have no idea what you're getting into."

"I'm not scared. These people are cowards, picking on vulnerable old people."

"You can't fight them. You're way out of your depth."

"Look – if you're not going to help me then go home and do some knitting. Now, let go of my door."

With a determined last effort, Natalie pulled the door from Margot's hand. She switched on the car and started to reverse.

Margot's head boiled. She ran around the back of the car, forcing it to stop abruptly, and then grabbed hold of the passenger door handle just as it got moving again. The backwards motion succeeded in opening the door for her, the chunk of metal tugging at her shoulder. Seeing what was going on, Natalie slammed on the brakes.

"What the hell are you doing, you nutcase?"

Margot took the opportunity to quickly hop in. She pulled

the seatbelt across her chest and clicked it into place. "Saving you from yourself," she replied, and then casually pulled down the vanity mirror to check her hair. Something told her she was going to regret this, but it was too late now. The woman in the driver's seat didn't look in the least bit impressed, but Margot subdued her with a conquering smile. "Don't worry, you'll thank me later."

The fire went out of Natalie's eyes. One-all, Margot reckoned.

16

It quickly became apparent that Natalie was familiar with the roads in the area. By taking a route closer to the coast, she managed to avoid the tourist traffic clogging up the D914, and then, on the outskirts of Perpignan, she found a cut-through on an industrial estate that linked to a junction on the autoroute that Margot had not even known existed. Twenty minutes after leaving Argents, she was accelerating away from the toll booth and merging into the stream of fast-moving traffic.

"Which junction should I get off?" Natalie asked.

The car was an electric one; a top-of-the-range model if the plush leather seats were anything to go by. Its fancy panoramic dash looked like something out of a spaceship, and it still had that new-car smell. It must have cost an awful lot of money. Margot didn't know exactly what Natalie did for a living (Madame Janvier had said she worked for a large multinational, something to do with cosmetics), but whatever it was, the job clearly paid well. The woman at the wheel was just as stylish as her vehicle. The V-neck Dolce & Gabbana top she was wearing was just like one Margot used to own. And Margot was pretty sure her skinny jeans were the same brand as a pair she had in her own wardrobe, though no doubt Natalie's were a couple of sizes smaller.

"You said the station was just outside Nîmes," Natalie prompted a short time later when Margot failed to answer her question. She busily checked her mirrors as they closed in on a slow-moving truck. Margot watched how she completed the manoeuvre: pulling right up to the truck's rear end and then swooping into the passing lane at the very last moment, exactly the way Margot liked to overtake when she was at the wheel (often to her passenger's annoyance). The rear windows of the cars in front began to dazzle in the sun, so they both pulled their sunglasses over their eyes in unison. Margot shifted uncomfortably. This was becoming uncanny.

"Why did you bother getting in if you're not going to say anything?" Natalie went on as Margot, arms folded, continued to remain mute. "You want me to take you on a mystery tour, is that it?"

Now that was an idea. She could direct her to some random set of woods, let her wander around for an hour or so, give her a chance to work this out of her system and then go home, pretending to share her frustration. It might get her out of her hair for a while. Then again, Natalie would probably see right through it.

"All right," Natalie hissed. "Have it your way. But I'm not taking you back to Argents until you've shown me those woods."

"In that case," Margot unmuted herself, "it's going to be a very long day."

"Fine. I hope you've got nothing planned."

Still in the outside lane, Natalie planted her foot on the floor. She tore past a glut of slow-moving traffic, the car's electric motor effortlessly whooshing them well over the speed limit. At this rate, Margot was going to have to come up with a plan pretty soon.

They continued without speaking for the better part of an hour. The landscape rolled by, flat and featureless in the main, with only small wooded hills visible in the distance. Margot went to and fro in her mind, trying to decide how best to play this. Captain Bouchard had sworn her to secrecy, but she couldn't hold out forever. Natalie deserved to be told something, and Margot was uncomfortable lying. As they closed in on Nîmes, she decided she would take her to the edge of the woods and then reveal a little bit more.

She tapped the icon on the screen to access the sat nav. A highly detailed map came up. Natalie watched suspiciously as Margot typed in the name of the station. It was twenty kilometres from their current position. After setting it to navigate, the first instruction appeared. "You need to get off at the next junction."

"Why?"

"Because that's the way to the station."

"Are you sure?"

"Of course I'm sure," Margot replied irritably. She wished now she had typed in some random set of woods. "Look at the screen if you don't believe me."

Natalie still seemed suspicious, but she did as instructed and came off at the next junction. The sat nav went haywire as they went through the toll booth, but then recalibrated and issued its next command. This time, however, Natalie sailed straight past when the turn came up.

Margot did a double take. "You missed the turn."

"No I didn't."

"Yes, you did. She should have taken the N road back there."

"This way's quicker."

"Says who?"

"Says me. I know these roads. I used to travel around this area for work."

Margot narrowed her eyes. "I should have known you'd be smarter than the computer," she muttered.

Much to Margot's chagrin, it turned out Natalie was right. The sat nav had predicted a seventeen-minute drive from the autoroute to the train station, but when they pulled into the station's car park, Margot's watch showed that less than fourteen minutes had elapsed. The car park looked full, but Natalie managed to find a space and neatly slotted the car into a gap between a big white van and a giant SUV. Pleased with herself, she pushed the button to turn off the *wundercar*. They sat in silence for a few moments, staring at a brick wall.

"Okay," Natalie said, giving Margot an expectant look. "Where now?"

Margot was craving a cigarette, but she resisted the urge. She couldn't help noticing the fancy titanium water bottle in the cup holder between them and suspected her annoying companion was a health-kick junkie – one whiff of nicotine and she would probably feel the need to detox herself with chia seeds.

"I'll take you to the edge of the woods, but that's as far as we go."

Natalie gave it a moment's thought. "All right."

Still, Margot's limbs still wouldn't move. A voice in her head was screaming at her, telling her she was doing the wrong thing. Twenty years ago she probably would have ignored it, but right now it was putting her on edge.

"Well," Natalie prompted.

"It's a twenty-minute walk."

"So?"

"I'm just saying."

"Well, if it gets too much for you, we can stop for a sit-down."

Margot clenched her jaw. "And bear in mind it'll be dark in a couple of hours."

"In that case we'd better get a move on, hadn't we?"

Margot looked deeply into the younger woman's eyes. *If this goes badly, you'll be to blame.* Reluctantly, she pushed open her door.

They crossed the railway line via the road bridge and then followed the winding lane that Margot had previously accessed through the gate in the fence. When they got to the gap in the hedge, Margot ducked under the overgrown branches and set off along the dirt track. After two or three minutes, it occurred to her that Natalie was lagging behind; when Margot paused to look back, she found her intentionally keeping her distance, watching Margot's every move with suspicion. Was she paranoid or something? She met Margot's eye, perhaps questioning why she'd paused. *I'm leading you to a lonely stretch of railway line,* Margot responded in her thoughts. *I'm going to tie you to the track and then run off. Perfectly understandable, don't you think?* With a disbelieving shake of her head, she carried on regardless.

The lights of a train appeared in the distance. The ground began to shake as the loco loomed large on the rails, and they took cover in a group of small trees. Carriage after carriage after carriage sped by, just metres from where they were crouching. It could have been the same train Margot had taken just a few days ago; she'd most probably sat there, gazing through the window at this very group of trees. After giving it ten seconds to get away, they stepped back onto the track, flapping their arms at the cloud of dust that was still swirling.

They continued in silence. No one was around, apart from a scruffy brown dog that emerged from the bushes to give them a curious look. It looked like a stray, but it had a friendly disposition and trotted happily alongside, seemingly keen to know where they were going. It accompanied them to the point where the trail split into two, but then pricked up its ears and hesitated. Eyes wide and alert, it watched to see which way they would go. It seemed disappointed when Margot chose the path to their right, and it let out a little whimper. *Adiós amigos. It was nice knowing you.* The dog turned around and went back the way they had come.

Another five minutes and they reached the underpass. The wind must have been blowing from a different direction this time because the traffic noise was loud. Margot located the path that led into the woods and halted a short way back from the tree line, her skin tingling at the sight of the chain strung between the two posts. The *CHASSE EN COURS* sign was still there.

Natalie came to her side, a questioning look on her face. "Is this it?"

Margot nodded. "Just as I came out of the underpass, I saw them go into these trees." She looked for the spot where the bullet had hit the dirt. It was probably still buried there if she cared to look.

Natalie nudged by. She went right up to the chain and took a closer look at the sign. Margot watched in alarm as she reached down to unhook it.

"What are you doing?"

"Going in."

"You can't."

"Why not? It's not hunting season. The sign must have been left here by mistake."

Of course she would know that.

"The sign's a fake. This is Ministry of Defence land."

She gave Margot a puzzled look. After thinking for a few moments, she took a step back and gazed along the tree line. "In that case, why are there no Ministry of Defence signs?"

"Look at the maps app on your phone. The satellite imagery is all blurred."

Natalie still seemed doubtful. With some reluctance, she took out her phone. She studied the screen, pinching to zoom in and out, then cleared her throat, clearly unwilling to accept what she was seeing. "It's probably a poor signal."

Margot scoffed. Could this woman be any more stubborn?

"It's not a poor signal. It's blurred out because it's a sensitive site." She took a friendly step closer. "Look, Natalie. I haven't been entirely honest with you. One of the people who conned your grandmother is an undercover police officer."

Natalie flinched. "How do you know that?"

"Captain Bouchard told me. I was sworn to secrecy in case it jeopardised the officer's safety."

"You mean it's someone from Argents *Gendarmerie*?"

"No. Someone more specialised. The captain was taking orders from Paris."

Natalie remained puzzled. "But why would an undercover police officer con my *mamie* out of her savings?"

"I honestly have no idea. We're guessing it's an anti-terror operation, but we don't know any details. But the point is, these woods are off-limits. And so are the people who stole your grandmother's money."

Natalie bit her lip. For once she seemed lost for words, and Margot knew exactly how she was feeling. In her shoes, she would have been just as reluctant to give in. But some fights you can't win.

"I know it's not what you wanted to hear," Margot went on, "but we really can't go in there. Let's just go back."

"Wait a minute." Natalie frowned, deep in thought. "If this is government property, there would be signs warning people not to enter."

"Natalie—"

"I'm perfectly within my rights."

"Didn't you hear what I just said?"

"Yes, I did, but they're not going to scare me off." Natalie reached for the chain. "You go back if you like. I'm going in."

Margot glared. "You're making a big mistake."

But this time her words fell on deaf ears. Natalie unhooked the chain, dropped it to the ground, and then stepped into the woods.

———

Powerless to do anything else, Margot stepped over the chain and followed Natalie into the woods, certain that she too was making a very big mistake.

But her annoyance soon melted away. There was something about entering a forest that felt good on a primal level, and within minutes of setting out, Margot felt transported to another realm. The wind had dropped, the sound of the autoroute had disappeared, and a sense of stillness pervaded. Cut off from the outside world, this was a land dominated by trees: oaks, chestnut and pine, surrounding them in every direction. It seemed inevitable that no matter how far you travelled, the trees were still going to be there. From the research she'd done, Margot knew that the woods around here were extensive. In the past, they had been part of an even larger forest covering the land all the way up to the Cévennes and the Ardèche. And much of it was primal forest, untouched by the hand of man. The Romans had made minor incursions, but the ground was too hilly for arable farming, the conditions too dry for pastoral. The trees were not giants, but they looked like they'd been alive for centuries, their branches twisted like the fingers of mythical woodland creatures.

Margot looked down at her feet, careful where she trod. The ground was covered in exposed roots ready to trip up the unwary. It was hard to see why the chain had been put there since there wasn't much of a path. Nothing indicated that anyone had passed this way recently, but the builder and his companion must have been heading somewhere, and they can't have been alone. Whoever had fired that shot had to have been waiting for them. Thorny dry shrubs threatened to prick at her skin so Margot rolled down her sleeves.

They passed the remains of a dry stone wall, beyond which a vague, rectilinear shape was discernible in the ground. It looked like the foundations of a small building, an ancient hut of some kind. Margot paused to look at the old, weatherbeaten stones, imagining the hands of the men that had originally shaped them. She wondered if people had been happier back then, before the advent of agriculture. At some point back in the day, someone (a man, no doubt) had decided that it would be a good idea to cut down all the trees and plant crops instead. Sure, it fed the masses, but when immersed in a place like this, Margot couldn't help feeling that something more than just trees had been lost.

Natalie had forged on ahead. Striding along, not looking back, acting like someone who knew exactly where they were going, even though she didn't have a clue. Ahh, the arrogance of youth. Margot gave her some space, though she was careful not to lose sight of her. For some reason, Madame Janvier was clearly very fond of her, and Margot couldn't help but feel a duty of care, hard as it was. Determination was one thing; pig-headedness could land you in all kinds of trouble, as she knew to her cost.

The further they went, the denser the forest became. After they'd been walking for maybe half an hour, Margot paused to take stock. The sky was darkening and it was getting hard to see. Scanning around, she felt a slight sense of panic as she realised she'd completely lost her bearings. The trees appeared to be closing in on her, like the jaws of a trap.

"I think we should go back," Margot called out.

She wiped the sweat from her brow. The air was still hot,

despite the fact that the sun had nearly gone down. She took out her phone, surprised to find she still had a signal. When she tried to open any of her apps, however, nothing worked.

Natalie still hadn't responded. Margot put away her phone and scanned around again. Her impulsive companion was nowhere to be seen.

"Natalie!"

Margot listened. No response came back, apart from the flap of a wing. A vague dark shape moved at the edge of her vision, and Margot's eyes discerned a large black bird perched on a bough. An ugly looking thing, the size of a large crow, but with dark blue markings on its wings, a species she was certain she had never seen before. It fixed its beady eye upon her, less than ten metres separating them, confused perhaps as to why this alien creature had invaded its world. Margot sometimes wondered what would happen if the animal kingdom ever decided to fight back. Surely one day they would put two and two together and realise that it was the humans who were responsible for destroying so much of their habitat. They would band together to enact their revenge. It wouldn't be pretty. (*You bastards!* cried the giant panda, shaking an angry paw). Birds were smart, they could figure it out. This particular specimen clearly hadn't received the memo, however, and promptly flew away.

Margot frowned in consternation. "Natalie," she called out again. "Where the bloody hell are you?"

A small patch of Dolce & Gabbana appeared in a gap up ahead. "Over here," Natalie called back.

In spite of everything, Margot was relieved to see her.

She tramped through the bushes to catch up. Natalie was staring at the screen of her phone, tapping the screen in frustration. "This is weird."

"Don't tell me – you have five bars yet nothing works."

Natalie looked up, the wind taken out of her sails. "It's like something's jamming the signal."

Maybe that was normal on Ministry of Defence land, although Margot had never heard of such a thing.

"Anyway," she said. "It's a moot point. We need to go back now. We can't stumble around in the dark."

For once, Natalie seemed keen to agree.

After a final glance around, she moved to Margot's side. Just as they were about to set off, however, something that sounded like a scream pierced the air.

They froze.

A prickle ran down Margot's spine. "It was probably just a bird," she said, though no bird she was familiar with had ever made a sound like that.

They listened again. Whatever it was had gone quiet. Margot concluded their minds had been playing tricks on them, but then Natalie suddenly came back to life.

"Look."

She pointed.

Margot followed her line of sight. At first, all she could see was a sea of grey trees, but then a faint light appeared, blinking in the distance.

"I see it."

The light appeared to be moving. It continued to blink for a while, then went out. Natalie turned and locked eyes with Margot, her mouth slightly hung open.

"Someone's out there."

"It could have been anything," Margot responded with little conviction. "A car; someone walking a dog." But they were miles from any road, and they'd seen no sign of houses.

"There's only one way to find out."

Margot was itching with curiosity. Despite her better judgement, she nodded in agreement.

The forest was growing darker by the second, making it difficult to see where they were going. They didn't spot the fence until they were almost upon it – a seven-foot-high barrier made of thick alloy wire, supported by sturdy steel posts. Margot's eyes lingered on the coils of razor wire attached to the top. A deep ditch prevented them from getting close enough to scale it. It was difficult to be sure in the dim light, but the fence continued unbroken in both directions, no end in sight. It must have enclosed a considerable area of land. On the far side, the ground looked like it had once been cleared, but saplings had taken root here and there. There was no sign of the flickering light.

They exchanged an uncertain look. Natalie, still keen to take the lead, pointed to their right. They walked parallel to the fence, pushing their way through an area of thicker undergrowth, taking care not to slide into the ditch. A short upward slope led them to higher ground, where they paused at the sight of a wooden watchtower. Originally, it must have risen high above the canopy, but the top section had collapsed, leaving a pile of broken timbers on one side. Beyond it was a squat concrete hut with an aerial attached to its flat roof. Judging by the state of the exterior, the building hadn't been used in some time.

They walked on, hoping to find a gate or some other means of entry. The ground sloped down into a hollow where a large tree had grown close to the fence. One of its branches had grown through the chainlink and detached a small section of the razor wire. Margot reckoned the gap looked wide enough to climb through.

"I could get through there," Natalie said, clearly having the same thought.

"It might be electrified," Margot cautioned. Despite her own warning, she was tempted to touch it, her reckless streak not having entirely deserted her.

Natalie shook her head. "You would hear it buzzing."

They listened.

It wasn't.

A pause grew. Once again, they looked into each other's eyes. Despite their earlier differences, it seemed they were now of one mind. They were going in, come what may.

Natalie went first. She stepped to the edge of the hollow and then leapt the ditch, clinging onto the fence with both hands. With the benefit of her four long limbs, she moved spider-like to the top, easily feeding herself underneath the detached section of razor wire. She rotated through three hundred and sixty degrees and then jumped down to the ground. Looking back, she smiled smugly. "Need a hand?"

Margot regarded her coolly. "I can manage, thanks."

Determined not to be outdone, Margot mustered her courage. She climbed the fence with ease, manoeuvred herself through the gap, and then climbed down to the ground, taking just a few seconds longer than Natalie had. Dusting off her hands, she was pleased to find her companion had nothing to say.

Their attention switched to their surroundings. Even though they had only travelled a few metres, there was a distinctly different feeling to being on this side of the fence. If they hadn't been trespassing before, they certainly were now. Moving past the concrete hut, they spotted a group of buildings in the distance – large, rectilinear shapes, with no lights coming from any of them. Despite being a long way off, there was an ominous feel to them.

A dog barked loudly.

Margot's eyes widened in alarm. The solid grey outlines of two powerful attack dogs were honing in on them at speed.

17

Less than twenty-four hours after the group had voted for bombs, Sébastien called another meeting of the Strategy Committee. At 11:00, every available brother reconvened in the classroom block, eager to hear what their leader had to say. Dion got there early. He sat on a bench at the front and listened closely as Monika put forward her plans for a campaign of summer bombings. She'd clearly done her research. For two hours straight, she presented the facts and figures, filling the whiteboards with text and diagrams, all delivered with her usual high level of confidence. She handed out detailed reports and pages full of diagrams. At one point, the lights were dimmed, and with the aid of a projector, she showed them photographs of the electricity substations that were to be targeted in the first wave of attacks, aerial shots and close-ups, the exact locations where the vans were to be parked. Someone in the group had certainly been doing their field work. Each location came with a risk assessment, detailing the dangers the operatives would encounter and the level of risk to the public. The risks were colour-coded – green for little or no projected casualties; red for carnage. She'd also mapped out the routes the operatives would take to get to the locations and indicated contingency plans should any of the missions need to be aborted. Nothing, it seemed, had been left to chance. The vehicles they would be using had already been sourced and were being prepped in the warehouse. Once the electricity grid had been paralysed, they would follow up with further attacks on the autoroute and the TGV network. With the bombers now in charge of the group, the country was set for a summer of carnage.

Dion memorised as much of the detail as he could, and took a few notes. When Monika had finished her presentation, Sébastien stepped forward and asked for questions. Most of the people in the room were still digesting everything they'd heard, but one of the academics stood up. He proceeded to attempt to pick holes in Monika's plans, claiming that she'd miscalculated the quantity of explosives required, that she'd underestimated the number of potential casualties in all of her models, that the strategy was far too risky and was bound to backfire. But Monika proved more than a match for him. She patiently countered every point he made and backed it up with figures from her notes. The man's arguments eventually ran out of steam, and he had no choice but to give in and return to his seat, tail between his legs. Monika's combination of intellect and ruthlessness was sometimes devastating to witness. The only thing they hadn't decided yet was the dates, but given the appetite for something to happen, it was going to happen soon.

Finally, Sébastien called for volunteers. Five teams of three were needed for the first wave of attacks: one driver; one back-up driver; someone with knowledge of explosives to deal with any last-minute hiccups. He made no bones about the dangers. Even if the plans went off without a hitch, the operatives would have bounties put on their heads, be hunted like dogs for the rest of their lives. Branded as terrorists, reviled by large parts of society, with no sympathy for the cause they were fighting for. The group would do what it could to help, he said, but there were no guarantees. Their only compensation, he claimed, was that history would look kindly upon their achievements.

Despite the warnings, at least ninety per cent of the people in the room raised a hand. Esmée was amongst them. So was Dion. Sébastien and Monika went through the sea of hands, taking their time to make their selections. Allowing for reserves, twenty-five people in total were chosen. Neither Esmée nor Dion were amongst them.

———

Dion hung back as the meeting broke up. While everyone else was making their way to the mess room for a late lunch, he risked calling in at the Command Centre. Unusually for this time of day, the radio room was empty. Seizing the opportunity, he inserted his flash drive into the nearest laptop and then double-clicked on his messenger app.

She wasn't on-line. He typed a message, waited five minutes, typed out another. He chewed on a fingernail while he stared at the blank screen. Maybe she wasn't home. Maybe she was in the bath. Maybe she was with *him*.

A noise came from the stairs. Dion's heart pounded. Part of him wanted someone to come in and expose him. He was in the mood to hit someone hard. He waited until the very last second and then snatched out his memory stick.

But he must have been hearing things because when he looked down from the top of the staircase, no one was there. Even so, he descended quickly. He leapt the last few steps to the half landing and rounded the corner, only to find himself face to face with Golem. The moron sent a surprised glance up the stairs, the cogs in his brain beginning to whir.

"What were you doing?"

"Get out of my way." Dion attempted to push past.

"You were in the radio room!"

Golem sidestepped to block him. Big mistake. As the red mist descended, Dion grabbed him by the lapels and wrestled him to the ground. He had him pinned down with a knee in the sternum in zero seconds flat. Right fist clenched hard, he was all set to give him what he deserved.

"Dion!"

Dion spun round. Esmée was staring up at them from the foot of the stairs. He loosened his grip, allowing Golem to crawl free.

"Sébastien's going to hear about this! You won't get away with it, not this time!"

Dion gave him the finger as he stormed off. He'd reached the next set of doors before he realised that Esmée had come after him. She grabbed his arm. "What's going on?"

Dion recoiled. "Nothing," he said, and turned to move on.

"Hey – we're friends, aren't we? You can talk to me."

Dion stared at her hand, still holding onto him. For a moment his brain was unable to compute. Friends? It had been a long time since he'd thought of anyone in that way.

"You annoyed you didn't get picked?"

"What?"

"For one of the missions. I saw you raise your hand."

He caught on. Remembering where he was, he made himself calm down. He looked back down the corridor. Golem had gone, but Dion remained jumpy.

"Come on," he said. "Let's get out of here."

They went into C-wing. Dion took turns at random until he was confident no one would be able to keep track of them. After four or five minutes, they paused to look back. No one was there.

They resumed at a more leisurely pace. Torch beams carving the darkness, they continued through a warren of long dark corridors. Ducts and pipes running along the ceiling made it feel more claustrophobic. Dion wasn't sure if he'd been in this part of the base before. The corridors were a different design from the others – the walls were painted brick, the ceiling precast concrete. Blue-green mould grew in many of the cracks. His internal compass told him they were moving underground, though it was most probably an illusion.

"So what did Golem do to wind you up?" Esmée asked.

"Just seeing him's enough to wind me up. You reckon he was that ugly at birth?"

"The midwife probably died of a heart attack."

They both smiled.

"It gets you down sometimes, doesn't it?" Esmée went on. "Being cooped up in here."

That wasn't really it, but she wasn't to know. He was more scared of not knowing what was waiting for him on the outside, where he would be, who he would be with.

"I doubt we'll be here much longer," Dion said. "If what they're planning comes off." It was always the direction Sébastien had been heading in. He'd been stockpiling weapons for months, spending more and more time with the more radical members of the group. What had happened in Berlin was the catalyst they'd needed.

They came to a low door, partly busted off its hinges. It led to a staircase, and they descended to a basement the size of a tennis court. It was full of old mechanical equipment. Dion was no engineer, but if he had to guess, he would say it was an air filtration system. They shone their lights over hulking metal containers linked by stainless steel tubes and ducts. Many of the tubes had sections missing, cannibalised for other uses, no doubt.

"Wow!"

Esmée was shining her light across the room. Dion moved to

see what had caught her attention and found a skeleton hunched up in a corner. He was less than surprised than his companion. According to the brothers who had been here from the beginning, it hadn't been uncommon to discover human remains when they'd first moved into the base.

They went to investigate. Standing side by side, they shone their lights over the poor wretch. A few tatters of clothing covered some of its bones, but the skull was completely exposed. A few tufts of hair were attached to a small, leathery piece of scalp, and the hands were raised up to where its ears had once been. Whether he'd died in his sleep or cowering in fright was impossible to tell.

Esmée crouched for a closer look. The width of the pelvis and the length of the arms suggested it was male. Dion shone his light around the rest of the space, but there was no sign of any others. Perhaps he'd been hiding down here alone, then died of starvation. Which begged the question: who had he been hiding from?

"I looked at that file," Dion said. "You were right – they were carrying out a drug trial."

Esmée nodded.

"They were experimenting with a drug that would eliminate the need for sleep. Trying to create a super-soldier. Can you believe that?"

Esmée stood and faced him. "The term 'mad scientist' springs to mind."

"And it wasn't just here. They had trials going on all over the place."

"You sound surprised."

"Aren't you?"

"Not really. If you think the conspiracy theories are wild, you can bet the truth will be a whole lot worse."

"But they were experimenting on *people*, using them like lab rats." He still couldn't get those images out of his head, those poor young men with their tortured faces. This guy in front of them didn't look like he'd been physically harmed, but he had obviously been terrified of something.

"Have you told Sébastien?"

"Not yet."

"He needs to know."

In the right hands, that kind of information would be incendiary, as potent as any of their bombs. The anti-vaxxers in the group would love it. But where did his loyalties lie? With a government that had lied to him, or with these people who now held his life in their hands? When he'd been in the army, Dion had taken his orders, just like the other soldiers, believing that those above him were acting in the nation's best interests. Yet at the same time, things like this had been going on. He felt he'd been lied to his whole life.

"They lie to us all the time," Esmée went on as if reading his thoughts. "If you believe the government, the bioweapons programme ended in the 1970s, but you can bet it's still going on somewhere. All they have to do is call it classified, say it's for security reasons."

The cooler air in the room made Dion suddenly feel cold. He'd had enough of staring at skeletons and suggested they leave. Whoever this poor fellow had been, they left him to rest in peace.

Dion normally prided himself on his spatial awareness, but when he tried to reverse their route, he realised he was lost. He picked a corridor at random, and they set off along another narrow passageway. He wondered how big this place really was, how many unexplored rooms there were down here. Sébastien claimed they had fully explored the site soon after the group had moved in, but Dion couldn't see how that could be true. The base could still be littered with skeletons, people whose stories would never be told.

"It makes you wonder whose side they're on," Esmée said, moving ahead as the corridor narrowed. "I mean, why do governments keep secrets?"

"To protect people, a lot of the time."

"The US Government classified fifty million documents last year. They can't all be about protecting people."

"True, but the communists are worse. Look at the Soviets."

"The Soviets never achieved true communism. The communists in here will say it's wrong to judge those failed regimes, particularly as capitalist countries went out of their way to make sure they never succeeded. But then, the Soviets were equally determined to destroy capitalism, so who won? The capitalists. Why? Because it's more in tune with human nature."

Dion had listened to dozens of these kinds of debates, had sat on the fence whenever anyone had asked for his opinion. It had seemed the safest option.

"We need your socialist guy," he said. "Give us all a hand with our wheelbarrows."

They walked on for a while in silence. They came to a section where there was more rubble than floor space, chunks of concrete with metal sticking out. They climbed over small mounds, ducked under swathes of cobwebs, until they came to a crossroads. Left went down another dark corridor, while to the right was something that looked more familiar. A distant green light suggested they were nearing the occupied area of the base. Fearing they would encounter a crypt full of zombies if they went the dark way, Dion suggested they go right.

"The problem is that people always want to put themselves in positions of power," Esmée said, walking by his side now that the corridor had widened. "Whether it's politics or religion or the Pilates club. Once they have it, the temptation's there to abuse it."

"Maybe that's just you," Dion said, grinning wryly. "You don't like other people telling you what to do."

She didn't deny it.

"Think of the social pyramid," Esmée went on. "The pharaoh is up there at the top, looking down on his underlings. One of the slaves looks up from the bottom and says: 'Hey, Mr Pharaoh. Why are you up there and I'm down here? Who put you in charge?' It's not like anyone voted for him. The Egyptians didn't all sit down one day, have a big think, and decide yeah, that guy Amunhotep – he's the one we want as our leader."

"Who was Amunhotep?"

"The one who threw prisoners of war into a pit and set fire to them."

"Nice guy."

"A lot of them also married their own daughters, some when they were only twelve years old. Yet these people were treated like gods."

If you looked back through history, Dion suspected that most rulers were either mad, bad or drunk on power, usually the men with the strongest armies, or the wiliest, most ruthless politicians willing to stab their nearest and dearest in the back. You didn't get to the top without climbing over others.

"Our democracies aren't much better," Esmée continued. "We can only vote for the two or three people on the ballot paper, and they're only there because they've used money and influence to get to the top. Why should we put up with it?"

"We shouldn't. But what's your solution?"

"I didn't say I had one. But I know what I would do first."

"What?" Dion asked, intrigued.

"I'd set fire to the pyramid. You can guarantee the guy at the top will be the first to jump off."

Dion smiled to himself. He should have seen that one coming.

They were interrupted by the strident sound of an alarm. Someone shouted, and then two armed men ran past the end of the corridor. Dion gave Esmée a curious look.

Hurrying to the end of the corridor, they realised they had looped back to A-wing. At the entrance to the Command Centre, a small group of brothers was having a lively discussion. Dion was surprised to see that the front door was wide open, the dogs barking outside.

Another man ran by. Dion grabbed him by the arm. "What's going on?"

The brother was high and reluctant to slow down. Before he ran out the door, he blurted out one thing: "Intruders."

18

The adrenaline kicked in and Margot turned on her heels and ran. Ran faster than she'd ever run in her entire life, her limbs powered by the strongest force known to man: self-preservation. Her instinct was to follow Natalie, but after a few seconds her mind snapped into searching for an escape route instead. Her roving eyes honed in on the concrete hut, and she gave a quick shout to Natalie. Margot veered towards the hut, found herself running down a grassy slope, and then up to a wooden door. Jiggling the handle, she caught a glimpse of Natalie fleeing in the opposite direction, either not having heard or choosing to ignore her.

Inside, Margot slammed her back against the door, gasping for air. Blood was pounding through her temples with such force that she feared her heart would burst. Her fingers searched for a bolt or any kind of lock, but finding none, she wedged the side of her foot against the bottom of the door and pressed one shoulder against it. Her eyes scanned the room she was in. The space was little bigger than a shed; a tiny slit window its only source of light.

Several long moments went by. No one came knocking.

Margot strained to hear, but everything seemed to have gone quiet. She searched her memory of the past sixty seconds, trying to picture how close the dogs had been, which direction Natalie had been heading. It had all happened so quickly, however, that nothing was clear.

Still, no one came. Margot's thoughts slowed. Realising she was not in any immediate danger, she released her hold on the door and had a longer look around. Apart from an old Cold War propaganda poster, the walls were bare. The slit window looked more like a gun slot – through it, all Margot could see were the thick dark lines of tree trunks, with an occasional flash of light moving through the branches. Soon, they too were gone and the feeling that she was all alone out here grew stronger. She waited another five minutes, and then cautiously exited the hut.

"Psst. Over here."

Over to one side, Natalie was waving from the cover of a jeep. After checking the way was clear, Margot ran over. She hunkered down with her back to the flat metal door and locked eyes with her companion. In an instant, the bickering of the past few hours was forgotten.

"Where did they go?"

"That way." Natalie pointed to her left. "The dogs must have picked up another scent."

"I think there was three of them."

Natalie shook her head. "There were at least four. I hid under the jeep and counted their boots."

Margot's mind raced again. Without breaking cover, she scanned around. The jeep was an old army model. It lay in a ditch next to a tarmac road. Any thoughts of using it to escape, however, were quickly dashed when she saw that all four tyres were slashed. Craning to one side, her eyes followed the course of the road as it weaved its way around the clearing. The contours of the land had all but disappeared, but the complex of buildings still loomed large in the distance.

"Ok," Margot said. "So what now?"

A short pause, then Natalie said: "We need to see inside those buildings."

"Are you mad?"

"If they're using guard dogs there must be something going on here."

"All the more reason to stay away."

"I'm not going back."

"You do realise we're trespassing on an army base."

"So are they," Natalie countered. "They weren't army. One of them was wearing jeans."

Margot hated to admit it, but she had a point. Despite her misgivings, part of her was as eager as Natalie to find out what was going on here.

"All right," she said. "We'll take a look. But the first sign of trouble, we leave. Okay?"

Natalie didn't disagree.

There was no sign of where the dogs had gone. Margot suggested they keep to the road, so they followed it around the edge of the clearing. Curious structures became visible along the way: a concrete cylinder rising vertically from the ground; a rusty metal cube; a series of wide shallow pools, the largest easily ten metres across. Margot paused to look into one of the pools, wondering what they might be. Science experiments gone wrong? Or the work of an avant-garde base commander who'd wanted to turn the place into a sculpture garden? The pools were only a few inches deep, and the water had gone stagnant. Hearing the *zizz* of mosquitoes, she quickly moved on.

After around half a kilometre the road re-entered the trees. Margot suspected they'd reached the periphery of the site, but a few minutes later, the trees thinned and gave way to another large clearing. The complex of buildings was now no more than two hundred metres away.

Even for an army base, the buildings were stark. Cold and uninviting, like something out of Stalinist Russia. At the heart of the complex, a building shaped like a cross stood out, at least three storeys high, its bare, featureless walls offering no clue about what might be going on inside. It could have been an abattoir, or a nuclear power station. The buildings around it were equally anonymous. Some of them were linked via overground corridors while others were partially obscured by mounds of earth. It looked like the whole thing was sinking, or that someone had tried to bury the place. Everything was bland and utilitarian, seemingly devoid of life.

The complex was bordered by a grassy embankment, with a ditch at the bottom holding more stinky water. They moved along the top of the embankment until they reached a point where the wing of one of the buildings jutted out from the others. Deciding to take a closer look, Natalie ran down the steep slope, leapt the ditch and arrived safely on the other side. She waited for Margot to join her. Margot's legs were not as young as they once were and she hesitated, fearing she would slip and end up sliding into the ditch on her rear. But she went for it, held her breath as her legs ran away from her, and cleared the ditch with a confident leap, mildly elated she made it without twisting an ankle.

The walls of the building were featureless concrete, pockmarked with what appeared to be bullet holes. There didn't seem to be any way in. On the ground, loose coils of razor wire prevented them from getting too close, and large piles of rubble and earth had been pushed against the walls in two or three places, presumably blocking what must once have been entrances.

"Were they shutting people in or trying to keep them out?"

Margot wondered out loud. It didn't look like a standard way of decommissioning a base, if that's what had gone on here.

More and more buildings were revealed to them as they circumnavigated the site. A large warehouse stood out to one side, fronted by an expanse of tarmac. Five large sliding doors were closed but hadn't been blocked. They followed an inner fence around an old car park, then continued along a concrete path that took them around the back of the warehouse. The walls were made of sheet metal, and the fire escape doors were only partially blocked with a few pieces of scrap. The third door they came to offered the easiest way in. Working together, they managed to shift a small steel beam and pull away some chicken wire. Natalie reached for the door handle and, with a firm tug, managed to get it open.

They squeezed through. Once inside, they quickly switched on their phone torches. Margot's eyes scanned a large room, empty except for two desks, both with their drawers pulled out. Archive boxes were lined up at the base of one wall, full of what appeared to be vehicle parts. A hole had been punched in one of the partitions, and parts of the ceiling were missing. Chunks of plaster crunched under their feet as they picked a way to an inner door.

They entered a short corridor. Their torches moved across the faces of a dozen closed doors, and briefly pinged back from a mirror at the end. Selecting a door at random, Margot eased it open. A similar scene of abandonment greeted them: desks overturned, glass smashed, rubble everywhere. A sudden movement on the floor caught her eye; she moved her phone just in time to catch a glimpse of something brown and furry disappearing down a hole. At her side, Natalie gasped. "What was that?"

"Just a mouse."

Sensing fear coming off her companion, Margot was briefly amused. "You're not afraid of them, are you?"

Natalie straightened her back, saying nothing.

The mouse didn't appear to have any friends, so they moved on. The door at the end of the corridor was locked, so they turned around and retreated, only to halt again at the sound of a vehicle reversing outside. They immediately switched off their lights. This time, Margot took the initiative, and in pitch dark, she felt her way along the corridor until she found an unlocked door. They entered an inner room where large glazed panels gave a view into the main bay. One of the large sliding doors had been opened and a van was backing in.

The high-level lights were on, but it was unlikely they could be seen, frozen like statues, in the unlit inner room. Two men guided the van in, and then opened the back doors. A forklift came over from the far end of the warehouse, orange light spinning on the roof of its cab. Together with the two men who got out of the van, they quickly started unloading. They worked efficiently, like they'd done it many times before. Margot moved a little closer to try and see what they were unloading. Large wooden crates in the main, clearly quite heavy. After sliding them onto the forks of the forklift, the driver took them down to the far end of the warehouse and then came back for more. There was little in the way of chat. They all had serious expressions on their faces and wore no kind of uniform.

The unloading went on for at least ten minutes. Margot hadn't been counting but she reckoned at least a dozen crates had been shifted to the far end of the warehouse by the time they were finished. They closed the van doors and parked the forklift, then stood around, chatting for a while. Margot drew Natalie into the cover of a steel stanchion just in case they came their way, but four of the men walked out through the main door while the fifth stayed behind to close it. After securing it with a padlock, he turned off the lights and then exited via a personnel door.

They waited, listening to the silence. When a couple of minutes had gone by, it seemed safe to assume the men were not coming back.

"Let's go and see what they've got in those crates," Natalie said. She switched on her torch and set off before Margot had chance to say anything.

They peered in through the van's front windows. The cab was empty and clean, the doors locked. Moving on, the light from their torches picked out the outlines of another three vans, lined up in a row. At the far end of the warehouse, a row of shipping containers was neatly lined up, each door secured with a strong padlock.

"Look at this."

Natalie was moving towards a partition behind which dozens of crates had been stacked. Beside them, a row of benches was covered with a variety of electronic equipment, cables and circuit boards. A chemical smell tainted the air. Spotting a loose lid on one of the crates, Natalie veered off again.

"Careful," Margot said as Natalie moved the lid to one side.

Inside, was a layer of straw, and underneath that was a wooden box, too big to take out with one hand. Margot held her phone for her while Natalie reached in. The box contained a tray full of green tubes, the size of aerosol sprays. Margot's heart skipped a beat when Natalie pulled one out.

"Hand grenades."

They carefully put them back.

Few of the crates had labels on. From those that did, familiar sets of initials popped out at them: AK-47; TNT; M16... Margot did some quick mental arithmetic. There must have been at least fifty crates surrounding them, not including whatever was in the shipping containers. There could be enough weaponry in this warehouse to supply a small army. And all the electronic equipment on the benches? Margot was no expert, but she had the strongest suspicion they were in the middle of a bomb factory.

"Is this why they stole my grandmother's money?" Natalie said. "To make bombs."

It seemed the logical conclusion.

"I neglected to tell you," Margot confessed. "Someone took a shot at me last time."

"When?"

"When I got to that chain on the edge of the woods. They were obviously trying to warn me off. Now I know why."

"Why didn't you say so before?"

"Would it have made a difference?"

"No."

"Well then. Look." Margot was done with this. "Whatever's going on here, it's out of our league. We need to go."

Natalie appeared to waver, but only for a moment. "I haven't got my grandmother's money back yet."

This woman's stubbornness might have been admirable had she not been so infuriating. "Fine," Margot replied resignedly. "Stay if you like, but I'm leaving."

Before she could take another step, however, one of the big lights came on. Margot was on the point of turning around when a man said: "Don't move."

There was a click of metal on metal. Margot froze. There was no doubt in her mind that a gun was being held to the back of her head.

19

Sébastien stood with a small group of brothers, anxiously watching the monitors in the Command Centre. For someone so paranoid, he'd done nothing to upgrade the base's CCTV. Only six cameras on the entire site, and all of them were old models: black-and-white pictures; no sound; probably dating back to the days when the base had last been occupied. Their leader preferred old-school methods: the dogs; men on the ground; tripwires and man-traps.

Dion knew the location of every single one of those cameras and had checked every square metre of ground each one covered. He didn't want anyone spying on him. All he could see on the screens right now was a series of grainy images, ghostly outlines of trees, an occasional flash of light. The base was so big that whoever had got in would have an easy time evading detection, but only for so long. To Sébastien's credit, old-school methods usually worked.

Standing beside him, Esmée gave him a nudge. She would be wondering why he hadn't yet told Sébastien about the file, but Dion wanted to keep it up his sleeve. Besides, this wasn't the time.

"Let me through."

Sounds of a commotion came from behind. They turned to see a man pushing through the crowd, keen to get to their leader. Golem came to the fore, an excited look in his eyes.

"What is it, brother?" Sébastien asked, giving the man his full attention.

"We've found them!"

"Where?"

Overexcited, Golem's words tumbled out of his mouth: "Snooping around the warehouse. Two women. And one of them was *her* – the woman who followed *him*." He pointed an accusing finger into Dion's face.

Suddenly it seemed like everyone in the room was looking at him. Dion's ears burned as Sébastien's blue eyes locked onto him. He scrutinised him for a few moments, and then turned back to Golem.

"Where are they now?"

"They were kicking up a fuss so we took them down to the old laboratory."

"You locked them in?"

"Yes."

"What about their phones?"

"Here."

Golem pulled a crumpled Faraday bag from his pocket and handed it over. Sébastien reached inside and took out two pink iPhones. He carefully checked they were switched off before putting them back in the bag and handing them to one of the beards. "Take these to the tech team. Harvest everything you can from them."

The beard took them away in double quick time.

"You going down there?" Golem asked eagerly.

Sébastien considered. He cast another look in Dion's direction, but said nothing. Whatever he was thinking, he was still holding fire.

"We'll leave them for now."

———

Sometimes, as a child, Margot would play a silly game. On a dark night, she would keep her eyes tightly shut and try to work her way out of her bedroom, imagining what life was like for a blind person. Hands on the walls, she would feel her way to the door, then onto the landing, and then down the stairs. The stairs were the trickiest part, of course: holding tightly onto the handrail, toes searching for the edge of each riser, knowing that one wrong step could be fatal. Occasionally, she made it all the way to the front door before the urge to open her eyes became too great to resist. In her youthful naivety, it didn't seem so hard, but the key difference was that she had the option to see again whenever she liked, unlike a blind person.

Margot was reminded of that game now as she felt her way around the walls of the place they'd been put in, her eyes probing a deep, deep darkness. Her palms moved across a smooth concrete wall, gingerly at first, then with more confidence as she encountered no hazards. Finding an internal corner, she turned her body through ninety degrees and continued until her fingers encountered a cold steel panel. A door? She traced its outline with her fingertips, hoping to find a gap, but it was sealed as tight as a submarine hatch, not even a breath of air making it through. It appeared to be locked with a smooth metal wheel. Maybe they'd been put on a submarine.

"Hold on."

Behind her, Margot could hear Natalie rifling through her bag. A few seconds later, a light came on and the younger woman's face appeared, bathed in the glow of a mobile phone screen.

"Where'd you get that?" Margot asked in surprise.

"The phone he took was my work phone," Natalie explained. "This one's my own."

How resourceful. Margot's relief was tempered by a pang of annoyance. She could have done the same had she not left the phone she'd borrowed from work in the car.

"I don't suppose there's a signal?"

After a pause, Natalie drew in a disappointed breath. "No."

Hardly surprising considering the walls felt a metre thick.

They had no idea where they'd been taken. After being blindfolded in the warehouse, a group of men had marched them across the tarmac and then into a building. They'd been relieved of their phones, jostled down a series of foul-smelling corridors, pushed to their knees, and abandoned in this... whatever this was. The last thing they'd heard, Margot now realised, was the closing of that heavy steel door.

"Switch on the torch."

An annoyed tut. "What did you think I was going to do?"

Seconds later, the glow from the screen was replaced by the piercing white light of the phone's torch. Natalie shone it in Margot's eyes (probably intentionally), then scanned the space around them. They were in a short narrow corridor, the steel door at one end, a plastic strip curtain at the other. Natalie went straight to the door and tried the handle, but the wheel spun uselessly whichever way she turned it. "Brilliant."

"We need to find another way out."

"No shit, Sherlock."

Margot gnashed her teeth.

Natalie switched her attention to the opposite end of the passage. With no light of her own, Margot had little choice but to follow. They pushed through the thick plastic strips of the curtain and entered a much larger space, an infirmary of some kind. Natalie's torch picked a row of gurneys lined up against the longest wall, complemented by side stands full of equipment, though it clearly hadn't been used in a very long time. The walls were covered in green mould. Puddles were scattered across the floor, the liquid in them smelling like it had been there for decades. Natalie's light illuminated a tray full of surgical tools: knives, scissors, saws. Barbaric things that looked like something out of the Dark Ages. You wouldn't want to get treated in here, Margot thought. The plastic topper on one of the gurneys had four small tears in it, like someone had clawed it with their fingernails.

"What kind of army base was this?" Margot mused out loud.

"Whatever it was, they didn't want anyone finding out about it."

There had clearly been a fire at some point. Clumps of burnt plastic littered the floor, and the gurneys at the far end were blackened with smoke damage. Natalie shone the light up at the ceiling to reveal rows of sprinklers, which might have explained the puddles. Either the place had been ransacked after its occupants had departed, or whoever had been using it had left in a hurry.

They moved through an opening into a room that looked like a laboratory. A line of stainless steel tables ran down the centre. Cabinets and shelves to the side were full of old-fashioned equipment, although most of it had been trashed. Broken glass was everywhere. It looked like a wild animal had been let loose. Margot couldn't help noticing all the hazardous warning signs affixed to the cupboards, hating to think what might be getting into her lungs.

The light blinked. Natalie's shadowy face reappeared as she looked at her screen. "Damn."

"What is it?"

"My battery's down to ten per cent."

It looked like there were more rooms to explore down the corridor, but Margot wasn't disappointed. She'd had her fill of delving into dingy, mysterious places of late.

"Best save it," she said. "There's no knowing how long we'll be in here."

For once, Natalie didn't argue.

They went back out through the plastic curtain and sat down on the floor of the corridor. Natalie switched off her phone and plunged them back into darkness. Margot looked at her watch. Six o'clock. They hadn't tried banging on the door or shouting for help – wasn't that obligatory in situations like this? It would undoubtedly be futile. No one was going to hear them through all that concrete.

A silence formed, which soon became uncomfortable. What were you meant to talk about in situations like this? Chat about the weather? Discuss what was on TV last night? Natalie wasn't the easiest person to talk to at the best of times. Margot moodily folded her arms, dark thoughts beginning to gather in her mind. The gravity of their predicament was beginning to sink in. No one knew they were here. Madame Janvier knew about the woods, but she had no idea of their location. How long would it be before someone realised they were gone – a day? A week? A month? Depressing to think how much time might go by in Margot's world before anyone realised she was missing. The more she stewed on it, the more she began to resent Natalie for getting her into this mess. This was all her fault – pig-headed, tempestuous little minx. She exhaled heavily. "Remind me again why we're here?"

"You know very well."

"I know I should have trusted my instincts."

"And what was that – stay at home and do some knitting?"

Margot exuded malice into the darkness between them. "I don't knit, and never have."

"That does surprise me."

"Not that there's anything wrong with it."

"No one forced you to come."

Margot laughed a harsh, dry laugh. "Oh right. And what was I meant to do – let you go charging off on your own?"

"I'm perfectly capable of looking after myself."

"Your grandmother would never have forgiven me."

"Really? She told me you were an interfering old busybody."

"I very much doubt she said that."

"Maybe it was just the impression I got."

"At least I'm not afraid of mice."

"It wasn't a mouse – it was a rat."

"A rat!" Margot laughed again. "I really don't think so."

"Yes it was. I was closer to it than you were. It was definitely a rat, and a big one."

Margot mentally threw her hands in the air. "All right. You win – it was a rat. A huge feral sabre-toothed rat from the back-streets of Nîmes. It must be hard being right all of the time."

"It's not my fault other people are idiots."

"And yet here we are, stranded in this hell-hole, and whose fault is that, hmm?"

"I didn't hear you object when I climbed the fence."

Margot exhaled tiredly. They could go on like this forever. And it was difficult arguing in the pitch black, unable to read the other person's body language, not knowing how they were reacting.

"Anyway," Margot said. "Why don't we just sit here in silence?"

"Finally, a good idea."

Otherwise one of us might end up strangled to death, Margot was tempted to add.

She took another look at her watch. What would she be doing right now if she had stayed at home? Curling up in front of the TV, or strolling down to La Lune Bleue for a meal? She could have been sitting beside the sea, enjoying a nice cold glass of wine, talking about weddings with the boys. It seemed a world away now.

The silence grew longer. Margot got to her feet and felt her way to the door. She pressed her ear to the cold steel panel, but all she could hear was a faint ringing sound at the back of her head. She couldn't help shuddering as she thought of all those weapons, piled up in the warehouse, hidden away in this apparently peaceful woodland. And the men with their guard dogs. It was like some terrifying parallel universe, just one step outside of normal life. Like being in a big city, shopping on famous boulevards, just one wrong turn away from its seedy underbelly.

Returning to her place on the floor, Margot hugged her knees. She looked at the space where she imagined Natalie to be and tried to think nice thoughts. Bickering wasn't going to get them anywhere. If they were going to be here for a while, they could at least try to be civil to each other.

"How long do you reckon they've been gone?"

A pause. "Twenty minutes."

Margot hadn't been keeping track of time, though she had a suspicion it had been quite a bit longer. "I hope they haven't forgotten about us."

"Unlikely. They're probably looking through our phones, trying to find out who we are."

Margot shuffled uncomfortably. With half your life on your phone these days, it was worrying what they might find out. "Who do you reckon they are?"

"Arms dealers? Militia?"

"Or some kind of doomsday cult, preparing for the next apocalypse."

"At least if there's an undercover cop in here, they can't let us come to any harm."

"I wouldn't bank on that," Margot said. "They won't want to risk blowing their cover." And given the fact she'd been told to stay away, they could hardly expect a warm reception. If they did encounter them, they would have to be careful not to give the game away. The builder from Narbonne, the woman with the long black fringe... *Nice watch*... ironic to think that the unlikely pair of fraudsters could be their best way out of here.

"You must be very close to your grandmother," Margot ventured. "Going to all this trouble for her."

Nothing came back from the darkness. She sensed Natalie shift, then clear her throat, perhaps reluctant to open up. Finally, she said:

"*Mamie* has always been there for me. This is the least I could do for her."

"You see her often?"

"I did when I was growing up."

"I guess you're lucky. I never really knew my grandparents. Two of them died before I was born, the other two I barely remember."

"She had a hard time raising my mother."

"Did she?"

"My mother has various issues. Like being a heroin addict, for one."

"Oh. Right." Margot felt like she'd stepped on a landmine. "That can't have been easy."

"It wasn't, but *Mamie* never gave up on her."

"That's good of her."

"It's what families do."

It wasn't quite the backstory Margot had imagined. Natalie, the daughter of a heroin addict. But maybe it explained one or two things about her.

"Is your mother getting any treatment for it?"

This time Natalie didn't respond. Perhaps she feared she'd opened up too much. Margot sensed a shift in the air, and tracked her progress to the door. When she got up and followed, she found Natalie stooping, an ear pressed to the steel.

"We could do with a safe cracker," Margot joked. "Or some of that dynamite. Blow this place to Kingdom Come."

"Shush."

Margot frowned. "What is it?"

A pause.

"I think someone's coming."

20

Natalie hurriedly turned on her phone. The instant the light came on, they ran through the thick plastic curtain and into the room with the gurneys. Continuing through the old laboratory, they paused in the corridor. Natalie pointed her light to the far end, but Margot grabbed her arm.

"Through here."

They went into a small office and closed the door behind them. There was a desk they could use as a barricade, but too late – loud voices and tramping boots came from the direction of the laboratory. Margot hunkered down behind the desk; Natalie looked for somewhere else to hide, but finding nothing, joined Margot behind the desk. Light out, they held their breath.

The tramp of heavy boots came closer. A man shouted; someone shouted back in reply, making no attempt to hide their presence. The gaps around the office door lit up as footsteps halted right outside. A moment later, the door was flung open.

The room filled with light. Peeking out from under the desk, Margot saw a jumble of heavy black boots. Shadows moved across the wall, and then a man wielding a floodlight came to the fore. Margot's heart nearly exploded as they were caught in the powerful light, cowering behind the desk.

"Down here!"

It was impossible to see with the light in her eyes, but Margot sensed dozens of bodies crowding into the office. After a few moments, the room was filled with the pungent aroma of heavily breathing men.

"That's her! She's the one who followed him."

The light dimmed a fraction. As Margot's retinas recovered, she opened her eyes to find a group of ten or twelve men gathered around the desk. A wiry, twisted figure was holding the floodlight, but another man was staying his hand. Blond hair and very pink lips – he was a slightly built man, but he commanded the attention of those around him.

"Stand up," he said calmly.

Margot was not one to blindly follow orders, but she rose to her feet without hesitation. A beat later, Natalie followed suit. The blond man moved a step closer, regarding them with intensity.

"What are you doing here?"

It was a simple question, and Margot would have given him a straightforward answer had her tongue not been frozen to the roof of her mouth.

"I know who you are," the man went on. "I've looked through your phones. All I want to know is why you came here."

Margot cast a glance to her side. Natalie was putting on a brave face, but Margot could tell she was petrified. Losing patience, the man with the twisted features lurched forward, brandishing the floodlight like a weapon. This time, the blond man pushed his arm away more forcefully.

An uneasy silence ensued. The blond man turned to look over his shoulder and signalled to someone behind him. A bigger man came to the fore. Margot tried not to react when she recognised the outline of the builder from Narbonne.

"Do you know this man?"

Without hesitation, Margot shook her head.

He turned to Natalie. "What about you?"

Natalie hadn't seen him before, but there was a chance she would guess who he was. Margot tried to catch her eye and transmit a warning – if he was the undercover cop, they had to be careful not to give him away. After giving it some thought, Natalie raised her head. "I've never seen him before in my life."

The blond man didn't look convinced. His frown deepened as he turned back to Margot. "Why were you following him?"

"What?"

"You followed him from the train station to the woods. You were seen."

Margot tried to look baffled. "That was days ago. I lost my way. That's all."

"And now? You lost your way a second time?"

Margot lowered her eyes. There was an intensity about this man that was unnerving, and she couldn't help feeling sheepish. She tried to guess what they might have gleaned from her phone – contacts, texts, emails, browsing history; all her communications with Captain Bouchard and Madame Janvier. It wouldn't take them long to put two and two together. Margot steeled her resolve. "I don't appreciate being shot at, that's for sure."

The man with the floodlight grunted like a pig. He tried to lash out, but this time the blond man took charge of the light and sent him to the back. A few words were exchanged with the other men, after which they slowly backed off, all except the builder, who remained by his side. The builder's face offered no clue as to what they should do. Margot remembered that night in Narbonne, the force of that punch. She was far from certain they could consider him a friend.

"I apologise if you feel you've been mistreated," the blond man said, no hint of sarcasm in his voice. "I have no wish to harm you. All I want is an explanation."

Margot was tempted to take him at his word and tell him the truth when Natalie blurted out: "You stole my grandmother's money. I came to get it back."

A look of bemusement passed across the man's face. That probably was not the answer he'd been expecting.

"We don't steal anything."

"*He* did." Natalie pointed at the builder. "He conned her out of forty thousand euros, and I want it back."

A ripple of amusement passed through the crowd; someone even laughed. The blond man seemed intrigued. "You just said you'd never seen him before."

"I haven't. It was an educated guess."

"So is that why you came – to get your money back?"

"Yes."

"Both of you?"

Margot nodded in agreement.

He gave it a little more thought. He didn't seem entirely convinced, but he stopped clenching his jaw.

"In that case, you've had a wasted trip. We only take what we need, and whatever we take is put to good use. I'm sorry, but you can't have it back."

He turned around and instructed the men to leave. They immediately began to file out.

"Wait," Margot cried out, beginning to panic. "Where are you going?"

They all ignored her. In single file, they trooped out through the laboratory and across the room with the gurneys. Margot

212 | RACHEL GREEN

and Natalie followed closely as they passed through the plastic curtain.

"Is that it?" Margot asked in confusion. "Are we free to leave?"

It seemed too good to be true, yet no one was attempting to stop them. The men exited via the thick steel door but then, when the last man was through, they turned as one to block the way. Catching the builder's eyes, Margot gave him an imploring look, but his face showed no emotion as the door began to close. Natalie tried to rush through, but the men shoved her back. The last thing Margot registered before the door sealed them in was the leering grin of the man with the twisted face, triumphant at the end.

———

Many of the brothers were still hanging around the mess hall, keen to find out what was going on. They clustered around the brothers who'd returned from the old laboratory, and everyone was brought up to speed. Dion remained in another small group that followed Sébastien into the Command Centre. Their leader said nothing until they'd reached the hub at which point he drew Dion to one side. "Can I speak to you in the ops room, please? Alone."

Dion looked back at him. Sébastien's face was a blank canvas. It was impossible to judge how angry he was.

"I've got a shift on laundry duty."

"It will only take a minute."

It wasn't a request.

They took the stairs to the first floor. Two brothers were working in the ops rooms, so Sébastien detoured into a side room. He waited for Dion to close the door.

"Before you ask," Dion began, "I have no idea who she is. Either of them."

"The woman who followed you works at the *Palais de Justice* in Argents-sur-Mer," Sébastien said. "She's friends with a bookseller who I believe was one of your targets."

Dion nodded. He hadn't seen any of the data they'd harvested from their phones. He had no idea what she might have on him.

"The younger woman is the bookseller's granddaughter," Sébastien continued. "Did she not come up in your research?"

Dion shook his head, relieved he didn't have to lie. "We never set eyes on her. The bookseller lives in an apartment over the shop. She never mentioned a granddaughter." Esmée had done the research and hadn't mentioned a granddaughter. She obviously hadn't considered her important. Many of their targets had been rich widows or widowers. Isolated people with no family close by.

Sébastien still seemed conflicted. "Tell me again what happened."

Dion recounted the sequence of events, how they'd arranged the hit, the story about the car park. He thought carefully about what he was saying, not just for his own benefit, but also eager to get to the bottom of this, just like Sébastien. The bookseller had been one of the easier hits, happy to hand over her money in the hope of making a fast buck.

"You're sure nothing went wrong?"

"Nothing," Dion replied. "She already had the cash hidden in a bag in a wardrobe. She asked the usual questions. We watched her for a few days afterwards, but she didn't go to the police."

"So how come the granddaughter just recognised you?"

"I don't think she did. She obviously realised I was the one her friend was following."

"And why was she following you in the first place?"

Dion shrugged. "She must have picked up our trail at some point. I honestly have no idea."

"Could Esmée have tipped her off?"

Dion recalled the image of the two of them seated at the bar. But he shook his head. "I can't imagine why she would."

Sébastien turned away. He moved to one of the consoles, looked at something on the screen of a laptop. After a few moments, he turned again and looked Dion straight in the eye. "Is there anything you're not telling me, brother?"

Dion swallowed. Sometimes, when Sébastien looked at him, Dion was certain he could see right through him. He wondered if now might be a good time to tell him about the file, to prove his loyalty, if it were in doubt. But then, he wasn't sure where his loyalties lay anymore.

"You can trust me, brother. You know that."

Sébastien took a little more time making up his mind, but finally he spoke. "All right. If you do remember anything, come to me first, please. Everything we do here relies on trust."

Dion nodded his agreement, relieved to be off the hook. "What will you do with them?"

"What would you do with them?" Sébastien fired back.

Caught out, Dion hesitated. The two women may not have known anything, but they'd seen too much. They would have to be dealt with, one way or another.

"Luckily I don't have to make those kinds of decisions," Dion said, half as a joke.

But Sébastien wasn't amused. Their leader had never shied away from making the tough decisions, and something told Dion he wasn't about to start now.

21

You there?

Dion stared at her avatar, willing the green light to come on. He had been sitting in the empty radio room for over ten minutes, and she still hadn't acknowledged him. He picked up a pencil, rolled it between his fingers, tested how much stress he could put on it before it snapped. He flinched when it did, then rubbed his thumb from where the broken end had cut into his skin.

Voices came from outside. It was early – not yet ten o'clock. He'd been lucky to find the place empty. Dion logged out of the messaging service, snatched the flash drive from the computer, and then turned off the monitor. He slipped into an alcove unseen, realising too late that he'd left the desk lamp on.

Two men entered the room, but then came to a sudden halt: Tik and one of the electricians. They had been chatting casually, but both abruptly fell silent, as if sensing something was amiss.

"Anyone in here?" Tik called out.

Dion watched them cast a suspicious look around the room. Tik knew the radio room like the back of his hand and would probably know in an instant if anything was out of place. They passed the alcove where Dion was hiding – two metres away, maybe less. All they had to do was turn their heads. Dion ran through contingency plans: which he would take first? Tik was the smallest of the two; he could easily break his neck. The electrician was bulky; tackling him would be messy. Tik spotted something on one of the desks, and seemed relieved. Whatever it was, he picked it up and they left, turning off the lamp on their way out. Dion let out his breath.

He made his way into B-wing. Some of the stresses melted away as he traversed the corridor to the laundry room. He liked the laundry room. It felt detached from the rest of the base. It had a high ceiling, smooth plastered walls; the gentle rumble from the washing machines was soporific. There was also proper lighting – multiple strip lights, on all the time. Added to which, it smelled a whole lot better than the rest of the base.

He loaded a basket of dirty linen into one of the washing machines. He took a pile of freshly-washed sheets out of the dryer and began feeding them into the ironing machine. It was satisfying to watch how smooth they came out. Crisp, clean linen. Like something reborn. He folded them carefully, making sure every line was straight. It was monotonous work but he could do it for hours.

A knock on the door took him by surprise. He looked across the room to see Esmée's smiling face framed in the small observation panel.

"There you are," she said, coming to join him. "I've been looking all over for you."

"What have I done now?" Dion smiled back.

She gave him a curious look as she circled the ironing machine. "So this is what you get up to in your spare time?"

"It's therapeutic."

"I'll take your word for it."

She turned around and jumped up to sit on the counter. "You heard about our new arrivals?"

"Sébastien's locked them in the old lab. One of them was the granddaughter of that bookseller in Argents-sur-Mer."

"I remember her. What's she doing here?"

"She came to get the money back."

Esmée laughed. "No refunds – didn't she read the small print?"

"That was what Sébastien said. He seems to think I had something to do with it."

"Why would he think that?"

"That woman from the hotel in Narbonne."

"It's not your fault she followed us."

"I'm not sure Sébastien sees it that way."

"If he suspects you, he'll suspect me, too."

"Maybe."

Dion fed another sheet into the ironing machine. When it came out, he neatly folded it and added it to the pile. Perturbed to find something contaminating the fresh odour, he sniffed the air. His eyes were drawn to Esmée's pink hoodie. "You want me to wash that?"

She gave him a curious look back. "You saying I smell?"

Dion stifled his grin. She wasn't the worst in the camp, but that wasn't saying much. Esmée gave the collar a sniff, seemed to concede he had a point, and took it off. Dion caught it as she tossed it over, then slung it into the washing machine.

"Going back to that bookseller," Esmée went on, re-perching on the countertop. "She owned four apartments in that town, as well as the bookshop. Forty grand would have been nothing to her."

She'd played the part of the sweet old bookseller, but had been anything but. In the course of her research, Esmée had hacked her Impots account and found she'd been pulling in over fifty k a year in rents alone.

"It doesn't seem to matter how much you've got," Dion said, "some people always want more."

"The con works best on the greedy. Just say those magic words: double your money. They can't wait to hand over their cash."

Dion nodded his agreement. He had no sympathy for people like that. Her stuck-up little granddaughter could whistle for the money.

He folded the last of the sheets. 23:00. The washing machine still had another ninety minutes to go. He looked at Esmée. "You busy?"

"I was thinking of washing my hair, but otherwise, no. Why?"

"Want to go look at the moon?"

"I've seen it before, thanks."

"Not like this you haven't." Dion grinned. "Come on."

He took her back to the hub. They had to wait a few minutes for some people to move on before ducking through the hole into C-wing. Once they were safely in the corridor, they switched on their torches.

"I didn't think there was anything in here," Esmée said, shining her light down the fire-blackened corridor. In places the walls were totally black; some of the partitions were coated with melted plastic. Bizarrely, a single white door handle remained unblemished, a sole survivor of the inferno. An intact teacup on the Titanic.

"Is this where God lives?" Esmée quipped, halting next to the door with the white handle.

"He used to," Dion quipped back. "He's not been seen in a while."

He opened the door. They looked inside. The room was no different to any of the others.

Dion continued down to C-5. He hesitated when he got to the door, shining his light onto Esmée's face. "I can trust you, can't I?"

Esmée made a cross over her heart. "Tell me your secrets. I promise I won't tell."

Dion unlocked the door. Inside the gym, a perfect shaft of moonlight was shining down through the hole in the roof.

"Cool," Esmée said. "Escape from Colditz?"

"Sort of."

"Did you make that hole?"

Dion moved to the base of the ladder and took hold of the ropes. "The hole was already there. But I made the ladder. "

"I'm guessing Sébastien doesn't know about this."

Dion shook his head.

"So what's out there?"

"You'll see." Dion tightened his grip on the ropes. "You go first. Wait for me at the top."

Esmée seemed eager to take on the challenge. Dion steadied the ropes as she slowly climbed up, but Esmée didn't put a foot wrong. She bravely pulled herself up through the hole and waited as instructed. A few seconds later, Dion was back by her side.

"The roof sheets are brittle," he said. "So be careful. Stay on the line of the purlins and you'll be okay."

He walked to the verge, checking to make sure Esmée was following his instructions. When she reached his side, she held onto his arm, peering over the edge.

"We need to jump down there." He indicated the mound of soil.

"What is this – an assault course?"

Dion went first this time. Esmée followed without hesitation.

She held onto his arm as they scrambled down the side of the mound.

"Where now?" Esmée said, breathless with excitement.

"See those trees?"

She nodded.

"Follow me and don't look back."

Dion set off at full sprint. He waited again when he reached the trees, checking to make sure no dogs were around. Esmée caught up without mishap, and they continued into the avenue together.

Bathed in moonlight, the antennae array was an arresting sight. Esmée paused to take it in. "What the hell were they doing – communicating with aliens?"

"Listening in on the Russians, more like. The equipment's all Cold War-era. And so is that."

Dion pointed to the copper dome. He took her down the overgrown path and in through the service door at the base of the structure. As they climbed the winding staircase to the gantry, he was pleased to see Esmée's face light up.

"That is one large telescope."

"It's one seriously large telescope," Dion said as they reached the gantry. "It would have been one of the largest refractors in the world at the time it was built." He had no idea why they needed an optical telescope of this size. An idiosyncratic base commander, perhaps, with money to spare.

He removed the lens cap and wiped the lens clean. The moon was coming into view, filling the observatory with waxy white light. Dion turned the wheel to adjust the azimuth, focused on one of the craters, and then stepped aside so that Esmée could take a look. "These days it's all done on computers," he said. "But nothing beats seeing it with your own eye."

Esmée made some appreciative noises.

"See those two big dark patches on the centre right?"

"I see them."

"The lower one is Mare Tranquillitatis. That's where the first moon landings were made. The one above it is Mare Serenitatis, one of the eyes of the 'man in the moon'."

"The detail's amazing."

Dion craned over her shoulder, pleased she was enjoying it. "There are all different types of crater. Bowl-shaped ones, big ones with a mountain in the middle. Then there are the really, really big ones, more like walled plains. A lot of those used to be filled with lava."

"There was lava on the moon?"

"Oh yeah. They've not been active for millions of years, but there are volcanoes and lava tubes. The lava tubes could be used as underground bases if people ever decide to build a colony up there."

Esmée came away from the eyepiece and smiled at him. Dion looked back at her, not sure what was amusing her. "What?"

"Why are you so interested in astronomy?"

He shrugged. It was a reminder of his youth, he supposed, a way of escaping. "It passes the time," he said, and took her place at the eyepiece.

They were silent for a while. Dion let his eye rove the lunar landscape, mentally transporting himself there. As a young boy, he'd read about the Apollo moon landings and had been amazed to think that people had actually set foot on its surface. Earthrise had to be one of the landmark moments in human history, a giant leap in anyone's book. It had seemed inevitable that by the time he grew up there would be bases in space, routine missions to Mars, fantastic ships that would transport people to far-flung regions of the solar system. As the years went by, it had depressed him to realise that it was never going to happen, at least not in his lifetime. The human race could have achieved so much more if all the energy that had been wasted on war and religion had instead been put to good use.

"I appreciate you sharing this with me," Esmée said.

Dion came out of his thoughts. He pulled his eye away from the eyepiece. His wife had never been interested. He'd had no friends who'd shared his hobby. Lots of people went through their lives without finding anyone who got them. It was no big deal.

"I spent a lot of time out in the fields when I was a kid. Looking up at the night sky."

"Where'd you grow up?"

"On a farm."

"That must have been nice, having all that space around."

"Not really." Dion moved to the control desk. He started cleaning one of the spare eyepieces. "It was out in the middle of nowhere. Big empty fields. It always seemed to be windy." Or maybe that was just how he remembered it: grey skies, flat fields, devoid of warmth and humanity. "My parents were cruel."

"Were they?"

Dion put down the eyepiece and started cleaning another. He remembered the box his childhood telescope had come in. Bought from the local *brocante*. Tatty around the edges, but one of his treasured possessions. It had come with three extra eyepieces, a cleaning cloth, a booklet on basic astronomy that he must have read a hundred times over.

"There was this room at the back of the house," he said. "They didn't really use it for anything. The only thing in there was a chair. Whenever I misbehaved, my dad would tie me to the chair and leave me there. Sometimes all night."

"Jesus. How old were you?"

"Six."

"Did your mother not say anything?"

"She was probably afraid to. I don't think he hit her or

anything, but she was timid. Never spoke up for herself. Maybe it was their way of calming me down. I think I was a boisterous kid."

"It's sick."

"Could have been worse, I suppose."

"They still alive?"

Dion shook his head. His parents had been dead to him long before their actual demise. He'd left home at fifteen. Joined the army as soon as he could. He'd met his wife on a training exercise in New Caledonia, and had only gone back to see his parents when he'd heard of their deaths. They'd perished in the farmhouse, died of natural causes, ten days apart. It had been two weeks before a neighbour had discovered their bodies. A fitting end, Dion had always thought.

He put the lenses back in the box and looked up at the moon with his naked eye. "There'll be a super blue moon in a few weeks' time. Should be quite a sight."

"Is that when it appears bigger than normal?"

"It's when the moon is closest to Earth. If you get two full moons in one month, the second one's called a blue moon. Get them both together and you have a super blue moon."

"Cool."

"It might be twenty years before it happens again."

"Be a shame if it's cloudy, then."

Dion smiled.

"Before I came in here, my wife and I agreed we would look at the moon every night at midnight. A way of staying in touch. Now she won't even talk to me."

"You've tried talking to her?" Esmée asked, surprised.

Dion froze, realising his mistake. He was getting sloppy, letting his guard down. He was going to trip up if he wasn't more careful.

"Not for a while, no," he said, and then closed down the telescope.

———

They made their way back to C-wing with little further chat. They parted company at the hub: Esmée went off to the bunkhouse while Dion continued to the Command Centre.

He went up the stairs to the ops room. He asked one of the geeks if he knew where Sébastien was and was pointed to a side room. Dion paused at the door, looking in through the observation panel. Sébastien, Monika, and Tik sat around a desk, engrossed in an intense discussion.

The door was too thick for him to hear what they were saying. Dion knocked. When all three faces turned to look at him, he couldn't help but suspect they'd been talking about him.

Sébastien got up and opened the door. "What can I do for you, brother?"

Dion looked past him to Monika and Tik, still seated at the table. Monika's face was blank; Tik wouldn't meet his eye. Had he found something on one of the computers?

"I was wondering about the two women," Dion said.

"What about them?"

"Have you decided what you're going to do with them yet?"

Sébastien lightly shook his head. "They're safe for now."

"They still locked up?"

"One night down there won't do them any harm."

And then what? Dion wondered. Sébastien wouldn't want any loose ends. The chances of them getting out of here alive were slim, but was that really his problem?

A silence formed. Sébastien and Monika were looking at him like they expected him to leave. Finally, Dion got the message and went.

22

Minutes grew into hours and still no one came back. Margot stared into the all-encompassing darkness, experiencing a weird state of disconnect. It felt like her mind had escaped and dissolved into the void, leaving her body a husk.

"I suppose we'd better think about getting some sleep," the thing that had once been Margot said, the words sounding hollow even to her own ears.

"*Sleep*!?" boomed the Voice of the Universe. "*I give you a miserly one hundred years living on your puny planet and you choose to spend one third of it ASLEEP?*"

"*I know,*" Margot's mind replied. "*When you put it like that it does sound wasteful. But then, beds are rather comfortable, and dreams are a nice way of escaping from the world, especially when the world's being mean to you.*"

"*Pish,*" cried the Voice of the Universe. "*If you are not happy with your world then change it. Have some backbone.*"

Margot's mind gave this some thought.

"*Would the universe mind if I improved my world by strangling someone?*" she ventured.

A pause. "*Did you have anyone in particular in mind?*"

"Oh, I don't know – an annoying new acquaintance, perhaps?"

"Hmm," pondered the Voice of the Universe. *"How would you go about this proposed strangulation?"*

"Creep up on them from behind?"

"In the dark!?"

"Smother them with a pillow?"

"While they were sleeping!?"

"It was just an idea."

With a sudden change of heart, the Voice of the Universe chuckled. *"Of course the universe wouldn't mind! You think any of the billions of other insignificant dots care what you do?"*

"Well—"

"Release yourself from this tyranny. Crush that long white neck with your bare bony fingers."

The real Margot wobbled her head, attempting to lasso herself to reality. You could easily go mad in a situation like this.

"Natalie?"

No response.

Margot had completely lost track of her companion's whereabouts. The fear that she'd found another way out and had gone off without telling her jolted Margot to life, and she quickly got up. Unable to sense anything at all, she felt her way through the thick plastic curtain and into the laboratory, relieved to see a small light coming from the far end.

"Natalie – is that you?"

"No, it's the Queen of Sheba."

"What are you doing?"

"Hold on."

There was the sound of tinkling water, followed by an *ugh* of disgust. Seconds later, Natalie emerged from the opening, buttoning up her trousers.

"There's a toilet back there," she said, picking up her phone from where she'd left it, leaning against the base of the wall. "Or at least, I hope that's what it was."

The mention of a toilet made Margot want to go.

"Can I borrow the light?"

Natalie was reluctant. "Be careful with it," she said, slow to release her hold.

Margot worked her way down a pokey corridor. She came to a dented steel door which opened into a tiny space where a cracked, stained bowl half-filled with rubble looked up at her. It was bad, but she'd used worse.

On the way back, Margot stuck her head through a few more doors. She found a room that resembled a mess hall and eyed up the furniture. There was a sofa big enough to stretch out on and an armchair that looked reasonably comfortable. Natalie appeared by her side. She immediately took back her phone and wiped it with a tissue. Margot tried not to look offended. "I don't think I peed on it. At least, not much."

The light was enough to catch the disgusted look on Natalie's face.

"We should try to get some sleep."

"In here?" Natalie was horrified.

"It's either that or one of those gurneys back there."

Having a closer look around, Margot spotted an empty bottle of Grey Goose in the wastepaper bin. It looked like it had been put there recently.

"I'll take the sofa," Natalie said.

"How very gallant."

"You'd better not snore."

"Don't worry, I'll be fine – once I've hacked up some phlegm."

"*Ugh.*"

Natalie gave the cushions a thump. The disgusted expression remained etched on her face as she grumpily settled down.

Margot slumped into the armchair and put her feet up on the coffee table. This time, when the light went out, she happily surrendered to the void.

———

Margot managed to sleep despite the annoying sound of dripping water coming from the toilet. When she woke, a dull green light was creeping in from somewhere. It wasn't the light from a torch. Margot sat up and looked at the illuminated dial of her watch. Five-thirty. Most probably morning, though how could you tell when it was permanently dark? Noticing the sofa was empty, the thought that Natalie had done a runner once again crossed Margot's mind, and this time she found herself unmoved, toying with the idea that she would be better off alone. She hauled herself up out of the chair, put on her shoes, and went into the laboratory, only to find Natalie striding towards her.

"The door's open."

"Which door?"

"The big one. Come and take a look."

Her brain still fogged from sleep, Margot had difficulty believing it. Without uttering a word, she walked straight past Natalie and went out through the thick plastic curtain. The steel door was wide open; the green light that had woken her was coming from the next corridor.

"It was like that when I found it," Natalie explained.

"Have you been out there?"

"I only saw it a minute ago. I was coming to fetch you."

Margot felt a sudden urge to flee. Fearing a trap, however, she held back. She exchanged an uncertain look with Natalie, who, for once, seemed reluctant to take the lead. Margot looked back at the plastic curtain, not sure why she was even hesitating. Anything was better than staying in that place.

Keeping their wits about them, they stepped through the door. They walked to the end of the corridor and found the next door unlocked. It opened onto a much wider corridor where the emergency lighting was on. At regular intervals, a large capital 'D' was painted on the wall. In silence, they pushed through a further set of doors and continued along another long corridor. It was like being lost in the world's biggest, most depressing hospital; the only thing missing were coloured lines to follow. Finally, a bright white light appeared before them.

They approached yet another pair of doors. They peered through wired glass observation panels into a space where people were milling around. No one seemed to have noticed them.

"They don't look like militia," Natalie whispered.

Margot didn't recognise any of them from the group that had come to question them. One of them must have been in his seventies. A couple of young men were laughing and joking. A man and a woman walked by, yawning, looking like they'd not long got out of bed. The thought they'd been kidnapped by a band of rogue hippies crossed her mind until she remembered all that weaponry in the warehouse. They watched them for a few moments until Natalie unilaterally decided to go in.

Margot held her breath, but no one batted an eyelid. A man walking by turned to look at her, but then carried on walking, completely unsurprised. One of the young men even smiled at her before he and his companion turned to move on. There was no sense of malice in the air. After a few seconds, Margot came out from behind the door.

Everyone appeared to be heading in the same direction; it seemed only natural to follow them. They arrived in a busier place where several corridors converged. Most of the people were heading through an opening labelled 'B-wing', but this time before Natalie could do something impulsive, Margot grabbed her arm. She pulled her to one side and pointed to another sign, this one spelling the word 'EXIT.'

No one was paying them any attention. In silent agreement, they followed the signs through a series of short corridors until they sighted a fire escape door. Margot quickened her pace, her heart pounding with excitement as they approached, but just as she allowed herself to think they'd escaped, a voice came from behind:

"Stop."

They turned sharply.

"I wouldn't go out there if I were you."

Three men were watching them from the other end of the corridor. Margot quickly recalibrated.

"Why not?"

The men appeared amused, almost as if they were laughing at them rather than trying to warn them off. Choosing to ignore them, Margot turned to Natalie and lowered her voice, "As soon as we get through that door, run as fast as you can. Okay?"

Natalie looked unsure, but then nodded her agreement.

A panic latch made the door easy to open. They looked out into a sandbagged alley, the ground rising on either side. It was a bright sunny morning, and after being cooped up in that laboratory for eighteen hours, the smell of fresh air was a tonic. Despite her own instruction, Margot hesitated, conscious of the men still watching them, smirks on their faces, keeping their distance. Was this some kind of prank? She took one step over the threshold, then almost jumped out of her skin at the sound of a dog barking aggressively. Something that looked very much like a Rottweiler came charging down the sandbagged alley towards them.

They were back inside in less than a second, slamming the

door so hard it echoed. The dog threw itself against the metal barrier with such force that Margot jumped again. She flushed as she looked back at the laughing men.

Amusement over, the pranksters went on their way.

———

The smell of food cooking drew them back to the place where the corridors met. Margot's stomach began to churn, and she realised that she was in fact very, very thirsty. They tagged onto a steady stream of people making their way down one of the main corridors and followed them into a large, noisy room. Margot realised it was the mess hall. Dozens of people were sat at benches on either side of two very long tables, eating and drinking with gusto. Seated at the far end of one of the tables was the blond man who had spoken to them last night. He noticed them, but didn't seem at all surprised. Margot scanned the crowd for the builder and his spotty companion until she was interrupted by a nudge from behind. She turned to find a man pointing to a stack of trays at the end of a counter where the food was being served. It seemed they were being invited to have breakfast.

Reflexively, Margot thanked the man. The world became surreal as Natalie and she took their places in the line of people waiting to be served, just like workers at a staff canteen. The kitchen was a hive of activity, with two men in chefs' outfits doing most of the work. There was plenty on offer, and it all smelled good. Maybe they were a cult, and this show of friendliness was a prelude to brainwashing them, though not everyone here was friendly, Margot reminded herself. Someone had taken a shot at her, and the person responsible was probably sitting at one of these tables.

Regardless of what the truth might be, the various dishes on offer soon had Margot's attention. The array of food was impressive, and Margot loaded her plate with Parma ham, sliced cheese, pain grillé and half a dozen little plastic tubs of butter, jam and honey. Behind her in the queue, all Natalie took was an apple. Margot also picked up a 2-litre bottle of mineral water and chugged some down as they shuffled along. They each had a coffee. Best of all, when they got to the end, there was nothing to pay.

Trays in hand, they stepped away from the counter. The surreal nature of the scene continued as they stood, scanning the tables for somewhere to sit. There was a space on the bench directly in front of them, but a man further down noticed their predicament and shuffled up to make space. It seemed rude not to accept his offer. After feeding her long legs over the bench, Natalie got a hipster for company, while Margot had to sit next to the man who'd shuffled up. She started eating her breakfast, trying to convince herself that what they were doing was perfectly normal.

Her eyes travelled around the room as she ate, taking it all in. A melting pot of faces surrounded them: hippies next to hipsters, studious-looking men with glasses opposite women with weather-beaten faces. The oldest looked about eighty, the youngest in his late teens. The skinheads were probably the most intimidating, with their neck tattoos and their vacant, nihilistic expressions. But despite the differences in appearance, the mood around the table was convivial. Almost everyone was talking, yet there was no sense of confrontation. Whatever bond these people shared, it was a strong one.

Margot glanced over her shoulder, hoping to catch sight of the builder. It took her a while to spot him, eating with his head down. Beside him was the woman with the black hair and neck scarf, wearing the same pink hoodie. Margot was transported back to that Saturday night in Narbonne. *Nice watch.* The briefcase full of cash. The force of that punch. She glanced their way two or three times, and then watched as he went to the counter to get more food. In a room full of oddballs, he certainly blended in. He looked a little jumpy. As he waited at the counter, his eyes darted around, assessing and evaluating everything. He caught Margot's eye as he returned to his seat, but he gave no reaction.

A burst of laughter brought Margot's attention back to her own table. The group around her had been discussing the situation in Russia, and the man beside her nudged Margot's arm and asked for her opinion. Reluctant to get involved, Margot indicated her mouth was too full to speak. Despite the friendly atmosphere, she could hear some extremist views being expressed. There was talk of the Berlin bombings, and the word 'patriot' was being bandied around. If alarm bells hadn't already been ringing in Margot's mind, they certainly were now.

It took her all of ten minutes to clear her plate. Beside her, Natalie had long finished nibbling her apple. Everyone around them was still busily talking, and Margot began to feel anxious and self-conscious. She sat, staring at her hands, desperate to avoid being drawn into any of their discussions. When it became too much to bear, she grabbed their coffee cups and rose from her chair. "I'll get us a refill," she said, and headed back to the counter.

She chose a circuitous route, one that would take her past the builder. She stared at the back of his head as she walked by, wondering what he was thinking. Neither he nor his companion looked round.

At the counter, Margot asked for two coffees. While she was waiting, the blond man got up out of his seat and headed for the door. On an impulse, Margot left the coffees and went after him.

She caught up with him in the corridor. "Excuse me," she said, touching his arm.

He turned in surprise. For a moment, Margot caught a glimpse of someone very different – a little boy who was not used to being touched.

"Yes?" he asked irritably.

"Can we have our phones back, please?"

"No."

"Why not?"

He blinked several times. "Phones aren't allowed in here. Besides, you won't get a signal."

"We got a signal outside, but something was jamming it."

He looked her in the eye. Perhaps he wasn't used to being questioned so directly. Two of the men he was with closed in, but Margot didn't back off. "Are we free to leave?"

"We're not in the business of taking prisoners."

"Then call off your dogs and let us go."

He firmly shook his head. "The dogs are there for our protection. You never know who might be snooping around in the woods." If he was making a joke, his eyes weren't in on it.

Margot's anger began to rise. "So what do you expect us to do – sit around, twiddling our thumbs?"

"You can do whatever you like. Try talking to people. You might learn something."

Just then, a noisy group of people spilled out of the mess hall. As a tide of bodies passed close behind her back, Margot sensed someone touch her rear, though when she spun round, there were too many faces to see who it might have been. She turned back, but the blond man and his companions had gone, vanished into the crowd of departing people. Frustrated, Margot went back to the mess hall.

The room had quickly emptied. A few people were standing at the counter, returning their dirty crockery, but the builder and his friend had gone. Natalie came over to join her. "What happened?"

Margot folded her arms, stumped. "Unless we want to take our chances with the dogs, it looks like we're stuck here for now." But she wouldn't remain defeated for long. One way or another, she would find a way out.

They collected their trays and dutifully returned them to the kitchen. Out of habit, Margot reached into her back pocket for her phone, only to find her fingertips touching a piece of paper instead. Curiously, she took it out. It was a photocopy of a floor plan, the room D-229 circled in red ink. Scribbled at the top was a handwritten message: *Meet me here in one hour.*

·

23

The floor plan showed a cross-shaped building with four wings labelled A to D. If Margot was reading it correctly, the mess hall occupied a large space in A-wing. From there, a hand-drawn red line worked its way down a series of corridors into D-wing, and then up a staircase to room 229, which appeared to be on the second floor.

They were soon the only ones left in the mess hall, except for the people cleaning up in the kitchen, banging pots and pans. Spotting the note in Margot's hand, Natalie was keen to see what had grabbed her attention.

"It was in my back pocket," Margot explained.

"Is this from the cop?"

"I guess so." The noisy group in the corridor, someone touching her rear – the builder could easily have slipped it in as he'd walked by.

Assuming they were under surveillance, Margot tucked the note away. When she scanned the walls, however, there didn't seem to be any cameras. These people were either remarkably trusting or extremely confident that no one was going to escape with their secrets.

Margot pointed to the door they'd come in by. They found their way back to the room where the corridors met, and from there located the entrance to D-wing. While no one was watching, they slipped through the doorway.

Following the red line on the map, they continued down a long corridor. Emergency lights lit their way, but after two or three turns, they were back in the dark.

"Any battery left on your phone?"

Natalie switched it on. "Five per cent."

"Wonderful."

Not that it made much difference – the torchlight barely extended a dozen meters before being overwhelmed by the inky darkness.

They blundered along. The floor was littered with debris and wet in places. Water was dripping from a pipe running along the ceiling. There were numerous doors – most had dents in them or handles hanging loose. Everywhere Margot looked there were signs of destruction. Hard, cold objects imbued with a past full of anger. A little ghoul inside her wanted to open every one of them, uncover its secrets, find out exactly what had once gone on here, but there wasn't time. Five per cent battery wasn't going to last very long.

They came to the stairwell indicated on the plan. A sign guided them up to 201-229. Beyond that, the signs ran out, so Margot started counting the doors with her hand. "This must be it," she said, tapping gently on what she reckoned was 229.

The hinges creaked noisily as they opened it. Natalie's light revealed a box-shaped room with a barrel-vaulted ceiling, along with two arched windows covered with louvred shutters. A vertical stanchion looked like it had once held up a floor, but the concrete was broken and lay in chunks at their feet. The ends of cut pipes and torn cables protruded from the walls. A partitioned-off area in the corner looked more promising, but there was nothing behind it. Noticing that one of the shutters hadn't been fixed very securely, Margot moved to the window and with a little effort managed to open it. Peering out, she looked down on a small, drab courtyard. It offered no means of escape, but it did provide some light.

"What now?" Natalie asked.

"We wait, I suppose."

Margot looked at her watch. It had only taken them ten minutes to get there. He'd said an hour.

They looked for somewhere to sit. Margot chose a lump of concrete to perch on while Natalie leaned against an old wooden workbench. Silence fell. Margot wasn't in the mood for talking. Or maybe she just wasn't in the mood for talking to Natalie. After a little while, the younger woman's impatience got the better of her and she got up and went to look out from the door. She came back after a few moments, disappointed.

"Did you hear what they were saying at the table? Calling each other 'brother' and 'comrade.'"

"Perhaps they're communists," Margot replied.

"Whatever they are, they're seriously deranged."

Margot thought of all those weapons in the warehouse. Guns coupled with ideology were a dangerous combination. Irritatingly, Natalie started pacing back and forth.

"Why do you suppose he wants to meet us?"

"Who said it was a man? It could be her."

"The insurance lady?" Surprised, Natalie shook her head. "It's not her."

"How can you be sure?"

"*Mamie* said she was nice. And she was too young to be an undercover cop."

Probably true, but it didn't stop Margot from hoping Natalie would be proved wrong.

Thankfully, her annoying companion stopped pacing after a

few more minutes. She sulkily returned to the workbench and contented herself with brushing dirty marks off her trousers.

Time slowly ticked by. Fifty-five minutes after finding the note, Margot thought she heard a noise. She went to the door to investigate, but the corridor was still empty.

She was about to go back in when an amorphous grey shape appeared out of nowhere. The next thing she knew, a hand was pushing firmly into her sternum and forcing her backwards into the room. When the hand stopped pushing, Margot was stunned to find the builder from Narbonne glaring into her face.

After a rapid check of the room, he returned to close the door, then quickly marched back. "What the hell are you doing here?"

There was steel in his voice, anger in his eyes. Margot took a moment to recover.

"You told us to meet you here."

"Don't be smart. In the base, I mean."

There were few people in Margot's life who had truly intimidated her, but under his gaze she felt half her normal size.

"How did you get past the fence?" he persisted.

"We climbed over it," Natalie responded combatively, crossing the room to join them. "It wasn't that hard."

"You were lucky you didn't trip one of the snares."

"Do we look stupid?"

"You were stupid to come here."

"Oh really? If you're so smart, why did you lead us here?"

He shot her an angry look before switching back to Margot. "You were told to stay away."

"And *you* conned my grandmother out of forty thousand euros," Natalie persisted, determined not to be ignored.

"We conned her out of nothing."

"Yes you did! You took a bag full of cash from her."

"The old woman got what she deserved."

Natalie's eyes blazed with anger. "You bastard!" She swung her right arm, aiming for his face, but he was too quick. He caught her wrist long before her hand got anywhere near his face.

He didn't let go. Natalie struggled to free herself, whimpering like a puppy as he squeezed, harder and harder. Something primal seemed to have taken over him.

"Let. Go. Of. My. Hand!" Natalie said through gritted teeth.

But the builder continued to hold onto it, making a point. Finally, after bringing Natalie to the point of tears, he released her. "Now do yourself a favour and shut up."

Natalie rubbed her wrist, glaring daggers.

Margot moved to her side. She did what she could to comfort her, but Natalie looked like she was in the mood to claw the skin from his face.

"To be fair," Margot said, "if you go around stealing from people you can't expect them to sit back and do nothing."

"Forget about the money. You're not getting it back. All you need to think about is staying alive."

"Who are these people?"

"The less you know the better."

"Oh come on. He suggested we talk to them. He said we might learn something."

A look of uncertainty crossed his face. He cast a cautious glance back at the door.

"We know you work for the GIGN," Margot continued, making his eyes snap back to her. "Maybe you could start by telling us your real name. I'm guessing it's not Rémy Demis."

Noticing the window was uncovered, he strode over there and looked out. He closed the damaged shutter, but not far enough to shut out all of the light. Returning, he stood right next to them, his face mere inches from theirs.

"My name is Dion. That's all I'm telling you. You do anything

Red Summer | 241

to blow my cover and I swear it'll be the last thing you'll do. I'll do what I can to protect you, but you got yourself into this. Don't expect me to get you out."

"He said we were free to leave."

"Sébastien's not going to let you leave. You step out of that front door and you're dead. If the dogs don't get you, the man-traps will."

"Sébastien's the blond guy?"

Dion nodded.

"And who are these people – terrorists?"

He regarded her as if she were naïve. "They don't see them-selves as terrorists. They're fighting for a cause."

"And what cause is that?"

"Nothing specific. General unhappiness with the state of the world."

"And he's their leader?"

Dion nodded again.

"What are they spending all that money on?"

"You've seen the warehouse."

"If these people are terrorists," Natalie put in, "then I want to know about it."

"So you can do what exactly – ask them to stop?"

"Isn't that your job?"

He gave her a smouldering look. Still massaging her wrist, Natalie backed off.

"Why were you sent here?" Margot asked.

"To gather intelligence."

"Are they planning some kind of attack?"

"I can't say."

"They must be planning something. There's enough weaponry in that warehouse to start a war."

"What I'm doing here is classified. You need to forget every-thing you've seen and stop asking questions."

Margot changed tack. "Where's your friend?"

He frowned. "Who?"

"Your partner in crime."

"Esmée?"

Nice watch. "Is she a cop, too?"

He scowled. "Don't be ridiculous."

"You're not allowed to break the law," Natalie interjected. "Whether you're a cop or not."

"And you're trespassing on Ministry of Defence land," Dion fired back. "How many laws do you imagine you're breaking right now? What I'm allowed to do is between me and my handlers. My conscience is clear."

After a short pause, Margot said, "I assume you have a contact on the outside."

Dion hesitated, but then nodded.

"How do you get in touch with them?"

"A secure messaging service."

"Have you told them we're in here?"

He shot her another irritated look. Without giving a reply, he went to the door, listened out for a while, then came back.

"That's enough questions. I have to go."

Margot reached for his arm. "Wait a second... What are we supposed to do?"

"Does anyone know you're here?"

"No."

"Then I suggest you stay out of the way and don't make trouble. Stick to the places where the lights are on. And a word of advice – don't approach Sébastien again. Next time he might not be so polite."

"How long do you expect us to stay here?" Natalie asked, indignant.

"As long as it takes. If I can find a way to get you out, I'll contact you. But don't come to me, not for any reason."

"And where are we going to sleep?"

"There's plenty of space in the bunkhouse."

"What's to stop us taking one of those guns from the warehouse and shooting our way out?" Natalie asked, apparently serious.

Dion grinned, taken aback. "Do you know how to fire an assault rifle?"

"Aim the barrel and pull the trigger," Natalie replied sarcastically. "It can't be that hard."

He almost laughed. "Right. If you want to try that, go ahead."

Margot cleared her throat. "Don't worry. We'll stay out of the way."

He looked at both of them in turn. For a moment, he seemed uncertain. It was almost like there were two different people inside him, neither of whom was quite sure of what they were doing. He quickly refocused.

"After I leave this room, stay here for another ten minutes. Got that?"

Margot nodded.

A moment later he was gone.

24

Dion shone his torch into every dark crevice as he made his way back to the Command Centre, inspecting every shadow, checking each concealed doorway. The skin on the back of his neck prickled when he thought he saw a movement. He kicked a wooden box out of the way, shone his light into a damp corner, fully expecting someone to jump out on him. He almost looked forward to it – if it was Golem, Dion was in the mood to punch him flat. But it was just a rat, spooked by the torchlight.

He turned off his torch and walked in the dark for a while. After all this time, he reckoned he could navigate much of the base blindfold, moving through the passageways on instinct alone. In answer to the stupid woman's question, he had not told AL they were in here. It was too risky going to the radio room right now. There were too many eyes upon him, too much suspicion in the air, and in any case, there was nothing AL could do other than pull the plug, bin the whole operation, send in a snatch squad, and there was no way in the world he was going to do that.

A heavier feeling set in as Dion neared the Command Centre. Perhaps the truth was that he was more angry with himself than with either of them. The spunky one was right – he was the one who'd led them to the woods. He'd let Sébastien down, and at some point he was going to have to answer for it.

It was busy in the hub. Esmée, leaning against a wall, looked like she'd been waiting for him. "Everything all right?" she asked, coming straight over.

Dion nodded. He hadn't told her where he'd been. He hadn't told her lots of things. Maybe she was better off not knowing. He told her that he was fine, that everything was okay, and he wondered if what he really meant was that everything was fine when he was with her, that these past few days had turned his world upside down and that if it weren't for her, he might well have gone insane. She was like a ray of sunlight that had shone into his head. But he didn't say any of those things to her. He just looked into her youthful eyes, hoping she understood.

They were about to move on when Sébastien came out of the ops room. Catching Dion's eye, he asked them to wait. He briefly disappeared before returning with a plastic carrier bag. He took them to a side room and, when they were alone, opened the bag. "We're getting another van. Would you mind going to collect it?"

The bag was stuffed full of cash.

"Okay," Dion said.

"Where?" Esmée asked.

"The shopping mall in Nîmes. Jevon will take you. The guy will meet you in the car park. It's all been arranged." Sébastien handed over the bag. "There's fifteen thousand in there."

Dion held it in the air between them. It could have been full of tins of beans as far as Sébastien was concerned. In the time he'd been here, Dion must have handled more notes than he had in his entire life.

"Why another van?"

"No time to explain. Jevon's waiting in the warehouse."

Sébastien moved to usher them out, but Dion held back. Something wasn't right. Jevon was one of Sébastien's inner circle, an ex-university lecturer who'd been with the group from the beginning. He wouldn't normally be tasked with driving a van. Dion looked Sébastien in the eye, but their leader's face gave nothing away. When the pause grew longer, Sébastien reached out to shake his hand. "Good luck, brother," he said.

Good luck, or goodbye?

————

They sat up front, Dion by the door, Esmée in the middle seat. Dion pulled the seatbelt across his chest but didn't click it in. Ready for any eventuality. Over in the driver seat, he eyed Jevon up, looking to see if he was carrying a gun. There was no sign of a shoulder holster, no bulge in his pocket. Dion imagined them being driven to an out-of-the-way lay-by, told to get out, a short walk into the woods followed by a bullet in the back of the head. There was only one thing Sébastien demanded of his brothers, and that was loyalty. Let him down, and it was the last thing you would do. But once they were on their way, Jevon stuck to the main roads and took the route to Nîmes that Dion would have expected. Half an hour after setting out, he was swinging the van into the sprawling commercial zone on the outskirts of town. Dion told his paranoia to have a day off.

The looped round the huge car park, searching for the rendezvous point. Jevon finally located it, next to a car wash. No one was there so he parked in the shade. It was baking hot inside the van, even with the windows down. Jevon made a quick call and then pocketed his phone. "The guy's running late. He can't get here until noon."

Dion looked at his watch. It wasn't even ten. What were they meant to do for the next two hours? Sit in this oven and stew to death?

"Sébastien wants me back at base," Jevon went on. "Okay if I leave you two here?"

"No problem," Esmée said.

Grudgingly, Dion nodded.

After bumping fists, they got out of the van.

Standing in the shade of a tree, they watched Jevon depart. Esmée put her sunglasses on; Dion kicked the kerb, feeling like a fish out of water, marooned in the ginormous car park with fifteen thousand euros hanging from the end of his arm. Everyone else was having a normal day, shopping for sofas and shoes, booze and baguettes.

"Fancy an ice cream?" Esmée said.

Dion grinned. "Go on then."

They went off to explore.

The mall was so big you couldn't see one end from the other. According to the floor plan, it boasted ninety-five shops and sixteen restaurants. All the major high street chains were there, vying for your attention. Fancy displays behind plate glass windows screamed: *come in and buy me.* Shop assistants prowled the aisles, ready to pounce. For years, France had resisted the rise of mall culture, yet now they were everywhere, on the edge of every main town, flanked by the hypermarkets and the ubiquitous drive-thru fast-food joints.

Dion pointed to a couple of places where they could get ice cream, but Esmée carried on walking. Perhaps she wanted to buy something – there were plenty of sales on – but then, apart from the bag full of cash, they only had pocket money. Dion wondered if she had other thoughts on her mind, and after they'd traipsed from one end of the mall to the other, he jokingly asked if she'd got any powder paint on her. Esmée came out of her trance-like state and looked at him with a beatific smile on her face, like someone who'd solved one of life's great conundrums. Maybe this was what she'd been like in Monaco.

"I left it back at the camp," she replied. "Besides, I don't think many billionaires shop at Claire's, do you?"

Fortunately, there were no designer boutiques in sight.

They went to get ice cream. The place was full of little kids, and the incessant piped music was enough to turn even the most level-headed shopper into a crazed spree-killer, so they opted for smoothies to take out. They wandered across the giant car park to another huge store where a pergola alongside the storefronts gave them some shade. Strolling along, looking at ever more window displays, Dion had to remind himself that this is what normal people did with their free time. They went to the shops, they ate ice cream, they met friends for lunch. It all felt alien to him now.

They binned their empty cartons and, with an hour still to kill, went into a homeware store. It was a maze of merchandise, offering everything from beds and light fittings to hot tubs, wardrobes and barbecues. Was there any piece of homeware you *couldn't* buy in a place like this? But most of it was wants rather than needs, Dion reflected. No one *needed* to spend three hundred and fifty on an all-singing, all-dancing coffee machine when they most likely had a perfectly good one at home. He remembered a time he and his wife had been in a store like this, shopping for a new sofa. They'd disagreed about which one to get: Yvette had wanted the one that matched her new colour scheme; Dion had thought the one with the deeper seats would be a better fit for his frame. In the end, they'd got the colourful one, and then, a few years later, Yvette had changed her mind and they had trailered the once-new sofa down to the *déchèterie*. Depressing to think that most of these shiny new things would one day end up in the dump. Needing to pee, Dion went off in search of a toilet.

When he came back, it took him a while to find Esmée. He'd left her in the artificial plants department, but when he eventually located her, she was on the mezzanine level, browsing the soft furnishings. Going to her side, he found her staring at a rack of cushions. "Looking for something to spruce up the bunkhouse?"

She didn't appear to hear him. "What is the point of a cushion?"

"What?"

"These." She pointed at the shelves. The cushions stretched the entire length of the aisle and continued around the corner. There were plain ones and flowery ones, fluffy ones and shiny ones, some made out of leather, some out of suede. Cushions with scalloped edges, cushions with tassels, cushions with sparkly silver crystals sewn into them. One even had gold rhinestones fixed into the braiding, while others had words like 'amour' or 'bonjour' sewn into them. The choice was mind-boggling when you came to look.

"And look at the prices tags," Esmée went on. "Forty, fifty... *sixty*-five euros."

"Everything's expensive these days."

"For a cushion!?"

Dion shrugged. He doubted he'd ever actually purchased a cushion in his entire life, but he supposed sixty-five euros was rather a lot to ask.

"If I bought one of these," (she was not letting go) "I'd be sixty-five euros poorer, and what would I have to show for it?"

Dion regarded her steadfastly, feeling slightly confused. "Well... you'd have a cushion, wouldn't you?"

"Exactly. And what is the point of that?"

He shook his head, bemused. "You're a capitalist worse nightmare."

They strolled on.

"They do have a practical use," Dion said. "They're something nice to curl up on."

"I can roll up my hoodie if I want something nice to curl up on. I mean, seriously – who needs all these tassels and frou-frou bits?" She flicked them in disgust. A woman passing by gave them an odd look.

"You could argue it gives someone a job," Dion went on. "People have to make cushions, deliver them to the stores, stack them on shelves like these."

"And how rewarding is that? There'll you be, at the end of your days, and along comes God: 'So tell me, puny human, what did you do with your life?' Me: 'I made cushions.' God: 'Well done. Now go and make me a sandwich.'"

Dion laughed.

They turned the corner. The next aisle was bed linen and throws, then towels and lampshades. Then came something that made Esmée stop dead in her tracks. "And oh God, here we have it, the most overpriced piece of consumerist crap on the planet: scented candles."

An entire tier of shelving was devoted to them, but Esmée had failed to notice that the woman in front of them had evidently just added a dozen of the offending items to her trolley. Judging by the price tags, she must have had a hundred euros' worth in there. She seemed quite well-to-do: fake plastic face, designer shades. She'd heard what Esmée had said, and when she moved on, deliberately ran into her ankle with the trolley. Snooty bitch; Dion felt like shoving her face-first into the shelf.

"You okay?"

Esmée gave him a nod. There was a pause while she mentally chewed something over. Dion got the feeling she was not yet done.

"Wait here."

Like a lion stalking a gazelle, Esmée set off in pursuit. Dion watched from a distance as she shadowed the woman along the aisle, and then around the corner into the cutlery section. When the unfortunate gazelle left her trolley unattended, Esmée swooped. She snatched the trolley and wheeled it off into the maze, leaving the snooty bitch looking around in confusion.

It was a while before Esmée rejoined him, dusting off her hands. A job well done.

"What did you do?"

"Put everything back."

Dion grinned in disbelief.

"Come on. Let's get out of here."

They went back to the car wash. They'd only been waiting five minutes when a silver Sprinter pulled in, the registration confirming it was the one they wanted. They greeted the driver as he jumped out of the cab, then kicked the tyres, just because it seemed like the customary thing to do. Few words were exchanged as they did the deal. The driver didn't even count the cash before he handed over the keys. He wished them good luck and then set off to the bus stop like this was something he did every day of the week.

After filling up with diesel, they hit the road. The van was an old model, but the engine was fruity. A tap on the accelerator got them swiftly away from the lights. The autoroute was the quickest way back, but when they came to the junction, Dion ignored it. He switched off the sat-nav and navigated the old-fashioned way instead – read the road signs, followed the map in his head. The weather couldn't have been more perfect, and there was no rush to get back. So they stuck to the old roads whenever they could, struck lucky when they found a quiet D-road that weaved through some scenic countryside. They drove with the windows down, hot air spiralling around the cab.

"Just out of interest," Dion said, feeling playful. "What would God have on his sandwich?"

Esmée put her DMs up on the dash and gave it some thought. "I'm guessing it would be something from the ocean. Something big and meaty."

"Tuna?"

"No – bigger than tuna."

"Filet of whale?"

"No way. God loves his mammals."

"Something plain and simple, then. A fish finger butty?"

"That's more like it." Esmée snapped her fingers. "A crunchy lettuce leaf, a couple of cod goujons, and a big dollop of tartare sauce."

Dion smiled. "He would have to be careful not to spill tartare sauce down his robe."

"Wouldn't matter. God doesn't do his own washing, you know."

"I don't suppose he does. But then, he's hardly likely to get dirty, frolicking around in those fluffy white clouds all day."

"Just imagine how clean his underpants are."

Dion laughed so much he almost steered them off the road. Coming the other way, an old guy at the wheel of a camping car got the fright of his life. They drove on, a little more sedately.

"You're not religious then?" Dion asked.

"Nope."

"Me neither."

His parents had been. They'd gone to church every Sunday, could quote passages from the Bible, yet they'd thought it was perfectly okay to tie a six-year-old to a chair.

"If there is a god," Esmée went on, "why does he let good people suffer? The only conclusion is he doesn't exist."

"As simple as that?"

"You can't argue with logic."

Maybe she was right. 2 + 2 would never equal 5, no matter how much you wanted to believe it.

Esmée rummaged in the glove box. She found an old Tom Petty CD and slid it into the player, then turned up the volume on *Free Fallin'*. With the sun shining brightly and the ribbon of black tarmac unwinding before them, Dion felt happier than he had in years. He didn't want the road to end, and when the final turn came up, he was tempted to keep going. Keep heading south. Drive until the tank ran dry.

———

They were back at the base by three. The warehouse doors were open, so Dion drove straight in and parked the van in line with the others. When Esmée jumped out, however, he remained at the wheel. All the anxiety he'd been feeling at the start of the day came back to him. He was convinced his cover was blown, that Sébastien had found out – all those head-to-heads he'd been having with Tik. It had been bound to happen sooner or later. Dion ran through his escape plan for the umpteenth time: he would start a fire in the Command Centre, use the confusion to give himself time to get out through the hole in the gym roof. He would escape via the antennae array and hightail it through the woods. He sent a glance to the stockroom door, toying with the idea of arming himself. There was a box of Glock 17s in there, ripe for the taking.

"You coming?"

Dion snapped out of his thoughts. Esmée was looking in at him through the open window. He might have to adapt his plans. If things turned nasty, he wouldn't want her getting caught in the crossfire.

Despite his fears, everything appeared normal as they walked the corridors that led to the Command Centre. Four o'clock in the afternoon, everyone seemed relaxed. The heat of the day had worked its way through the walls, and the mess hall was sticky, full of people in tee-shirts and shorts, chatting away. Jevon acknowledged them with a nod, unsurprised to see them back. Dion caught sight of the two blonde troublemakers, keeping themselves to themselves, and although they saw him, they wisely stayed out of his way. Hopefully, they'd learned their lesson. They found Sébastien in the ops room, where Dion handed him the keys to the van.

"One Mercedes Sprinter. As ordered."

"Good work, brothers."

Sébastien paused for a moment as some people walked by, then drew them into a huddle. He seemed unusually shifty. "Can you meet me back here at midnight?"

After exchanging a glance, Dion and Esmée nodded.

"Any particular reason?"

It was Esmée who had asked the question, but it was Dion whom Sébastien looked in the eye. "We need to talk," he said, and left it at that.

25

In many ways, the base was more akin to the campus of a dot-com giant than a hotbed of political dissent. Everywhere they went, people were having earnest discussions about the implications of climate change. Bearded intellectuals stood around, swigging water from reusable bottles, talking about ocean pollution. Only the dinginess of the surroundings gave it away, although even that might have been explained as the grunge chic aesthetic favoured by a tech giant maverick. Nothing hinted that what these people were working on was not the latest version of a software package, but something more akin to France 6.0. Even the skinheads Margot and Natalie encountered as they roamed the dimly lit corridors, looking for something to do, seemed harmless enough, although word must have gone around to tolerate but not engage. Whenever Margot got the chance to ask anyone what they were doing, she was met with a blank look.

Two hours after Dion had left them to fend for themselves, they were back in the crowded mess hall, drawn by the smell of lunch. Elbow to elbow with the motley crew, Margot paid a little more attention to the conversations going on around them, and this time tried to chip in. Although she was listened to, no one engaged with her or followed up on what she'd said. The whole hour went by without any sign of Dion or Esmée, so avoiding them wasn't an issue. It wasn't until four o'clock that Margot spotted them, passing through the space where the corridors met. She watched them go into the Command Centre and then, a few minutes later, come back out again. They seemed remarkably pally all of a sudden. Margot's instinct was to follow them, but she held back. Better to do as they'd been told. For now.

As the day wore on, things quietened down, so they decided to take another look around. They steered clear of the populated areas and found themselves in a building that wasn't on the floor plan. The main corridor was illuminated, but all the side passageways were totally dark.

"I don't suppose there's any charge left on your phone?" Margot said, trying to make sense of some faded signs on the wall.

"It's flat," Natalie replied. "But I do have this." Out of nowhere, she raised a hefty Maglite, easily twelve inches long. "I found it in the mess hall," she explained, and might as well have said: *Three-nil. You lose, old timer.*

Once again, Margot had no choice but to follow Natalie's lead. She traced her hands along a smooth concrete wall as they moved along, surprised to find it was warm. Either it was a blisteringly hot day outside or they genuinely were inside a nuclear power plant. They ascended two sets of stairs. Natalie spotted an opening, but when they advanced upon it, they nearly plunged to their deaths. Before them was a disused lift shaft, the cables cut, a crumpled cube of metal at the bottom. Dust motes caught in the beam of light, rising on currents of air.

"I've never liked lifts," Natalie said with a shudder.

Imagine being trapped in one, with two ferocious rats for

company, Margot was tempted to say. Her inner voice could be cruel at times.

Almost every room they looked in was trashed and burned, either gutted by whoever had abandoned the base or ransacked by looters. Spotting a sign to the Guardhouse, Natalie led the way down a spiralling concrete ramp until they came to a barred door. The door opened onto a short central corridor lined with cells. A bucket and a bunk in each, a rusty chain fixed to a ring in the floor at one end. This time it was Margot who shuddered, remembering a similar place she'd visited recently.

Without waiting for the light, she turned around and blindly retraced her steps. Natalie caught up and guided them back to the corridor.

Another random turn led them to a metal door, which, when opened, triggered a series of lights to come on. They walked onto a gangway crossing a room that looked like a former armoury. Beneath their feet, a rats' maze of heavy-duty racking covered an area the size of a tennis court. All the weapons were gone, and the many ammunition boxes that were scattered around looked empty. Peering down through the metal grid floor, Margot spotted an inner room, more like a cage, that reminded her of the Cabinet War Rooms. One wall was covered in a map dotted with red pins – some kind of battle plan, by the looks of it. Papers were scattered across the desk along with several modern laptops and some aluminium drinking bottles. It all looked recent. Margot was keen to take a closer look, but the only way down was a locked ladder. Hearing a noise, they quickly moved on.

Back into another dark corridor. They should have brought a ball of thread, Margot thought, fearing they might never get out. But then the torch picked out a homemade sign pointing to the Command Centre, and soon they were back at the place where the corridors met. They asked someone the way to the bunkhouse. A short walk took them to an anteroom where two pairs of sliding doors were labelled A and B. Both led to an identical large space filled with rows of bare metal bunkbeds. Screwing up her nose, Natalie ventured no further than the threshold. "I'd sooner sleep in the room with the gurneys," she said, stepping away.

Margot took her place and sniffed the air. Fifty men sleeping in a communal space... Natalie did have a point.

A third door was labelled "STORES". This one was full of all manner of bedding and supplies. Much of it looked like army surplus. Whatever they were up to, they were in it for the long haul. The final doorway led to the latrines.

Margot looked at her watch. Twenty past six. Someone earlier had told them dinner was served at seven. She looked at Natalie. "You hungry?"

Natalie pulled another face.

Margot sighed, hot and fed up. "All right," she said, frustrated. "What do you want to do?"

"Well I'm not sleeping in there. We'll have to find somewhere else."

"Like where – the on-site Hilton?"

"Ha. Ha."

Margot gave up.

They took their pick from the stores – sleeping bags, blankets, towels, and toothbrushes. Fully loaded, they looked for somewhere a little more appealing to bed down. They found a hallway a short walk down from the bunkhouse that didn't appear to lead anywhere. The floor was reasonably clean, and with the doors closed they would have some privacy. Margot dumped her things on the floor. Her clothes felt sticky and she was craving a wash but had to wait while Natalie made herself the perfect little bed. She used one of the blankets as an underlay and carefully rolled out the sleeping bag on top. A second blanket served as a pillow protector. She improvised a bedside table from a concrete block, and after converting the Maglite to candle mode, used it as a lamp. Margot watched in disbelief. Shame there wasn't a teddy bear back in that store cupboard.

"You done?"

Natalie primped it a little more before finally nodding, completely missing (or ignoring) the implicit sarcasm.

They returned to the latrines. Natalie was horrified to discover that there was no segregation. Stalls on either side, a circular *pissoire* in the centre. The sanitaryware looked like it had been built to last. Next door was the bathhouse where one large communal shower ran along the wall. Everything apart from the ceiling was clad in white tiles, which, for the most part, were spotlessly clean. It looked like one of the few places in the base that hadn't been left to rot. Margot tried to imagine what life must have been like for the base's original occupants. Young soldiers, miles from home.

Thankfully, with everyone else having dinner, the place was deserted. Margot quickly stripped off. "Shout if anyone comes."

She got into the shower, opened one of the valves, and waited for the water to warm up. Natalie looked on aghast as Margot danced under the lukewarm spray for five minutes. She must have looked a comical sight, but it was marvellously invigorating.

Natalie handed her a towel when she came out, her face screwed up again.

"You not having one?" Margot asked.

"No thanks." She couldn't have looked more disgusted if she'd tried. Her loss.

After brushing their teeth, they made their way back to their makeshift beds without another word.

———

Natalie took as long getting into her bed as she had making it. First, she took off her shoes and placed them side by side at the foot of the sleeping bag. Then, she adjusted her pillow to make sure it was sitting dead centre on the hood of the sleeping bag. She started to unbutton her jeans as if planning to take them off, but then had second thoughts and buttoned them back up again. She seemed the kind of person for whom everything had to be perfect, and only when everything was finally done to her satisfaction did she slip, fully clothed, into the sleeping bag. She turned off the torch without even asking if Margot was ready.

It was far too hot under the covers, so Margot flung her blanket aside. Bored, she looked at her watch. It hadn't even turned eight o'clock. In the total absence of natural light, it was hard to know what time of day it was; it could have been midnight, it could have been ten in the morning. The silence deepened. Margot grew increasingly frustrated. It wouldn't have been so bad if they had something to talk about, but she clutched at straws trying to think of something to say to her prickly companion. Her stomach rumbled. It had certainly been a mistake skipping dinner.

"I'm hungry."

Natalie tutted loudly. "Do you ever stop thinking about food?"

"Occasionally."

Margot had to admit, she was one of those people who looked forward to what they were going to eat the next day.

"Wouldn't hurt you to skip a meal or two," Natalie mumbled, adjusting her bedding.

Margot flinched, not sure she'd heard correctly. "What did you just say?"

"Nothing." It sounded like she was speaking into her pillow. "Other than you could do with shedding a few pounds."

"Thanks."

"Sorry – did I say that out loud?"

Margot recalled the look she'd received when she'd come out of the shower. *Bitch*. "You think I'm overweight?"

"Not really." (Normal voice). "For someone your age." (Sotto voce).

Cheeky minx.

"I suppose you get by on a lettuce leaf per day."

"Better than shovelling pastries in my mouth."

"Thanks again."

"You're welcome."

Margot thumped her pillow.

She tossed onto her side and stared belligerently at the wall. It came to everyone eventually, no matter how few lettuce leaves you nibbled on. In her forties, she had resolved to exercise more and had got back into her swimming, but all it took was one short lapse and the pounds piled back on. It was a constant battle with gravity. "Wait till you get older," she responded moodily. Gravity always wins.

They lay with their backs to each other for a while, but Margot didn't stay angry for long. At least age brought wisdom, she reflected. You learned to rise above these things. She rolled over onto her back again.

"I remember when people were obsessed with size zero, but who cares? Pastries are a lot more fun than dieting."

Natalie, it seemed, had given up talking to her. Margot carried on regardless.

"This reminds me of boarding school. I used to lie there with my eyes wide open, thinking of ways to escape." And wondering why her parents had abandoned her. It really hadn't seemed fair.

Natalie still didn't respond. She'd started making some heavy breathing noises, but Margot wasn't fooled. "I know you're not asleep."

An exasperated sigh came from the other side of the room. "What do you want?"

"To talk."

"Why?"

"Can you think of something better to do?"

"Yes – lie still and go to sleep."

"Bor-ing. It's only eight o'clock. How can you even think about sleeping?"

"Quite easily, thanks."

"When I was your age I rarely went to bed before midnight."

"Good for you. Was that when the world was in black and white?"

"Totally. We didn't even have electricity. Or cars. Or beds, for that matter. We used to have to go down to the—"

"All right!" Natalie snapped. She pulled the pillow from her face so hard that Margot felt the draught. (Margot smiled devilishly.) "What do you want to talk about?"

"I don't know. Something. Anything." Despite having got the better of the little exchange, Margot was again stuck for something to say. "What would you normally be doing at this time of night?"

"Right now? Sitting in my apartment, replying to emails probably."

"That doesn't sound like fun."

"It isn't. But it's my job. And it's pretty intense at times."

"Do you enjoy it?"

The question seemed to stump her. Margot imagined she was on a high salary but had maybe reached that stage of life when she was questioning whether it was worth it. Kudos to her for turning her life around, she supposed. It can't have been easy growing up with a drug-addicted mother. Perhaps her obsessive neatness had been her way of coping, bringing some order to the chaos.

"It's not so bad," Natalie eventually replied. "I don't get much time to socialise."

"Sucks."

"But I do get to travel, so that's good."

"Any kids?"

"No." A pause, then, "What about you?"

This time it was Margot who went quiet. That particular well of sadness was never far away, threatening to pull her in. "No," she said, and left it at that. "You got a partner, or a husband?"

"Not at the moment."

"Me neither. I do hope someone is going to start missing us. Otherwise, who knows how long we'll be in here?"

"You reckon he's going to help us?"

"The cop?"

A worried tone had crept into Natalie's voice. "He didn't seem very keen."

They couldn't really blame him. They'd jeopardised his operation and put his life in danger. Years of work might have gone down the drain, and it was all for nothing. There was no way they would be getting Madame Janvier's money back. And worse: *Sébastien's never going to let you leave.* They'd seen too many faces. Discovered that bomb factory. Found the location of his lair. They would have to find a way of escaping soon.

"If I did have children," Natalie went on, "I wouldn't send them to boarding school."

"Good on you. I suppose the only consolation is you get to put your parents in a home when they're older. See how they like it."

After that, the conversation dried up. Margot turned onto her side and plumped up her pillow, her high spirits replaced by anxiety. Eyes wide open, she stared into the darkness, finding it hard to believe what was happening. On the one hand, it seemed she was worrying over nothing – no one had been hostile towards them, the food was good, and they had somewhere warm and reasonably comfortable to sleep. Yet, with every fibre of her being, Margot loathed the prospect of spending another day in their company.

26

They were back in the Command Centre at five to midnight. Sébastien asked them to wait in one of the offices while he went to find a couple of the others.

Five metal chairs were lined up against the wall. Esmée sat down, but Dion was too keyed up to settle. He moved from the desk to the door and back again. "Where's he gone? He said he would only be a minute." He'd been gone five.

"He said he wants to speak to everything at the same time," Esmée said. Then, with a little annoyance: "Will you please stop doing that?"

"Doing what?"

"Pacing."

Dion froze, realising what he'd been doing. It was a classic sign of a man on the edge. He'd learned that in a class once. He made himself sit down.

Two minutes later, the door opened. Sébastien came in, followed by two beards and one of the skinheads. Dion instinctively rose to his feet. He knew the beards well; they'd been in the group longer than he had, but the skinhead was a recent arrival, a kid from the slums of Paris. Dion was immediately suspicious. The skinhead hadn't been integrating. Lazy and argumentative, he'd been picking fights and ridiculing some of the others. And, if the rumours were true, one of the beards had also been causing trouble, questioning Sébastien's leadership and demanding the group move to more radical methods. Why would Sébastien bring the five of them together in this room? They closed the door behind them and pulled out chairs. Sébastien perched on an edge of the desk.

"Dion, please take a seat."

Dion realised he was the only one standing. All five faces were looking at him as if he were doing something wrong. Finally, he sat down.

"Thank you," Sébastien said calmly. "And thank you all for joining me."

The skinhead gave him a pissed-off look. In his case, it probably hadn't been optional.

"I know this all feels a bit cloak and dagger," Sébastien went on. "Normally we share everything in the group, but these are not normal times. What I'm about to say to you is for our ears only. It's not to be discussed with anyone else. If any of you feel that's too great a burden, I invite you to leave now." He indicated the door.

No one moved.

Sébastien seemed pleased.

"We've set a date," he said.

The five of them regarded him in surprise.

"For the bombing campaign?" the older beard asked, sounding hopeful.

Sébastien nodded. "The main event."

"When?" Dion asked.

"August the 28th. A day that will go down in history."

Less than a month away. Dion committed the date to memory.

"We still have a few loose ends to tie up, but we'll start spreading the word in the next few hours. There's no going back now, brothers."

The two beards looked pleased. The skinhead still seemed peeved.

"So why can't we tell anyone?" Esmée asked.

"Monika has been working on a whole range of strategies. August the 28th is the earliest we can implement the main attack, but given what happened in Berlin, we want to keep the momentum going."

"By doing what?" one of the beards asked.

"Let's call it an *amuse-bouche* ahead of the main course. A simple plan: five cities, five simultaneous attacks. A lone operator will leave a backpack full of explosives in a busy shop, and then walk out and detonate it remotely."

He paused to let that sink in. There were mixed reactions around the room: the beards remained excited, the skinhead frowned, Esmée shifted on her seat, looking a little uncomfortable.

"What kind of shops?" the beard asked.

"Top-end stores in high-profile locations. Monika has worked it all out."

"It's a risky strategy," the other beard commented, though he didn't seem fazed.

"You could be looking at dozens of fatalities," Dion put in.

Sébastien nodded, unperturbed. "There'll be a security crackdown, of course. But just when they think it's all over, we'll hit them with the big one." He slammed his right fist into his left palm with force. Sometimes, the zeal in their leader's eyes was intoxicating. "We have to make our voices heard, brothers. And if that means taking deadly action, then so be it. You can't break down a corrupt system by knocking politely on the front door."

"I'm guessing we are the five," Esmée said.

"The reason I've chosen you is that you've each impressed me in some way. Some of our brothers are squeamish when it comes to the more extreme methods. That's not a criticism, we're a broad church. But you are different. I wouldn't have asked you if I didn't think you had the stomach for it."

"And if we say no?"

Sébastien shrugged. "It's entirely up to you. What I'm giving you here is the chance to volunteer."

Both the beards looked up for it, but the skinhead and Esmée were less forthcoming. A hundred competing thoughts were running wild in Dion's head. The difference between him saying yes or no could be the flip of a coin.

"When are you thinking of doing it?" Esmée asked.

"Saturday."

She flinched. "That's pretty short notice."

"Everything's set up. It'll take thirty-six hours to get everyone into position. You'll leave the base on Thursday night and then make your own way to the target locations."

And afterwards? Dion wondered. What was the plan for that?

"All I need from you now is a simple yes or no. But whether you're in or not, it's crucial that no one outside this room knows what we've discussed. I can't stress that enough. I want the rest of the group focussed on August the 28th, not distracted by this operation. Other than myself and Monika, the only people who know are the five of you. I'm sure I can count on you all."

Nods of agreement went around the room. Dion looked away.

Sébastien got off the desk. "So, lady and gents, it's decision time. Are you in or out?"

He came to them one at a time. The beards nodded without hesitation. The skinhead paused before giving a sharp nod of his head. Sébastien moved on to Esmée. "What about you, Esmée?"

Esmée thought about it for a moment, then nodded. Finally, Sébastien turned to Dion.

"Dion?"

Dion looked at Esmée. He waited, but she didn't look back at him.

"If you don't feel up to it, I can ask someone else," Sébastien prompted. "For an operation like this, you need to be fully committed."

But he didn't need any more encouragement. Dion had already made up his mind. "I'm in," he said, and felt a little fizz of excitement.

27

Margot tossed and turned for the few remaining hours of the night. By five o'clock, she was wide awake and itching to get up. She clambered across to Natalie's side of the room, patted the floor until she found the Maglite, and then switched it on. It wasn't intentional, but the light shone directly into her sleeping companion's face.

"Sorry," Margot said, only half regretting it. Natalie covered her eyes.

"What time is it?"

"Five o'clock."

Groan.

A few minutes later, they staggered off to the washroom together.

They were in the mess hall by seven, waiting in line for breakfast. Margot was starving, but conscious of Natalie's eyes on her plate, she resisted the urge to load up on pastries. She settled for a bowl of *fromage blanc* instead. Along with two pieces of *pain grillé*. And a slice of holey cheese. Natalie had an apple.

More people came in. The tables filled up, and although the mood seemed a little more subdued than the day before, everyone remained polite towards them. Margot kept a keen eye out for Dion and Esmée, and when they appeared, watched them take their seats on the other table, head to head, engrossed in each other's company. No one would have guessed they were the same moody couple she'd encountered at the hotel in Narbonne. As soon as they'd finished their breakfast, they took their trays back to the kitchen and left, looking like they were joined at the hip. Dion didn't even glance their way as the pair of them went out the door.

"Where's he off to?" Margot wondered out loud.

"Looks like he's forgotten us."

Whatever he was doing, he didn't seem in any great hurry to help.

Twenty minutes later, when the others had left, Margot became despondent. All she could see ahead of her was another long day of boredom. As they nursed their second cups of coffee, she entertained a few wild ideas: they could steal a steak from the kitchen, use it to throw the dogs off the scent, make a dash for the fence. How far could it be – a kilometre or two? She could cover that ground in, what... nine or ten minutes? They would be fine just so long as they didn't stumble into a man-trap. Margot shuddered as she imagined the rusty steel jaws snapping shut on her leg, blood pouring out, the dogs honing in. It was far too dangerous to risk. By nine o'clock, the kitchen crew had washed up and gone, leaving them totally alone. With nothing else to do, Margot suggested they go for another wander.

They stuck to the main corridors this time. They followed the signs to the Command Centre and found it full of busy people. When someone noticed them, they were told they weren't allowed in.

Another corridor took them to a well-lit room where a large printer was spewing out sheets of A3. Beside it was a long desk where four people formed a production line. The first was folding the sheets, the next two collating and binding them, the final one was stacking completed pamphlets into a cardboard box. Margot recognised the box-stacker as the man she'd sat next to at breakfast yesterday. When he appeared to recognise her, too, she approached and took a closer look at what they were doing. The pamphlet featured a red banner bearing the title "*La Vérité*".

"Would you like to take a look?"

The man offered her a copy. The headline on the front page read: *Has France lost its ideals?* Below it was a picture of Philippe Rio, the well-known French Communist, once voted "the best mayor in the world". Margot accepted it from him and skimmed a few pages. It was very wordy, the text interspersed with a few amusing cartoons. The articles she glanced at covered a range of topics from politics to history to economics. She was intrigued enough to ask the man a question, but was distracted by a voice from behind:

"You must be the ones everyone's talking about."

They turned to find a short woman with grey hair approaching. Her tanned, leathery face made it difficult to discern whether she was smiling or not. Feeling they'd done something wrong, Margot handed back the copy of the magazine. "Sorry," she said as the woman drew near.

"What did you think?"

The woman seemed interested to know. She was probably a foot shorter than Margot, but Margot hesitated before replying, not wanting to risk antagonising her.

"Some of the slogans seemed a bit trite. Real life is more complicated than a soundbite."

"We know that. But slogans motivate people, and motivated people are the most potent force in the world. Don't you agree?"

Margot nodded without conviction. The woman spoke with the calm assurance of a zealot explaining their religion as if there could be no doubt about the truth of her words. If you didn't agree, you needed to be educated. She was keen to talk and went on to ask them a lot of questions, seemingly genuinely interested in why they'd come to the base. Margot thought it wise to keep her opinions to herself. There was no point trying to reason with people like that. Their minds had been made up, their brains washed. When Natalie explained about her grandmother's money, the woman listened patiently, but then proceeded to lecture them about Marx's monetary theory and how the concept of private ownership didn't exist. Like Sébastien, she claimed that the group had done nothing wrong by taking the money since the country's resources belonged to everyone. Despite her friendly attitude, there was something about this old leathery woman that Margot found frightening. Masking extreme ideology in intellectualism didn't make it any less extreme. Like an iron fist inside a velvet glove. As soon as an opportunity presented itself, they moved on.

They continued their tour of the corridors, but Margot soon realised they'd picked up a tail. A wiry, misshapen man appeared to be following them. It was the same man who had been wielding the floodlight the other day, if she wasn't mistaken. At one point, Margot stopped and stared at him, prompting him to duck around a corner. He reappeared when they carried on, and then repeated his comic disappearing act when they stopped for a second time. Clearly, he wasn't the sharpest tool in the toolbox. Margot gave Natalie a nudge and a wink. They turned left at the next corner, then left again, then hid in an unlit doorway. A few moments later, the confused gimp hurried by, as clueless as a slug.

———

Lunch time slowly came around. Neither of them were particularly hungry, but they took their places at the table and kept their eyes peeled for Dion and Esmée. It was twenty minutes before the two of them arrived, choosing the same spot as at breakfast and eating with their heads together, deep in conversation. What on earth were they finding to talk about? Meal hurriedly consumed, they returned their trays to the kitchen and left, disappearing into the corridor without so much as a backwards glance.

"He's ignoring us again," Natalie commented.

Margot sighed in annoyance. She had half a mind to go after him.

The day dragged on. Wandering dark corridors soon lost its appeal, and they resorted to playing chess in the mess hall. Margot felt a little pot of anger simmering inside. Bored and frustrated, hanging around like two spare parts – she had better things to do with her time. It didn't help that Natalie, despite playing without any discernible strategy, beat her 2-0.

When dinner time arrived, Margot was determined to do something. Once again, Dion and Esmée were late arriving, and for the third time that day they sat and ate without once looking over. Margot kept a close eye on them, and as soon as they got up to return their trays, she made her move. "Wait for me back at the bunkhouse," she whispered to Natalie.

Margot followed them out of the mess hall. At the place where the corridors met, they turned into B-wing. There were lots of people around, so she kept her distance, biding her time. Then, as soon as they were alone, Margot quickly closed in.

"Excuse me."

They turned around in unison. Dion flinched as soon as he realised who had called out. Margot couldn't guess how much Esmée knew, but she couldn't risk giving him away.

"I think I'm lost. Can either of you help?"

Esmée gave her a piercing look. *Nice watch.* She went to say something, but Dion touched her arm. He gestured for her to leave. Reluctantly, Esmée complied.

In silence, they watched her walk off down the dark corridor. Once she was out of earshot, Margot turned back to Dion. "I'm guessing she doesn't know who you are."

Dion regarded her intently. Then, in a burst of movement that caught her completely off-guard, he grabbed her by the arm, kicked open the nearest door, and pulled her into a small dark room. He slammed her against a wall, switched on his torch, and aimed it directly into her face. "You think you're smart?"

"Not particularly."

"I told you not to come looking for me."

"Your magnetic personality keeps drawing me back."

He pressed his forearm firmly against her chest. Two inches higher and he would have been crushing her windpipe. His face was so close that Margot could feel the heat radiating from his skin. Struggling to speak, she said, "Will you please let go of me?"

He pressed more firmly, as if to make a point, but then stepped back. The moment she was free, Margot moved closer to the door.

"You're meant to be helping us."

"I said I would do what I can."

"Have you contacted your people?"

"Not yet."

Margot flinched in astonishment. "Why not?"

"I can't just waltz into the radio room and use one of the computers. It's too risky, especially now, thanks to you. Besides, it's not going to be their top priority. You were told to stay away. If anything happens to you, it's not on me."

Margot could have slapped him, but she restrained herself.

276 | RACHEL GREEN

They couldn't really blame him. After a few seconds, they both calmed down.

"You can at least tell me what's going on here."

"I told you, it's classified."

"Don't give me that. We found the armoury. They've obviously got something planned."

He looked at her more closely. "You saw what, exactly?"

Margot shrugged. "A big map. Lots of papers."

"Stay away from the armoury."

"You can't keep information like that to yourself. People need to know."

"I can do what I like."

"Why do they need all those weapons?"

"To blow up the world."

"And you're just going to stand by and let that happen, are you?"

For a moment, he looked worried. Margot thought she'd touched a nerve. He suddenly moved past her to get to the door. After checking that no one was outside, he quietly closed it again.

"My mission was to gather intelligence. And that's what I've been doing."

"So the police know what they're up to?"

He may have nodded; Margot couldn't really tell. There was barely enough light in the room to see his face, let alone read his expression. The thought that he might have succumbed to Stockholm syndrome crossed her mind.

"The police have known for years what they're up to," he said. "The people here are only a fraction of what's going on. There's thousands more online, waiting for the call."

"To do what – start a revolution?" Margot scoffed.

"Maybe," he replied defensively. "There are a lot of angry

people out there. All you have to do is light the blue touch paper."

"Like the *Gilet Jaunes*?"

"Something like that."

"All that disruption, and it achieved nothing."

"Well, maybe that's why they want to switch to more radical methods."

Margot gave him a closer look, wondering whose side he was on. He seemed very jumpy. There was clearly a lot going on in his head.

"How long have you been in here?"

"Eighteen months."

"That's a long time to be away."

"I've had easier jobs."

"Your family and friends okay with that?"

He shrugged. Margot watched as he went to the door again, opened it a fraction, and peeked out. He didn't seem entirely in control of himself, like something inside him was unravelling. After eighteen months of listening to their rhetoric day after day, it wouldn't be surprising if he had become sympathetic to their cause. Margot gave him a few moments. At least one thing was becoming clear – they couldn't rely on him to get them out.

"Where does your spotty little friend fit in?"

He flashed her an angry look. "Don't call her that."

Touched another nerve. "You lied to her in Narbonne. That guy you punched. I saw it all."

He took a step closer, forcing Margot to retreat to the door. "Keep your nose out of other people's business."

"Could you get us our phones back, please?"

"No."

"I'm guessing they jam the signal."

"Aren't you the clever one?"

"Have you tried *un*jamming it?"

278 | RACHEL GREEN

Dion stared at her like he was struggling to figure her out. Then he backed off. Margot feared she'd pushed him too far.

"I'm leaving now. Don't approach me again."

"Wait! You can't just ignore us."

"Wanna bet?"

"And if he kills us. Do you want our deaths on your conscience?"

He paused. "I'll give you just one piece of advice: find somewhere to hide. Things are starting to heat up in here, and it might turn ugly."

"What's that supposed to mean?"

"Exactly what I said."

"And you?"

He looked confused. "What about me?"

"If things turn ugly, have you got a way out?"

He looked at her for a very long moment without speaking. A calmness settled over him. "Don't worry about me," he said, then pushed her aside to escape out the door.

———

Anything to report?

AL's message stared back at him from the computer screen. The monitor went into sleep mode, so he woke it back up. It was three in the morning, and the radio room was deserted.

You've been silent for a couple of days, AL went on. *Do we need to be concerned?*

Dion moved his hands to the keyboard, ready to type a reply. He had been sitting in front of the computer for fifteen minutes straight, thinking what to say. Where did his duty lie? He'd done his job for over twenty-five years, never once stepped out of line. He'd followed his orders, done as he was told, never questioned the authority of those above him. They were higher up the chain of command, they were called your superiors for a reason, they'd earned their place... or so he'd believed. A soldier blindly followed orders, it was drilled into them. You weren't meant to ask questions, or think for yourself. That was the way it worked.

But not this time.

Not this soldier.

Dion took a deep breath, settled in his mind.

No problems here, he typed back. *Nothing to report.*

28

Sébastien came for them at breakfast time. As soon as they'd
finished eating, he joined them at the counter as they were
returning their trays. He called them into a quiet corner, away
from the crowd.

"Your backpacks are ready. Would you meet me in the
armoury in one hour, please?"

Dion and Esmée exchanged a look. Then gave him a nod.

"Monika will brief you. You'll leave tomorrow at midnight.
The attacks will take place at two o'clock on Saturday afternoon." Sébastien smiled. "We'll be worldwide news by five."

They bumped fists. Comrades in arms. Dion felt a buzz
inside him, a sense of belonging he hadn't experienced in years.

They arrived at the armoury ten minutes early. Sébastien
and Monika called them into the cage where five black backpacks were already lined up on the table. Cheap ones, the kind
of thing a schoolkid might use as a daypack, though these
contained something rather more potent than textbooks. They
waited a few minutes for the beards and the skinhead to arrive.
As soon as they showed up, Monika locked them all in. Class
assembled.

"Try them on," Sébastien said. "They're all identical."

They formed a line in front of the table. It was like trying on suits for a wedding; there was a heavy dose of self-consciousness in the air. Esmée and the others swung theirs nonchalantly onto their backs, tested the weight. Dion took a little more care, having seen firsthand what explosives could do. He picked his up and eased his arms through the loops.

"Get comfortable," Sébastien continued. "You're going to be carrying them for the next two days. Treat them like your best friend. "

"Or your worst enemy," Monika quipped.

They stretched and straightened, adjusted the straps. "How do I look?" the beard quipped back, doing a little twirl. "Like the world's worst nightmare," Monika replied without missing a beat. Dion half expected her to wheel out a full-length mirror, just so they could check themselves out. *Ooh! Suits you, sir.*

"What exactly are we carrying?" the younger beard asked.

"Two kilograms of TNT," Monika replied. "Enough to blow up a small building."

"Wow."

Guns and ammo. Bombs and bullets. You couldn't deny their elemental appeal.

Dion loosened the straps on his. He reckoned his weighed more like five. Certain death for anyone standing within three metres.

"How do we arm it?" the skinhead asked.

"You don't," Monika replied. "The device is set up and ready to go. Do *not* open them and do *not* fiddle with them. All you need to do is detonate them."

"And how do we do that?" the beard asked.

Monika reached under the desk and brought out an old ammunition box. She pulled out a Faraday bag from which she took five mobile phones. Basic, anonymous Nokias. She handed them out. "Only switch them on when you're ready to use them. There's one number programmed into the contacts. All you need to do is call it."

Dion looked at the phone in his hand. Ubiquitous pieces of plastic and silicone. He wondered if whoever had invented these things had ever imagined they would one day be put to such a use.

"Okay," Monika said. "You can take them off now."

They took off their backpacks and set them down on the table.

"Next, your targets."

She produced another metal box and from it took a bundle of papers. She handed each person two laminated sheets: a street plan and an itinerary. Dion's heart skipped a beat when he saw he'd got Cannes. A detailed route had been plotted, starting from a drop-off point on the outskirts of town and leading to a final destination on the Boulevard de la Croisette. At two o'clock on a Saturday afternoon, the place would be packed.

"Let me just emphasise this," Monika continued, "stick to the routes I've plotted. We've scouted each of these locations and chosen a route that avoids every known security camera."

"There's bound to be others," Dion said. "Every other shop will at least have a door cam."

"True, but the cameras I'm talking about are the ones used by the security forces. Avoiding them will buy you some time."

"Just wear a hoodie," the skinhead put in. But it wasn't quite that simple these days. Software recognition was much more sophisticated.

"Any questions?" Sébastien asked.

"Yes," Dion said, turning to look their leader in the eye. "What happens after it's done? Where do we go?"

"Good question," Sébastien said. "And I'm afraid there's no easy answer. The truth is, you'll be on your own. One operative, working alone – that's how these missions were conceived. We can't risk sending anyone to pick you up. I'm sure you understand."

"Your best option is to make your way from the scene on foot," Monika added. "Act as quickly as possible, but don't run. The police will throw up a cordon so try to get out before they get organised. Head for a station on the outskirts of town – I've marked their locations on your plans. Get on the first bus or train you see and don't look back."

"And come back here?" one of the beards asked.

"No," Sébastien responded immediately. "We'll be evacuating the base at the end of next week."

"How come?"

"We can no longer be sure we're safe here."

Dion lowered his eyes, hoping that wasn't a dig at him.

"Once this kicks off," Sébastien went on, "people are going to come looking for us."

"Where will you go?"

"We'll split up. Spread out across the country."

If their campaign had even half the desired impact, nowhere would be safe. Monika took over:

"As far as the five of you are concerned, I suggest you lie low for a couple of weeks. Pick up a copy of *La Vérité* as soon as you can. I'll hide a phone number somewhere in the back pages. Call it and we'll be in touch."

Dion felt a little spaced out. All this had come out of the blue; he'd not even picked up a whisper. How many other things might he have missed?

"Pack up your things and we'll see you back here at midnight tomorrow," Sébastien said. "Good luck, brothers."

They filed out. Sébastien and Monika shook everyone's hands in turn. "What's happened here today will go down in history," Sébastien said. "I'm proud of you all."

He held onto the handshake when it came to Dion's turn. Their eyes locked. "I'll see you on the outside, brother," he added, so quietly that only they would hear.

Dion nodded, not entirely sure what he'd meant.

———

When the briefing ended, Dion and Esmée left the armoury together. Dion felt numb. After eighteen months of being cooped up in the base, he wasn't sure how he felt about leaving. He wouldn't miss the gloom, that was for sure. And he wouldn't care less if he never saw a tree again in his life. But who knew where he would end up, what direction his life would take?

"Where did you get?" Dion asked as soon as they were alone.

"Toulon. What about you?"

"Cannes."

"Wow." Esmée's eyes widened. "You'll be making a splash."

Lost in thought, they worked their way back to the Command Centre. It dawned on Dion that this could be his last full day at the base, and despite its drawbacks, he had grown accustomed to it. There were people in here he would miss. At the hub, he drew Esmée to one side.

"You busy?"

"I'm due a shift cleaning the latrines."

Dion smiled. "Lucky you."

"But not till tonight. Why, what are you thinking?"

Dion checked to make sure no one was watching. "I was thinking we could go to the observatory after dinner. Last night here and all that."

"Okay." Esmée nodded. "I'd like that."

"Let's meet back here at eight."

———

It was a cloudy night. They couldn't even see Venus. Dion contented himself with admiring the telescope, tracing his torchlight over its smooth, clean lines, marvelling at the skill of the engineers who'd built it. He remembered the day he'd found it, the thrill he'd experienced when he'd torn through the vegetation and discovered the door at the bottom of the dome. It had been too much to hope that a telescope would still be inside, but there it had been, in all its glory.

"I guess you'll miss this place," Esmée said, joining him on the gantry.

Dion nodded. All those dark nights he'd spent gazing up at the night sky. "What about you? Anything you'll miss?"

"I won't miss cleaning the latrines." They both smiled. "But no, not really."

It was different for her. She was young. She had a lifetime of new experiences ahead of her.

"To be honest," she went on, her face betraying a look of nervous excitement. "I can't wait to go. I'm glad Sébastien chose me."

Dion wondered if she would have gone if he hadn't been chosen. Or vice versa.

"You sure you're up for it?" he said.

"Absolutely."

"There's a world of difference between throwing powder paint and planting a bomb."

"What I did in Monaco didn't even get mentioned in the national news. Ninety-nine per cent of the time we're invisible. But this... Chances like this don't come along often."

She was right, of course. The world was going to hell in a handcart and nothing would change unless someone did something drastic. But people were going to get killed. Even if it was just one person, could he live with that?

"How are you feeling about it?" Esmée asked.

Dion looked her in the eye. During those six weeks on the road together, she was the last person he would have confided in, but now he wanted to tell her everything.

"There's something you don't know."

"Is there?"

"About me."

"Go on."

Dion hesitated. "I haven't been entirely honest with you."

"Okay."

"I'm not a farmer."

"Aren't you? So, what are you?"

"I'm a police officer."

She didn't even blink. He couldn't tell if she was surprised or building herself up to punching him.

"I'm working undercover. My mission was to infiltrate the group and report back. I've been passing on intelligence for months."

Esmée nodded thoughtfully. "So they know about Sébastien?"

"He's been on their radar for years."

"You've told them everything?"

"Not everything, no," Dion stressed. "I haven't been in touch with them for a while. They know nothing about what's gone on in the past few days. And I won't be telling them."

"Why not?"

He stopped for a second to think about what to say. "I've been a cop for fourteen years. Before that, I spent ten years in the army. I served my country. I was loyal, patriotic. I did everything that was asked of me, and I trusted the people giving the orders were doing so for the right reasons. But after what I've seen in here, and what we found in that lab..." He shook his head in dismay. He still couldn't shake those images from his mind. "I feel I've been duped. They break the rules, then cover things up. People's lives mean nothing to them."

"And now what – you've turned against them?"

Dion gave a firm nod of his head, more certain than ever. "Sébastien has his faults, but he's got more integrity in his little finger than any of them."

Esmée studied him for several long moments. Then she lowered her eyes and walked away. She kept her back to him for a while, but when she did turn around, Dion was relieved to see that she was smiling.

"So you didn't dump horseshit on the Champs-Élysées?"

He grinned. "That was just my cover story. But I did grow up on a farm. And what I told you about my parents is all true. I wouldn't have lied about that."

"And your wife...?"

He nodded. "She's real. The guy I went to see in Narbonne is her lover."

"So why are you telling me this?"

"Because... I thought you should know. I'm committed to this mission. I'm putting my life on the line, just like you."

They went quiet again. Dion felt like a weight had lifted, regardless of what she might say. For the first time in ages, he knew he was doing the right thing.

"So," he asked. "Are we good?"

"Am I the only one who knows?"

Dion nodded. "I thought you would understand."

She smiled again. "We're good. And thanks for telling me. But we'd better go. I've got toilets to clean."

———

They parted company in the hub. Esmée headed off to the bunkhouse while Dion detoured into B-wing. He left the sanctuary of the illuminated corridors and walked in the dark for a while. When he was sure he was alone, he switched on his torch. A dozen mangled doors punctuated the walls around him. Choosing one at random, he opened it and went inside a small dark room.

He reached into his pocket and took out his flash drive. Holding it under the torchlight, he thought of all the chats he'd had with Yvette, the talks with AL. In the early days, he and AL had chatted for ages. He had no idea who AL was, the person behind the avatar, but their chats had been a lifeline, a link to the life in which he'd had a house and a job and a wife who was faithful. But that was all gone now. The only thing that remained was this little piece of silicone and wires.

Dion dropped the flash drive to the ground. He shone his light onto it one final time, and then crushed it with the heel of his boot.

29

Watching the day slip away, feeling powerless to change their situation, pushed Margot deeper into despondency. All they could do was bide their time and see what happened, jump at the first opportunity. They kept their heads down. Their cubby-hole made for a safe, if rather depressing, out-of-the-way place. And since sleep seemed as good a way of passing the time as any, they bedded down early for another night, settling into their sleeping bags at nine o'clock. Not since she'd been a child had Margot gone to bed so early.

It struck her that she hadn't seen a single ray of sunlight in over twenty-four hours. As sleep finally crept up on her, Margot drifted into a nightmare about being buried alive. When she woke up and remembered where she was, it was a toss-up as to which reality was the nightmare.

It was still only ten-forty-five; she'd slept for less than two hours. Needing a pee, she got up and started feeling her way towards the door.

"Where are you going?"

Margot looked round to where she imagined Natalie to be. "I need to pee."

"Wait. I'll come with you."

She wasn't sure why they were whispering.

An entire ensemble of snoring greeted their arrival at the bunkhouse. If someone sampled and rearranged all those sounds they could probably have composed a German opera. They gave the entrance a wide berth and went into the latrines. No one was in there, apart from someone mopping the floor in the bathhouse. They chose stalls far apart and swiftly disappeared inside.

Margot was the first one out. Eager to cool down, she filled a washbasin with cold water and lowered her head, cupping her hands to splash the water over her face. Bliss. Less appealing was the sight that greeted her in the mirror: sallow skin, horrendous panda eyes, hair flatter than roadkill. She felt compelled to do the world a favour and start wearing a bag over her head.

As Margot dried herself off, her focus shifted to a different part of the mirror. Framed in the bathhouse doorway, the woman who had been doing the cleaning was standing stock still, staring back at her. Turning, Margot was surprised to see that it was Esmée. An awkward few moments of silence passed before the younger woman adjusted her scarf and went back to mopping the floor.

Margot saw an immediate opportunity. With Natalie, they outnumbered her two to one. They could kidnap her. Bundle her off to their cubbyhole, and use her as collateral to persuade Dion to do something – he'd clearly grown attached to her. Despite it being a ridiculous idea, Margot gave it some serious thought.

Natalie was still in the stall, so Margot drifted across to Mrs Mop. She halted a few feet away, the mop-head moving in wide arcs between their feet. Esmée carried on with what she was doing for five or six seconds. Finally, she stopped and raised her eyes to Margot's. "Fancy meeting you here."

"What are the odds?"

"You've missed a spot."

"Thanks," Esmée said, but didn't move her mop.

They stared each other off. Margot found herself uncharacteristically lost for words. This woman was less than half her age, yet there was an intensity to her that was unnerving. The young woman widened her eyes, as if encouraging Margot to speak, but Margot still had nothing. Seemingly disappointed, Esmée squeezed out her mop. "Well... nice talking to you. But I must get on. These floors won't clean themselves."

Margot didn't budge.

"That night," she said at last. "Why did you ask about my watch?"

"What watch?"

Margot held up her wrist. Even in the harsh lighting of the bathhouse, the jewels sparkled brightly. "We were sat at the bar. 'Nice watch,' you said."

"Did I?"

"Yes, you did. You know very well you did."

They both looked at the twinkling diamonds. It was hard to interpret the look on Esmée's face. Her eyes were sparkling, too, but not, Margot suspected, with appreciation.

"What did you mean by it?" she persisted.

"Why does it bother you?"

"It doesn't bother me."

"Clearly it does. Otherwise you wouldn't be standing there."

Margot looked deep into her eyes. "I assumed you were commenting on how much it cost."

"So what if I was?"

Anger rose within her. "It's no business of yours how much it cost. My husband bought it for me."

"Lucky you."

"He worked hard for a living. *Damn* hard." Margot gritted her teeth. How could someone so young look so smug?

They were distracted by Natalie coming out of the stall. She gave them both a curious look, and the heat went out of the moment. Esmée dipped her mop into the bucket and went back to cleaning the floor.

They left moments later, though at the door, Margot couldn't resist a parting shot.

"I know what you're fighting for, but it'll never work. You can't stop people wanting nice things."

Esmée nodded knowingly, not believing a single word.

———

Unable to sleep, Margot rolled out of her sleeping bag. Five o'clock. She sat in the corner with her face in her arms until Natalie stirred at six, and then went off to breakfast, doing a wonderful impression of a zombie.

She sat at the table with her head down, picking at her food. *Nice watch.* Margot wasn't sure why it bothered her so much. She was adamant she was right. These utopian ideals were all well and good, but they never worked in practice. People are different. Some are talented, some are lazy. Some will always want to get ahead by putting in the long hours, while others are happy to drift along, not giving two hoots. Besides, who wanted to live in a world where there was no differentiation – no stylish clothes, no way of expressing yourself? People are individuals, not part of a herd. All these things were true to Margot's mind, yet she still couldn't shake off her feelings of guilt. Until she pictured what a herd of humans might look like, naked hairy bodies galloping through the latrines. She shuddered. The image was disturbing enough to pull her out of her funk.

They remained at the table for over an hour, but neither

Dion nor Mrs Mop put in an appearance. By now, they had perfected the art of staying out of the way, and nobody seemed to notice them. Everyone around them appeared to have a lot on their minds, and no one wanted to talk, which suited Margot since she wasn't in the mood to ask any more questions. All she wanted to do was curl into a ball and sleep until it was all over. She wondered if this was what being in prison was like.

Another day ebbed away. Margot wasn't even sure what day of the week it was anymore: Wednesday, Thursday...? She would have to count on her fingers to be sure. When night and day were indistinguishable, time lost all meaning. How Dion had survived it for eighteen months without going mad was beyond her.

They went back to the mess hall for dinner. There was still no sign of anyone coming to rescue them so they went to bed and were tucked in by eight-thirty.

———

Margot drifted up through the layers of sleep, disturbed by something cold and hard being pushed into the small of her back. Realising it wasn't a dream, she opened her eyes. A split second later, she registered someone lying on the floor directly behind her. She turned her head instinctively, but a man's hand instantly clamped over her mouth.

"Don't make a sound," Dion's voice whispered into her ear.

Margot's heart beat like a drum.

"I have a gun in your back and won't hesitate to use it. I'm giving you just one chance to get out of here so keep quiet and listen. Understand?"

With his hand still clamped over her mouth, Margot could only nod.

"I'm leaving," he went on. "A few hours from now I'll be

gone, and I won't be coming back. I don't know what they've got planned for you, but it's not going to be good. Take this." His arm moved over her, his hand seeking hers. When he found it, Margot reluctantly opened her fist and felt something small and metallic being pressed into her palm. "This is the key to the old gymnasium. You'll find it in C-wing, behind the door marked C-5. There's a hole in the roof. Climb up the rope ladder and then jump down onto a mound of soil. You'll see what I mean when you get there."

"But—"

He pushed the barrel of the gun harder against her spine.

"Be careful on the roof. The sheets are brittle so make sure you follow the lines of fixings. Got that?"

Margot nodded.

"From there it's a short run to the fence. Head due east. After two kilometres you'll come to a road. Go straight to the nearest police station and..." He trailed off, breathing heavily. The heat coming off him was almost suffocating. While he was still paused, Margot managed to wiggle her mouth free from his hand.

"And what?" she prompted.

He snapped out of it, and tightened his grip. "And tell them to prepare for Armageddon. There's a plot to blow up the electricity grid, substations all over France. August the 28th. You got that?" He seemed keen that she remember. Margot nodded quickly.

His grip slackened again. Their cheeks touched when Margot turned her head. "Why can't you tell them?" she asked, but he didn't appear to hear.

"They're moving out of the base at the end of next week, but don't hang around. Wait for daylight. It's too dangerous at night." He pulled himself up onto his knees, moving the barrel of the gun to the side of her neck. "August the 28th. Make sure you warn them."

A dozen questions flashed through Margot's mind, but she didn't get the chance to ask any of them. The next time she blinked, Dion had gone.

30

Somehow, Natalie had slept through the whole thing. Margot crawled to her side of the room and gave her shoulder a shake. "Natalie. Wake up."

Her right knee connected with the Maglite and slipped on the smooth metal shaft. Banging her knee on the floor, Margot cursed. She picked up the torch and switched it on, this time deliberately shining it right into Natalie's eyes. "Natalie! Bloody wake up, will you?"

Sleeping Beauty scowled. "What is it?"

"Dion was here."

"When?"

"Just now."

"What did he want?"

Margot filled her in on what had happened, and watched Natalie's eyes light up with anger. She lifted herself up onto her elbows. "You mean he's abandoned us?"

"Not entirely." Margot showed her the key. "He said there's another way out. A hole in the gym roof."

There was a pause while Natalie took it all in. But she wasn't sharing Margot's enthusiasm.

"Don't you see what this means?" Margot stressed. "We can leave."

"Not without my grandmother's money, we can't."

"Oh come on."

"No! I'm not letting them get away with it. Especially after what we've been through."

There was stubbornness, and then there was outright foolishness. Lacking the energy for another argument, however, Margot let it drop. It wouldn't be safe to do anything for hours, anyway, since he'd told them to wait until daylight.

They sat for an hour, thinking things through. At four o'clock, they went to the latrines.

The noise reached them in the corridor. It seemed like the entire group had assembled in the bathhouse: there were queues for the toilets; every washbasin was taken; the showers were a steaming hot mash of brown and white flesh. Everyone seemed to be in a hurry. When Margot's turn came, she used the toilet as quickly as she could, splashed her hands in one of the sinks, and then exited as swiftly as possible. Outside, another group was emptying the storeroom, pulling towels and blankets from the shelves and loading them into laundry bags.

"What's going on?" Natalie whispered when she caught up, giving the men a curious look. "I thought he said they were leaving at the end of next week."

"He did," Margot whispered back, confused. Surely he hadn't been lying.

She glanced over her shoulder as they set off back to their cubbyhole. Two men promptly detached themselves from the group and started following them down the corridor. When they came to the door to their cubbyhole, Natalie moved to go in, but Margot gave her a nudge. "Don't look round, but I think we're being followed." She steered them into a different corridor instead.

298 | RACHEL GREEN

As soon as they'd rounded the corner, they sped up. The skin on the back of Margot's neck tingled. At least when Dion had been here, there had been someone to protect them. The two men appeared behind them, their actions now more urgent.

"Hey, you."

Margot halted and turned to face them. The two men continued to approach, their attitude distinctly unfriendly. It seemed the rules of engagement had changed.

"Sébastien wants to see you."

"Does he?"

"Come with us."

"Okay."

A glance in Natalie's direction was all it took. One second later, they were sprinting away down the corridor.

―――――

The advantage of being trapped in such a large base was that it was easy to find somewhere to hide. This time, they stuck together (even held hands as they fled down a rubbish-strewn corridor) and after three or four turns, managed to give their pursuers the slip. Hearts pounding, backs to the wall, they waited a few minutes, just to be sure.

Switching on the Maglite, they found themselves in an unfamiliar part of the base. The corridors were long and wide, and the rooms had a very different feel – high ceilings and brick walls; a few of them had windows. Graffiti covered many of the walls, and there were empty beer bottles around, some of them with modern labels. What looked like a used condom was festering in one grubby corner.

They came across a room that was a little more promising. The air was fresher and the floor cleaner than anything else they'd seen.

"So what do we do now?" Natalie asked.

Margot was fresh out of ideas. "Sit here and wait, I suppose." She had no idea how to get to C-wing. She'd seen no signs, and had never heard anyone talk about the gymnasium. In any case, it was academic right now. Dion had told her to wait until daylight, and for once Margot was keen to do exactly what she'd been told.

They found places to sit. A few hours went by. Margot sat quietly with her eyes closed, and when she reopened them was surprised to find the room had got a little lighter. She looked around, and realised the light was coming in through a grille at floor level. It was too low to be an air duct, but it looked big enough to fit a body inside.

Margot went for a closer look. Getting down on her knees, she managed to wrench the grille free. Beyond it was a short concrete tube, wide enough to squeeze into, although thick metal bars at the far end prevented any hopes of escape. A dank smell pervaded, and tall weeds were growing on the other side of the bars.

"What's that?" Natalie asked, coming to see.

"Some kind of sluice gate by the looks of it."

"Where does it go?"

It was hard to tell, though the light that was coming in was definitely daylight. Margot looked at her watch. 06:35. Her companion showed no sign of wanting to do the decent thing.

"I suppose I'll crawl through and take a look then, shall I?" Margot said.

Natalie stood, folding her arms. "Age before beauty."

Pearls before swine, Margot countered in her head.

The concrete was marked with some ugly brown stains. Inching forward on her elbows, Margot hoped it was only rust.

"What do you see?"

"Wonderful things."

Natalie gave her a kick.

"Ow!"

"You deserved it."

"Thanks."

Margot pressed her left ear to the top of the tube to get her eyes as high as possible. She found herself looking across the flat expanse of tarmac, and could see as far as the warehouse.

"Something's going on over there. Those vans we saw are parked outside the warehouse." The orange light on the forklift was flashing as it moved in and out.

"Are they packing up?"

"It looks like it."

"So he was lying to us?"

Margot tried to remember every word Dion had said, read between the lines and figure out what he was up to. August the 28th was four weeks away. So why all this activity now? Perhaps he was enacting a bigger plan – getting the group to evacuate now and then leading them into a trap. A hundred armed police officers might be waiting in the woods, but she doubted it. Had he abandoned not only them but his duties as well? She shuffled back out on her elbows, and accepted Natalie's helping hand to get up.

"We could go and see what they're up to," Margot suggested.

No one had come looking for them. Maybe the two men had been acting alone rather than being part of a concerted effort to round them up. The group obviously had more important things on their minds.

"All right," Natalie agreed.

They kept their wits about them as they retraced their steps back to the bunkhouse, avoiding using the torch wherever possible. The bunks were empty, the storeroom ransacked. The latrines were also deserted, and there was no sign of Mrs Mop. But noises were coming from several places nearby. They froze when they heard people running down a corridor, though the sound must have been conducting through the walls since no one appeared. They cast a tentative look through an observation panel and saw trolleys being wheeled by, loaded with all manner of things. At this rate, the base would be empty by the end of the day.

With little option but to wait it out, they retreated to their hiding place.

———

"I think they've finished."

Slightly delirious from the lack of sleep, food, and water, Margot raised her head. She was sitting on the floor, her back against a lumpy chunk of concrete. Remarkably, Natalie was lying face down in the drainage tube, hidden from the waist up.

Margot got to her feet and joined her. "What's happening?"

"Nothing, by the looks of it."

"Let me see."

They swapped places. It was broad daylight outside and the warehouse doors were closed. There was no sign of the vans. After shuffling back out, Margot consulted her watch. It was three o'clock in the afternoon. "You reckon they've gone?"

"There's only one way to find out."

They made another trip to the bunkhouse. This time, the corridors were eerily empty. Listening out, they couldn't hear a single sound. The fact the group had departed didn't seem in doubt. Their thoughts turned to sustenance, and with no further ado, they set off to the mess hall.

They passed through the place where the corridors met. The scene couldn't have been more different: loose papers were strewn across the floor, a trolley lay overturned and some boxes were upended. The emptiness felt even stronger now, especially given the hubbub of before. The same was true of the mess hall, where all the chairs were out of place and unwashed cups and plates were piled high on the counter. It felt like the Marie Celeste. Fearing they might have taken all the food, Margot strode into the kitchen, relieved to find some tins in one of the cupboards. Natalie found a multipack of bottled water and clawed through the plastic packaging to liberate two 1-litre bottles.

They took their time slaking their thirst. Given the state the place had been left in, it was safe to assume the group had gone for good. As Margot's brain got back up to speed, she realised the imperative now was to get out as soon as possible. They needed to pass on Dion's warning and avert whatever attacks had been planned. With everyone gone, there was nothing to stop them walking out the front door, though she hesitated to believe it was going to be that simple. Margot found a tin opener in a drawer and opened a can of peach halves in syrup. She was so hungry she ate them straight from the tin with her fingers. The smell of food piqued Natalie's appetite and she joined her behind the counter. Margot offered them up, but Natalie opened a tin of her own.

They ate for a while without speaking. After a minute or two, Natalie put down her half-empty tin and gave Margot a curious look. "Where would they keep a safe?"

Margot swallowed her final peach-half and rinsed her mouth with water. "I doubt they'll have forgotten to empty it."

"You never know."

It was worth a try, Margot supposed. They might as well see this thing through to the end.

The Command Centre was the obvious place to start. Roaming the empty base was like going into school after dark – being somewhere you weren't meant to be, seeing things you weren't supposed to see. Margot picked up a discarded torch as they entered the ground floor of the Command Centre. She'd expected it to be all high-tech – banks of monitors, computer equipment galore – but it was nothing like that. A dozen old-fashioned desks occupied the space, and although there was a small bank of screens, the monitors looked decades old. There was even a typewriter on one of the desks, along with a fax machine, and something that looked very much like a telex machine. Who were these people communicating with – the 20th century? Margot sensed the place had only been evacuated in the past hour: the chairs were still warm; papers had been left lying around. Other than a few smashed-up keyboards, they hadn't done a particularly good job erasing their presence. There must have been thousands of fingerprints on these surfaces; the SOCOs would have a field day gathering evidence. It was surprising someone as apparently professional as Sébastien hadn't bothered to cover his tracks, unless there was more going on here than met the eye.

"Bastards."

Margot looked round. Natalie had evidently discovered the safe and was pointing her light inside. The door was wide open and the safe was bare. Even so, Natalie got down on her knees and ran her hands around its smooth metal insides. Not a centime had been left.

"I'm sorry, Natalie. We did our best."

Natalie rocked back on her haunches, hissing with frustration.

The dutiful thing to do would be to go back to the armoury and check out those battle plans, but Margot felt a sudden chill. "I think it's time we got out of here, don't you?"

This time, Natalie was quick to agree.

They located the corridor that led to the exit. Margot expected it to be barricaded, but the path to the front door was clear. There was nothing, it seemed, to stop them from walking straight out. As Natalie was about to do just that, Margot spotted something that made her take fright. She grabbed Natalie's arm.

"Don't move."

Natalie returned a puzzled look. Margot pointed down to her feet where a strand of what looked like fishing line had been stretched tight across the corridor, maybe twelve inches above the floor. One more step and she would have caught it.

"I'm guessing that's a trip wire," Margot said.

Fresh weld marks were visible on the door frame where a steel contact had been attached. A matching one had been fixed to the face of the door. A pair of red and black wires ran from the contact, down the wall and then into a wooden crate tucked away in the corner. Suddenly, the lack of concealment made sense. No point disposing of evidence when a bomb could blow the base to smithereens.

31

They bobbed and swayed on the bench seat as the van made its way along narrow winding roads. Side by side in the back, Dion and Esmée had barely exchanged a word since they'd set out, each deep in their own thoughts. The beards had gone west in a separate van. They'd dropped the skinhead on the outskirts of Marseille. Next it would be Esmée's turn, then Dion would continue alone to Cannes. They would each spend the night in an anonymous hotel, one last night of normality before unleashing hell on the streets. Five bombs, five cities – saturation coverage on the evening news.

They lurched sideways as the van sped up, then rolled again as it navigated a roundabout. Hyperaware of the deadly cargo at their feet, Dion kept a tight hold of the straps. On the other side of the grille, the driver was in a world of his own – earbuds in, humming along to his tunes. He could have been delivering groceries, or ubiquitous brown parcels.

With time to kill, Dion allowed his mind to wander. He recalled another time when he had sat in the back of a van – his early days in the army, at the tender age of eighteen. He and his fellow new recruits had been on their way to a training exercise,

306 | RACHEL GREEN

and the van had been full of chatter and camaraderie. They'd been an interesting bunch. In those first few weeks, Dion had made more friends than he had in his entire adult life, and he often felt sad that he'd lost touch with them. The army had been his escape from the place where he'd grown up – that lonely old farmhouse, his parents, that chair. Many of the young men who'd travelled with him that day had been in similar boats, orphans in everything but name, never having felt the warmth of a parent's love. The army had become his family, it had fed and nurtured him. Then later, a similar experience with the *Gendarmerie Nationale.*

And then came the group. A different kind of family, wayward and disparate, yet united in a cause. Guided by a man with a vision rather than a functionary passing on orders. For the first time in his forty-five years, Dion felt he was doing something meaningful with his life, and the more he thought about it, the more he realised how grateful he should be to Sébastien for entrusting him with this mission. Many more back at the base would have been eager to be in his shoes.

Would there be casualties? Dion shifted uncomfortably on the hard wooden bench. As a soldier, he'd been sanctioned to kill, but if the people doing the sanctioning were corrupt, didn't that already make him a murderer? Armies fought armies, but if civilians got caught in the crossfire that was their bad luck. *We're sorry for the loss*, the generals would say, *but the bombing continues.* Politicians and armies were no different from the terrorists; they just hid behind cloaks of civility, as if putting on a uniform or a suit gave them immunity. Their methods were just as extreme, their motives often more murky. Dion was done with them. Hypocrites, the lot of them.

"I'm going to give a warning," he said quietly to Esmée. "Leave the rucksack in the shop, and then tell everyone to get out."

His cause was just, but he couldn't condone killing innocent people. He didn't care what anyone said, he'd made up his mind. He was the one who would have to live with himself afterwards. Esmée was giving him a doubtful look.

"Admit to a group of shoppers that you've just planted a bomb in the store?" she said. "You'd be mobbed before you got to the end of the street."

Dion lowered his eyes. He hadn't thought of that. He was aware that his mind had grown woolly of late, his thinking a little ragged at times. He rubbed his forehead in frustration, trying to knock some sense into himself.

"You could telephone a warning instead," Esmée suggested. "Phone the store from outside and tell them to get everyone out."

Of course, that was the best solution. Esmée was much smarter than he was. She settled his thoughts. He felt grounded when he was with her.

"Will you do the same?" he asked.

She gave it some consideration and, after a pause, nodded. "I didn't sign up to kill people."

"Sébastien's not going to like it."

"It'll still be his *amuse-bouche*."

"You think he'll want us back?"

"In the group?" Esmée sounded surprised. "Why wouldn't he?"

Dion shrugged with his eyebrows. "Maybe we shouldn't go back."

"And miss his great hurrah?"

That's if there would be a great hurrah, Dion reflected. He hadn't told Esmée he'd tipped off the woman, and he wouldn't. Whatever happened on August the 28th it wasn't on him. He'd done what he'd needed to do it to appease his conscience.

"What would we do without the group?" Esmée mused.

"Live a different kind of life."

"Be *normal,* you mean?" The contempt in her voice was strong. Dion had to smile.

"We could get hobbies," he suggested.

"Like what – play golf?"

"Join the tennis club."

"Pilates?"

Dion leaned into her side. "We could go to the homeware store on Saturday afternoons and buy cushions at sixty-five euros a pop."

Esmée laughed. Dion felt his heart grow warmer. He would miss these times.

They were quiet for a while. It was close to midnight. They must have been nearing Esmée's drop-off point by now, and right on cue, he noticed a sign for Toulon flash by.

"We should meet up," he said. "When this is all over."

Esmée looked back at him. "Where were you thinking?"

He shrugged. "Paris?"

"I know a bar."

"I thought you might."

"Your typical left-bank kind of place: pretentious intellectuals sitting up at *le zinc*, talking shite."

"We'll fit right in."

She gave him the address. Dion committed it to memory. They bounced on the seat when the van clipped a kerb. The driver glanced back and apologised. Maybe he'd only just realised what a sensitive cargo he was carrying. "Two minutes," he called out, and Dion felt butterflies in his stomach.

"You want to set a date?" he asked.

"How about next Wednesday? Six o'clock."

"Okay. Just in case we don't make it, look up at the moon at midnight."

She glanced into his eye, perhaps misunderstanding his meaning. But then nodded.

They bumped fists. "*Vive la revolution*, and all that."

"*Vive la revolution*, and all that."

The van pulled up. Silence fell when the engine turned off. The driver got out and walked around to the back.

"I guess this is me," Esmée said.

"I guess it is."

The doors opened, letting in a waft of cool air. The driver stepped aside to light a cigarette. Dion took charge of the rucksacks while Esmée got out.

"Be careful with that," he said, helping her slip the bomb onto her shoulders.

Esmée tightened the straps. "Don't worry. I will."

The van had parked on an elevated spot, offering them a panoramic view of the city. In a few hours' time, another fine day would be dawning, baking the streets in hot sunshine. He imagined people stirring in their beds, having no idea what was about to hit them. For most of the time, the average Joe lives a powerless life, unable to change a single damn thing in the world, yet all it took to wreak havoc was a singleminded individual, armed with a backpack. And there was nothing the authorities could do.

"Good luck, brother."

Dion looked her solidly in the eye. In years to come, he knew he would look back with fondness on the time they'd spent together. But all good things come to an end.

"Good luck, sister."

They shared an awkward embrace. For the first time since they'd met, Esmée looked a little nervous. She set off without another word, and with a heavy heart, Dion watched her walk away. Halfway down the hill, she turned to look back. Dion waved, but too slow for her to notice. He burned the image into his memory, just in case it was the last he ever saw of her.

32

Margot and Natalie stared into the wooden crate. It appeared to be a simple device: three brown tubes of dynamite held together with black tape, resting atop a pile of straw. Only two wires – red and black – joined the lump of explosives to what must have been the detonator. Cut either of the two wires and that would break the circuit. Basic electronics. As easy as that.

"You seen any wire cutters around?" Margot asked.

"Probably."

Neither of them looked.

Red or black? She'd seen it enough times in the movies.

"You think we should risk it?" Natalie queried. She seemed up for it, but that alone gave Margot second thoughts. She smiled wryly and put on her sensible head.

"Let's find this gymnasium instead."

They worked their way back to the hub a little more carefully this time, on the lookout for tripwires. It took them a while to find the entrance to C-wing. A pile of rubble blocked what appeared to be the entrance, and the only way in was through a nearby hole in the wall. There was so much rubble around it looked like a bomb had already gone off. They picked their way along, checking the numbers on every door. Finally, the faded white letters of C-5 appeared in their torch beams.

"I guess this is it."

There was nothing to suggest it led to a gymnasium. Being the only one they'd seen that was secured with a padlock, however, it had to be the right one. Margot took Dion's key out of her pocket and tried it in the lock, relieved when it fit.

"Hold on," Natalie said, quickly staying Margot's hand. "How do we know this one's not booby-trapped?"

Reflexively, Margot pulled her hand away. They shone their torches around the edges of the door. There were no obvious alterations, nothing to suggest it had been tampered with.

"Why would he have given us the key and then booby-trapped the door?" Margot asked. If he had wanted to kill them, he'd had plenty of chances.

"Who knows. But I certainly wouldn't trust him."

He hadn't seemed in full control of his mind, but Margot couldn't believe he would have set them up. On an impulse, she snatched off the padlock and pushed open the door.

KA-BOOM! said that mischievous voice in her head. In reality, all that followed was silence. Natalie gasped like she'd just dodged a bullet.

They entered a hallway, and then a changing room. The benches were covered in dust, and the lockers were old and battered. Incredibly, the smell of stale sweat still lingered. Light was filtering in through a pair of swing doors; pushing through, Margot was cheered to find a shaft of daylight streaming down through a hole in the roof. A homemade rope ladder dangled from one side of the hole, just as Dion had described.

They went to stand at the foot of the ladder and looked up at a jagged circle of sky. It would be dark in an hour or two, but that would probably be enough time to get clear of the woods. Dare they believe this nightmare was finally coming to an end?

"I'll go first," Natalie said, gallant as ever.

"All right. I'll steady it." Margot took a firm grip of the bottom of the ropes.

Natalie wasted no time climbing up and reached the top in less than half a minute. Once she'd pulled herself through, she promptly vanished.

"Wait for me!" Margot called up in consternation.

Natalie's face came back to the hole. "I am. As long as you get a move on."

Margot looked at the rope, wondering if she could fashion it into a noose.

With no one to steady the bottom of the ladder, she had a much harder time of it. The ropes began to swing, gently at first, but then more erratically as she climbed higher. It was like wrestling two giant pieces of spaghetti, and she was exhausted as she neared the top. Natalie reached down to give her a hand, but Margot ignored it and pulled herself up by her own strength. She clambered a short way across the roof sheet and lay flat on her back, filling her lungs with lovely fresh air.

Margot quickly recovered and looked around. The roof had a shallow pitch. They were around six metres down from the ridge, ten metres up from the eaves. A jumble of buildings surrounded them on three sides, with forest stretching out on the fourth. Growing impatient, Natalie started walking towards the ridge, setting off an alarm in Margot's head.

"Wait! You need to keep to the line of the fixings."

"What?"

They both looked down. Margot spotted the smooth heads of the fixing bolts running in straight lines from one side of the roof to the other. She realised that it marked the line of the supporting beams, making it the strongest place to bear weight. However, Natalie was standing pretty much halfway between two of the lines, on a sheet that looked ropey at best. The realisation came too late – before she could even think about moving, there was a loud crack and the sheet ruptured. Natalie disappeared as if a giant hand had reached up and grabbed her.

———

A blood-curdling scream was followed by the crunch of soft matter hitting hard ground. Margot looked down through the newly formed hole in a state of amazement. Shock turned to panic, and she shouted Natalie's name. As the dust began to settle, the outline of a figure appeared on the floor below. Face down and unmoving.

Adrenaline pumping, Margot quickly lowered herself down the ladder. Twenty feet away, surrounded by bits of broken roof sheet, Natalie still hadn't moved. A cold hand grabbed Margot by the throat as she saw the pool of blood, slowly expanding. The fact that Natalie was dead seemed undeniable, but Margot knelt beside her and checked for a pulse. And then, before her amazed eyes, a miracle happened. With a series of feeble groans, the corpse rolled onto its back.

"Oh God, Natalie! Are you okay?"

The stupidest of questions in the most surreal of circumstances. Her left eye had swollen to the size of a tennis ball, and her breath was coming in raspy gasps. When Margot looked down, she could see that her right leg was bent horribly out of shape. Margot's mind went into freefall. She'd been trained in first aid, but in those vital first moments, her clumsy hands had no idea what to do.

A word started to come out of Natalie's mouth. Margot placed a comforting hand on her shoulder. "Don't try to talk. Just lie still. I'll do everything I can to get you out of this. I promise." Calming words yet Margot felt utterly useless.

She took a deep breath, trying to steady her nerves. A closer look at Natalie's legs revealed that the right thigh of her jeans was soaked with blood; her left leg was twisted so far around that her foot was facing the wrong way. She was beyond first aid. If she were a horse, a vet would have put her down.

"Look at me, Natalie." Margot brought their faces together. "I need to get some supplies. Remember the store room we found? I'm sure there was some medical equipment in there. I'm going to leave you here for a while, but I'll be back. You understand?"

Natalie's hand flailed out and grabbed Margot's arm. Despite her injuries, her grip was strong.

"I'll be back as soon as I can. I promise." She prised Natalie's fingers apart, then grabbed a torch and ran.

Margot sprinted down the corridors, blasé to the danger of tripwires. Part of her hoped she did trigger one – it would at least put an end to all of this. After a few wrong turns, she made it to the barracks. The shelves in the storeroom had been ransacked, but they hadn't taken everything. Margot found a stash of first aid kits and loaded them into a laundry bag. Then she spotted a much larger boxed-up medical kit, and took that too. She filled a second laundry bag with towels and pillows, tucked a couple of blankets under her arms. Spotting a broom on the way out, she added that to her haul, having a feeling the handle might prove useful.

She took a little more care on her way back to the gym. By the time she got there, Natalie's condition had worsened. Her breathing had become shallow, and she appeared on the brink of unconsciousness. Margot dropped her things and knelt beside her, gently tapping her cheek. "Stay with me, Natalie. I've found a medical kit. Everything's going to be fine. But first..." Her voice trailed away as she looked down at the mangled leg. *But first I'm going to have to wrench your bones back into place.* This was not going to end well. Even if she managed to straighten the leg, how would she stem the flow of blood? The chances of her surviving before an ambulance arrived were slim, and that was assuming Margot could even find a way of calling one, which seemed unlikely.

But she soldiered on. A job needed to be done and she was going to have to do it. "Your leg's broken," she said simply. "I'm going to try and set it."

Margot took a pair of scissors from the medical kit and cut through Natalie's jeans all the way from ankle to thigh. She paused at the sight of a small grey lump poking up through a gash in the skin, realising it was the end of a broken bone. Steeling herself, she snapped the broom handle in two and arranged the makeshift splints on either side of the limb. Then she cut one of the towels into strips and laid them out ready.

"I'm sorry, Natalie, but this is going to hurt."

Understatement of the year. Margot took a deep breath, grabbed the lower half of the floppy limb, and twisted it back into shape.

A primal, guttural scream filled the gymnasium. Natalie's fingers, hard as screwdrivers, dug into Margot's arm. If only she had some painkillers. Margot bound the splint with the strips of towel and then mopped up the worst of the blood. She cleaned the wound with water and dressed it with some swaddling from the medical pack. When she'd finished, the leg still looked a mess, but at least the outpouring of blood had slowed. The strips of towel were acting as tourniquets.

Gradually, Natalie sank back down. Margot took the opportunity to look for other injuries. There didn't appear to be any more broken bones. She wanted to do something about that puffed-up eye, but guessed it was the body's own defence mechanism in action. Her wheezy breathing suggested internal injuries that she had no hope of treating. Not sure what else she could do, Margot tried to make her as comfortable as possible, and used some pillows and rolled-up towels to try and stop her from moving around too much.

Margot looked at her hands, covered in blood. As were her trousers, and most probably her face. Imagine being a surgeon, doing this kind of thing day in, day out. She rifled through the rest of the medical pack to see what else might be useful. Her eyes alighted upon an internal zipped pocket which had been secured with a cable tie. She cut the tie with the scissors and inside found two small vials. Holding them up to the light, Margot realised they were liquid morphine. Bugger. Fortunately, Natalie had already slipped into unconsciousness.

———

Did surgeons ever get squeamish? Or did being so up close and personal to the inner workings of the human body on a regular basis make them desensitised? Despite having washed her hands several times, the blood still wouldn't come out. Now that the adrenaline had worn off, memories began to form, and Margot couldn't stop seeing that twisted limb, that dark grey end of bone. The horrible sound of Natalie's body hitting the floor was starting to torment her. Margot hoped she never became desensitised to such things.

At the first sign of Natalie coming round, Margot gave her a little of the morphine. There were no instructions on what dose to use, so she used a syringe to draw a small amount from the vial and then added a few drops to her lips. Fortunately, the drug took effect almost immediately and Natalie lost consciousness again.

Margot grimly took stock. She may have patched up the broken leg, but the wheezy breathing was still a worry. Could she have broken a rib and punctured a lung? How long could you last with an injury like that? Margot had no idea, but she was beginning to realise there was no good outcome from this. Moving her wasn't an option – she certainly couldn't carry her up that rope ladder. The best thing she could do would be to escape and find help, but even then, it might be hours before assistance arrived, and chances were Natalie would have passed away by the time she got back. Added to which, night had now fallen and it would be foolish to go into those woods in the dark. The default option was to stay put, nurse her as best she could, try to make her final hours as comfortable as possible. The morphine would help. While she was settled, Margot went to see if she could find any other options.

She roamed the lonely corridors. The power had gone off, and the areas of the base that had previously been illuminated were now completely dark. Margot carefully retraced her steps to the front door. She approached the crate and shone her light on its deadly contents. She touched the wires, tempted to risk it. The odds were different now. What did she have to lose? She froze when she thought she heard growling on the other side of the door. A dog left behind? No one left to feed it, growing hungrier by the hour. Even if she managed to disarm the bomb, she wouldn't make it past one of those hounds.

Margot strolled into the Command Centre. Her torch traced another length of fishing wire stretched across the bottom step. She carefully stepped over it and ascended to the first floor. One large room, a dozen empty desks. Seeing some old radio equipment, she wondered if she might be able to use it to contact the outside world. She scanned the array of switches and dials, pushed a few buttons, hoping something might come to life. But it was as dead as a doornail.

Her next thought was the armoury. Margot wasn't entirely sure of the route they'd taken last time and it took her a while to find it. She came upon it by chance and entered from the opposite end of the gangway. The ladder that led down to the lower level was now unlocked. Once she'd descended, Margot navigated her way through the shelving bays and approached the inner cage, only to find it padlocked. But she found a metal bar that would work as a jemmy and was soon inside.

The laptops were gone, but many of the papers remained. Margot picked up a bulging file and leafed through photocopied pictures of power stations, railway lines, factories and industrial sites. Another file contained pages and pages of technical specifications. There were plenty of hand-drawn diagrams and detailed calculations, and all of it looked recent. Margot had no doubt this was the heart of the operation.

The map on the wall was a large-scale map of France. Coloured pins had been affixed in at least fifty locations, scattered across the country. As Dion had said, electrical substations had been targeted. The A1 autoroute was also in their sights, with pins inserted at every major junction from Paris to Lille. A thread linked each pin to a cluster of documents: satellite images; locations of security cameras; technical details. Each operation had been given a codename, and there were at least a dozen of them. If they only bombed half of these targets, there was going to be carnage.

But something didn't add up. Many of the pieces of paper bore the date August 13th, and when Margot went back to the desk and scanned through some of the other documents, she found the same date written in numerous places. Yet there was no mention of August 28th.

She turned and looked at the map from a distance. Her eyes travelled south to where a series of yellow pins were clustered around the Côte d'Azur. It looked like five towns had been targeted, but the information on each was sketchy in comparison with the others. A note was appended to each city: "Cédric P." to Toulouse; "Cédric D." to Bézier; "Fab" to Marseilles; "Esmée" to Toulon; "Dion" to Cannes. Each name was marked with an asterisk, and lower down, someone had written "Dummy" to signify its meaning. Margot stared at the list for a very long time, not sure what to make of it.

Coming out of her thoughts, she exited the cage and took a look around the rest of the space. Most of the shelves were empty, but on the far side, a bright red digital display caught her eye. The numerals read 03:45, but Margot was pretty sure that was not the correct time. As she moved closer, an uncomfortable thought passed through her mind.

The digits were on a small black box, the only item on the shelf. A bundle of multicoloured wires ran from the back of the box and down the upright of the shelving bay. Margot dropped to one knee as she followed its progress along the floor, up the next upright, and then into an unmarked metal box, the size of a water tank. She peered in hesitantly and saw that the box was packed full of explosives – five times the quantity they'd seen by the front door. This one wasn't attached to a trip wire, however. Margot glanced back at the clock at the very moment the display changed from 03:45 to 03:44. Unless time had started to go backwards, she was looking at a timer, not a clock.

33

The driver pulled up on a slip road at a large motorway junction. Hazard lights flashing, Dion got out of the van and went round onto the verge. He gave the side panel a knock; stepped back as the van sped away. There was no *bon chance*. No manly bear hug. The driver didn't even check his mirrors.

Despite the late hour, there was still plenty of traffic around. Dion tromped along the dark, lumpy verge, his rucksack slung over one shoulder, careful where he trod. He got tooted at by a couple of cars; almost got pulled off his feet when a lorry thundered by. The hotel where he would be staying was less than a kilometre away, but keen to get away from the road, Dion stepped over the barrier and pushed through a thin hedge. He leapt a ditch and crossed a dark field, his eyes fixed on the neighbouring commercial zone. Arriving at the edge of a floodlit car park, a high chainlink fence blocked his way, forcing him to go round.

The hotel reception was bathed in bright light. A minute before midnight, a pissed-off receptionist was about to lower the shutter. She pointed him to the self-service check-in booth outside, but since Dion only had cash, he was forced to feign ignorance. Luckily, she took pity on him and gave him a keycard.

He left his backpack in the room while he went to the burger joint on the edge of the roundabout. He took a stool at the window and watched the lights from the cars pass by. His mind jumped back to that day in Montpellier with Esmée. It seemed a lifetime away. It struck him that this could be his last night of freedom. Twenty-four hours from now, who knew where he would be? Even if everything went to plan, he had nowhere to go. Sébastien had given him two hundred in cash, but that was all he had in the world. He could head north. Stick to the wild places. Live rough for a couple of weeks. It didn't bother him. He'd been trained to survive, he knew how to hunt, he wouldn't go hungry. As for Esmée, she could always go back to her parents. Meeting up in Paris was just a pipe dream. Happy things like that were something that happened to other people. Not him.

A gang of partygoers staggered in, drunk out of their skulls. A dishevelled old guy in the corner started singing La Marseillaise. Outside, someone was pissing into a bush. All life was here. Dion slipped quietly out of the side door and skirted the car park to return to the hotel, avoiding the floodlights and cameras. The moon was out, lighting his way. Inside the room, he looked at the rucksack where he'd left it on the bedside chair. Tick-tock. He was tempted to open it, make sure the device had been set up correctly (he was familiar with IEDs; he didn't want it going off accidentally), but he left it untouched, just as Monika had said.

He longed to speak to Esmée. He missed her already. But even if he'd known her number, he wouldn't have called her. Standard procedure. No communication was allowed with any of the others. Plausible deniability, if any of them got caught.

He closed the blackout curtains and took Monika's notes out

of his pocket. He spent an hour memorising the route. Afterwards, he cut the two sheets into tiny pieces and flushed them down the toilet.

His mind still buzzing, he lay down on the bed, fully clothed. Didn't even take off his boots. He switched on the TV and watched it with the sound turned down, but it soon started to annoy him. He switched it off and turned out the light. Outside, a hum came from the traffic passing by. Down the corridor, a door opened and closed. Hands behind his head, Dion stared at the ceiling.

————

Margot hurried back to the gymnasium in a daze. 03:39 the display had read when she'd left the armoury. Three hours and thirty-nine minutes to figure a way out of this. It seemed plenty of time, but the moment she got back to the gym, she froze with indecision. There was the rope ladder, her route to safety, and there, squirming uselessly on the ground, was Natalie.

"Margot – is that you?"

Several seconds went by while Margot stood and did nothing. Her selfish gene switched on and assessed the chances of her climbing the ladder without Natalie noticing. At some point, difficult decisions would have to be made.

"I'm here," Margot replied at last.

Despite her injuries, Natalie appeared to smile as Margot drew near. Her breath was still raspy, though her swollen eye had gone down a little. Margot checked the makeshift splint, pleased to see that the bleeding had stopped.

"I'm sorry, Margot. This is my fault, isn't it? Why oh why didn't I listen to you? I'm so stubborn. I could slap myself." Her hand flailed out, missing her cheek by miles. She was half-delirious, clearly still under the influence of the morphine.

"Shush now. Don't try to talk. You need to save your strength."

"Okay," Natalie replied like an obedient child. She drifted back to the land of nod.

Margot knelt down beside her on the floor. She looked at her watch. Three hours and fifteen minutes to come up with a solution. She ran through her options. She could escape on her own, raise the alarm and hope that help arrived before the bomb went off – the moon was now out so she wouldn't be stumbling through the forest in the dark. She could make a sled, improvise a block and tackle, try to haul Natalie up through the roof... Even as she thought it, it seemed ridiculous. Escaping out the front door, even if she could disarm the bomb, wasn't an option unless she wanted to get savaged by the dogs. Then there was the problem of what to tell Natalie. *Listen, Natalie. There's a bomb about to go off. I would love to stay here and comfort you, but it makes much more sense if I save myself. You do understand, don't you?* None of the options came with a happy ending.

As if hearing her thoughts, the patient shifted irritably. Margot took on the role of nurse once more and tried to calm her down. Natalie wriggled and riled and tried to push her away. Another few drops of morphine did the trick.

Time went by. Margot's mind raced with ideas, but her prospects seemed increasingly bleak. Maybe on some level, she had already accepted her fate.

"Why did he tell me August the 28th?" she said, thinking out loud. Had he given her the wrong date intentionally? It seemed unlikely, given that what he'd said about the targets appeared true. Everything in the armoury had spoken of August the 13th, and for whatever reason, Dion had got it wrong. If she was remembering the days correctly, August the 13th was just nine days away. Didn't Margot have a duty to get out and warn someone? Sitting here waiting to die was going to help no one.

"I think he's rather handsome."

To Margot's surprise, Natalie was smiling.

"I know he's done wrong," she rambled on, "but I wouldn't mind him kissing me. He could take off my clothes, kiss me all over, do..." Clearly this was the morphine talking.

"Try to rest," Margot said, having no desire to hear any more. "You need to conserve your strength."

"You won't leave me, will you, Margot?"

A sharp pang of guilt hit home. "Why would I leave you?"

"I don't want to die alone."

"That's not going to happen."

"I know you hate me."

Margot tutted. "I don't hate you."

"You think I'm a horrible person."

Would it kill her to lie? Margot took a long, slow breath. "I don't think you're a horrible person, Natalie. And I certainly don't hate you." And that was no lie. The world had wasted far too much energy on hate.

"I don't blame you," Natalie went on, seeming not to have heard. "I'm not a very likeable person. It's my fault we're here. I should have listened to you. I'm pigheaded and stubborn and—"

"Stop thinking like that. You were looking out for your grandmother. I totally get that."

Natalie stewed for a while. "He stole her money. I don't like people who steal."

"I suppose he was only doing his job."

"My mother used to steal from me."

"Did she?"

"She stole my birthday money once. I was saving up for a dress."

"That wasn't very nice."

Natalie paused to cough. It wasn't very pleasant to watch. Margot thought about giving her the rest of the morphine, putting her out of her misery, allowing her the dignity of a peaceful demise. How did you decide when someone had reached that point, when death was preferable to suffering? It seemed an impossible decision to make.

"I'm so lonely, Margot. I don't mean to be horrible to people. I assume they are going to be horrible to me so I get in first. Push them away. I have no friends, not real ones."

Margot squeezed her hand. It felt intrusive, listening in on her private thoughts like this. She could only imagine how hard it must have been for her growing up. One of the girls at Margot's school had been the daughter of an heroin-addict. She'd often overreacted or acted impulsively, causing people to resent her.

Natalie's grip slackened. Margot was relieved to watch her slip back into unconsciousness. She stared at her watch, though all she could see were the bright red numerals on the timer in the armoury. Looking on the bright side, the gym was a long way from the bomb – the explosion might not reach them – but there were bound to be other devices. Sébastien would want to destroy all trace. Staying here meant certain death. An act of self-sacrifice. If their positions had been reversed, would Natalie have sacrificed herself? Would Margot, aged thirty, have stayed? Perhaps not. Her selfish gene would probably have won out. But with age, it seemed that doing the right thing had become more important to her.

She took off her watch and stuffed it into her pocket. No point torturing herself. Better to accept her fate, admit she was powerless, realise she'd done all that she could do. At times like this, weren't you meant to look back on your life and think about what you'd achieved, conclude you'd not done too badly? Margot thought about the milestones in her life: the day her father had died; the little baby she'd had to say goodbye to; the phone call from Pierre telling her that Hugo had been killed.

She looked at the grim walls of the gymnasium, depressed to think that this was where she would be ending her days. Would anyone shed a tear when their bodies were recovered from the rubble?

Natalie stirred. "Is the ambulance here yet?"

Margot forced a small, sad smile. "It's coming," she said. Unable to resist, she pulled her watch back out of her pocket. "Not long to go now," she added forlornly, and wiped Natalie's brow with the towel.

34

Routines were a hard thing to break, even when your life had been turned upside down. Dion rolled off the bed at 06:00, washed his face in cold water, brushed his teeth and combed his hair, exactly as he had done for the past thirty-five years. After he'd finished in the bathroom, he sat on the end of the bed in the anonymous hotel room and turned on the Saturday morning news. The British king was visiting. A news reporter was standing outside the Palace of Versailles gushing about the pomp and ceremony that was about to be unleashed. A lavish banquet would be followed by a flyover of the Red Devils, there would be military parades and handshakes galore. Ironic that the French had got rid of their own monarchy only to become obsessed with their modern-day counterparts across *la Manche*.

Unable to settle, Dion switched the television off. He shifted his gaze to the rucksack on the chair beside him. An everyday item, something you might buy in a market, yet this innocuous piece of nylon would be pushing the royals off the news tonight.

07:37. Less than seven hours to go. Plenty of time to get into position, but Dion wanted to keep moving. With Esmée not around, he was finding it harder to stay focused.

He stripped the bed, picked out any stray hairs, wiped the door handles. He sterilised the remote and the light switches. The bathroom got cleaned to within an inch of its life. Satisfied he'd left no trace, Dion lifted the rucksack onto his back and quietly left, dropping the key card in the return box on his way out.

The sun was rising over the rooftops, heralding the start of another great day. Dion could smell the sea in the air, even though the beach was four kilometres away. He crossed a busy main road, followed his route through the outskirts of town, and called into an anonymous café. He ordered a double espresso, two croissants and a bowl of fruit. He replied good-naturedly when the waiter brought it over. Rucksack clamped between his feet, he ate without meeting anyone's eye. He didn't want to stick out in anyone's memory. Finished by 08:25, he got up and left.

The route Monika had plotted to the Croisette would take an hour and fifty-five minutes (twice as long as a direct route), but Dion wanted to be there with time to spare. He still had to decide on a target, and he wanted to take his time, walk the strip, immerse himself in the surroundings.

He set off along a palm-lined street. There was something about seaside towns that had always appealed to him. Laidback people in flimsy clothing. Kids on scooters in flip-flops. Everything he was not, and maybe that was the point. The temperature was rising, but Dion kept his hood up. He pictured Esmée and the others doing the same. Five walking bombs, five ticking disasters, closing in on their targets. He was confident that Esmée would keep her word and telephone a warning, but that still left three killing machines on the loose. He imagined the coverage on the evening news: the roving reporters, the dramatic mobile phone clips, the hysterical eyewitnesses. The rest of the group would be watching back at the base as the pundits in the studio speculated about the motive behind the attacks, wondering if there was more to come. Maybe this time they would finally get the message – we've had enough and we're going to fight back.

A mother pushing a stroller rounded the next corner, heading straight for him, a second kid by her side. As they drew near, Dion caught the little boy's eye and registered his shy smile. When they came to pass, Dion gallantly stepped into the street, though a parked car didn't give him much room, and his rucksack brushed the mother's arm. She turned to say something – a thank you or an apology – but Dion didn't acknowledge her. In the days to come, maybe they would see his picture on the news. Vaguely remember him. Realise how close they'd come.

He turned left, then right, then left, then went straight on. He was surprised to spot a few cameras high up on poles. Maybe Monika hadn't done her research as well as she thought. Dion lowered his eyes as he passed a police surveillance camera. He remembered his training: try to look normal, act like he was on his way to buy bread from the shop, but his palms still moistened. One clear image was all the camera needed. His mugshot would be out there before the end of the day, his name on the alert list of every police force in the country. Was that the future he had to look forward to – checking over his shoulder for the rest of his life?

The sound of a siren distracted him. A police car raced by before pulling up at the kerb. When two cops got out, Dion considered crossing over. A single man, walking with a heavy rucksack, sweat on his brow, crossing the street to avoid them... it wouldn't look good. So he held his nerve and watched the cops zero in on a Rasta loitering outside a kebab shop. They were busy searching his pockets when Dion walked by.

He walked past tenement blocks and bland concrete housing. He walked under cranes and next to workmen patching up roads, jackhammers pounding the tarmac. The back streets of Cannes were just like any other big town. But soon the route took him into a better neighbourhood, past houses fronted by lush green tropical gardens, and villas hidden behind tall, ornamental screens. Here it was, the domain of the rich and powerful. Some wanted to flaunt their wealth, others were keen to hide it. Taking a cut-through on a narrow street, he caught his first glimpse of the sea and then, a few minutes later, he emerged on the sunny Croisette.

Dion slowed his pace, keen to take it all in. It was all there, the glitz, the glamour, just like in the postcards. Ultra-smart buildings stretched along the seafront, opulence oozing from every white-washed façade. Islands of palm trees, languid in the heat, towered over his head. He caught glimpses of a golden sandy beach that seemed to go on forever, and a forest of masts on the yachts in the marina. A perfect sun shone from a clear blue sky as if nature itself were in on the act.

An open-top Ferrari rumbled by, a bronzed Adonis at the wheel. The street was their playground, a parade ground for their ultra-expensive toys. Stopped by a red light, the Adonis put on a show for the pedestrians, pretending not to notice the attention he was getting while simultaneously sucking it in through every pampered pore. When the lights changed to green, he gunned the engine for a whole two seconds before enjoying an encore at the next set of lights.

The scene continued to unfold as Dion walked on, the ostentatiousness undiminished. The designer boutiques were all there: Chanel, Dior, Prada. Spoilt for choice, he could take his pick. He passed Gucci and Yves Saint Laurent, and paused to look in the window of Fred. Trinkets that cost more than he'd paid for his last car, watches that could have fed a family for a month. Dion saw with absolute clarity what Esmée had been telling him these past few weeks. He'd worked hard his whole life. He'd followed the rules, done as he was told, yet all of this was still miles out of his reach. He was never going to be able to walk into a shop like this, slap down a credit card and walk out with a nice fancy bag, no matter how hard he worked. The architects of this world had got it very, very wrong.

Which would he choose? It wouldn't make much difference; the impact would be the same whichever designer boutique he blew up. He discounted the ones that had apartments above them (he wouldn't feel comfortable blowing up someone's home), and narrowed the choice down to those that were single-storey. He picked one and went inside for a recce.

The beefcake on the door looked at him like he was something the cat had brought in. Dion had a quick look in the fittings rooms. Everything you would expect: stool, curtain, mirror. He could leave the rucksack under the stool, march straight out, duck around the corner and make the call. It was that easy... Or was it? The doubts began to creep in when Dion spotted the cameras. Two of them, watching his every move. And the assistants all had their eyes on the ball. The beefcake hadn't stopped looking at him since he'd come in. They were bound to notice if he tried to leave, minus his backpack. Panic set in and Dion felt dizzy. What the hell was he doing here? He was never going to succeed. He'd made a big mistake and needed to get out.

Back on the street, he gulped in air. He was starting to overheat inside his hoodie. He became hyperaware of his surroundings and cowered as a shadow loomed over him: a coach pulling in, air brakes hissing. Dion watched as day-trippers emerged from the air-conditioned box. Wish you were here? Maybe... but not today. He walked around the front of the bus and crossed the street without looking. He went down a ramp onto the beach where he tore off his rucksack and dropped it on the sand, then did the same with his hoodie. Closing his eyes, he counted to ten.

The dizziness eased. Dion gathered his things and sat down on the sand. 11:00. Still three hours to go. He had plenty of time to sort this out. His mind came out of the rut it had got itself into, and his thoughts began to clear. There might not be enough time to phone a warning, but he could shout one on his way out. Get away in the ensuing chaos and make the call as soon as it was safe. It didn't really make any difference. Last-minute jitters, that's all it was.

Two women in bikinis walked by. Dion stared at their feet, sand on the tops of their little white toes. He watched a jet-ski for a while, way out at sea, pounding the glistening blue water. Further down the beach, a little kid squealed; ice cream dropped in the sand. A wave of emotion rose up inside him as Dion thought about his hopes of having a family of his own. A period in his life when all he'd wanted was to have a kid. He would have done anything to make it happen – adopt, foster, IVF – he'd been open to them all. He reckoned he would have made a pretty good dad. At work, he'd spent hours listening to his colleagues talk about their kids, doing the things that families did: helping with homework; buying presents at Christmas; going to the beach on days like this. Surely his time would come, he'd thought. But it hadn't. Life was like being stuck on a freeway with thousands of lanes. You could see other cars moving by, doing much better than you, but there was no way of switching. Like the trinkets in the shop windows – look but don't touch.

Dion thought about the chair and what his parents had done to him. He thought about Esmée's neighbour with the treehouse and her rich daddy boss. It was the luck of the draw which lane you got put in. It shouldn't determine who you are, but all too often it did. He made slits of his eyes as he gazed out to sea. There was nothing left for him in this lane now.

Dion could feel the heat rising up from the sand. The noon sun was directly overhead. Two hours to go now. All he had to do was sit here and wait.

35

A distant clanging sound jolted Margot to her senses. She had been hugging her knees, forehead buried in the crook of one arm, trying to hold onto a dream. She raised her head, not sure if the sound had been real or part of the dream. But then there it was again: *clang, clang, clang*. Metal hitting metal.

Margot looked at her watch. Seven-thirty. Daylight was streaming in through the hole in the roof which meant that it had to be seven-thirty in the morning. Saturday morning, if she'd got her days correct.

Natalie was still zonked out. Heart pounding, Margot got to her feet and moved to the door. She shone her light down the long, dark corridor, picking out cobwebs and rubble and dust motes swirling in the air. She remembered the scream she'd heard in the woods. Was someone in here? She jumped when she thought she saw a flash of light move across the ceiling, but it was merely the light from her own torch, reflecting in an odd way.

Margot walked to the end of the corridor. She ducked through the hole in the wall, into the place where the corridors met. Empty, dark spaces surrounded her. Devoid of life. Or were they?

Clang, clang, clang.

Margot's skin turned to ice. It wasn't clear where the sound was coming from, but it didn't seem to be far away. She continued along the corridors, every one of her senses turned up to the max. Five minutes went by without a repeat of the sound. Maybe it was something mechanical. A ghost in the machine? A generator running out of juice? She heisted to believe it was a straggler left behind. Margot thought of the man with the twisted face and balked at the prospect of being trapped with him, but then, did it really matter? If she was doing her sums correctly, the bomb was due to go off in less than twenty-five minutes.

Clang, clang, clang.

Margot froze. She was definitely getting closer. Entering the Command Centre, her eyes were drawn to the passage that led to the exit. Outside, she thought she could hear voices.

Clang, clang, clang.

Someone was knocking on the front door.

Jehovah's Witnesses?

Hmm. When would that voice get out of her head?

Margot jumped when a gunshot rang out. Closely followed by another. And then, if she wasn't mistaken, came the pitiful sound of a dog whimpering. She ran to the front door.

"Who's out there?"

"This is the police. Open up."

Margot was elated, but also alarmed. "Stop hitting the door! It's wired to a bomb. I'm going to climb out through a hole in the roof. Look for me there." Without waiting for a reply, she turned tail and ran.

Back in the gym, Margot climbed the ladder as fast as she dared. She pulled herself up through the hole in the roof and, choosing her footsteps wisely, moved to the edge. Relief washed over her when she saw three uniformed policemen moving cautiously between the buildings, guns in their hands.

"Over here!" She desperately waved her arms. "Come quickly!"

The men spotted her immediately. One of them broke away from the others and sprinted for the mound of soil. All Margot could see as he began to climb was the top of his *kepi*, but when his face appeared, she blinked in disbelief.

"Captain Bouchard!"

"It's all right, Madame. I'm coming."

In no time at all, the captain had reached the top of the mound. Despite the heat, he was still wearing his tunic. He paused to catch his breath. "Are you all right?"

Margot remained in a daze. "How did you get here?"

"You hadn't been seen for days. Madame Janvier told me you'd come looking for the woods. You'd already given me the location."

"So you came to find me?"

"Of course." He appeared surprised, as if it had been his only option. Margot could have hugged him, but there were more pressing matters at hand.

"Natalie's injured. She's broken her leg and I can't risk moving her. And there's a bomb about to go off."

Captain Bouchard didn't bat an eyelid. "Where's the bomb?"

"In the armoury. It's set to a timer."

"How long?"

"Ten or eleven minutes."

"Are there any other ways out?"

"There's a fire exit below me, but it's blocked by this mound of soil."

Captain Bouchard quickly appraised the situation. Margot could sense his mind working as he looked at the bulldozer – no time to try and get that started – then up at the sky – perhaps hoping for divine intervention. Finally, he looked back at the two men and told them to start digging.

"Jump," he said to Margot, holding up his hands. "I'll catch you."

But Margot shook her head. "I can't leave Natalie. I'll go down to the door and call to you from inside."

"But—"

"No time to talk. Get digging."

He wasn't very happy about it, but the captain tore off his tunic and went to join his men.

Margot descended the ladder at breakneck speed. She sprinted to the emergency exit and pounded the door with the heel of her fist, shouting the captain's name. Margot admired his spirit, but felt a sense of hopelessness. They didn't even have shovels. The chances of them digging a way through in time were remote.

Scraping sounds came from the other side of the door. Margot could hear the captain shouting encouragement to his men. She threw a shoulder against the door, but it didn't move an inch. She was desperate to be out there, helping them dig. An uncontrollable fury rose up inside her, and she screamed at the door, kicked it as hard as she could, and then picked up a piece of the broken roof to use as a battering ram. The door shifted a little, then a little bit more. A chink of daylight appeared. Margot caught a glimpse of a face at the end of a short, rough tunnel. The captain and his men were digging with their bare hands and scraps of wood. Margot lent her right foot to the effort, loosening it with her heel, and as soon as the hole was big enough, hands reached in and grabbed her by the arms.

Brusquely hauled out on her back, the captain helped her to her feet. His face was covered in sweat and dirt, and his finger-nails were torn, but he didn't pause for a moment. He told the men to keep digging. "We need to get this door fully open," he stressed, and then he got down on his hands and knees and crawled back in.

Margot called after him. According to her watch, there were less than two minutes left. But the captain ignored her pleas and disappeared inside. Margot joined the gendarmes and began pulling clumps of soil from the mound, then improvised a spade with a flat piece of wood and dug until her fingers bled.

She knew it was coming, but the explosion still took her completely off guard. A deafening bang was followed by a powerful rush of air that knocked them all off their feet. Margot ended up flat on her rear, a full two metres away from the base of the mound.

Stunned, she watched in horror as a series of explosions began tearing the base apart. The realisation soon struck – the two gendarmes were recovering nearby, but Captain Bouchard was nowhere to be seen.

———

Margot's eyes widened in disbelief as she took in the scale of destruction. At least a dozen explosions had ripped through the base. An entire wing of the cross-shaped building had been reduced to rubble, the warehouse was in flames, and the building that had housed the gymnasium was teetering on the brink of collapse. As the dust began to clear, Margot could see that only one of its walls still stood.

A voice was calling to her, faint and distant, like she was deep underwater, even though the gendarme was standing right beside her. Margot realised her hearing had been affected by the blast. The gendarme was holding her arm, gesturing for her to move back, but she pushed his hand away. There was no way the captain and Natalie could have survived, but Margot could hope for a miracle.

She began picking her way over the rubble, heading towards what remained of the gym. There was so much debris it was impossible to make out what had once been what. A shout rang out; Margot paused to watch the final wall come down. She hunkered down, shielding her face from the billowing cloud of dust.

She rose again, almost gagging on the dust in her nose and throat. Her eyelashes were matted, her vision blurred. When her eyesight did begin to clear, Margot was convinced she was hallucinating. A figure had materialised out of the cloud and was heading towards her – a man, burdened by a heavy weight, carefully stepping over the chunks of broken concrete. Only when the figure got close enough to see his face did Margot accept that it was real: Captain Bouchard with Natalie in his arms.

"She's still breathing," the captain called out. "Call an ambulance!"

Miracles, it seemed, were real.

36

13:53. Dion eyed up the boutiques across the street, having chosen his target. He switched on the phone while he was waiting for a gap in the traffic. Only one number had been programmed into the contacts: BOOM. Monika's warped sense of humour.

The traffic kept coming, costing him precious seconds. Timing was key. He had not allowed for contingencies. He'd given himself one minute to walk to the store, two minutes to get inside and leave the bag under the fitting room chair, thirty seconds to turn around and walk out. If he hadn't been rumbled by the time he got to the door, he would shout a warning. Crazy guy shouting a bomb threat, but they'd better believe him. Three minutes for everyone to get out before he made the call.

Dion crossed the street. Walking steadily along the sidewalk, he was slightly perturbed when his ears began to ring. People around him became a blur, streaks of multicoloured light, oblivious of what he was about to do to them. Should he feel guilty? Angry? Excited? Truth was Dion had no idea how he was feeling. His mind felt like it was fading away.

He was brought up sharp by a commotion up ahead. A

group of people were gathered outside a shop, looking anxious and confused. Dion's mind came back into focus when he spotted a blue uniform. Someone said something about evacuating a building, and people started filming with their phones. The crowd thickened, more cops appeared, the ringing in his ears was replaced by the sound of sirens. As confusion spread, people started to leave, quickening their pace in their eagerness to get clear. In no time at all, Dion's route to the target was blocked.

He rapidly reassessed. There was no plan B. What could he do? Leave the rucksack in a dumpster; toss it into a bush across the street? As panic took hold of him, he was grabbed by the arm from behind. "This way, brother." Suddenly, Sébastien stood facing him.

Dion flinched. "What's going on?"

"Follow me. There's a quick way out."

"It's not done yet."

"It's over, brother. We need to go."

Sébastien pulled his arm, but Dion resisted. He was flabbergasted. How had the police found out? What was Sébastien doing in Cannes? Questions bombarded his brain.

Chaos was spreading along the Croisette. Flashing blue lights were popping up here, there and everywhere. The streets were gridlocked and motorists were starting to get angry. People bumped into them in their haste to get by.

"Come on," Sébastien urged. "We don't have much time."

But Dion wasn't budging. There was something different about Sébastien that didn't quite compute. Dion realised it was the first time he'd seen him outside of the base, and he was struck by what an oddball he was. Six inches shorter than he remembered, bug-eyed and thin, wiry hair and ashen skin. He looked lost in an oversized flak jacket. The nutter on the bus.

Another rush of people flowed by. The police had formed a

line and were corralling pedestrians off the sidewalk. Remembering the deadly cargo on his back, Dion realised it would be wise to get out of the way.

They fled through a warren of backstreets. Sébastien seemed to know exactly where he was going and only once looked back to check that Dion was still with him. He turned a corner, ran down an alley, emerged in a short, shady street, surrounded by tenement blocks. Another short passage took them to a courtyard where Sébastien ran up to a garage door, unlocked it with a key, and rolled it up. After ushering Dion inside, he rolled the door back down, sealing them in.

Lights flickered on. The garage was quiet and empty, save for a pile of fishing tackle in the corner and a freezer by the back door. A strong smell of fish bait hung in the air. There was a pause as the two men caught their breath, searching each other's faces, gauging reactions. Dion was the first to recover.

"Why were they evacuating? The police were all over it. What are you doing here?" The questions tumbled out.

Sébastien took longer to regain his breath, and another few seconds went by before he was able to stand upright. "They were obviously looking for bombs," he said.

"They wouldn't do that without reliable intelligence. It can't be coincidence."

"Who said it was coincidence?"

"What else could it be?"

"They must have found out."

"But how?"

"You tell me."

Dion faced him squarely, not sure what Sébastien was getting at. "How would I know?"

"Because you tipped them off."

The words were like a slap in the face. Dion was too stunned to speak.

"The only people we told about this mission were the five of you," Sébastien went on. "How else do you explain it?"

Dion's mind reeled. It must have been one of the others. He wracked his brains to think which of them might have a motive. Certainly not Esmée. The skinhead perhaps. He'd never trusted them.

"I had doubts about all of you," Sébastien continued. "That's why I chose you. But you, Dion – you were always the prime suspect. And now you've confirmed it."

Dion sustained his gaze, the pieces falling into place. So that's what this was about? A hastily conceived mission. Nothing to do with an *amuse-bouche*. But Sébastien had got it wrong. Dion advanced on him. "It wasn't me, I swear. I was all set to go. Another five minutes and it would've been done."

"We know about AL."

"What?"

"Tik found your messages. You thought you'd covered your tracks, but you weren't smart enough. Everything leaves a trace, you should know that."

Dion looked away. Sébastien was right – he should have been more careful – but this wasn't how it was meant to end. He wasn't going down without a fight.

"Okay, I admit it. I was communicating with someone. But that was then, this is now. I'm totally with you on this."

"I trusted you."

"You still can."

"I took you in as a brother, accepted you into the group. But you were spying on us the whole time."

"Not any more."

"You betrayed us."

"I—"

Sébastien took a step back. He reached behind him and suddenly a gun was in his hand. He levelled his arm at Dion's face. "There's a price to be paid for disloyalty," he said. "And now's the time to pay up."

Dion swallowed. It wasn't the first time he'd stared down the barrel of a gun, and he wasn't scared. "You're making a mistake," he muttered, but Sébastien squeezed the trigger anyway.

———

Margot watched the traffic drift by as they sat in the back of the police car, racing along the autoroute. Her world had been a silent movie for the past few hours with her hearing still impaired from the blasts. She had barely heard the thwack of the rotor blades as the army helicopter had come into land, and had watched the troops rush in like a video game on mute. The air ambulance soon followed, and Natalie had been whisked away within minutes. The medics had wanted to take Margot too, but Margot had refused.

Captain Bouchard had immediately raised the alert in all five cities, and Margot had persuaded him to take her to Cannes, assuming that was where Dion had gone. Reluctantly, the captain had agreed. Seated beside her, he nudged her forearm. "That was the hospital." He indicated his phone. "They've taken Natalie to the ICU."

Margot acknowledged him with a slight nod. Something in her head cleared and she began to hear a little better. "I hope she'll be all right."

"She's in the best hands."

A thin trickle of fresh blood seeped from the wound on his brow. *Just a scratch*, he'd said when Margot had pointed it out earlier. The tale of how he'd survived had indeed been miraculous. He'd managed to get Natalie to the fire escape door just as the explosion had hit. The roof beams had fallen in such a way as to create a protective cage. Despite being hit on the head by a few small pieces, the captain had emerged unscathed. He'd eschewed the attention of the medics, preferring to be stitched up by a gendarme.

It was after two when they reached Cannes. The driver remarked that the traffic seemed unusually heavy for a Saturday afternoon. Soon, the news came through on the radio that the town was being placed under lockdown. Roads quickly became gridlocked. Even with the siren on, they got nowhere. Margot feared they'd arrived too late. Realising it was useless, Captain Bouchard unbuckled his seatbelt. "Stay here, Madame." He reached for his door handle.

But Margot was having none of it. "I'm coming, too," she replied and promptly got out. Across the roof of the car, she gave him a look that made it clear it wasn't up for discussion.

It was a five-minute jog to the seafront. A police roadblock had been set up at the entrance to the Boulevard de la Croisette, but after speaking to an officer, they were allowed through. Margot stayed close to the captain's side as they ducked under the tape and worked their way through the crowd. The scene was confusing, but there was no indication that a bomb had gone off.

They came to another cordon where a group of officers in combat gear were gathered. Judging by the way they were holding their machine guns, it didn't look like they were preparing for action. The captain managed to capture the ear of one of the officers, and after a brief conversation, he turned to give Margot a grave look.

"There's reports of a gunshot. One man dead. No sign of the shooter."

The crowd parted to let an ambulance through. The barrier was removed to let it pass, and when the medics jumped out and continued on foot, Margot and the captain tagged on to a group that followed them.

They hurried down a series of narrow streets, into a shady courtyard. A garage door was wide open and bright lights on tripods revealed crime scene technicians at work. A plainclothes officer told them to stay back, but not before Margot had gotten close enough to get a good view of the body. Eyes wide open, a bullet hole in the centre of his forehead – it only took one second to see that it was Dion.

37

Margot removed her shoes before heading along the rocky headland path to the cove. The feel of hot rock under her feet was bliss. The sun appeared to be rising faster than normal today as if determined to give them another hot roasting. August was probably her favourite month of the year, and now that the 28th had passed, this year felt more special than most.

She swam for an hour. Back on the beach, she put on her beach sarong and left her hair to dry naturally as she walked home. Returning to her courtyard, she paused to look down at the hot flagstones, watching how quickly her wet footprints evaporated. Here one minute, gone the next. Just like life in many ways.

She went into the salon and switched on the TV, eager to watch the news. Margot was relieved to hear no mention of bombs, terror attacks, or outbreaks of rioting. August the 13th had been a similarly unremarkable day. The lights had stayed on, the autoroutes had remained open, the trains had kept running. People had been left blissfully unaware of how close to catastrophe they'd come – no point spreading panic when the danger had apparently passed. Margot switched off the TV, made her breakfast, and took her tray out to the courtyard.

Usually a lover of the heat, Buster had instead chosen a shady spot under the table. Margot reached down to fuss him, but the thought of returning affection was clearly too much and all he could manage was a long lazy yawn, opening his mouth so wide it was a wonder his jaw didn't fall off. A notification popped up on the screen of her laptop. Margot's eyes widened in surprise when she saw that it was an email from the *École Nationale de la Magistrature*.

Chère Madame Renard,

Further to your application for a place on the direct integration course at Bordeaux, we are pleased to inform you that...

Margot felt a lightness in her chest. She read the text twice, just to be sure, then stared at the screen, dumbfounded. It took a moment for her to register that the cat had moved to the side of her chair.

"Sorry, Buster. My mind was elsewhere."

Margot looked down at him, but the cat soon lost patience. He departed with an angry *meow*, climbing the wall and disappearing next door without a single glance back. Which raised another question in her mind: if she went to Bordeaux, what would she do with His Lordship?

She was ready for work by nine. On her way to the *Palais*, Captain Bouchard phoned and asked to see her. Margot took Rue Garenne to the Gendarmerie and found Lieutenant Martel outside, watering the window boxes. His face brightened when he noticed her.

"Madame Renard – good to have you back." He leaned forward as if to kiss her on the cheek, but then remembered himself. "How are you doing?" he smiled instead.

The day after she'd got back from Cannes, Captain Bouchard had informed her that someone from the GIGN would be coming to debrief her. A car had pulled up outside her house at eight the next morning. Two plainclothes men had taken her to an anonymous grey building in Perpignan, put her in an interview room, and questioned her for hours about what she had seen and heard during her time in the camp. At times it had felt more like an interrogation than a debrief.

"I'm okay," Margot said, touched by his concern. "Thanks for asking."

"The captain told us what you'd been through." He puffed out his chest. "If I were in charge, Madame, I would give you a medal."

Margot smiled fondly. She couldn't help thinking that if Martel were in charge, the Gendarmerie would be a very different beast.

"He wanted to see me?"

"Yes. Go through. The door's open."

Margot stepped into the lobby, but then had a sudden thought. "Are you busy this evening?"

"Not especially. Why?"

"They're having a party at La Lune Bleue. Raymond tells me there's a rare blue supermoon."

"That's when the wall turns blue." The lieutenant smiled. "He told me all about it yesterday."

Margot smiled back. "That boy's wasted serving tables."

"I'l be there."

"Tell all your friends."

"I will."

Captain Bouchard was in the detectives' office. Their eyes met through the corridor windows, and he joined her at the door. "Madame Renard, thank you for coming in." He showed her into his office where he made a point of closing the door behind them. It seemed that whatever they had to say to each other was still to be kept secret. He poured her a glass of water from a decanter and then one for himself. "I hope you were well treated by my colleagues in Perpignan." His tone suggested he might have some doubts.

Margot accepted the glass and took a sip. "They didn't actually shine a bright light in my eyes, but it did feel like I'd done something wrong."

The captain looked a little embarrassed. "I can only apologise. I did explain the circumstances, but there's procedure to follow. You do understand?"

Margot nodded. "I suppose they were only doing their jobs."

Captain Bouchard settled into his chair. He selected a file from his tray. "I managed to get some information out of the police in Cannes. Naturally, they were very cagey. They confirmed that the man found in the garage was Lieutenant Dion Langlois, formerly of the GIGN. Cause of death was a 9mm calibre bullet in the forehead, point blank range."

He gave Margot a moment to digest that. Margot had been through so many emotions in the past few weeks she didn't know how to feel. No doubt in time the numbness would wear off.

"Any idea who killed him?"

"Not yet. A man was seen acting suspiciously, but no one got a good look at him. It seems what actually went on is still a mystery. The rucksack he was carrying contained an explosive device, but luckily he didn't have time to detonate it."

"I still can't fathom out why he told me the 28th and not the 13th." Margot recalled the earnestness in his voice when he'd come to her that night. The way he'd talked about the group's ambitions, she had no doubt he'd grown sympathetic to their cause, but he'd been a difficult man to read. She was sure he hadn't been lying to her.

"If he was being set up," the captain replied, "they would have given him the wrong date on purpose. They would have wanted to keep the element of surprise for August the 13th, which was clearly the intended date. Vans packed with viable devices were found close to several of the sites you identified."

He showed her some photographs. It took her right back to the armoury, all those pins in the map. "What about the other four people on the list?"

Captain Bouchard slid the page back into his file and then took out another. "A device was exploded in Toulouse, another in Béziers. Twenty-seven people were injured, but there were no fatalities, apart from the perpetrators, both of whom were shot dead by the police. And in Toulon, the body of a young woman was discovered in a dumpster. She's been identified as Esmée Pelletier." He showed her another photo, this one of a young woman in a pink hoodie, lying face down in the rubbish. Margot remained cold. *Nice watch.*

"She played the part of the insurance agent when they conned Madame Janvier," Margot explained.

"She was the youngest of the five, just nineteen years of age. She was offered a place at the Sorbonne, but turned it down. Six months ago, she was arrested for throwing paint in a store in Monaco."

"How was she killed?"

"Same as her friend in Cannes – a single bullet in the forehead."

"And the bomb she was carrying?"

"It didn't go off. She was caught on CCTV outside a jewellery store opposite Galeries Lafayette. The footage shows her walking back and forth outside the store, looking agitated. After a few minutes, she's seen disposing of a mobile phone in a street drain. The footage goes on to show her fleeing the scene with the rucksack still on her back."

Margot frowned. "So she changed her mind?"

"It looks that way. The footage also shows her being pursued by a man in a hoodie. The dumpster where she was found was just two streets away. A suspect matching his description was arrested yesterday afternoon. He's admitted to being a member of the group."

Executed by her own people? Margot found it hard to sympathise. Live by the sword, die by the sword. Whatever had been going on in her mind, she must have gone there with the intention of detonating the bomb, potentially carrying out mass murder.

"And Sébastien – have they caught up with him yet?"

The captain glanced at the door before giving a reply. "The press haven't yet been informed so keep this to yourself. Sébastien was apprehended close to the German border last night. The police picked him up when he stopped for fuel at a motorway services."

"Let's hope he's rotting in a cell somewhere."

"A dozen other arrests have been made, mainly people who were already on the intelligence service's watchlist."

Margot exhaled in relief. "Thank god it's over."

The captain leaned back, a sceptical expression on his face. "It may be over for now, Madame, but the threat hasn't gone away. This group, and others like them, pose a credible risk to our way of life. In many ways, they are the most dangerous kind of terrorist: no clear demands; only interested in anarchy."

"Frightening, isn't it?"

He nodded. "It would be nice to think this is a cosy little town, but the signs are there if you look for them: roadsigns turned upside down; a piece of graffiti; a pamphlet on a notice-board. Some people are not happy with the way things are, and perhaps one day they'll succeed in tearing it all down. We live in dangerous times."

It was a sobering thought, yet Margot doubted it would ever come to that. Even within the group, there had been dissenting voices, those who had been adamant that peaceful methods were the best way of achieving their goals. Common sense had to prevail at some point.

"And the base...?" Margot asked hesitantly. "I don't suppose we'll hear anything about that in the news."

Captain Bouchard firmly shook his head. "Anything they do recover will remain top secret."

Margot was unhappy with his answer. "Terrible things went on there, Captain. You didn't see that lab. They were experimenting on people."

He held her eye for several long seconds, perhaps reluctant to be drawn into offering an opinion, but finally he conceded. "Coming from an army background, I can assure you, Madame, that I share your disgust."

Unfortunately, such incidents occurred far too frequently. It was more than just a blemish on the army's reputation. Things needed to change, otherwise next time they might not be so lucky.

"Anyway," Margot said, rising from her chair. "Thanks for updating me."

"You're most welcome."

She paused at the door. "Oh, by the way – in all the excitement, I never got around to thanking you. If it weren't for you, I wouldn't be standing here."

"I was just doing my job, Madame. That's all."

"Nevertheless, I really do appreciate it."

The captain smiled. Something that looked like pride glinted in his eyes.

―――――

At lunchtime, Margot walked down to the harbour and followed the crooked lane that led to Madame Janvier's bookshop. The door was locked, and when Margot peeked in through the glass, there was no sign of the proprietor. Deciding to try around the back, she took the lane that led to the car park and approached the back door, which she found wide open. "Madame Janvier?"

Inquisitively, Margot craned her head over the threshold. Her eyes alighted on a suitcase inside the lobby.

"Margot – is that you?" Madame Janvier appeared on the stairs, carrying another suitcase.

Margot looked up, smiling. "I haven't called at a bad time, have I?"

"No, it's all right."

"Need a hand?"

"I can manage, thank you." She placed the second suitcase beside its companion and heaved a tired breath. "Anyway, Margot. How are you?"

"Me – I'm fine. More to the point, how's Natalie?"

Madame Janvier returned a grave look. "She had her last operation yesterday, so hopefully she's over the worst of it. But she's still very unwell."

"If there's anything I can do, just say the word."

Madame Janvier shook her head. "Thank you, Margot, but no. I'm going to go and stay with her for a while. She will need a lot of support. They said it could be six months before she can walk again."

That explained the suitcases. Margot tutted in sympathy. "She's a strong woman. I'm sure she'll get through it."

"Hmm." Madame Janvier didn't seem so sure.

They migrated through to the shop. With the lights out, the place seemed different. The shelves were all dark, the books hidden away. Millions of stories, just waiting to be discovered.

"I've spoken to Natalie about what happened," Madame Janvier said. "She wouldn't say much. It must have been a very frightening experience for her."

"For both of us," Margot pointed out. "It'll take some time to process."

"How long did you stay with her?"

Margot thought about it. "Seven or eight hours. I thought about going for help, but I didn't want to leave her."

The hospital had told her she'd done the right thing. Without the crude splint, Natalie would have bled out in minutes. Madame Janvier was still scrutinising her.

"It's lucky Captain Bouchard came along when he did."

"It is," Margot agreed.

Looking into her eyes, Margot was unsure of her meaning. Had she meant that as a criticism? She couldn't help thinking that Madame Janvier was blaming her in some way. But there was no point arguing. She changed the subject instead.

"What will happen to the bookshop while you're away?"

"A friend has kindly offered to look after it. She'll be here at the weekend."

"Glad to hear it. I always love coming here."

"Anyway, my taxi will be here soon. I must get on."

"Of course."

Madame Janvier showed her to the front door, but halfway there Margot remembered something. "Actually, while I'm here... I seem to remember you had a first edition *West with the Night*."

"Quite possibly, yes."

"Do you still have it?"

"Erm... Let me just check."

They started scanning the shelves.

"Here." Margot's heart rose when she spotted it. As she took the book down from the shelf, she flipped it over to see the price tag, which made her heart sink. "Oh. Is this right?" A new label had been stuck over the old one: €550. Margot was sure it had been four hundred the last time she'd looked.

Madame Janvier came over to check. She nodded. "I'm afraid I've had to put up some of my prices," she explained. "Losing all that money. I'm sure you understand."

Margot looked into her eye, hoping the shopkeeper might relent. But a few seconds passed and Madame Janvier offered nothing.

"Of course." Margot returned the book to the shelf. "Perhaps next time."

Madame Janvier showed her out.

In the lane outside, Margot passed a café. A pamphlet had been left on one of the pavement tables, the red banner of *La Vérité* instantly catching her eye. Margot looked round to see if anyone was watching, and then picked it up. It was the latest issue, dated only a week ago. The front page carried a picture of the devastation caused by of one of the Berlin bombs. The headline read: *COMING TO A STREET NEAR YOU?*

Margot put the pamphlet back down. Dangerous times indeed.

———

As Margot descended the steps to La Lune Blue, a funky poprock beat drifted up from the sea. She arrived at the base of the defensive wall to find a small stage set up on the terrace upon which the Amy Winehouse lookalike was giving a full-on rendition of *Valerie*, resplendent in a full beehive wig. The restaurant was packed.

Spotting a few familiar faces, Margot mingled for a while. Lieutenant Martel was there, canoodling with a woman Margot very much hoped was his wife. Florian was there, along with a few of the other assistants from the *Palais*. She had hoped Stéphane might come down, but he was visiting Célia in Lake Garda. When Margot finally reached the bar, she found Raymond collecting a tray full of drinks, looking stressed.

"What a turn out," Margot said, slotting into a gap beside him. Cerise, busy behind the bar, smiled as she landed more drinks onto his already crowded tray. "I've never seen the place so busy."

"It wasn't meant to be this busy," Raymond complained. "We don't know who half of these people are!"

"Oh," Margot said guiltily, realising she might have been partly to blame. She'd been mentioning it to pretty much everyone she'd met. "Still, it's good for business."

"Not so good for Rogier," Raymond said covertly while Cerise was fixing another cocktail. "He was going to propose tonight. That's why the band's here."

"Well, he still can, can't he?"

"Try telling him that. He's a dithering wreck."

Margot tutted. "Where is he?"

"Hiding in the stock room."

She patted him on the shoulder. "Leave him to me."

Margot fought her way to the end of the bar, dodging a suspicious look from Cerise. A low door opened onto a narrow passageway that gave access to the toilets, but beyond that, smooth stone steps curved and sloped downwards into another passageway. The noise from the bar faded as Margot entered the old cave where the booze was stored. The air was a refreshing ten degrees cooler.

She looked around. Rogier was lurking in the shadows, swigging from a bottle of beer. "So this is where you're hiding?"

He returned a sheepish look. "I'm not hiding."

"So what are you doing?"

"I'm drinking a beer, if that's okay with you." He took an ugly slurp, spilling a few drops down the front of his clean white shirt. He cursed. "Great. Just what I needed."

Margot grabbed a towel and sat down beside him. She dabbed his front like a mother hen. "Drinking alone never solved anything. Trust me."

"It makes me feel better."

"Not in the long run, it won't." She dried the spilled beer as best she could. It was going to leave a stain, but hey ho. Margot folded the towel away. "Raymond said tonight's the night."

"That was the plan."

"So what's the problem?"

He glared at her as if she'd gone temporarily insane. "Have you seen how many people are out there? I can't ask her in front of all them!"

"Of course you can."

"What if she says no? They'll laugh at me, and think I'm stupid. I'll never live it down."

Margot drew in a long, sad breath. "No one's going to laugh at you, Rogier. They'll all be rooting for you. In any case, you can't live in fear, not taking a chance, just because something might go wrong. Sometimes you have to step out of your comfort zone. It's what makes life exciting."

Rogier mulled it over for a while. "You really think she'll say yes?"

"She'd be mad not to. Especially when she sees you going out on a limb."

Rogier grinned bashfully. Finally, he drew in a deep breath and straightened himself. "All right. I'll do it."

And with that, they went back to the bar and out onto the terrace. Rogier held his head high as he approached the stage and interrupted the singer to ask for the microphone. A surprised hush descended. The music cut out as Rogier got up onto the stage. Like every amateur stand-up the world over, he tapped the microphone (*testing, testing*) before calling for Cerise to come out and join them. Everyone watched in eager anticipation. And when, a few moments later, an uncharacteristically bashful Cerise emerged from the bar, Rogier got down on one knee and asked Cerise if she would do him the honour of becoming his wife. And of course, Cerise said yes. Everyone applauded, just like it was meant to be.

It seemed that nothing could break the spell that had been cast that night, not even when Raymond let off the fireworks and one of the rockets veered off course, hit the wall, and tumbled to the ground just feet away from where people were standing. To top it all off, the moon came out and put on its show. By some trick of the eye, it looked twice its normal size, and as the bright white light struck the wall, the huge stone blocks did, if you used a little imagination, turn a slight shade of blue (not quite up to the billing but impressive nonetheless). Margot smiled, full of the joys of life. It was undeniably true that the world was a dangerous place, but it could, at times, be a pretty magical one too.

———

The revelry looked set to continue into the small hours, but by midnight Margot was flagging. Craving a break from the noise, she stepped over the chain that separated the terrace from the sea and, wine glass in hand, climbed down some rocks to get to the water's edge. The moon, high overhead, cast a ghostly silver glow over the water.

She checked her phone: one missed call from Stéphane. Despite the late hour, Margot called him back. He answered right away.

"I didn't wake you, did I?"

"No. I was hoping you'd call back. How are you?"

"I'm okay."

"From all that music in the background it sounds like you're having a good time."

Margot told him about the proposal.

"Poor foolish boy."

"That's not a very nice thing to say."

"Too bitter?"

"I'd say."

"Sorry, Margot. I'm just feeling sorry for myself. Do pass on my congratulations to the happy couple."

Margot instinctively reached into her bag for her cigarettes, only to remember that she had left them at home. On purpose. Seven days since she'd last had one. Pretty good going under the circumstances, though she did need to find something else for her hands to do.

"Any news on Natalie?"

Margot told him the latest. "I feel I ought to go up and see her, but to be honest I can't face it."

"Why's that?"

"Not sure. I do feel sorry for her, but she was a difficult person to get on with."

"A clash of personalities?"

"Just the opposite. I think she reminded me of what I was like at that age."

"What – pig-headed and inflexible?"

Margot oozed contempt down the line. "No, Stéphane. That's not what I meant."

Stéphane laughed. "Margot, you may be a little pig-headed at times, but some of us like you that way."

A large wave came in, spritzing her legs with water. Margot shuffled back a few inches. "Maybe she reminded me of some of the things I've lost."

"Such as?"

"Energy and enthusiasm."

"If you're lacking those things now, I hate to imagine what you were like twenty years ago."

Margot enjoyed a smile with herself. If only he knew. "Anyway. Changing the subject: I received an interesting email today."

"Go on."

"The ENM wrote back. They've offered me a place."

"Really? That's wonderful news."

"You think so?"

He hesitated. "Don't you?"

Margot raised her right hand to her mouth, realising at the last moment she wasn't actually holding a cigarette. She picked up a small stone instead and tossed it out to sea. "I'm not really sure. I've spent most of the day trying *not* to think about it." She couldn't help but imagine the looks she would get from the other students, the questions they would ask: *What are you doing here at this time of your life? Shouldn't you be at home, knitting?* It was a different world now. Sometimes it seemed her youth was too far away to row back.

"When do you have to give them an answer?"

"A week, or two. They didn't really say."

"Then take your time. After what you've been through it's a lot to take in."

"It is. Anyway, I'd better get back to my party. They've got an Amy Winehouse cover band on."

"Have they?"

"Rock 'n' Roll Rehab."

"Oh dear."

"She's actually quite good." Right on cue, the singer launched into an encore of *Valerie.*

"Okay. Well, have fun."

"Give Célia my love."

"I will."

Margot stood, but then was struck by an idea. "Before you go... What are you doing right now?"

"Me? I'm sitting in my apartment, drinking beer from a bottle, watching mindless TV."

"Do me a favour."

"Okay."

"Go outside and look at the moon."

"Is that it?"

"That's it, Stéphane."

Margot ended the call. She gazed up at the night sky and focussed on the bright white disc of the moon. The air was so clear that she could see individual craters. A warm glow filled up her insides as she lost herself in thought, sharing her soul with a thousand fellow moon-gazers.

AUTHOR'S NOTE

A quick note to reiterate that this is a work of fiction. As far as I am aware (nudge-nudge, wink-wink), no secret drugs trials were taking place in France in the 1970s, and the Ministry of Defence has certainly not covered up the use of any secret army bases. That would be unthinkable. In the words of one great writer: a novelist makes stuff up.

Project MKUltra, on the other hand, is a very well-documented affair. In the 1950s and 60s, the CIA spent a reported $25 million experimenting with mind control techniques out of fear that Russia and China were doing the same. MKUltra consisted of 149 sub-projects covering a range of programmes from the effects of behavioural drugs to electroshock treatment to analysis of ESP. Many of the participants were experimented on without their knowledge or consent.

The Canadian government was also involved. Some of the experiments took place at the Allan Memorial Institute, a Gothic mansion near Montreal with a nickname of "The Allan". Many patients went in with minor psychological conditions, only to emerge months later as zombies. The treatments involved keeping patients in chemically induced comas before using electroshock therapy to "destructure" their brains. According to the researchers, the aim was to reduce the patients to a "plant state", from which they would regain a healthier state of mind. Scary stuff.

Reading about "The Allan" got me thinking that it's not unusual for buildings to become synonymous with scandal and atrocity: the Watergate Apartments; Auschwitz; the Twin Towers. An illustration, perhaps, of how something as simple as bricks and mortar can have a lasting impact on our socio-political landscape.

The idea for the army base originated from a family holiday in my childhood, when we stopped in a lay-by backed by woods in a densely forested part of Europe. My brother and I went off to explore. In the mind of an imaginative six-year-old, it seemed we had trekked for hours along a deserted path through the trees before coming to a chain-link fence. The sight of some mysterious buildings lurking in the distance sent us scampering back to our parents.

On a not entirely unrelated note, some of you may be interested to know that Buster the cat is also very much based on a true-life individual.

À la prochaine,

Rachel.

PLEASE REVIEW THIS BOOK

Please don't underestimate how important reviews are to authors, particularly independent authors who don't have the backing of a huge marketing machine. If you enjoyed *RED SUMMER*, please consider leaving a review on either Amazon or Goodreads – it will be very much appreciated.

FREE SHORT STORY

To receive a free short story featuring Margot Renard visit:
https://www.rachelgreenauthor.com/freeshortstory

WHAT NEXT?

Look out for the next book in the series, coming soon to Amazon

For updates, sign up at: www.rachelgreenauthor.com

FOLLOW:

https://twitter.com/AuthorRachelG
https://www.instagram.com/authorrachelg/
https://www.facebook.com/AuthorRachelG
https://www.bookbub.com/authors/rachel-green?follow=true

Printed in Dunstable, United Kingdom